THE BARISTA'S GUIDE TO ESPIONAGE

DAVE SINCLAIR

THE BARISTA'S GUIDE TO ESPIONAGE

Better shape up Bond. There's a new girl in town and she's come to kick some ass.

Meet Eva Destruction, the only thing quicker than her mouth is her talent for getting into trouble. It's true she's always had an eye for a bad boy but when she falls for billionaire super-villain Harry Lancing, it seems that even Eva may have bitten off more than she can chew.

Eva hurtles headlong into terrorist attacks, assassinations, car chases and the occasional close encounter with a dashing spy who seems determined to charm Eva into bed as he is to thwart Lancing's plans to bring down every government on Earth.

As the odds begin to stack up in Lancing's favour the fate of the world lies in Eva's hands. Luckily for the world, Eva Destruction isn't the type of girl to let a super-villain ex-boyfriend with a massive ego, unlimited resources and his own secret island get the better of her.

"High octane, wise-cracking, ass-kicking entertainment from the first to the last page…"

"As if Stephanie Plum had James Bond's (Australian) love child…I loved it. It's fun, it's funny, it's clever. I want a movie of this now. Brilliant."

PROLOGUE

Eva was out of bullets, out of luck and out of time.

Crouching low in the tropical vegetation, she inhaled slowly to steady her nerves. The metal tang of blood mixed with the rich scents of crushed foliage, almost heady in its intensity. Blood had smeared across her forehead and cheeks, like gory war paint. *You can do it*, she told herself. There was a good fifty metres of open ground between her and the beach. The odds weren't with her making it without being seen, but she had no choice. If she faltered, people would die and the world would be plunged into chaos.

She stood on unsteady legs and did her best to block out the exhaustion. Ignoring the pain from her countless lacerations, Eva broke into a run. Ducking low, she sprinted from the jungle and headed towards a small pier with its nearby powerboat. With every stride, her hope grew. Could she do it? Was there still a chance? Her breath sawed in and out as her legs and arms pumped. Bullets splintered the wood at her feet and she skidded to a halt.

The sound of footsteps thudded behind her, and Eva turned. Three black-clad guards stepped carefully onto the tiny pier, the wooden slats screaming in protest at the added weight. They approached her slowly; a couple of their compatriots had made the fatal mistake of underestimating her. Their corpses littered the island. But these guards needn't have bothered with their caution. She'd spent both magazines from her Sig Sauers.

Bikinis were nice and all, but completely rubbish for storing extra ammunition.

The tropical sun scorched her exposed skin, which was slicked with sweat. She'd been so close. *So close.*

Now she'd never get to him.

The guns fell from her hands and clattered noisily on the wooden slats. She didn't remove the tiny umbrella tucked under her bikini strap like a samurai sword. Slowly, Eva placed her hands on her head. Her mind rapidly processed the scene. Three to one. Not the best statistics, but she wasn't out of options. Her eyes lingered on the barely-healed scar on the middle guard's cheek.

The guards circled, careful to ensure there were several metres between them and her.

She smiled. "So, what brings you fellows here?"

The guards jolted. One even took a step back.

Eva widened her grin. "How's everyone doing? Much on, boys? Who's up for Boggle?" Her bravado was forced, but she refused to show weakness. There was too much at stake.

The guard on her left favoured his right leg, a dark wet patch glistening on his black trousers. His mouth was pinched, with pain or annoyance, she couldn't say. It was probably a bit of both. Privately, she patted herself on the back – she'd managed to hit something after all. Eva had been shooting so wildly she assumed she'd had the accuracy of a concussed Stormtrooper. Running through the jungle with blood in her eyes hadn't helped her aim.

The middle guard – who happened to be the shortest and oldest – stepped forward, outside striking distance. Van Buren. Since they'd first met, he'd had a perpetual sneer, as if she was comprised of nothing but spoiled milk. They'd had run-ins before. The month-old red scar on his cheek was a vivid reminder of their last little dalliance. "Drop the umbrella."

"Nope," Eva said.

"Why are you even carrying that out here?"

"Sun protection?"

"Yeah, I'm not buying it. What's with the umbrella?"

"It's magic," she said.

"Really?"

"No. What are you, five?" He had to know she was stalling for time.

"Then why carry it through the jungle?"

"Greta and I have been through a lot together."

"You called your frilly little pink umbrella *Greta*?"

Eva nodded. "Skeletor's Mighty War Hammer seemed overblown."

He aimed his gun at her head. "Drop it."

With few options available, Eva did as asked and reluctantly unsheathed Greta and dropped it on the pier. It was as if she'd betrayed a friend.

Satisfied with the small win, Van Buren said, "Right. Now, come back with–"

"Nope, VB," she said firmly. "I'm waiting for something."

Eva checked the expensive and bulky men's diving watch on her wrist. The timepiece was too big for her, but it wasn't a fashion statement. The watch had a purpose. As did she.

Eva was surprised how little time she had left.

"You have somewhere else to be?" Van Buren asked. His cockiness grew every moment Eva stood motionless.

"Don't we all?" Eva asked. "Oh. You asked because I checked my watch. Right. This little baby tells me when all sorts of interesting things are going to happen." She wriggled her wrist in the air.

His eyebrows drew together. "What kind of things?"

Eva held up a finger to silence him, but nothing besides an uncomfortable ten seconds of silence followed. "Sorry." Eva shrugged. "It was ripe for a dramatic pause, now it's kind of weird. Wait, okay…and, no… Okay, wait." She nodded at the watch. Confidently she repeated, "It tells me when all sorts of interesting things are going to happen."

Van Buren stared blankly at her. Eva nodded encouragingly. At first he shook his head in confusion, then realised he was expected to repeat himself.

"What kind of–?"

A thunderous explosion rocked the island, reverberating through Eva's chest. She fought the urge to clap her hands over her ears, but she saw two of the guards duck and use their fingers like earplugs. The explosion was followed in quick succession by two more. Tropical birds shrieked and fluttered into the air. Behind the men, huge black plumes of smoke belched into the clear blue sky.

When the last explosion died away, all three stared at the devastation Eva had wrought. But she had no time to admire her handiwork.

Launching herself at the nearest guard, she used a rugby tackle that would make an All Black proud. She caught the guard mid-back and off balance, and he staggered backward, arms flailing. His thrashing caught his neighbour and both men bounced off one another and careened unsteadily towards the edge of the pier. A well-placed Mae Geri front kick sent them both bowling over the side. They splashed unceremoniously into the clear, warm water.

And her Krav Maga teacher had said she lacked discipline…

Eva turned and bent her knees into a fighting stance, facing off against Van Buren. Even though he was two metres away and holding a gun, he looked petrified.

"Don't you move!" He waved the pistol at her.

"Sure." Eva placed her hands on her head.

"I said don't move!"

"You want me to put my hands down so you can tell me to put them on my head?"

"Yes. No. Shit!"

"One thing at a time, chill VB," Eva said.

"Stop calling me that." Van Buren waved the gun in her direction and peered over the side of the pier to determine what had happened to his lackeys. That was all Eva needed.

Stepping towards him, she pivoted to one side. Van Buren's

attention snapped back to her and he lunged. Eva grabbed his arm at the wrist and elbow, and pushed her thumb into the elbow joint, causing him to shriek in pain. She peeled his gun away and before he had time to blink, Eva had the weapon pointed at his head.

"Holy crap. That actually worked." She didn't know who was more shocked.

Van Buren's lips moved, but no sound escaped. He clenched his eyes closed, waiting for that final, fatal shot.

The tropical sounds of the jungle returned, timid at first, then stronger; the incessant background cacophony of birds and insects assaulted Eva's ears. Sweat trickled where sweat had no right trickling. Her trigger finger tensed and relaxed. Tensed and relaxed.

She exhaled. "Time for a swim, VB."

Van Buren pried one eye open. "What?"

"Jump. I won't ask again." Eva pulled back the gun's hammer.

He may have been many things, none of them good, but Van Buren knew when to do what he was told. Without hesitation, he leapt into the water. As soon as she heard the splash, Eva picked up Greta and ran for the end of the pier.

Fumbling hands undid the rope trying the boat and she pulled the starter cord. There was no time to check fuel levels. She wouldn't need much. All she needed was enough to get to the other island.

If it wasn't already too late.

She gunned the throttle and the boat sliced through the still crystal waters, towards the island on her right. She was probably meant to call it starboard or aft or whatever it was but, in her short time on the island, she hadn't bothered to learn sea-faring terms. She'd had more important things on her mind.

Faint popping sounds came from behind. Loud thumps hit the hull. Her head jerked around. One of the guards had managed to scramble onto the pier and was firing an assault rifle. He refocussed his aim, and leaned into his stance. Eva willed the craft to go faster, despite the throttle already being on full.

More distant pops. The bullets pierced the boat from the front, snaking their way up the hull towards her. Eva saw the other island loom larger and prayed she'd make it. Only a couple more minutes…

It was too much to ask.

A bullet ripped through her shoulder and at first all she felt was the *thud*. Then the single most excruciating pain ricocheted through her body. The throttle jolted from her grasp and the engine shuddered to a halt. Eva fell forward into the aluminium hull, and she pressed her palm to the wound. She could feel blood pooling and running down over her bikini top, and she knew the bullet had gone clean through. Scurrying towards the engine, it was suicide to remain where she was. More shots rang out as she reached for the throttle, while keeping one hand pressed to the bullet hole.

The piercing sound of more ammunition tearing through aluminium flesh reverberated through the boat. Rising to her knees, she peered over the lip of the hull and tried to get her bearings while her spare hand frantically grasped for the throttle.

A bullet grazed her temple.

"Fuck!"

Eva fell back, and she hit the side of the boat hard. Legs failing her, she tipped over the edge, plunging into the water. Gulping for air, her limbs refused to function, even though everything in her screamed *swim!* Stinging sea water flooded her lungs, and the boat drifted away as her vision started to grow dark.

Everything was lost.

CHAPTER ONE

Eva woke with a desperate gasp, her whole body shuddering awake.

Her arms jerked but didn't get far. The restraints saw to that. *Why am I sitting up? Am I handcuffed?*

A soothing voice said, "Woah, settle. You're okay, you're okay."

She blinked repeatedly. Everything seemed slightly blurry, the world seemed out of focus and devoid of colour.

There was a metallic *clang* and the same voice said, "Tell the Commander she's awake."

Commander? Of what?

Eva shook her head. Her mouth was dry and tasted of vomit. Her ears rang and her skin was bunched in places, especially her shoulder. Bandages? Stitches? Someone had worked on her while she'd been unconscious. Everything that could ache, did.

Eva struggled against her restraints. Her vision still hadn't returned, although it was a lighter blur. She needed to know where she was, who held her captive. Why she was shackled.

"Please stay still, Miss. You're safe."

Eva meant to laugh, but the only sound to escape was a hoarse wheeze. She attempted to talk, but couldn't form anything coherent.

Footsteps approached. "Here, this will replace the lost electrolytes." The accent sounded American.

He poured a sweet liquid into her mouth. Eva gulped it down, coughing at first. It was the single best thing she'd tasted in her life. It even got rid of the lingering flavour of vomit.

Eva rolled her tongue in her mouth. Everything still hurt, and she still couldn't see, but at least she felt only half-dead. Hoping her voice would work this time, she said, her voice croaky, "The eighties called, they want their handcuffs back."

"I'm...excuse me?"

Eva blinked. Her vision was returning; she could finally make out small details. In quick succession she checked every corner of the room for an escape route, a weapon, anything that she could use. She came up short on all counts. No windows, a hefty-looking bulkhead door and not much else. All she had to work with was a plain metal table and a balding sweaty sailor with a strong chin and weak eyes. The overall effect was a kindly face, if a little browbeaten.

"The handcuffs. I thought it was all about plastic restraints these days. You know, whatever you guys call those cable tie things."

"You guys?" he asked. She thought there was a hint of amusement in his voice.

Eva nodded in his direction. "The uniform. Either this is a US Navy vessel or you take *An Officer and a Gentlemen* cosplay really seriously."

The sailor sat and tapped his pen on the metal table. She wondered how long he'd been there while she was unconscious. The pad in front of him was blank. She assumed there was about to be an interrogation. The lack of flowers and candlelight, plus the metal restraints, excluded the possibility of a date. She assumed he wouldn't be asking about her favourite movie or if she had any brothers or sisters. Which was a shame, because she really had awesome taste in films.

While silence filled the room, her captor did his best to keep his eyes above her neck. He failed. She assumed the middle-aged man wasn't accustomed to grilling someone like her. The bikini probably threw him. And the tattoos. And the fact that all the blood hadn't washed off her body.

The sailor ran his hands through his thinning hair. The name tag above his right pocket read *Lieutenant Commander Cole*. There weren't as many ribbons above his left pocket as there should be for a man of his age.

The drink had revitalised her, refocussing what she needed to do and where she had to be. Neither of those things were here.

"The island. You have to send a party to the island. There's someone in danger. If you could send out a boat or something to search for–"

He shook his head slowly. "We won't be doing that."

"Why not?"

"For one thing, we're not authorised to. Secondly, we need to know your story first. The only thing we know for certain is we found you floating at sea."

"Then why tie me up?"

There it was, a slight hesitation. "Standard procedure."

A lie. It was plain to Eva that something else was at play. Handcuffing someone you rescued, especially with countless lacerations and a gunshot wound, was far from standard procedure. No, the sailor knew more than he was letting on. That made two of them.

Eva scanned the room and was overcome with dread. If they weren't going to do the saving, she'd have to do it herself.

"Did you find my boat? There was a pink umbrella in it."

"Pink...? I don't understand."

Eva shook her head and calmed herself. "No, you wouldn't. Sorry." There was no point pushing the issue. Chalk it up to another disaster for the day.

Cole regained his composure. "Now, Miss, could you please state your name?"

"Eva."

He made a note and smiled expectantly.

She sighed. "Destruction."

He wrote that too, stopped and looked up. "That's seriously not your name, is it?"

She shrugged.

He pressed on. "Age?"

"I've been carbon dated at twenty-eight."

"From?"

"Melbourne, Australia, but I've lived in London for eight of those."

"I see. Eva – may I call you that? I don't think I can call you… Could you please tell me how you came to be here?"

She thought about dropping the line, 'You'll have to ask my folks, they never told me' but remained mute instead. She was still sizing up her captor.

The Lieutenant Commander seemed lost. He appeared positively sick. Green didn't match the white crisp uniform. The poor guy. Surely he hadn't signed up for this. He was probably used to small time stuff; a Petty Officer caught with booze in his bunk, a recruit staying too long at port, a crap game that got out of hand. Not this. Definitely not this.

There was no movement from waves, so the ship must have been huge, maybe even an aircraft carrier. There was no engine vibration so they were probably anchored offshore or were nuclear-powered. If the ship wasn't moving, she allowed herself a semblance of hope. She doubted it would stay anchored for long, though. The ship would be leaving soon and no matter what, she couldn't be on it. She had unfinished business on that island. Her captor wasn't going to leave the room any time soon, let alone undo the handcuffs. He would be no use to her on the other side of the bulkhead.

There was no way of knowing what Cole knew. The truth had become so twisted Eva couldn't afford to trust anyone. By contrast, she had to gain his trust. In order to do that, she needed to talk. A lot. There was no way a sly comment and a flirty glance would result in him giving her the slightest of chances. She had to work hard, keep the dialogue going, win him over and only then could she hope to sway him. But say what? She didn't have time to spin an elaborate yarn. Then a crazy thought hit her. To keep him talking, she could tell him something she hadn't heard from herself in a while. The truth.

If she did actually manage to make it back to the island, there was every chance she'd never make it out alive. If this plump but pleasant-looking middle-aged officer wanted to chronicle how she came to be there, at least someone would know her story. There was a chance her friends might one day find out how and why she died. Perhaps they'd understand the sacrifices she'd made, the changes she'd forged. There was a chance they'd one day know their friend, the mouthy barista from Australia, had saved the world.

She cleared her throat. "Being born with the name Eva Destruction, I was either going to be a supervillain's girlfriend or a stripper." She had his attention. "Lucky for me, I've been both."

He stared blankly as if unsure how to reply, no words formed. She continued before he could regroup. "Neither would have made my staunch feminist of a mother particularly happy. The latter came about due to a chronic shortage of cash, an overbearing landlord and more bills than a duck convention. The former, well, that's a whole other story. If she were still alive my mother would have berated me about my poor choices, particularly in men. I should have made my own mark, become the change the world needed, you know? To never be reliant on a man and forge my own destiny in the name of womankind, all that crap."

"Ah, right...but what about the explosions, and er...?"

Eva wasn't going to be distracted now. But it was interesting that he'd mentioned those. They hadn't been in his two-step summary earlier.

"Which is all fine and good, and sentiments I wholeheartedly endorse, but when a man buys you a castle, you end up forgetting all about the sisterhood. Wait, that didn't quite have the right emphasis."

She leaned forward. The uniformed man across the table fought valiantly to keep his eyes above her shoulders.

"He. Bought. Me. A. Fucking. Castle. I don't care what moral fortitude you have or suffragette principles you lean towards, when a man buys you a fully decked out French castle smack in the middle of the Rhone Valley, you sit up and take notice."

"I see, yes, but…"

"It has a moat and everything."

"Sure, but, ah, there's the small matter of how you came to be on the island and ah…"

"How did a former stripper and the daughter of a vegan feminist hold the fate of the free world, literally, in her hands?"

He nodded.

Keep him occupied. She'd started picking one of the handcuffs with the bobby pin she'd had pinned to her bikini bottoms. She'd learned long ago to have one on her person at all times. She reassessed her surroundings. No windows. Bulkhead door, locked. She assumed armed guards on the other side. The room was bare, except for the metal table and chairs, a sweaty portly man, his folder and a pen.

The pen.

The pen was sharp enough to pierce his aorta. He wouldn't be expecting her to escape the handcuffs. She'd be too fast for him to stop, even in her weakened condition. His pain would be absolute, blood everywhere. Then the door. There would be at least two burly Marines stationed outside. Problematic, but not out of the question. They'd hear the screams and come running in. She'd have to overpower them without raising the alarm. Quick. Silent. Lethal. Then all she had to do was fight her way through a shipload of US Navy personnel using any and all weapons at her disposal, find her way out of an unfamiliar vessel. She'd have to commandeer a boat, navigate her way back to the island, which had been racked by explosions and much of it under water.

She'd faced worse odds before.

There was only one problem with her elaborate plan. A minor

one, sure. She didn't have a clue how to do any of those things. Not a one.

She thought it best to keep her interviewer distracted while she came up with a more practical plan.

"How did I come to be here?" Eva asked. "It's a long story."

CHAPTER TWO

ONE MONTH BEFORE THE ISLAND

Two Jets screamed fast and low over East London. The flyovers, male posturing bullshit at its finest, seemed to be more common since the heightened terror threats. Eva didn't know where they were headed in such a hurry. The English government wasn't facing the mutinous cries like the rest of Europe.

Not that anyone seemed to care. Not a single head rose to watch them careen overhead. Why would they? Folks had other things on their minds on a Saturday night. So did Eva. She was on her way to be set up by her mates, again. Despite the battlefield of dating casualties that made the current Russian civil war look like a garden party, they held out hope for her. Even if she didn't.

This guy was apparently 'nice'. An adjective that generally struck fear into the hearts of single woman everywhere but, as far as Eva was concerned, nice would be a pleasant change. Long overdue, in fact. She absentmindedly tugged at her sleeve as if to hide her tattoos and wondered why she'd felt the need to conceal them. If she hit it off with this guy, he'd see her intricate rose-themed sleeve tats decorating her body in all kinds of strategic places. They were a part of her, a manifestation of her treasured rebellious spirit, so why would she feel the need to hide them?

THE BARISTA'S GUIDE TO ESPIONAGE

Because you're not attracting the bad boys any more. You're done with that now.

Approaching the neon-lit corner bar, she exhaled the last of the cold night air and pulled the heavy wooden door open. She was hit by multiple sensations at once, but the warmth was the most shocking, given the chilly December night. The noise of laughter, mixed with the sound system pumping out some new band she probably should know, but didn't, assaulted her ears.

The TV in the corner blared the news headlines, which basically entailed the football results. In the corner, Nancy stood and held her hand high in the air. It barely came above most folk's heads. Eva waved back and removed her heavy black coat.

All day, she'd continually told herself it wasn't too late to pull out. Suddenly it was. Perhaps reading her mind, Nancy had weaved through the punters and stood between her and the door. *Sneaky bitch.* Another reason she loved her. They hugged and Nancy took in her outfit and gave an appreciative nod. It turned into a scowl when she saw the item under Eva's arm.

"Uh, my love, what's that?" she asked with her faint Irish lilt. The full Irish lilt tended to only come out when she was drunk or yelling at her husband.

"It's a book, they still have them you know."

"You brought a book to a blind date?"

Eva tucked a strand of raven hair behind her ear and shrugged.

"No books tonight, sweetie, you have a man to meet." Nancy took the heavy tome and slipped it in the pocket of her hanging coat.

Eva screwed her lips into a semi-snarl. "Is this one potentially Geronimo-worthy or am I just wasting my time?"

Nancy and Eva had many discussions, usually at ill-advised hours of the morning after too many drinks, about Eva's Geronimo theory. Not one to believe in predetermination or a god, she still clung to the hope that when she found 'the one', it would be a boots and all, blindly jump out of a plane without a para-chute kind of deal. So far life had not been kind to her Geronimo theory.

"How the hell would I know? I just put 'em up for you to knock down."

"What do I pay you for then?"

"You don't pay me anything. My reward is to live vicariously through your sexploits and tell derogatory stories about you when you're out of earshot."

Eva fought the grin creeping into the corner of her mouth. "Can this one at least be a good kisser? It's a seriously underrated skill."

"I didn't pre-kiss him to find out, sorry. I'll do better next time."

"Next time? Thanks for the vote of confidence."

"I have met you."

Eva tilted her head, regal. "Touché."

Nancy grasped her arm and half guided, half dragged her to their table.

Paul, Nancy's loyal bloodhound of a husband, greeted her with the requisite bear hug that lifted her feet off the ground. Eva was introduced to Stephen, 'with a ph, not a v'.

Eva offered a feeble, "Hi," sat and unzipped her leather jacket.

At least he was reasonably good-looking this time. Conventional straight back and sides haircut, a soft face and an affable demeanour. Brown hair, green eyes, nothing offensive, nothing jaw-dropping. He seemed designed by a committee to represent average. Nice and average.

The last one Nancy tried to set her up with had only left his mum's basement to pick up the latest video game, or an industrial-sized bucket of cold sore cream. Eva had had to fake period cramps to get out of a second drink. Stephen with a ph looked positively normal by comparison. Sensible trousers, a shirt and jumper. Not exactly neo-punk, but he had his own hair and a nice face. There was that word again.

A loud collective 'whoo!' filled the room, causing Eva to look around the bar. It was followed by a round of enthusiastic applause and cheering. Paul tugged one of the celebrators hollering at the TV and asked what was going on.

"Liverpool won. Holy crap!" Paul said. *English and their football.*

It was nice to see Paul out. He usually spent long hours at

the Treasury. When she asked exactly what he did the answers were long and tedious with no actual substance. Nancy was an administrator at HSBC. Her two best friend's vocations certainly didn't match their personalities. Paul rarely spoke of his job, in fact he was downright elusive about it. She sometimes wondered if it was because it was so boring it would make mere mortals slip into a coma if he were to explain.

"I guess a win is a good enough reason as any to have some booze." Nancy slapped her hands together. "Paul, can you help me with the drinks, love?"

Paul sighed, then muttered, "Since when did you have issues carrying four pints?"

Nancy pulled her lovably oblivious husband to his feet and shoved him towards the bar.

"Way to be fucking obvious, Nance." Eva mentally slapped herself. She had to watch her mouth around new fuckers. Nancy gave her a scowl and followed her husband towards the bar.

"So," Eva said sitting opposite Stephen with what she hoped wasn't a manic grin.

"So." He smiled a pleasant smile. "What do you do, Eva?"

That was his first question? Out of all the myriad of possibilities the English language offered, three thousand years of Western civilisation and four hundred years of freely available literature, and that's the best he could come up with?

One pint and she was out of there.

Eva forced a pleasant tone. *May as well play along.* "I'm a barista."

"Oh, fascinating, I've always been intrigued by the law. I thought about it in college, but I was put off by all that reading. I wouldn't have picked you for a lawyer, but I guess they aren't all the button-down type." He gave an odd half-shrug.

"No, I think you misheard me. I'm a barista, not a barrister. You know, coffee."

Half a pint. Tops.

"Oh right, must have been the accent. You're Australian?" He nodded in her direction, like her accent was a physical thing to be gestured at.

"Ah-huh. And you're from Yorkshire, a few years gone I'm guessing."

His dark eyebrows shot up. "How the did you know that? I haven't been there since I was five."

"The consonants. You hide it well by rounding them out, but they're still there just under the surface." Eva's fingers danced against the tabletop, but on the inside, she cringed and told herself to shut up. Why had she decided to pull out her party trick for accents? She was meant to be getting to know the guy, not showing off.

Stephen seemed to not mind. "Nancy didn't mention the Australian thing."

Eva forced herself to not roll her eyes. "Is that a problem?"

If he does a kangaroo impression I'm out of here.

"Not at all. Given the state of the world, Australians are getting to be the new ruling class, I guess, given recent events, I mean." He leaned forward then, giving her a megawatt smile. "Plus, I've always loved the accent."

Alright, a pint.

"You're kidding me, right?" Eva couldn't stop the teasing note entering her voice. "No one loves the Aussie accent. We barely tolerate it. All those flat vowels. It makes the South African accent sound positively French by comparison."

Nancy strode over and placed two pints before them. "They're just pouring ours, could be a bit." *Saved by the beer*, Eva thought.

Nancy nodded at Eva. "I like your scarf." She winked and returned to the bar where she put her arm around her lug of a husband.

"She's right you know."

Blinking, Eva asked, "I'm sorry?"

"Your scarf," Stephen said. "It really suits you, brings out the green in your eyes. I think you look fantastic."

"I was unaware there was a new definition of fantastic that means one's been pulled through a hedge backwards."

Before he could issue an answer, the TV blaring in the background became more obvious. Eva heard the news anchor state there was an escalation in the Horatio Lancing crisis. The crowd lowered its volume to a dull murmur.

Eva's jaw clenched and her eyes went wide. She broke into a sweat. Stephen with a ph probably thought she was having some kind of fit.

From the end of the bar, Nancy's head whipped around. Standing as high as a five foot four woman could, she squinted at the end of the bar and yelled, "Neville!" motioning to the TV.

The barman, who was busy giving change to a customer, gazed at Nancy, then the screen. "Shit, sorry Nance! Right." He reached for the rear of the bar and fumbled with the remote. The TV screen blipped off.

Heads turned in his direction, unimpressed. "What the hell, man?"

"Standing bar rule fifty-seven, no Lancing after nine on a Saturday night, mate."

"It's eight forty-five."

"My bar. My rules." Neville shrugged. He placed the remote behind dusty bottles of vodka. "It's not like it won't be repeated *ad nauseam* tomorrow. We could all use a break from that guy."

The crowd slowly turned away from the screen and the bar took on the familiar ambiance of a Saturday night pub.

Nancy and Paul returned to the table, concern in their eyes. "You all right, love?" Nancy asked stroking Eva's hand.

Eva nodded, taking a deep breath. "Yeah, fine. It's just, you know–"

"I know."

"Am I missing something?" Stephen asked, frowning.

"Got you a Newcastle Brown," Paul said, pointing at the beer on the table. "Hope that's alright. Kilkenny always gives me gas."

"Uh, yeah. Fine, thanks."

Nancy put on her best congenial façade. "Did Eva tell you about her Masters Degree?"

Stephen's frown didn't ease up. "No, she didn't."

"You know that's not quite true," Paul interrupted. "Evie has two. Political Science, and–"

Since the day Eva and Paul had met, Paul had called her Evie. He'd initially misremembered her name, and had since stuck with it. It was a quirk only long-time friends could understand. But it wasn't a nickname she normally liked.

Eva fought to dismiss the lingering malaise from seeing the news report. It was like her mind had temporarily seized and she had to fight to regain control. Finally she said, "History."

Stephen nodded his approval.

"And she speaks three languages. Four if you count Australian."

Nancy was incorrigible. Why didn't she put Eva in a pen and ask men to come up and inspect her teeth? Nancy failed to mention that she spoke as many languages as Eva. In fact, it was how they'd first met: Eva had been shopping in some snooty high-end store in Regent Street, when a shop assistant had started bitching about her under her breath in French. Eva had insulted her back with compound interest. In French. Nancy had been standing in line and laughed her arse off. They'd bonded and gone for coffee. They'd discussed how many languages they spoke and picked out all the best swear words. A lifelong friendship was born.

Nancy put down her pint and wiped away her little Newcastle Ale moustache. "In spite of all that, she's wasting her time making coffees for corporate wankers and hipsters. I don't get the appeal."

Eva gave a friendly shake of her head. "Hey, if I want to know how to properly spell something or lose an empire, then I'll talk to the English. Coffee, not so much."

Nance rolled her eyes. "What would an Australian know about coffee?"

"Bitch, please. I come from Melbourne, we rode Starbucks out of town on a rail." Raising an eyebrow at Nancy, Eva asked, "You've tasted my coffee, and?"

Nancy shifted uncomfortably, took a sip of her beer and mumbled something incomprehensible.

"You'll have to excuse me, I didn't quite catch that."

"It's like tasting angel semen, okay! Happy, Miss Awesome Barista?"

"I am now. Nobody's referred to my coffee like *that* before."

Paul nodded, patted his wife's leg, "And I hope they never do again."

"Two Masters, eh?" Stephen sounded impressed. "That's fairly amazing."

"What's probably more amazing is that they didn't throw me out for being a fraud before they handed me those considerably expensive slips of paper."

Stephen jutted his chin out. "You tend to put yourself down a lot, don't you? You really have no reason to."

Eva tucked her stray hair behind her ear. Maybe she could stay a bit longer. Two pints, but that was it.

Nancy gave them both a half-grin. "So, you two seem to be getting along, then?"

"Rather well, I think," Stephen said. "Definitely no faults I can find."

Eva let out an unintentional, "Ha!" Recovering, she cocked her head in Stephen's direction. "You're improving, Nance. He's nice."

"Ah." Stephen sighed, dejected. "Nice." Somehow, he managed to have 'nice' rhyme with 'loser'. "Girls don't go for the nice guys do they? They prefer a bad boy."

Nancy snorted. "Let me tell you something, Stephen. Girls going for bad boys is bullshit. I've seen it a million times." Eva caught Nance eyeing her. "If a woman wants someone to treat her like a servant and alternate between being smothered and ignored, she can get a damned cat."

Eva patted Stephen's knee. "Darlin', let me tell you something. Bad boys have their appeal, a lot of, well, let's just say, girls dream about the bad guy, but we always end up with the nice ones." She sipped her beer. "Bad boys are overrated."

As Eva glanced across the bar to the blank TV screen, she hoped he believed the lie. All her adult life, she'd dated men who were bad for her. Men who treated her dreadfully and under-

21

valued her worth. She knew that, she'd always known that, and yet she failed to break the cycle. There had only been one man who'd treated her with respect and as an equal. It was a shame he'd also threatened every government on Earth and drawn UN condemnation.

Eva ran her finger around the rim of her pint. Why were all the best kissers hell-bent on tearing down the world?

CHAPTER THREE

Notwithstanding outward appearances, Stephen with ph had some skill. He flipped her onto her back, hardly missing a stroke. All right, quite a bit of skill. In the small confines of her bedroom, he didn't seem to mind her tattoos. Though he did seem a little shocked when she suggested keeping her heels on, displaying a possible gap in his kink factor, but he was certainly giving it his all.

Eva wrapped her slender legs around his torso and dragged her nails down his admirably muscular back. When she bit his nipple he faltered and lost his rhythm. Okay, she would hold back a little, let him show her how far he was willing to go. Her heels met each other and knocked together pleasurably. They were hideously high and revoltingly expensive, just the way she liked them.

He slowed and teased by withdrawing, then entering ever so slightly more than the previous stroke. She admired his self-control, but it wasn't the time.

She grasped both sides of his face and said with all the forceful-ness she could muster, "Faster. Now."

"Certainly."

Eva closed her eyes and sank her head into her pillow. The

bedroom swelled pleasantly around her. Deep within her a familiar, yet long-absent primal feeling stirred within. *Christ it feels good.*
It was a pity it would end too soon.

There was no way she would be lucky enough to reach her
goal. That was far too much to ask. Even with Stephen's valiant
efforts she was going to be left disappointed and unsatisfied.

His breathing quickened, his thrusting less managed and more
urgent. Quiet moans emanated from his lips. She held on tighter,
knowing it would make no difference.

Heat spread to all parts of her body, her synapses popped. She
could have sworn she'd heard the sound of smashing glass.

Frantic, Stephen was visibly holding back. Bless him. A wave of
pleasure washed over her and black shapes filled the fringes of her
vision. He began to make *that* noise and it would all be over in a
matter of seconds. Almost pleading, Eva tried desperately to hold
on to the last vestiges of pleasure knowing it pointless.

When he made *the* face, it was too late for both of them. It was
ludicrous to think she could achieve climax with this guy. What
was she thinking? His thrusting frantic, she was waiting for an
orgasm that would never come.

Before she knew what was happening the dark shadows in the
corner of the room reached for Stephen and he was wrenched from
her grasp. His face displayed nothing but pure shock as it disappeared into the darkness of her room.

Eva threw her arms in the air, casting every ounce of frustration. "Every fucking time, guys!" she shouted at the four featureless black Kevlar masks. There was exhaustion in her words, she'd
had this conversation too many times. "Just once, once, I'd like you
to burst in after I come. Is that too much to ask?"

From the end of the bed came an exclamation of unintentional
pleasure. She looked in Stephen's direction. Okay, so he was very
close, then. The tip of the condom expanded with a pleasurable
ejaculate.

Stephen, still in shock, managed to utter, "Sorry."

"That's gross," one of the guards said.

Eva shrugged. "Could have been worse, he might have been

riding bareback and you'd have a nice white stripe down your trousers."

The other faceless guard said, "She's right. You know how hard it is to get that off a black uniform?"

His black-clad partner asked, "How would you know?"

She knew the voice.

Stephen laughed nervously. The shortest guard grunted at that. He stepped forward and backhanded Stephen. He went flying backwards and crashed into Eva's bookshelf. In an instant she leapt to her feet and launched herself off the end of the bed. The short guard received a foot to the chest and reeled backwards. She ripped off his mask and raked a nail across his face. A bloody red trench appeared on Van Buren's cheek.

Momentarily stunned, they didn't immediately retaliate to her attack. There probably wasn't a section in the manual advising how to deal with a violent naked and horny Australian woman. Probably. That, and she was sure they had orders never to harm her. How sweet.

Seething, her fists clenched, nails digging into her palms. "Boys! Naked, semi-screwed, frustrated woman here! I will tear off every one of your testicles and wear them as a necklace if you touch him again. You've done your job – and so has he–"

Stephen covered his manhood and addressed Eva, confusion covering his face like sweat, "Sorry again. Uh, what's going on?"

"–so if you don't mind, can you please fuck right off. You've achieved your orders, you've intimidated and terrified him. Well done. Now piss off. I'm angry and frustrated, and won't be able to sleep until I take care of something, so unless you boys want to watch, you'd better get the hell out."

Eva turned to the man who until several seconds earlier had been enjoying himself. She assumed he most likely hadn't expected to be interrupted by four heavily-armed private security guards breaking into the bedroom.

"Sorry Stephen. You seem like a genuinely nice guy. But I'm sorry, it never would have worked. You were looking for what was wrong with me before? You want to know what my fault is? I'll tell you. I'm a girl that has one fatal flaw. I have this," she tapped her temple, "chip in my head where I fall for bad boys. Always have. And these guys," she waved her hand at the Kevlar-clad guards, "are a reminder of my dalliance with the baddest of all bad boys."

"You don't mean–?"

"Yep. Can I pick 'em, or can I pick 'em?"

"Are they going to kill me?"

"No." Turning to Van Buren she asked, "You're not, are you?"

Wiping the blood from his cheek, he gave the slightest shake of his head. His cold expression told her he wished it were otherwise. He was a sadistic little Mussolini, but he was as loyal as they came. If his master said stay, he'd do just that until he was a surrounded by a pool of drool. Stephen wasn't in danger, as long as Eva kept her distance he would be fine.

"No, they'll just rough you up a bit, maybe give you a threat about never seeing me again and dump you someplace unpleasant. Sorry, it's been nice."

As they dragged Stephen with a ph away, she heard the second guard murmur, "Ooh, she said *nice*. The poor bastard."

Eva stared at the phallic insult to the London skyline. At least that's what he'd told her when he'd purchased it for his headquarters. His justification was that he'd funded free schools for females throughout the Middle East, so it balanced out a bit. The fact that the fifty-storey Lancing Tower supplied an unimpeded 360 degree view of the city, a three-storey penthouse apartment and his own helipad had nothing to do with it either.

It really was rather phallic though. The last few floors curved towards the tip to add that extra layer of penisisity

Seated on a park bench opposite the building, Eva sat freezing her arse off. She'd been so livid once the guards had hauled Stephen away that she'd tossed on clothes and stormed straight over. Actually, that wasn't entirely true. She carefully picked out a flattering outfit that would *appear* as though she'd thrown it on and then stormed straight over. Same same.

Eva went through the nine circles of abuse she'd throw at him. Her seething anger multiplied with each intake of the glacial night air. The only problem with acting these scenarios out was it involved leaving the bench, entering the building and actually talking to him. Not as easy as it sounded.

Sure, there were the multiple floors of security personnel, countless anti-intruder devices, including lasers, concussion blasts, knock-out gas and random trapdoors, but they weren't the main problem. It was seeing *him* again.

The man had taken her heart, loaded it in a skeet trap, raised his gun and yelled 'Pull!' He was also the man who had shown what a skeet trap was. The smug son of a bitch was up there, swanning about and probably laughing his head off about how he'd managed to ruin yet another date for her. Didn't he know she was perfectly capable of messing up her own relationships, thank-you-very-much?

She raised herself from the cold bench and ground her teeth. Eva shook. Partly because of the freezing London air, but mostly the unmitigated rage. Her mind was made up. She pivoted on the spot and walked away from the massive cock of a building and further into the park.

Her footsteps echoed in the cold night as she strode down the cobblestone path beneath the bare winter trees. She found the toilet block. The Gents door creaked open and she selected the third cubicle. Eva closed the door behind her. It had been a while, so it took some time to find the right brick. It slid into the recess of the wall. She counted to five, stood back and waited. A series of whis-per-quiet *clicks* and *whirrs* emanated from behind the wall until it swung open, toilet and all, to reveal stairs descending into darkness.

It took a few seconds for the lights to flicker on and she had a moment of doubt. It only took the memory of the private security guards dragging away another man she'd brought back to her apartment to steel her resolve. *Twat.* She pressed the button to close the door behind her and marched down the secret passage.

After the hundred-metre walk, she halted, dread enveloping her. Was she really going to do this? How would he react? Would he even be in? Would he see her? And if he did, would he turn her words around so his argument seemed like the most logical thing in the world, like he always did? Would he yell? Embrace her? Ignore her? What did she really want? *Damn Eva, how much did he mess you up?*

Before she had a chance to think about it, her black polished fingernails typed in the code and pressed the only button available – up. The code hadn't been changed, did that mean anything? She tried to steady herself. *Good luck with that.* She stepped into the elevator and it ascended noiselessly.

Only two other people had access to his secret elevator; Eva and his Security Chief, Van Buren. The latter had told her the small collection of individual contractors who made it were *apparently* no longer alive. Or so he said. She was never sure if his posturing was an attempt to propagate Lancing's legend, an attempt to shake her, or was actually true. She suspected a combination of the first two.

Lancing's political aggression of late was aimed at the corrupt and intensely greedy. It had won him greater favour even in the face of his less than subtle, or legal, methods. Putting a bullet in the head of an apprentice electrician wasn't really his style.

The elevator *pinged* far too loudly for her liking. The doors slid open with a gentle *hiss.* She blinked several times so her eyes could adjust. The harsh fluorescents of the elevator contrasted with the low-lit mahogany interior of his inner sanctum.

It never failed to impress. The stunning view, the massive open plan room taking up the entire floor, coupled with the décor that was at once stylish, but masculine. The grey colour scheme accentuated the wooden features, including the wet bar, the two-storey library, the huge raging fire in the centre of the room. In the countless times she'd been there, she'd never once wondered where the smoke went. *Yeah, because that's what you should be focussed on right now.*

If the fire was lit, he must be home. But she couldn't see him. Her chest constricted when she realised he might have company. Of the female variety. If he was entertaining some skank that would be all Eva needed to send her crashing through the nearest window.

A small cough emanated from the sunken floor lounge next to the fire. He was in, though she couldn't see him. It was possible to hide pretty well down there. They'd spent hours in it, wrapped in each other's arms, ignoring the world. Given who he was, that was quite something.

Without standing, he said, "So, Eva, I'm thinking of calling the new European currency ducats, what do you think? I'm leaning towards it partly because I need a name that's not currently used for legal tender, but mostly because it makes me laugh."

He raised his head above the polished Tasmanian Oak floorboards and shot her a devastatingly cheeky grin. *Bloody hell he was good-looking.*

With clenched jaw, she strode over but found herself unable to utter a single syllable. He lounged amongst the numerous cushions, dressed casually in jeans, a tight white t-shirt and bare feet. Myriad of computer pads at his feet displayed figures, stock ticker-tapes and footage from parliaments around the world shouting his name. Ignoring her anger, he waved pleasantly.

Smug git.

"Hi. I've missed you."

She held up a single accusatory index finger and pinched her lips together. Countless emotions bombarded her at once. The urge to throw something heavy at his flawless face, the need to scream abuse until her lungs bled, or maybe grab one of the logs from the fire and raze the whole bloody building to the ground.

But deep down, that wasn't what upset her most. The fact that despite everything she'd been through, including tonight, she still loved the bastard.

Finally able to gather enough willpower to speak, she croaked, "Where the hell do you get off sending guards into my apartment?"

"My men thought you were in danger." Harry gave a congenial shrug. "They said you were crying for help."

That was a new one. She issued an incredulous look. "I was crying, but the 'oh god' kind."

"And you the hardcore atheist."

This was not going how she'd envisaged. All she'd wanted was to send a little abuse his way, for him to make a full and unqualified apology, and to promise never to interfere in her life again. Was that too much to ask?

While Eva desperately tried to find the words to convey all that, he said, "Can I get you a drink? I always have a bottle of Jägermeister handy, in case you pop by."

Eva remained rigid and clenched her jaw. Bad memories came to mind of a drunken night in Algiers. Visions of her head in a gutter and Harry holding her hair back. She'd vowed never to touch Jägermeister again. How could he make jokes?

"Bring it on. I'll just chuck on your pretty floor."

Harry shrugged. "Lacking some of your usual tact, wouldn't you say?"

"Tact is reserved for people who haven't seen you naked."

That made him smile. Casually, he said, "Did you hear I have something cooking for tomorrow?"

It was a stupid question. Of course she had. The entire world had. If anyone else had pulled what Harry had in the last few days they'd have been hauled in front of the nearest firing squad. Harry wasn't like anyone else. Not that long ago he'd been a bona fide hero. A lot of the world, London in particular, still loved him and that had given him leverage. Unfortunately for Harry he'd pretty much squandered all of the goodwill he had left.

"Yeah, I've heard. You've pissed off the entire world, Harry. No small feat."

"Oh you're sweet, you still follow my career." He'd always loved teasing her. "The mild leaks I've released so far have ruffled a few feathers, yes. But I assure you that's merely a forewarning. Spirited foreplay, if you will. What's coming is going to be good.

It'll make Russia look like a schoolyard skirmish. As well it should, I spent a whole lot more time on it than I did on that."

"Wait, what? You? You made Russia happen? The civil war. That was you?"

"It was a little experiment."

"Russia, little?" He had influence, but to bring down a former superpower? Did he have *that* much power? "How the hell did you do that?"

"A sprinkle of truth here, a well-timed article there, a social media signal boost over here, a gentle nudge there and ta-dah."

"Death on a stupendous scale."

"Yes, that. But the Russian people have their country back. I'll do better next time."

"Next time? What exactly are you planning, Harry?"

"I'm planning what I always have, Eva. I'm planning on making the world a better place."

"Your definition of better."

"Which, as I recall, was also yours."

"This isn't a game, Harry. You're playing Risk with the world."

"I was never any good at Risk."

"I know, I kept beating your arse."

"I was always more partial to nude Twister." He cast her a cheeky grin. "And I'll be forever thankful to you for introducing me to it."

The mention of sex jolted her back to the reason she was there, with a side flashback to some very pleasant naked memories. And she had to stop thinking of that word. Naked. Naked. Naked. She had to focus on what she came for, not civil wars and world government problems.

Way to dial up the narcissism Eva.

She shook her head. "Look, listen–"

"You want me to do both?"

"I want you to shut up for a start. You have no right to send in your trained monkeys. I don't want your goons anywhere near me."

"They're there for your protection, if someone–"

She thrust her finger in the air again, and this time it worked. He stopped talking.

"Let's leave out the total creep factor that you've had me followed or bugged, or whatever it is you've been doing, but instead let's focus on the fact that you interrupted the first decent screw I've had in months. You have no idea what it's like to be that frustrated and to–"

"Yes I do."

"Wait, what? You haven't…in a year? Since we broke up?"

He gave a slight pitch of his head in acknowledgement and Eva was bombarded with a whole new set of emotions; less angry ones, but worse. Bordering on affectionate. Casting her gaze towards the London skyline, she tried to process what any of it meant.

No. This is what he does. What he always does.

Not this time.

She needed to gather her thoughts. She needed to shape them into a cohesive and adult response.

Eva sniffed. "I'm going to take a wiz."

She marched towards Harry's luxurious bathroom and didn't even wait to see his reaction. The door slammed behind her. She flicked the light switch and the enormous black tiled bathroom that was larger than her first apartment was bathed in soft light.

She stared at her face in the huge high-tech mirror. Stock prices and news feeds scrolled along its base. Even with the designer lighting she looked like hell. Eva was unsure if the wish for a less dishevelled face staring back at her was because it was the best form of revenge or because she wanted him to want her. If it was the latter, what would she do with that?

Her first instinct was to reapply her lipstick. She could have punched herself in the face. She stared into her bloodshot eyes. "He's really done a number on you hasn't he? You're a complete mess."

"I think you're positively adorable."

Her head snapped to the door, but it remained steadfastly

closed. Did Harry have the bathroom under surveillance? His *own* bathroom? That was beyond creepy.

But it wasn't Harry's voice, so who?

The bathroom was huge, but not large enough to conceal another human swanning around in it. Glancing up, her hand shot to her mouth to stifle the scream.

Suspended by wires hanging from the open skylight in the ceiling was a man in a harness, dressed in all black. Chiselled jaw, blond cropped hair and a smile so incandescent it made the sun look like a blown light globe.

Raising one eyebrow he said, "I can assure you this is exactly what it looks like."

CHAPTER FOUR

Eva wasn't a screamer.

That was a lie.

Eva wasn't a screamer in a non-recreational sense.

Staring up at the intruder suspended from the ceiling she re-evaluated her screaming philosophy. As he unhooked himself from the harness, Eva wondered why she didn't run into the other room and raise the alarm. His casual manner made her want to trust him. There were no fast moves. His actions, measured, unhurried. Confident.

That, and she'd met him once before.

It was eighteen months before, when she'd first started dating Harry. He'd tried to warn her off. It didn't take. He obviously knew nothing about her, otherwise he'd have known telling Eva to stay away was the perfect way to make her run directly for what-ever she was being warned about.

Using his impressive muscular ability, the intruder lowered himself and landed panther-like before her. He was tall, wide-shouldered. The smile never stopped beaming. His attractiveness was persuasive, yes, but there was more to it. His eyes. Oh she remembered those eyes. At once charming and mischievous. It was a shame the whole package came wrapped in a big blanket of chauvinistic piggery.

Was he the bad guy? Was Harry? She didn't know any more. What Harry was trying to achieve on a world scale was breath-taking and audacious. If he could manage to pull it off the world would be much better for it, she honestly believed that. It were his methods she had issues with. So did every other Western govern-ment. Did blackmail and government manipulation justify the end?

If the man standing before her was there to stop him, where did she stand? Who wore the white hat and who wore the black? Espe-cially in light of the Russian thing. Whose side was Eva on?

"Thank you for not alerting him," he said in a whisper. "I spent a good hour and a half scaling this bastard in the middle of winter and didn't fancy being tossed off straight after all that effort without so much as a gold star and a stiff whiskey."

When Eva first met him he'd said he worked for MI6. She'd taken him at his word as she doubted he carried a business card.

"Give me one reason why I shouldn't scream my head off?" she asked in a harsh whisper.

"Oh, my dear, I think that's exactly the wrong phrasing. One thing at a time."

Eva hated herself for letting a smirk escape. Then she saw his shoulder holster.

He followed the direction of her glance. "I'm not an assassin if that's what you're worried about."

"I'm not."

She was.

Eva had been in the bathroom too long. Harry would be getting suspicious.

He tilted his head, sizing her up, taking his time, lingering on her sleeve tats. "You've changed your hair. I like it. I was led to believe you and Mr Lancing were no longer an item."

"We're not. Just looking up an old ex."

"How ex?"

"The ex-iest there is."

"Good." He seemed pleased by that. "And you're still not easily rattled, I see."

"You'd be surprised how many men I meet suspended from the roof."

The corners of his eyes crinkled. That amused him. "Somehow I believe everything about you would be surprising."

Those eyes. Jesus. She could swim around in those baby blues for hours.

"Well, what are you here for?" she asked determined not to be swayed by his casual charm.

She saw him weigh up his answer. A darkness fell over his face. The smile remained, but was tainted by a hardness. His tone remained unconcerned. "You may have heard Mr Lancing has threatened to divulge certain information publicly tomorrow? Well I'm here to retrieve it as a matter of national security." He glanced at his thick black wristwatch. "Before the airstrike."

Eva spluttered, "Airstrike?"

"Yes, and…" he glanced at his watch again, "every moment I spend in your company, while thoroughly delightful, means I'm failing in my mission. So, if you'll excuse me."

He made to walk past her, but Eva's palm hit his chest. Hard as rock.

"Hang on there, Spiderman. You said airstrike. Here? You mean the English are going to fire on a civilian building in the middle of London?"

"Not us, no," he replied peeling off her hand. "Now, if you could momentarily distract him, I can make my way to his study on the second floor. We haven't much time."

"You expect me to trust you? Just like that? Nope, it doesn't work that way, Sunshine. You have to wine and dine me, put in the hard yards. I'm not going to metaphorically open my legs for you because you flash me a naughty smirk and spin me a tale about national security. This is our second date, at best you could expect a handjob if you're lucky."

A wicked grin crept across his face.

"Again, metaphorically," she said quickly. "You have to earn my trust." Eva shook her head. "Is that the way it normally works for you and women? Give them a story, slide them a sneaky smirk and they're yours? Mission accomplished, cocktails at midnight and back to your place for a one-night stand they'll never forget?"

He glanced at his watch and longingly spied the door. "To be honest, well, yes."

Swamp donkeys, he was telling the truth. Were women disposable to him? Something to be conquered then discarded?

Eva clenched her fists. Priorities. This wasn't about her. She had to decide if she trusted this man and, if she did, would she allow him to accomplish his mission? Did she still believe in Harry's goals any more? His methods? Him?

"This is going to sound boorish," he said interrupting her thoughts, "and as much as I'm enjoying our little tete-a-tete I really must insist that you–"

"Shit or get off the pot?"

"Yes, ah, that." He glanced at his wrist.

"I'm going to need some proof."

"I'm terribly sorry, my top secret dossier and wax-sealed orders from the PM are in my other trousers."

"Hmm, mighty snarky for someone desperate for my help."

"I will concede there may have been the slightest hint of snark, but you must appreciate there's no time. You have to trust me or not. There's no time to get the PM out of bed, plus she's a heavy sleeper and gets most cranky when one calls her in the middle of the night. I can only implore you to have faith that I am on the mission I stated and it is of the utmost importance that I be allowed to complete it. We're out of time."

"What are you going to do?"

He held up a small USB stick. "The boffins have a program, but it needs a physical access point. In this case, Mr Lancing's office computer. It will identify the hackers he's been using, suck all the secrets he has and delete it at the source while retaining a copy on this."

Eva mulled it over. "How about this for a compromise? I let you in and distract Harry long enough to get what you need. Then you hand it to me, all of it, at which point I get you out via a private elevator, alleviating the need for all that pesky building-scaling business. Then you prove to me you are who you say you are. If I'm satisfied, you may have your precious information. But no harm is to come to Harry."

He nodded.

"Repeat it," Eva said harshly.

"No harm will come to Mr Lancing."

"Right. So how does that all sound? And before you answer, that's the only deal on the table. The next best option is for me to run into the next room yelling, 'There's a spy in the bathroom, there's a spy in the bathroom!' Your call."

His eyebrows met and he frowned approvingly. He almost appeared impressed. "What sort of madman lets a woman like you get away?"

"The kind of madman who thinks a man has any right to allow or disallow a woman to 'get away'. Jesus, this isn't the fifties. You know women have choices these days, right?" Eva didn't attempt to hide the contempt in her voice. He really did believe women were objects. "Do we have an accord?"

"We do." He motioned to the door. "Ladies first."

"And patronising pricks second."

Not waiting to see his reaction, she entered the open plan apartment. Harry was nowhere to be seen.

Holding the bathroom door open, she tentatively called out, "Harry?"

No answer.

She couldn't usher in the spy or whatever he was until she knew where Harry was. The spy. *You don't even know his name.* What the hell was she doing?

"Did you fall in?"

Harry stood behind the bar, shaker in hand. The city lights extended as far as the hazy London night sky allowed. The view left her speechless every time she saw it. Which had been a lot.

Eva grinned. "I'll have an Old Fashioned, heavy on the bourbon."

Harry looked despondently at the shaker in his hand. "I was making Illusions."

"Sorry, I was unaware this was a nightclub in the nineties. Old Fashioned thanks."

Harry turned as she knew he would. The bourbon was on the top shelf of the well-stocked bar. With her hand, she motioned the spy to go and she took the long way to the bar. From the corner of her eye she observed him sprint towards the stairs to the study. He didn't make a sound.

"I don't want to know what you were doing in there, do I?" Harry asked.

"You really don't."

Placing bottles before him, Harry paused. "I miss you, Eva. Every single day."

"I haven't missed your goons, I must say."

"An overreaction."

"An understatement."

Harry placed a highball glass on the bar, filled it with ice and free-poured the ingredients. He asked, "Orange slice or cherry?"

"Neither."

"Of course." He slid it over.

Eva downed it one and slammed the glass on the bar. "Again."

"Thirsty?"

"Pissed."

"At?"

"Seriously?"

Harry poured another cocktail. "By the way, your gentleman caller is safely home, unharmed. He probably won't call you again, but my men didn't injure him."

"It's hardly the point."

"Then what is?"

"Letting me go, Harry. That's the point, it's always been the point."

"I know it's going to sound all teenage angsty, but I love you, Eva. It's not even the fact people don't generally say no to me, it's...well..." He poured the Illusion into a martini glass and took a

39

sip. She could always tell when he was gathering his thoughts, the slightest crease formed above the bridge of his nose. "If you want, I'll stop. Everything. The protective surveillance, the drunken 3.00 a.m. calls, the satellite tracking–"

"The what?"

"–everything. I'll stop it all if you answer one question. It doesn't even matter how you answer it, just look me in the eye and reply."

Eva knew what the question would be. She didn't want to answer it. She really didn't. For all sorts of reasons.

"Do you still love me, Eva?"

How does he do that?

Before she could answer, two small flashes caught Eva's eye in the sky somewhere over Waterloo. She was about to look away when she witnessed the unmistakable trails of two missiles. The jet fighter banked and bugged out. The missiles were headed straight for them.

"Uh, Harry, you might want to have a gander out the–"

Claxons blared and red lights flashed, piercing the soft lighting of the penthouse. His mobile rang and he grabbed it.

"What's going on, Van? Can we–? All right, get everyone out. Go!"

Without hanging up, he tossed the phone aside and raced around the bar. He grabbed Eva's hand and led her towards the centre of the vast apartment. Matter-of-factly, he said, "We'll never make it in time."

"A helicopter?"

"Not enough time. Sorry." He stroked her chin and for an instant, it was if the last year hadn't existed. His head swung towards the window. "It's almost here, but we can–"

Harry stopped abruptly when he heard the thudding footsteps on the stairs. The dark-clad spy halted when he saw both sets of eyes on him.

The spy tossed a USB stick in the air. "Got it, cheers, Eva." He grinned cheekily at her.

Harry's head snapped around to her.

The expression of betrayal was absolute.

Eva had never been so gutted in her life.

Stepping away, Harry reeled backwards. In all they'd been through, the hardships and losses he'd suffered, she'd never seen him so distraught. So lost. So betrayed.

He half staggered, half fell into his sunken floor lounge and scrambled for a wooden panel. It slid across and he pressed a glowing red button. Steel shutters slammed together above his head forming a silver floor where there wasn't one a second before. A whirring sound was closely followed by a *whoosh* of an escape hatch disappearing into the depths of the building.

It took a moment for Eva to realise what had happened.

"He left me. I can't believe he left me."

The spy grabbed her hand and wrenched her from her malaise. As they broke into a run he drew a pistol and fired at the window before them. It took four bullets before the floor to ceiling window shattered. The spy didn't slow his pace. Eva did. Skidding to a halt, she realised the missiles were nearly on them.

He extended his hand. "Come with me if you want to live."

In defiance of the situation, Eva said, "I can't believe you just said that."

Fragments of glass cracked underfoot. The wind buffeted them as they stood on the fifty-storey precipice.

Time had run out. With no time for debate they leapt out the building.

The missiles smashed through the windows on the other side of the building. In a deafening instant, reds and oranges assaulted her eyes as the terrifying roar, smoke and debris engulfed them. All air in her lungs was punched out only to be replaced by razorblades.

And they fell.

And fell.

And fell.

She desperately tried to clutch empty air. The spy's grip was a vice on her wrist.

She was going to die. Like this. Because of Harry. Eva always suspected she'd die because of him.

Being well read, she knew the whole unconscious-before-you-hit-the-ground thing was bullshit. People died horribly, fully cognisant. Eva awaited her death. She waited for the impact.

It came sooner than she thought.

The landing was hard and unexpected. They hit the hard glass curvature of Lancing Tower's forty-eighth floor. She had always derided the rounded upper portion of his tower as being far too phallic. No longer. The two of them spun out of control. The spy's grip never faltered, it was as if he were part of her.

Their speed increased and soon they'd run out of the tower and careened over the edge into the abyss and certain death.

Eva wouldn't allow that.

She kicked. Frantic, desperate kicks. The accumulated effect gave her some semblance of direction over their unrestrained slide. The spy didn't know what she was doing, but joined in when he realised their skid was less out of control. They both kicked. They increased speed, but in one direction.

She was aiming for something.

The world shook around them. Explosions shook the floors above. Fingers of fire ignited the air.

This was it. Their one shot.

It wouldn't be pretty and it would hurt. A lot. Even if it did work, and it most likely wouldn't, the impact would probably kill them. But it was all they had.

Realisation flashed across the spy's face and he doubled his efforts. The window-washing rig. When it wasn't in use it was hidden on the edge between the curvature of the top of the tower and the rest of the building. It was the only non-smooth surface of the entire structure, and they were hurtling towards it.

They were going to overshoot it.

Eva dug her heels in and skidded. The spy spun around and slingshotted over her. But it was enough. They were back on target. Probably. With their feet, they slowed their descent as much as they could, which wasn't a lot. All they had to do was hope their momentum didn't fling them too far. Then they really would be done for.

The crash was painful and ugly. They both hurtled into the thin window-washing scaffold with a bone-crunching thud. Limbs flailed and cries of pain were issued. The scaffold bounced off the building and creaked. It crashed back into the edifice before leaning to one side. The winch groaned. Then...nothing. The scaffold stayed fast.

For the first time in forever, Eva breathed.

What was once Harry's penthouse rocked with blasts above them.

They collectively sucked in half of London's available air.

After what seemed like hours, Eva finally gathered her wits and asked, "That was your grand plan? Jump out of a building?"

"The fact we're discussing it seems that the plan was not without merit."

"Thanks to me."

"Thanks to you, yes." He touched his rib and winced. "You handled yourself gracefully and with more guts than I've seen highly trained specialists muster in far less harrowing circumstances. In short, you done good."

"Living is good."

"It is indeed."

A wall of flame blew out a window above them, showering them in glass. The spy slid towards the control panel for the washing scaffold. The controls were hidden behind a sheet of plain metal locked in place. He rattled it once, shrugged and left it.

"What, that's it? Give it a wiggle and then give up?" Eva asked.

"Do you have a better idea?"

"It seems like I always do." She leaned over and assessed the lock. "Five pin Yale. Piece of piss."

"What, you're going to..."

The spy didn't finish his sentence once he saw Eva pull out her small leather lock pick case from her jeans pocket. It was a habit she'd never been able to give up. Her chequered past had given her the skill, and her adventurous spirit meant she'd continued to carry it with her in the present. That, and she hadn't been one hundred percent sure Harry would let her in.

"A half diamond and a flat tension wrench should do the job," she said more to herself.

She plunged the pick in and within a minute the lock clicked open to reveal the panel. Eva didn't even attempt to hide the smugness. With a theatrical flourish she pressed the down button for the scaffold. Nothing happened.

The spy crossed his arms and nodded below. "No power." Not a single light shone anywhere on the building. "But an impressive show of nefarious skill there. You very nearly showed me up. It could have been uncomfortable for both of us."

"What, you couldn't handle being saved by a woman? Twice."

"Oh, you're one of those?"

"What, a woman? What gave it away? Was it the boobs? It was the boobs wasn't it?"

"No, one of those feminist types. I can do anything better than a man, and so forth."

"Have an issue with feminists there, bub?"

"I have no issue with equality. But feminists take it too far. We're all equal these days, you might have heard you even have the vote. It's not a competition."

"Yeah, you're right. We should probably let that whole feminist thing slide as there's nothing left to do. That wage gap is sorted, there's no such thing as rape culture and domestic violence is just something from those picture shows. All us feminists can do now is sit around and bitch about our periods."

Eva wasn't sure what part of the statement made him most uncomfortable. Actually, she did. For a man like him, all women existed just like they did in porn movies. They were always up for it, travelled commando, and periods didn't exist.

He stared at her mutely. Eva sighed. In order to change the subject, she said, "I guess we're stuck. Don't you have a mobile or a homing signal or something?"

"No, dropped it, but this turns into an inflatable raft." He shook his bulky black diver's watch. "Probably not useful now, I suppose." He issued a shrug and one of his charismatic smiles.

"Shame. You don't have a jetpack stuffed in your shorts, do you?"

"You're very flattering, but no."

Eva asked, "Can you shoot through the window? We could get out via the stairs."

"Unfortunately my pistol probably landed somewhere in Piccadilly."

"So, we're stuck."

"Stuck, but luckily with such scintillating company. I wonder what two attractive people could do with so much time to kill, isolated and all alone in the middle of the night. The options are endless."

In response she crossed her arms over her chest. Then crossed her legs for effect. He seemed to get the gist of her less-than-subtle rebuff.

The spy pulled out a silver lighter and a metal cigarette case. He offered the contents to Eva. Ignoring several smoke-free years, she took one and he lit it. Taking a long drag, it settled her nerves. *That's the stuff.* Oh how she missed it. Unsurprisingly, a near death experience made her completely unconcerned with the health implications.

The spy slumped to the floor. "I could go for a kip up here. Wake me up if something interesting happens."

Eva nudged him, which resulted in a stabbing pain in her own ribs. "No sleeping on the job." She picked tobacco from her tongue. "No lock picks, no radio, no gun, no grappling hook, but you're packing ciggies. Good to see you've got your priorities straight...flaming cock-monkeys, I...I don't even know your name. I've been calling you 'The Spy' in my head all this time."

"Not, Devastating Cheekbones?"

"No, but Arrogant Arse-Donkey might also suit."

"It may, but I go by Charles Bishop normally."

Distant sirens seemed to come from all directions. Crowds

gathering below despite the pre-dawn hour. They were too distant to hear their cries even if they tried.

Picking glass from her hair, Eva asked, "So Mr Bishop, who shot the missiles if it wasn't you guys?"

"I believe the official story will be that a rogue Russian pilot had a technical malfunction and accidently sent two AA-10 Alamo missiles into a civilian target, which it chose as being the tallest structure, not due to the current political machinations. Officially."

"Unofficially?"

"American."

"American? Why the hell are they shooting missiles in the centre of London? I'm pretty sure that's still an act of war."

"Not if they told us first. It will be spun endlessly as a regrettable technical error. Since the civil war started, Russian preventative maintenance has been lax etcetera, etcetera."

"Even so, an airstrike? Surely a strongly-worded letter would have sufficed. You're English after all."

"Normally, yes. His majesty was even willing to go as far as issuing a stern look, but circumstances halted that kind of ugly confrontation. Mr Lancing has in his possession certain files that, shall we say, are of a sensitive nature. The leaks so far have already led to cabinet resignations. Possibly a suicide. He publicly threatened to release files if certain demands were not met. If the information were to be made public, certain members of the US and UK political systems would be compromised and highly embarrassed."

"Bugger that. Harry's going to ramp up his plans as a giant screw you and now he knows the US and British, and most likely every other Western government, is out to put a bullet in his head. All because the Yanks missed their shot."

"I will concede circumstances are somewhat worse, yes."

"You bloody well think?"

The eruptions seemed to have died down and were replaced by the cacophony of fire engulfing the building. It was several floors up, but by no means were they safe.

Eva shivered. The spy slid his arm of steel around her.

"Don't worry. We'll be out of here in a few minutes. Trust me."

~

"We were rescued by helicopter seven hours later." Eva stared at the naval grey wall. "I was suffering hypothermia, countless lacerations, and needed seven stitches."

Why had she decided to tell the truth to the sailor rather than fabricate a detailed tall tale? It was a good question. For one thing, she had to tell some sort of story to keep Cole in the room. Telling him what she knew took less brain power than inventing a coherent story, so she could use the remainder for planning her escape.

The other reason was that if she did somehow get back to the island, she wanted some chronicle of her story. It would probably be her last chance because there was every reason to believe she'd never get out alive.

"Miss...Miss..." Lieutenant Commander Cole shook his hand from writing copious notes freehand. "This is fascinating and all, but none of it is answering my question. How did you come to the island?"

"Context." Eva rocked her neck from side to side. "I'm putting things in context."

"Are you?" Cole seemed flustered. "Let's see, so far you've told me about a date, that you knew Mr Lancing and there was a British Secret Service agent. But none of it tells me why *you* were on the island. So far this tale seems to be a waste of time."

Speak for yourself, Eva thought. She aimed the bobby pin's end towards the locking arm of one of the handcuffs. *Not long now...*

The ex-boyfriend who had once left her handcuffed to the bed would never know how he had inspired her expertise at the life skill of handcuff picking. She might even forgive him for stealing her possessions as she'd screamed bloody murder. Who was she kidding? If she ever caught sight of that weasel again she'd knock him the hell out.

Every second she grew closer to escaping and getting back to the man she'd left behind on the island. She had to save him. She owed him that much. It was her fault he was there and probably dying if he wasn't already dead. It was her mistake and she was the only one who could fix it. First step was getting through the damn cuffs.

Eva nearly dropped the bobby pin when the bulkhead door was wrenched open. The crisp white uniform of an officer entered. He nodded curtly to Cole. Everything about him seemed officious and managed to an inch of its life. Unlike his comrade, his body was chiselled and toned. As if he lived for exercise, carrot juice and cleansing enemas. This one was a Commander. At this rate she'd be speaking to a Fleet Admiral by supper.

"Good afternoon Ms Destruction, my name is Commander Decker and I will be taking over the investigation from here on in."

This was news to Eva. And, by the expression on his face, Cole too.

Decker placed a thick manila folder in front of him. He interlaced his well-manicured hands on top of it. "I looked you up with the details you gave Cole here. It seems you've led a colourful life Ms Destruction."

"I believe it's important for one to live life with a rich palette."

"I have been supplied this dossier via Interpol–"

"Is that volume one?" she asked looking at the folder.

"–and it makes for interesting reading."

"I will admit I've burnt a few bridges," Eva said as Decker thumbed through the file. When he paused on one page, she added, "And a car."

Cole raised an eyebrow. He leaned over to have a read, but Decker angled the file so he couldn't spy its content.

"Cars seem to be a reoccurring theme." Decker tutted. "It says you stole four of them."

"That's wildly inaccurate."

"So you didn't steal them?"

"No, it was way more than that." The two men stared at her. Her joke falling flat, Eva changed tack. "I will admit that I do have a fairly chequered past. But that was done away with long ago.

What's the last entry there? What, ten years ago, more? I hardly see how it's relevant to–"

"It is all relevant Ms Destruction," Decker said authoritatively. "Now, could you please state the nature of your relationship to Mr Horatio Lancing?"

"If you want that, I'll have to go way back." Her mind raced to see how the change of circumstance could be used to her advantage.

Cole shook his head. "Here we go."

CHAPTER FIVE

EIGHTEEN MONTHS BEFORE THE ISLAND

Jimmy the Bastard had lived up to his name. For the third day in a row he hadn't shown up for a shift even after teary protestations over the phone that he would 'definitely' be there the next day. "Totally, no question, I wouldn't let you down, Babe!" He let her down, Babe. He was done. Life at the Kanga Brew café was definitely more lax than the Saville Row-clad clientele's workplaces, but you didn't abandon your mates. It was simple as that.

There must have been something about the uncustomary clear spring day had that brought Londoners out. Eva's café was under-staffed and she was over-tired. Last night she'd watched a succession of progressively shoddier bands at an all-nighter gig at some seedy East London club.

Eva was in no mood to play nice with customers. Working the coffee machine so hard she was sure its manufacturer in Italy would have conniptions, she plastered on her best fake grin and forged on. Surely there had to be a lull soon? She glanced up and wiped her brow with her forearm. The line was longer. It snaked out the door and past the window down the street.

Holy mother-tugging shit-kittens.

She was going to die at the coffee machine. She only hoped

they'd wipe the coffee grounds off her body before rolling it into the back alley to be eaten by wild dogs. She'd read somewhere caffeine was bad for dogs.

Each member endured the queue irritated, but stoically. They were English after all. Every person in the line possessed a sort of grim determination. No one had elected to leave. It was as if the English had been genetically bred to queue. They didn't like it, but endured it. A mini-Blitz every day.

One member of the queue stood out from the others. Unlike everyone else he seemed to be enjoying himself, as if the ridiculously long line was a big adventure. Eva had no time to ponder his pale, but kind of pretty face. She had exactly eleventy billion coffees to make before she was allowed to die.

"I take break now yes."

"Now, Anchor?" Eva asked the big lumbering Swede.

"I have work for seven hours no break. I break now yes."

How could she say no to those big puppy eyes?

"Alright, make it quick, this lot are likely to get right snippy if we slow down any more."

Anchor made a cutting motion. "Snippy?"

She punched him in the arm. "Go, ya lovable yob. Have a ciggie for me."

Anchor issued a, "Yar yar" over his shoulder as he left.

Eva headed to the counter and first in line was the grinning pretty idiot.

"Hello," he said pleasantly.

"Enjoy lines do you?"

"I don't get many, to be honest, it's a novelty. It's like old time Soviet Russia or something." A wide grin crossed his lips. What kind of bloke found a queue novel?

In spite of his foppish hair and three day growth the queue-liker with the vivid childlike green eyes intrigued her. It could have been the lack of sleep, stupid hours or excessive caffeine intake talking. But he was too much of a pretty boy for her tastes.

He rocked on his heels. "I've been a bit out of the loop. It's a bit sad when a line is a luxury, isn't it? I seem to have lost my common touch."

"You been in jail or something?"

Why did she ask *that*? She knew why. Of course she did. She'd much prefer her daydreams to have a bad-boy edge.

"No, why?" he asked.

Today was not the time for chit-chat. Eva pulled out her notepad, and asked, "What can I get you?"

"One coffee please."

She stared blankly at him. Between clenched teeth, Eva asked, "What type of coffee?"

"Oh, I see. There's more than one type? Right, what is there then?"

A collective moan emerged from the others in the tiny little shop. Those waiting for their orders frowned in his direction, the ones in the line behind him became visibly agitated.

A tiny smirk crept from the corner of Eva's ruby red mouth. There was no way this guy could be so naïve, he must have had an angle. She had no time to find out what it was.

"Darlin', we have so many we could be here all day. Long black, short black, mocha, ristretto, macchiato, affogato–"

He stared blankly at her.

"You look like a flat white kind of guy."

"That would be fine."

Raising an eyebrow, she asked, "Sugar?"

"Yes, Sweetie?"

"Okay, I see that you're trying to be cute, I do, but look at these guys behind you. Most of them have to either get back to work before the boss finds out, or are in the later stages of some serious caffeine withdrawal. I think you're about to be lynched."

"Right you are. One please."

"Alright then." Eva made a squiggle on the paper cup only decipherable by her, placed it to one side. "Next!"

The not-jailbird character faded into the crowd as she took further orders. Anchor's break was thankfully short and she returned to coffee making duties.

Orders were called. In accordance with a long-standing tradition the café had their own system of handing out orders. Regulars had their own nickname. Some obtained a moniker on their first visit that stuck for years. In quick succession Anchor called the names, 'Tiny Pete', 'Dwarf Head', 'High Hair', 'Low Tie' and 'Nice Bum'. Each resulted in the recipient handing over cash to him and taking their coffee, except for the last one. Again, he called "Nice Bum" but nobody came forward.

Eva popped her head above the steaming La Marzocco coffee machine and nodded to the non-jailbird. "Oi, Sugar, you're up."

Chuckling, he paid for his coffee, tucked a note in the tip jar and walked away. She returned to the scorching silver beast and went to work. With a bit of luck they would clear the line in time for the next day's shift.

Anchor tugged her coffee-soaked sleeve.

"Uh, Eva."

Without raising her head, she said, "You just had a break, Anchor."

"No. Not that. This."

She slammed a double shot latte on the counter and glanced up. Anchor was holding up the tip jar. At first she shrugged. Then she saw it.

"Cock juggling thunder twats..."

"My thoughts are also similar," Anchor replied.

~

Eva raced down the thin street, weaving around slow pedestrians. She squinted. The London sun was as bright as it was unfamiliar. Scanning the smattering of Londoners she clutched the paper in her hand.

Then she caught sight of him. If anything, he looked paler in the sunlight. She spied him about twenty metres away, several shops ahead. He took a sip of coffee and halted walking mid-stride. He took another sip and shuddered as though he was having an acid trip.

Eva called out, "Oi!" and he turned.

She marched towards him, certain steam was billowing from her ears.

"What the fuck is this shit?"

He reeled. "Excuse me?"

She waved a fifty-pound note he'd placed in the tip jar in his face. "Who the fuck pays fifty pounds for a fucking coffee?"

"You do swear a lot."

She gave a slight shake of her head and issued an interrogative gaze.

He held up the coffee cup. "It's very good coffee. Actually, this isn't coffee, it's bliss in a cup."

"I know. It's bloody marvellous. But you didn't know that before you tipped me, so what gives?"

"Uh, I honestly don't know. You think I have a nice bum?"

She smiled. He smiled. He had a lovely face. Warm and genuine.

"Me? Oh god no. That was Anchor."

"And Anchor is?"

"The tall lanky bloke who looks like the Grim Reaper, if the Grim Reaper was a skateboarder and Swedish."

It was a lie. Anchor wasn't in the café when he'd ordered, but she wasn't telling him that.

"I can genuinely say I hadn't paid attention to the other staff in the café. Well, I'd like you to keep the money. If you or your staff don't want it, you can give it to charity."

"Do you normally go about issuing stupid tips to complete strangers? You one of those eccentrics the English are so fond of?"

"You're Australian too? Thought so. What are the odds?"

"Pretty bloody likely in London, mate. We're a bit less popular than we used to be because of, you know–"

He paused, losing his confidence. "That Lancing guy?"

"Yeah, that guy. If you're an Aussie and a bloke, most wonder if you're him or if you're a chick, you know him. Kind of puts people off, yeah?"

His face softened. "Yes, he seems to be ruffling a few feathers of late, doesn't he? Do you like what he's doing?"

"What do I give a crap? I don't know much about it, to be honest."

But she wasn't being honest, again. She must be on a roll. In fact Lancing was a bit of a hero of hers. A modern day Robin Hood. A man that gave the middle finger to the establishment, always a way to her heart. She, like everyone else in her generation, had tried to hunt for his true identity but, like everyone else, she'd come up short. He remained a faceless man. The only personal information people had was that he was Australian.

Eva shrugged. "As far as I know he's a rich white guy giving away his cash and bullying others into not being gits. Not exactly up there with genocide or a Limp Biskit reunion."

She realised she'd lapsed into a civil discourse and glanced back towards the coffee shop. "Look, I have to go. You sure you–?"

"Keep it, please."

"Alright. Um, thanks. Enjoy the coffee."

"Would you like to go out some time? With me?"

He seemed as shocked as she was by the question, as if it had burst from his mouth without his knowledge.

Coldly she, said, "We are out."

"Right. Of course – I just thought – yes. Hmm."

She threw him a sympathy smirk. "You're not really my type. Sorry." Her face turned to stone and asked, "Is that what the tip was about? Coz if it was, you can shove–"

"No, no, I didn't…I wasn't… This isn't going well. Actually, my whole day's been terrible, to be honest. Sorry." He squeezed the bridge of his nose with his free hand. "Today was meant to be about the people. To see what was happening that wasn't filtered through reports, statistics or spin. I was meant to be familiarising myself with the area…"

"Familiarising?"

He continued on, "…it's the first time I've left the compound in, I don't know, years?"

"Compound? You in a cult?"

Again, no reaction. "It started when I missed my tube stop because the train was so packed. I couldn't move anywhere near the doors for another three stations. I'm almost certain I was mildly sexually assaulted by an old woman rubbing up against me. The term may be frotting, I'm not sure. What I am certain of, however, was she seemed to have crocheted a hat out of garbage bags. Her parting gift was to cough phlegm in my face. It was all downhill from there. So, you see, your coffee and unconventional customer relations were an island in an ocean of shit."

"Wow, way to flatter the girl."

"No, I mean…"

"Listen, I hope your day improves. This has been…interesting…but, like I said, you're not my type. I tend to go for the more dangerous kind."

He laughed. Was he mocking her? *Fuck you buddy.*

"I'm Harry by the way."

"I really don't care."

With that she swivelled on the spot and marched away. Eva was angry, but more at herself than the guy. She should dislike him based on her dealing with him, but against her better judgement was oddly attracted to him. She silently repeated to herself. *Not my type, not my type.* She wondered how he'd gotten under her skin so quickly. Not that she really had to worry. She was certain she'd never see him again.

"And that was your first meeting with Mr Lancing?" Commander Decker asked.

"My introduction to Lancing came later. Like I was saying to your mate Cole here, I'm supplying context."

"Supplying a waste of time," Cole muttered under his breath.

Decker ignored him. "Hardly Romeo and Juliet."

"I will concede that," Eva replied. "There was a distinct lack of teenage angst, suicide and codpieces. So I guess you're right on the money there."

She was still trying to figure the two out. Their interruptions and questions told her more than she was telling them. Cole was more officious, worried about the here and now. Decker wanted everything in detail, for her to paint a picture. Eva didn't know if that picture was for the CIA or late night stories in the officers' quarters.

Regardless, Eva needed to work them. They were her only means of getting back to the island. Guilt was a powerful motivator. Was it already too late? Was he already dead?

Her story was reeling in Decker. She needed him on side. She needed him to stay in the room.

Cole rubbed his wrist and shook his pen. "This still isn't relevant to the last twenty-four hours. The bombs, the UN crisis meeting, the whole mess..."

Decker frowned. "I guess you're right, Lieutenant Commander." He turned to Eva. "So, this man keeps buying coffee, leaves big tips, buys you expensive gifts, you fall for him, end up on the island...so, what I want to know is–"

"It didn't entirely shake out like that." Eva rolled her neck. "Of course there was the assassination attempt, terrorist attack and riot."

They both sat bolt upright.

She coughed. She didn't have something in her throat. It was subterfuge. A cover. With a pleasing *click*, Eva managed to free herself from one of the handcuffs.

"Right. Where was I?"

CHAPTER SIX

"Buzzcut, you're up." Eva held up a half-shot soy latte, heavy on the chocolate sprinkles, doing her best to stifle a snigger.

To her relief the line had cleared out some. "Anchor, I'm taking five, can you handle the orders?"

"Yar, no problem for me." Or at least that's what she thought he said. The lovable Swede always sounded like he had a mouthful of marbles coated in molasses. Oddly, he tended to become easier to understand the more booze he consumed. She still hadn't figured that one out.

Eva emptied the bins into a garbage bag and realised there was still more rubbish to go, a two-trip deal. Lugging the heavier of the bags she headed out the back to the alley. She arched her back, stretched and let out a thankful sigh. It had been a busy day, good for her business, but she hadn't had a break since they'd opened at six. That wasn't entirely true. She had had a whole five minutes while off yelling at the bastard who'd given her the fifty-pound tip. *What exactly was his issue?*

The background noise from the nearby hub of Trafalgar Square provided a constant hum in the small dank alley. As she lobbed the garbage into the skip she heard noises closer by in the labyrinthine cobblestoned laneway. She nearly ignored them, but didn't want to return to work so soon. Eva had given up smoking a painful six years earlier and had tossed her latest book into the bin in disgust at the Charing Cross station that morning, so didn't have an excuse to stay outside. Now she'd found one.

Muffled footfalls echoed on the timeworn brickwork, making it difficult to determine where they were coming from, but they were in a hurry. The running stopped and was followed by voices. Unable to work out the exact words, she could tell someone wasn't happy. Livid in fact. *This could be fun.*

There were two voices. One was raised, angry, the other was barely audible. Poking her head tentatively around the corner she froze. This wasn't the amusing domestic chav stoush she was looking for. As the smile drained from her face, she lost all humour. Perhaps it was the gun.

Both men were regaining their composure. The nearest of the two had his back to her and stood tall while the other held a handgun aimed at his forehead. The gun wielder was virtually manic in whatever he was saying. His accent was thick, he could have been Russian or from somewhere in the Baltic. His tracksuit and penchant for gaudy jewellery backed up the assumption. Her ear guessed Bulgarian based on the smattering of words she'd heard. Either way, he wasn't happy about something.

The tracksuit wearer panted, having exhausted himself with the run and subsequent rant. The man with the gun to his head remained unyielding and spoke evenly, almost kindly. Unable to see his face, she didn't know if it showed the panic absent from his voice. Did he not know a man with crazy eyes was holding a gun to his head?

"They are all very good points, really, they are. But I'm pretty sure you don't want to shoot me. Killing a man, any man, is not easy, no matter what they've done. I'm not going to beg, I think we both know that. But I can see you're having second thoughts, that's a rational reaction. Human. I can help you. I can get you out of whatever situation you've got yourself into. You know I can. Let me help you."

Mr Tracksuit thumped his temple as if the ideas hurt his brain-pan. He retracted the gun to rub both temples. Eva wasn't the only one to notice. The head of the man who'd been talking followed the gun's arc, but he made no move to grab it. Mr Track-suit took a step to his left and the two circled each other like prize fighters.

For the first time she could see who was talking. In quick succession she let out two tiny yelps. His arm was a mass of blood. His upper sleeve was a ripped and meaty mess, the rest of his arm was crimson red. That wasn't what made her eyes go so wide she was sure they'd spill from their sockets. This was the bastard who'd given her the ridiculous tip. That's why the voice had sounded familiar. *Who is this guy?*

Unaffected by the flesh bursting through his attire, the big tipper addressed his increasingly erratic companion, his back rigid and his words unaffected by the wound. What was his name, Harry?

"So I have made, what I believe is a fair and reasonable offer. Now comes the stick–"

From behind came a crashing sound. Eva leapt backwards, ensuring she wasn't seen by those she was spying on. She twisted and observed Anchor emptying the other garbage bag into the skip. He issued a friendly wave and returned inside.

Steadying herself with a few quiet breaths, she slowly inched her head around the corner. What she saw made her gasp, and considering the last few minutes that was saying something. Mr Tracksuit was positioned before Harry, all colour drained from his face. His arms dangled uselessly beside his body, he barely held onto the gun. His pale features a mixture of confusion and abject fear. Harry stood stiffly, silently watching the man with all the power crumble before him. He made no move to advance, just watched.

The silence ate away at Eva until it was unbearable. The two men stared at each other. One a disintegrating mess, the other a monolith of composure. Harry slowly raised his good hand, palm up, and held it in mid-air, unshaking.

"You have one hour. You know I keep my word. If I were in your shoes, I would start running. Don't stop until you reach the end of the world and, when you do, leap into the abyss. You don't want to be found. This is your one chance. The clock has started."

Eva didn't wait to see which way he ran. She scurried back towards her café, aware every footfall sounded like clashing symbols. Staggering through the back door, Eva attempted to lock it, but her hands refused to cooperate and became useless squids at the end of her arms.

"You right, Missy?" Anchor asked and she jumped.

He leaned over her and locked the door. Taking a step back, concern was etched across his Swedish mug. "You sweating?"

Unable to answer, she waved him away. She had to compose herself. Not entirely sure what she'd witnessed, it was none of her business. The locked door helped. It was a barrier from whatever it was that she'd seen. And if anything was going to make her feel better, it was distance from Harry.

How did an unarmed man unnerve a bigger, stronger bloke who held all the firepower and advantage? But he wasn't JUST unnerved, he was terrified. Shitting bricks, run-away-screaming terrified. How did that even happen?

Eva shook her head. Getting back to work would stop any further cloudy thoughts dead. A line had formed towards the door and her lumbering assistant would have no chance of clearing it himself. Clapping her hands together she stepped into the shop, picked up a pen and asked, "Who's next?"

After a few minutes she came to believe she'd imagined the worst parts of the confrontation in the laneway. The Baltic guy wasn't that frightened. The wound on Harry's arm obviously wasn't bad if he was still standing. No, her imagination was getting the better of her. Must have been a prop or a gag shirt. Maybe they were filming the whole thing gorilla-style and she'd see it turn up on ITV in a few weeks. She slapped a cap on a latte and felt better.

Well, she did right up until she saw Harry stagger through her front door, bloodied and pale.

He slipped past the crowd by the door and wandered unsteadily into the café. Holding his arm, his pasty face scanned the room until he found Eva. He smirked weakly. "I wonder if I could bother you for another coffee, and perhaps a napkin or two?" Nodding to his arm, "Lacrosse accident."

Eva grabbed a pile of serviettes and handed them over. In a voice sounding far more confident than she was, "Dangerous game. You should be careful. I'm a bit out of the loop with the latest rules and all, what's the regulation calibre size these days?"

He raised an eyebrow. "Clever gi–" His eyes rolled back and he collapsed backwards. Two latte-sipping suited regulars stepped back and cleared a path. A Gen Y copyboy dived to cradle Harry's head just before it hit the polished concrete floor.

For the first time, the room noticed Harry's bloody arm.

"Bugger me, he's been shot. Call the bobbies!"

"Call an ambulance!"

With a man bleeding on the floor, her floor, Eva pulled out her phone. Hand hovering over the keypad she couldn't understand why she hesitated. Surely this was someone else's issue. Why then did she feel somehow responsible?

"Uh Eva," Anchor said quietly in her ear. "I think he is dying. You might want to call a someone. The after work rush is coming, customers doing the step over dead guy is much bad for business."

"How do they manage to squeeze every conceivable ounce of happiness out of the designs of hospitals? There must be course on it someplace. Someone somewhere has a Masters in joy sucking." After a moment Eva said into her phone, "That sounded better in my head."

Nancy giggled on the other end of the line. "Paul I've already got one of those."

Eva snorted. "Eww, there are certain things I don't need to know!"

"I made you laugh, my work here is done." After a moment Nancy's voice turned less jovial. "So how long are you going to hang around?"

Eva glanced over at the man on the hospital bed, hooked up to an IV line and monitors. "Not sure. The doctor's said he's stable, should be okay. He even quoted the *Black Knight*, ''Twas but a flesh wound'. So, I'll probably be over at yours soonish."

"Alright, you be careful, Hon. I think it's noble of you to be looking out for him, but you're not married to the guy. There are professionals for that, doctory types, you know? You call me if you need, yeah?"

"Of course. Give my best to the big twat. See you in a couple. Loves."

Hanging up, Eva wondered why she was still there. She'd done the right thing and called an ambulance. The fact that the cops turned up as well wasn't her doing. Then again, the mention of 'gunshot wound' may have piqued their interest. The fact that he was handcuffed to the bed and an officer was stationed outside the door meant they took the whole situation seriously enough. That they let her stay in the room indicated it wasn't *too* serious.

She didn't know anything about the guy apart from the name he'd given her. Harry. It was a friendly name. Not one you would normally associate with people having guns held to their head. That was more of a Nigel thing.

He had no identification on him. None at all. In this world it was as amazing as it was alarming. No credit card, no driver's licence, not even a Subway loyalty card.

"I suppose I should thank you."

Eva twisted to see Harry sitting up and admiring his new police-issued jewellery. She hadn't even heard him stir.

"I'm sorry, they–"

"No, no, it's fine. I wasn't having a go. Standard operating procedure in the instance of a suspected firearm offence. It's fine, really. And thank you, sincerely."

Eva smiled awkwardly. She'd never been one to accept thanks well. Or compliments. There were so many questions, but she had no idea how to broach the subject. *So, are you a drug dealer? A terrorist? How the hell do you talk a guy out of killing you?*

"I should thank you properly."

"You already did, remember the tip? I think you're okay for a while."

"No, I mean properly."

Eva snorted. "What, like buy me a car or something?"

"What style would you like?"

She wanted to offer a reply but decided to remain mute. She wasn't willing to say any more in fear of him actually following through with it. *He is a drug dealer.*

"The doctors say you'll be fine. They patched you up, you'll be right to go in a day or so–" Eyeing the handcuffs, she added, "Uh, from the hospital, that is."

He grinned confidently, apparently unfazed by being bound to a hospital bed. Was he used to that sort of thing? Eva had plenty of experience with handcuffs herself, but in a recreational rather than professional capacity.

"Can you–?" He shook his head. "I don't even know your name."

"Eva, my name is Eva Destruction." She held up a hand. "Don't, I've heard them all."

"I like it. Suits you. Something pedestrian like Susan wouldn't cut it."

Alright, every one but that.

"Eva, can you tell me what happened after I came into your shop. That's the last thing I remember."

"I called an ambulance after you fainted."

"No I didn't."

"Yeah, you kinda did, Dude."

"No, I blacked out. That's far manlier."

"Oh, right. My mistake. So what caused this manly blacking out spell? Why would some Bulgarian guy shoot you?"

"How did you know who shot me?"

Shit. Shitty shit McShit.

"I might have seen something in the alley before you came in. Briefly. Hardly saw a thing."

"Right." A wry grin. His assessment of her wasn't malevolent, just curious. "Who knows why he wanted to take a shot? It's an odd world. Why do good people do bad things? Why do bad things happen to good people? Why can I only get hot cross buns up until Easter? Why is there no word in the English language for when you keep accidently glancing at someone and they think you're staring at them? How can Celine Dion have sold more records than AC/DC? The world can be messed up."

Against her better judgement, Eva chuckled. How could he be so blasé?

"Why me?" she asked. "Why my shop? Why did you come back?"

"I had to find someone I could trust."

"I told you to fuck off."

"All the more reason to trust you."

"Those drugs have kicked in now, huh?"

"No, I mean it. You had the fortitude to renounce a tip because morally you thought it disproportionate. You stood your ground, listened and were not afraid to share your opinion."

"I tend to do that."

"Don't apologise."

"I wasn't."

"Good, you shouldn't. The world's changing, Eva. The new Russian revolution, rumblings elsewhere in Europe. Things are finally changing for the better. People are demanding more of their governments, but their governments aren't listening. It takes people like yourself to shout until you're heard. Your voice should rise above the pettiness of politician's self-interest and fringe loonies like Freedom First. When I met you, you struck me as someone with morals, strong and kind. I make my living by trusting my instinct about people. I'm hardly ever wrong. So, I gravitated to you when I needed aid, so thank you."

Eva suspected she was glowing a little red. "You're welcome.

But in your little list there you forgot, 'and makes a kick arse cup of coffee'."

"And makes a kick arse cup of coffee, most definitely."

They let that hang in the air for a while.

Eva rubbed her legs. "I think I'll go. You seem okay, surprisingly okay, so I'm going to nick off. They'll look after you, they seem to know what they're doing."

"Well, yes, but I'll be happy when the NHS is funded adequately and staff are paid proportionately for their work. Like education, for example. Politicians seem to have forgotten who they've been elected to serve."

She gave him a frown. "You sound like a brochure."

"I've been accused of that before. I've been accused of many things."

She picked up her handbag. "You're a weird cat, Harry The Big Tipper."

"That, I don't think I've been accused of, but I like it."

A rush of blood to her cheeks and Eva let out a giggle.

Mesopotamian crap buckets, I'm giggling. Kill. Me. Now. Next Eva thought they'd be having disagreements over who should hang up the phone first. She needed to leave before they started arguing over which one should be called Schmoopy.

"Mind if I ask you a question, Eva of the Kick Arse Coffee?"

She said, "Shoot" and instantly slammed shut her eyes in embarrassment.

"Why are you here, Eva? If you realised I was shot, wouldn't you want to distance yourself as much as possible?"

"I wanted to see if you were alright."

"They have phones for that."

"I guess–"

She slipped out the door quietly, giving the officer stationed there a brisk nod.

It was a damn good question. Why was she there? Walking down the starkly painted hallway, Eva knew the answer. She didn't want to admit it, but she knew.

She'd told herself that Harry was far too much of a pretty boy for her tastes. It didn't matter. She was already smitten. He was smart, had strong moral fibre, and was well read and self-confident. These ticked some good boxes, but that wasn't what had flicked her switch. Deep in her chest, and further south, Eva knew why she'd come to the hospital. Underneath his classic attractiveness, Harry was a bad motherfucker. He'd taken on a gunman and made him run away in abject fear. He'd shaken off being shot like a piddly little knock to his arm. Nothing seemed to faze him. There was a dark black bad-boy streak in Harry and Eva wanted to see more.

Am I falling for a drug dealer? She'd dated worse.

Nancy upended another bottle of cheap French red into her glass and hooted her infectious laugh. Eva was cross-legged in front of Nancy and Paul's coffee table in their tiny welcoming flat. Indian takeaway boxes were strewn across the room. As always, the TV glowed in the background showing the news service Paul always had on. Two empty bottles adorned the mantle above a crackling fire.

"Oh beautiful husband of mine bought this from a guy in the pub." Nancy drunkenly motioned to Paul with the elbow of her pouring arm, managing not to spill a drop. "A good deal he said. Didn't drink it first, though, did he?" She shook her head.

"Tastes alright." Eva nodded encouragingly to her best friend's husband.

"Yeah, but you wait till tomorrow, it's chock full of chemicals. Hangover on this stuff's a bitch. Feels like the entire back row of The All Blacks have moved into your head and soiled the carpet."

"We've had two bottles, now you tell me?"

"Misery loves company. And Sweetie, you're going to be one miserable son of a bitch tomorrow."

"I get up at five!"

"That's what makes it so funny," Nancy said pouring herself another generous glass.

Paul rose unsteadily and mumbled something about the TV aerial and staggered towards the entertainment unit.

"So, how cute are we talking?" Nancy asked with her wicked grin she only pulled out when talking about men. "Was he worthy of an eye flutter or a lock the bathroom door we're doing it right now kind of cute?"

"Who, the shooting guy? No, it's not like that."

"So he's hideous." Nancy sounded disappointed. "Like Paul's hairy arse first thing in the morning kind of hideous?"

Paul popped his head up from behind the TV and yelled, "Hey" before his face was bathed in a contemplative gleam and he drew his mouth in, as if to say, *fair enough.*

"No. He's, uh, he's actually good-looking in a classic kind of way, like a Cary Grant type. But no, I have no designs on the guy. Not my type at all, darlin'."

"So he's not a prize douchepoodle who rides a Harley, has a face like a welder's armpit, treats women like garbage, sleeps around and turns up for a three a.m. booty call months after breaking up?" Nancy took a swig of wine. "I like him already."

"Yeah, well you suck," was the best Eva could come up with. This red really did have a punch to it. The lack of alcohol percentage on the label was worrying, as was the misspelling of Bordeaux.

Nancy unleashed *that* grin and asked, "Do you normally escort strangers to the hospital and hang around to find out if they're okay?"

Sometimes she hated how well Nancy knew her. Nance was pointing out the exact same questions she'd tried to suppress in her own mind and failed. With all the booze, Eva's defences were down. Not that it mattered with Nancy. She could read her like a book. A Little Golden Book, at that.

She hadn't been able to get Harry out of her head, not that she'd tried that hard. What was he doing? Was he thinking about her? Was there a way she could accidently bump into him and drag him back to her place for a week he'd never forget?

About to launch a barrage of half-arsed denials, Eva was distracted by a news break on the TV. It was the photo that grabbed her attention first. It showed a mug shot of a face she'd seen before. Quite recently. The picture showed Mr Tracksuit. The headline read, *Bulgarian man found dead at Victoria Station.*

CHAPTER SEVEN

"Roots, you're up." Eva handed over a tiny coffee cup to a peroxide blonde-haired woman with dark roots sporting a serious suit. Taking the cup, the woman hardly acknowledged her and continued her ostensibly important phone conversation peppered with words like, 'recalibration', 'strategy', 'synergy' and 'alignment' out the door. Eva wondered if she even knew what she was talking about.

Only a smattering of customers were around this late in the day. Anchor had left to deal with immigration for the tenth time in six months. It was becoming an issue, but it wasn't the big dopey git's fault. Plus mid-afternoon wasn't the time for a coffee break in Westminster, so it wasn't too busy.

Handing over two cups to 'The Jugheads', Eva sighed and glanced up. Her eyes went wide. "Holy jizz factory."

Harry stood before her. There was no sling, but she assumed the bulk under his t-shirt was bandages. A broad toothy grin stretched across his pale handsome face.

"Hello," he said with an apologetic smile.

"Uh. Good thanks," she said disorientated.

Blinking several times she wondered if the conversation had

skipped like a record and she'd missed something. She stared straight at him. He was neither agitated, nor threatening. There was an urge to say something but she couldn't think of a single useful word.

"Could I order a coffee possibly?" he asked politely.

"Uh, yeah, yeah you can, sure. Flat white?"

"Ah, no, I'll have a ristretto if that's okay? That's from the best part of the extraction, yes?"

"It is," Eva gave an appreciative frown and manipulated the silver coffee machine with expertise. "You've been doing your research."

"In my line of work, you have to."

"And what's that then?"

"Acquisitions."

"A suitably vague and nondescript explanation."

Eva caught the smirk before it spread across her face and resumed her serious disposition. She told herself not to be charmed by his casual charisma. Sweet face or not, he could stare down someone trying to kill him without batting an eyelid. And potentially despatch them with similar ease. That was enough to wipe any grin from her face. Harry was possibly a murderer. A killer.

For security, she scanned the café. There were only two customers huddled together at a table by the window engrossed in a discussion about case briefs and trial dates.

Harry lowered his voice. "I didn't kill him. He wasn't murdered."

Jets of steam burst skyward from the coffee machine. Eva's hands flew towards various knobs and buttons as she attempted to quell the eruption.

Eva's voice broke and in false calmness she asked, "Who?"

"Lars Schmit. The Bulgarian chap from the alley. I didn't kill him, if that's what you're thinking."

"Last time I saw you, you were handcuffed to a hospital bed, so, you know—"

"For the sake of clarity, I didn't have anyone murder him

either." He leaned forward and placed both palms on her bench. "For some reason I thought it important you knew that he wasn't murdered."

"Could you stop saying," Eva lowered her voice, "murdered."

"Certainly."

Passing him a coffee her hands trembled slightly, but not as much as she would have expected.

He took the coffee with a nod. "How much–?"

"On the house. I think you're entitled to a freebie, with the tip and all."

"Right. Thanks. Fell on the tracks. Third rail."

"I'm sorry?"

"Lars. According to Metropol he jumped the barriers at Victoria Station to evade paying a ticket and was chased by station staff. Jumped onto the tracks to get away and stepped on something he shouldn't have. Not even suicide."

"Right," she said.

Could she believe him? A simple internet search would confirm it. Eva was surprised by the wave of relief that enveloped her. Who was she kidding? It was a tsunami of relief. In retrospect, the thought of a tsunami of relief didn't sound that comforting.

She wiped her hands on her filthy apron. "You didn't need to tell me all that."

"For some reason I felt I did." He straightened his back. "Thanks for the coffee by the way. I've never tasted anything like it."

She gave a shrug with a *what are you gonna do?* look. Why on Earth did she feel like a fumbling teenager around this guy? She was better than that. Eva prided herself on her fierce independence, her unabashed need for freedom in all her relationships.

Though he did have pretty eyes.

There was something about his nature that was nigh on protective. Was that it? All the men she was used to dating were so far from protective that they'd need to take three bus lines and a taxi to even see what protective was. Though if she found herself giggling once more she'd be forced to drown herself.

"Thank you again, for helping me," he said interrupting her thoughts.

Between pursed lips she said, "Mmmm, mmmm," and glanced up as new customers strolled into the café.

He nodded. "I'll leave you to it."

Occupying herself with greeting newcomers, Eva expertly manipulated her now under control machine. Harry sat at the end of a long bench and glanced at the newspaper and sipped. His eyes closed and he may even have done a semi-jig.

Why was he still there? Besides the kick arse coffee. He'd explained the Bulgarian's death, he'd thanked her *again* and appeared uncomfortable in her presence. So why hadn't he simply left? Even Eva's own regard for her coffee making skills weren't enough to think that was why he stayed. Her heart fluttered at the possibilities.

Heart fluttering *and* giggling? Eva wondered if there was a way to commit suicide via coffee machine.

The three customers didn't actually order, they simply engaged in small talk as she prepared their beverages. Regulars. So regular in fact, she knew their real names. Not that she used them. Continuing their conversation they'd brought in from outside, they were discussing a good day's trading. Eva had never asked but judging by the cut of their suits, good results were a regular thing.

"...yeah, yeah, but nah," the youngest of them said animatedly. "It was at fifty-four when I bought. Closed at eighty-eight. Ron lost his mind. He said he wanted to increase my bonus next year. I said, 'Bullshit, after that you owe me a yacht'. Hell of a day. I wanna shake Lancing's hand. That dude made me a shit-tonne of cash."

Harry's head shot up. He was suddenly interested in the conversation.

"If anyone could find the bastard," said the oldest of the three.

They all nodded. The elusive Horatio Lancing. Apparently no one knew who he was. Apart from the fact that he was head of one of the biggest corporations on the planet. It never made sense to

Eva how someone could be so well-known, yet invisible to the world. Especially these days of instant everything.

"I still reckon he doesn't exist," said the middle man.

"What, Lancing Industries just run themselves?" the oldest of them asked. "I doubt your phone or laptop or overused Chirp account made themselves."

"No one's ever seen him," he replied indignantly. "It's probably a fictional figurehead like Colonel Sanders–"

"I'm pretty sure he was a real guy."

"–and all the different corporate heads run the show. They're the ones who take all the glory anyway."

"You're so full of it. He's a bloke. He's Aussie, like this one." The oldest motioned to Eva.

"This one?" She planted her hands on her hips. "This one has a name." All three stared at her. "Right. First bloke to tell me my name gets free coffee." Silence. "For life." It would have been an appropriate time for tumbleweeds to roll across the floor. "Thought so." Eva handed out the coffees. "There you go, Simon, Jason and Piers."

The three sheepishly took their coffees. Harry chuckled and said, "She's got your numbers, boys."

"Bloody hell," the oldest said, "another one. Are there any English people left in London?"

The other two appeared to want to dive into their coffees.

"I'm intrigued," said Harry, "why don't you think Lancing is real?"

It was the second time Harry had asked about Lancing. First was when they'd been on the street.

The youngest piped up. "I reckon he is." He eyed the sceptic among them. "He has to be. No corporation's gonna be doing all that philanthropy crap off their own bat. That's a human doing that. Has to be. He's made all his money from his tech, industry and media arms, right? So now he does all that charity bollocks in Africa and India and whatnot, which I still reckon is pissing it up against the wall."

The other two finance guys shared a smirk.

The oldest rolled his eyes, "Everyone knows when he's buying up debt and giving," he used his fingers to create air quotes, "'free' debt management to the shitty European counties. Which basically means he's buying power and influence and god knows what else."

"None of that has ever been substantiated." Harry seemed a little too defensive.

The oldest sceptic snorted. "Substantiated how? About a man no one's ever seen?"

"It doesn't mean it's not true," the youngest said with a shrug.

"The media think he's real."

"What? The media he supposedly owns? The social media platforms that spread the word of this supposed growing social revolution in Europe are all owned by him! Reported on his satellite TV networks. There's all manner of rumours about bribery, blackmail, vote rigging and extortion, you name it."

"But the people love him," the youngest said.

"The *idea* of him. How can you love someone no one's ever seen?" said his workmate.

"Like the bloke you've got on a cross around your neck?"

"What, he's the messiah now?"

"To some. To large parts of the population, maybe. Governments, not so much. They're scared shitless that he'll dump all the dirt he's supposedly accumulated."

"What's that?" Eva asked. She'd remained passive during the conversation, but that had caught her attention.

"There was this thing in *Wired* saying he's hiring hackers to gather up all this government data. Like a private Wikileaks or something. Didn't ring true. Sounded like some government git scaremongering, if you ask me."

Harry appeared to want to say something when the oldest glanced at his watch. "We've got that three o'clock."

"Yeah, right. Thanks for the coffee, ah–"

"Eva, Piers." She shook her head. "You've been in here every day for two years."

"Eva. Yeah, sorry Eva. See you tomorrow, uh, Eva."

The other two men waved goodbye. When they walked out, Eva discovered only she and Harry were left in the café. She collected the money and placed it in a wooden box. He checked his watch again.

"That's your system? A box?" Harry asked with a smirk.

Eva shrugged. "It works for me. Cash registers aren't really my thing. Technology and I don't get along. Like oil and water or Captain Hook and pap smears." She paused. "Sometimes I shouldn't be allowed to speak out loud."

Harry chuckled. Walking out from behind the bench, she collected cups and tidied up.

He scanned the men. "They're in for a bumpy few weeks on the market."

"How do you know that?"

"I know a few things."

Straightening magazines at the end of the bench where Harry sat, Eva shook her head. "So, not a drug dealer then?"

"Who said I was a drug dealer?" Harry tilted his head. "Pimp I could understand, but drug dealer?"

"Oh darlin', you really think you could pull off pimp?" She smirked. "I can't see you kneecapping a guy." The grin disappeared and her eyes wandered towards the floor. The alley and the image of the Bulgarian on the news came back to her. "Searching for a flat?"

"What was that?"

Eva nodded to the open real estate section of the newspaper Harry was reading. "I assumed–"

"Oh, right, yeah. Hunting for somewhere to set up," he paused, as if the word stuck in his throat, "home."

"Westminster isn't cheap, Dude. I hope you're sharing." Suddenly realising what she'd said, Eva added, "I mean, I wasn't fishing. You can live with whoever you want, or not, or do, whatever. It's really none of my–" Her head whipped around and she opened her mouth in mock surprise. "Oh look, a thing I have to do. Over there. That's not here. Excuse me."

Harry chuckled. "You're adorable when you're off kilter. Wait, did I refer to another human being as adorable?"

"I can honestly say without a word of a lie that no one's ever referred to me as adorable."

Harry politely wiggled his coffee cup in her direction to grab her attention. "I'll be paying for that one, won't I?"

Eva was suddenly struck by images of how she'd make him pay. None were suitable for children's viewing hours.

Rolling her eyes in a friendly manner, she took the cup from his hand. Her delicate porcelain fingers wrapped around his for a moment. In fact, it was a fraction longer than a moment. Their eyes met, and it was far from uncomfortable.

An instant later the world shook and turned blood orange. The explosion ripped through the windows, showering them in glass and debris, and knocked them both to the ground. The gut-punching blast engulfed them with crippling heat.

After the second explosion everything went black.

CHAPTER EIGHT

It was the smoke that panicked Eva the most. The acrid cloud descended like a dark spectre and cut her vision to no more than a metre or two. Outside sounded like the apocalypse. It was a horrifying cacophony of agonising screams, people calling out in panic, sirens and car alarms.

Eva staggered to her feet, took a step, slipped on glass fragments and fell. Before she could hit the ground a strong set of hands cradled and hoisted her up. She twisted and saw the granite jawed Harry. A trickle of blood flowed from a cut on his forehead. He hadn't seemed to have noticed.

"Are you alright? Are you hurt?" he asked. His jaw locked in place, his expression stern. He'd become a different person. Harder.

"I think – yes, I'm fine." She patted herself down to double check, but there was no pain, nothing broken, nothing cut as far as she could tell. Glancing about her café, the windows were completely gone. Tables and chairs were covered in glass shards. Bad but repairable. Outside an occasional figure staggered past. The thick smoke made it impossible to know what was happening beyond the footpath.

"Good." Harry took in the street scene with concern. "Stay behind the bench, lock the back door, don't venture out for any reason until you see the police or military, do you understand?"

"Like fuck I will."

"Pardon?"

"Jesus sodding Christ, who the hell do you think you are? I'm not some damsel in distress and I'm certainly not taking orders from a man I hardly know."

Harry seemed genuinely taken aback that his orders, and they were orders, weren't immediately followed. *Screw him.*

"Ah, right. Okay. Then I *recommend* what I just said, if you want. I'm going to go out there and see what I can do to help."

"Are you a doctor?"

"No."

Apparently the conversation was over because he marched into the darkness. Not knowing what to do, Eva reluctantly did exactly what he'd ordered, then suggested, she do. With no glass in her windows she was exposed and especially alone.

When did she become the cowering fragile type? Squatting, she reached under the bench and pulled out her non-English baseball bat. She'd only taken it out once in the café to emphasise a point to a couple of particularly persistent Mormon preachers. Clutching the wood to her chest she felt marginally less like a weakling.

The sirens refused to let up. The screaming and shouting continued, but there was so much it coalesced into an unrecognisable horrid shriek. About to venture to the doorway, another explosion tore through the darkness outside. Squatting in the foetal position, hugging the bat to her chest, Eva rocked back and forth, terrified.

Several minutes passed, silence replaced chaos, which was far worse. There were still relentless alarms, but all human noise seemed to have ceased. The dark smoke hovering above the street began to dissipate and morphed into an unreal white haze. Occasionally a black silhouette ambled past like a zombie.

Chastising herself for her cowardice, Eva made the decision to go outside and see what was going on. People might be hurt.

There hadn't been an explosion for a good five minutes, maybe it was over.

Standing unsteadily to her feet, she tentatively edged towards the front of her café. The occasional shout told her there were at least some humans left alive in London. Reaching the door, she was able to take in the street for the first time. An unnatural ashen mist hung over everything, the smell of burnt plastic and gasoline filled her lungs. Eva wandered cautiously towards the Strand where there were at least some signs of life. The source of the blasts seemed to be Charing Cross Station, which had black scorched wreckage of some description strewn across the entire street.

Her first thought was Freedom First. A fringe group of loonies whose ultimate aim was anything but what their name suggested. Driven by the current worldwide disillusionment with self-obsessed governments, they advocated near-anarchy. Their rhetoric made the IRA look positively Ghandi-like by comparison. Even though there had been vague threats and a few out of control protests, they'd remained all talk. Maybe that had changed.

People were about, but had completely contradictory reactions. Some were dazed. Others ran either away or towards the scene. There were several groups huddled together, arms around each other for protection. One woman stood in the middle of the street and screamed incessantly. Several hooded figures slunk about in the dark corners, trying to be invisible.

There was only one large collection of people about fifty metres down the Strand, closer to the station. Not knowing why, Eva hurried towards it. As she approached, she observed the damage to the shops along the strip. As with her shopfront, all the windows on the strip were blown in. No store had survived intact. Some shop owners were already cleaning up. And judging from the movement at the back of the pharmacy, some were already being looted. *Vermin.*

About twenty people formed the largest group. A strong voice was the only one she could hear. He seemed to be in charge. Of course he did. She couldn't see him because of those surrounding him, but she knew exactly who it was.

"–and then take her to St Barts. How you going there Liam, you okay with applying that pressure? Need a rest?"

"No, it's alright, I've got it."

"Good lad. Right, you, Red Shirt, I need you to go talk to the pharmacy over there, get all the bandages and gauze they can spare. If they have those car med kits, grab them all, it'll make it easy to distribute."

"That could be a problem." When Eva spoke she was surprised how her voice sounded.

All eyes turned to her. Including Harry's. He was huddled over an elderly man, tying a shirt sleeve, his own, around the man's leg as a tourniquet. Harry didn't show any emotion, but raised a questioning eyebrow.

Eva addressed him, "I think – I think they're already looting the pharmacy."

Harry's eyes narrowed and his lips went white. "Bastards, don't they know–" He tilted his head back and closed his eyes. He patted the hand of the old man and asked, "Charlie, you going to be alright?"

"Yes, yes, thank you."

Nodding, Harry rose. "Right, Red Shirt, UPS guy, and you," he said to a tall black guy, "if you want to do some good, you'll all come with me and we'll clear them out of the chemist. People need help more than some crackhead needs his pseudoephedrine. You with me?"

The youngest, with a red shirt, shifted uncomfortably. "They could have knives and all–"

"Yes, they could," Harry said without further encouragement. He gave a slight shake of his head, as if to say *and?*

The three men uttered their acquiescence, some more eagerly than others. They walked towards Eva. Sweetness returned to Harry's face, he leaned down to her. "I should have known you wouldn't have stayed put. Are you alright?"

Eva nodded, not knowing if her voice wouldn't break if she

uttered another syllable.

"Can I borrow that?" He motioned to the baseball bat in her hands.

She hadn't realised she still had it. Giving a brisk nod, she handed it to him. He ran his hand tenderly along her arm and broke into a run after his newly-formed citizen posse. Was he really going to–?

Before she could even finish the thought, Harry sprinted towards a hooded figure emerging from the window of the pharmacy, one arm cradling a collection of pill bottles. Without breaking stride, Harry leapt in the air and kicked the man in the centre of his chest, throwing him clear off his feet.

The pills went flying, the man – he must have been at least six four, to Harry's six foot – flew backwards and hit the ground with a thud. Before he'd had a chance to recover, Harry swung the baseball bat hard into his ribs.

The crack could be heard all the way down the street, it may have even echoed. Satisfied his victim posed no threat, Harry rose and turned to his somewhat stunned companions. Tossing the bat end over end, he caught it on the handle and grinned. "Who's next?" With a yank of his head, he motioned the others to follow and jumped through the smashed window. His posse followed him in, albeit with less enthusiasm.

Nothing happened for the longest time. Eva slowly edged along the street, but had no weapon to speak of and felt naked and exposed. Shaking her head, she chastised her helpless reactions. Sure, whatever had caused the explosions was bound to be catastrophic, but she was better than that. Stronger. She was no wilting violet. She wasn't a character in a Charlotte Brontë novel. Eva had seen off muggers who'd made the mistake of showing the slightest vulnerability. She'd sent exes to A&E that had dared raise a hand to her. Why would this be any different? Clenching her fists and straightening her back. *It's not different.* Under her breath she muttered, "Fuck weakness," and was better for it. People were dazed, but at least they were still standing.

More Londoners filled the street from the nearby office buildings and tube stations, either from pure curiosity or having been evacuated. Tourists, not knowing which areas were safe, seemed to be moving the fastest away from the scene. The street was less like a post-apocalyptic scene and more like her adopted city again, albeit a bruised and battered one.

Eva organised the uninjured office workers to form small groups to carry some of the wounded to the nearest hospital on Pall Mall. Most followed her orders without question, assuming the person with the strong voice knew what she was doing. She didn't have the heart to tell them it was all an act. But it was an act that worked.

From the dark recesses of the pharmacy came shouting and several crashes. Abuse, orders, names shouted in panic and viscous threats rang out. Scanning the street for a weapon, any weapon, she came up short. Relying on her new found bravery, Eva edged forward.

Two youths leapt out the shattered windows and hit the ground running. They sprinted up the street and didn't look back. Neither carried anything in their hands. Harry and his little group emerged from the pharmacy engaged in jovial conversation with two white-outfitted staff members. Red Shirt cradled his arm, but seemed elated. They had faced off against an enemy and had emerged victorious.

Alright, Eva was a little impressed. It was no wonder Harry captivated her. He had seemingly limitless ability to surprise her. More importantly, surprise her with being a mother-fucking bad arse. She could honestly say she'd never met anyone remotely like him.

A low murmur from the way they'd come, past her café on Craven Street, grew steadily in volume. The wall of sound was a horrifying mix of shouts, chants and smashing glass. Its source rounded the far corner and both Harry and Eva took a step back-wards. About one hundred youths of mixed size, age and race marched as one towards them carrying crowbars, shards of wood and wrathful temperaments. Many wore handkerchiefs to conceal their identity. One thing was certain; they weren't here to help.

There was no way Eva could get back to her café. They had to move away from the encroaching violent-looking throng, but that would mean moving towards the scene of the blast. They had no choice. Staying put would mean being beaten by a mob, or worse.

The office blocks weren't the only ones emptying of their inhabitants.

The mass of youths must have streamed out of somewhere. There weren't housing commissions this close to the city, but they must have been nearby. Even the looters in 2011 hadn't been this quick to react. They were organised, motivated. *How is that possible?* The bombs had only exploded ten or fifteen minutes before and the emergency services had only just managed to appear, so how did this crowd mobilise so quickly?

It wasn't the time to think about it. They were approaching, fast. Scanning the scene behind her, Eva saw wounded people still on the Strand with small groups surrounding them to assist.

Turning to face them, she shouted in a voice she thought herself incapable of, "You need to get these people out of here. Now." People turned away from the advancing rabble and gazed at her bewildered. Shouting as loud as she could, she said, "This place is about to become a war zone, you need to pick up the wounded and fall back to where the ambulances and police are at Trafalgar Square. And you need to do it right fucking now. Go!"

Red Shirt and another man from Harry's little mission were still positioned near the pharmacy. Pointing in their direction, Eva motioned to the wounded youth Harry had given a crack to the ribs. "That includes him, boys. You need to take him down there." The two men gawked at Harry for guidance. He gave a curt nod and they proceeded to pick him up under the arms and cart him away. The youth offered no resistance. Harry's lips cracked into a small grin and he gave Eva a wink.

Looking back at the faces of the office workers and shop owners, Eva saw nothing short of hopeless fear. Many took unconscious steps backwards recoiling from the oncoming hoard. Within minutes the street would be abandoned to the encroaching mass intent on looting and violence. Several workers had already broken into a run, not wanting to get caught in the crush. As much as it sickened Eva, she'd have to join them. There was no way she could get through them to protect her café against the sheer mass of viciousness coming her way. Nobody could.

Beside her, Harry climbed onto a Mini abandoned on the street. It seemed he had other ideas. The cuts on his forehead had dried and added to the drama of the moment. He faced the frightened, mostly suited, crowd.

Using his downturned palms to quell chatter, he raised his voice and addressed them. "Everyone, everyone! You all see what's coming, but we can stop them. Nobody wants to see our city looted and destroyed. We can stop them dead, but we have to work together. There's far more of us than them. We can hold them off."

A middle-aged man in a cheap suit, with ridiculously thick neck pointed at Harry and asked, "Who the hell are you, Mate?"

"I'm the guy saying if we work together we can do some good."

Eva eyed the street, the gathering at the far end seemed to have slowed their advance. It was as if they were waiting for a signal. *Christ there were a lot of them.*

Harry pointed at them. "These aren't soldiers. These aren't trained thugs. These are desperate people who think they're owed something they're not. They're not evil, they've just seen an opening that shouldn't exist. You can close it. We all can, but we have to do it together, as one. These guys are after goods, they're not expecting resistance. They're not expecting us."

Another voice called out, "People are going to get smashed, right? Look at 'em. You can't guarantee folks aren't in for a world of hurt."

"No. No, I can't. But let me ask you a question. Tomorrow, when people watch the news and someone asks if you were there, are you going to tell them you were part of the wall that held back chaos, or you ran away? Moments in life define us, right here, right now, this is one. What you decide now will define you for years to come. Were you part of the line that held, or did you turn tail and run?" Harry spun to see how close they were. "I for one want to hold my head high and one day tell people that I held The Strand Line and faced down anarchy. I was there the day Londoners said no more. The day we stood as one and took back our city. If you want to stand tall, look your kids in the eye and tell them about that moment in your life, that instant where you were asked to fight for what was right, what are you going to tell them? Did you run? Or did you hold that line?" Harry straightened his back and pushed out his chest. "Who's with me?"

At first a handful of people, all men, stepped forward. Eva joined them. Soon a trickle turned into a flood. Whether it was a need to do the right thing, a sense of civic pride or guilt, it worked. Harry continued to rally support and soon there were hundreds surrounding the Mini. People held up their phones to capture the moment.

Those that joined were a strange mixture of angry, scared and bemused. But they were there, and they were building. A few, probably more than Eva would have expected, turned their backs and either walked or ran away.

Using the baseball bat to punctuate the point, Harry continued. "We make a line there. You hold that line, do you understand? No matter what, you hold. Always keep Trafalgar at your back, kind of apt, really. If someone gets injured, you create a tunnel, get them out, then move the next rank up. Disciplined. You have each other's backs."

In quick order, Harry directed people where to stand, how to support the lines in front, how to keep a roving band of burly reserves that could be deployed at any time should there be a break in the line. He even set up the pharmacy as a temporary triage area. He'd also used his phone for a short conversation she'd been unable to hear.

Where the hell were the rescue crews? Downing Street was only a few blocks away, surely police and ambulance crews should have been here by now. The longer it went on, the more Eva felt they were on their own. It was fortunate the city had its own saviour.

In a few short minutes Harry had organised his band of volunteers of office workers, students and shop owners into a human barrier across the street. The term 'charismatic leader' was mostly misused but, in Harry's case, it seemed to have been created just for him. He was amazing. At that instant, if he'd told Eva he loved Margaret Atwood she'd have dropped her pants and demanded he do her up against Nelson's Column.

The mob continued to hold position. They were motionless at the end of the street, increased in volume but lacking action. Harry glanced at the halted rabble and confusion shrouded his face. He was probably thinking the same as Eva. Why weren't they attacking?

There was a disturbance at the front of the opposition's position. One of the throng was physically being held back, apparently prevented from attacking. He didn't seem too pleased about it. Finally shaking loose his compatriots, he ran full pelt towards Eva and everyone else. He carried a piece of metal pipe and a nasty disposition. Everyone around her tensed, but he remained the only one to break ranks. A few at the front of their position put out their hands holding back others, as if to say *not yet*.

As the young man ran, Harry jumped off the Mini and handed Eva the baseball bat. With a slanted grin, he said, "If you're staying, you'll need this."

"Try and stop me."

"Eva, from what I've seen, there's not much in this world that could." He ran his hand along the side of her face and she closed her eyes at the tender touch. He pulled back his hand. "Excuse me." With that he ran directly at the opposition's single threat. As he took off, Eva could have sworn he muttered, "Our first catch of the day."

Did he make an obscure Star Wars reference? But that quote was from a character in the Empire.

The two men ran at each other, neither slowed an iota. When they were mere feet away, the man raised his iron bar with both hands and let out a fierce battle cry. A mistake. Harry dropped his shoulder at the last second and plunged it into his ribcage.

Both men flew into the air. It seemed like minutes they hovered there. The man flew back, with Harry on top of him. The iron bar fell to the ground with a metallic *clang* and rolled away.

Dazed and hurt from Harry's charge, the man attempted to rise, but Harry grabbed the front of his collar, drew back his fist and punched him in the face. His head flew back and he struggled. He threw loose punches, but Harry's grip was strong. Successive punches were punctuated by words. "Not. In. My. Town."

Cameras and mobile phones recording proceedings.

With his prey subdued, Harry hauled him onto his shoulder and fireman-carried him back to the edge of Trafalgar Square. He flung him into the arms of his lieutenants. Trotting back, Harry mounted his Mini podium, and addressed his ramshackle troops. "That's how we do it. One on one. Help anyone that needs it. Watch your comrades, have each other's backs. Hold the line. We can do this. *You* can do this."

Eva believed him. Everyone believed him. But it was then that the low rumble at the other end of the street became a cacophony of fearful screams and shrieks. From around various corners more joined the mass of youths. So many more. The hundred turned into two hundred. They weren't holding back because of the resistance. They were holding back because they were waiting for reinforcements. *Grunting badger farts.*

The rumble became louder and louder as if they were gearing themselves up. Several in the crowd positioned near Eva pushed through as they fled from the frightening wall of hurt.

One second the rabble were taunting, the next they ran. Having been given a signal, the horde charged with a deafening war cry. They sprinted, gnarling and gnashing.

It was terrifying.

But Eva wasn't afraid. Deep within her core, logically, she should be, but wasn't. She was loving the danger.

Eva rolled up her sleeves, slid her back foot sideways to better repel force and spat on the ground. Staring down the attacking swarm, she forced air out her nose, and mumbled, "Come at me fuckers."

Time slowed. For the longest time it seemed like nothing happened. Then all it once it did.

With a nauseating crash the mob hit the mass of office workers, shop owners, tourists and students. There was an agonising *oof* sound, combined with the clang of metal on bone. Fist on skin.

Eva paid the sound little heed. She was too busy screaming like a banshee and swinging her bat at any target she could find. The world became a melange of weapons, limbs, teeth and blood.

If Eva had believed in hell, this is what she'd have imagined.

Cole and Decker stared at her. Neither spoke. For several seconds they just blinked. Finally Cole managed to form words. "You were there?" He asked with a tenor of awe. "The Battle of Trafalgar? On that day of all days?"

Eva didn't try to hide the proudness she still held. "I know."

"The day he...the day Lancing..."

"A little later, but yep."

They knew how the rest of that particular tale went.

Cole was about to ask something, but Eva cut him off. "Hey, who's telling this story?"

Both officers leaned forward in rapt attention, which was exactly where she wanted them. While she held them distracted by tales of yore, she was almost done with the other handcuff. It had been easier than she'd thought.

Her cockiness cost her. The bobby pin slipped and sprang from her grip. Her sigh covered the sound of it hitting the floor.

She'd been so close and now she was screwed.

In response to her sigh, Decker asked, "Are we being bothersome with questions, Ms Destruction?"

"Ah, no. Not at all. It's just, ah, I remember what happened after. The stuff after the news reports and such. The next night was when everything changed for me."

"How so?"

"That was the night I met Horatio Lancing."

CHAPTER NINE

The small gate creaked out the front and footsteps echoed across the tiny path. Eva was nervous. *When was the last time that happened?* The knock at the door made her jump. Through the slit in the curtain she watched him knock again, step back and wait.

She reprimanded herself for acting like a star-struck teen and steeled herself. She was tougher than that.

Before she moved from her voyeuristic position at the window, stomping footsteps echoed along the hall. The door was wrenched open and a lanky, dishevelled and slightly confused man stood perplexed before Harry. Bless Paul. Eva made her way through the lounge in the fear he'd scare poor Harry off.

She heard Harry's muffled voice. "I'm terribly sorry, I must be at the wrong address."

Paul let out a noise not dissimilar to a startled elk. After first exclaiming, "Fuck me sideways," he promptly slammed the door in Harry's face.

Turning to Eva, Paul shook his head at her open-mouthed. Before she could utter a syllable, Paul flung open the door to reveal a justifiably confused Harry.

"You're him. The bloke from the telly," Paul said in reverence. "The Battle of Trafalgar guy. Am I right?"

"Uh, well, yes, I was there–"

Paul turned to Eva. "Evie, you never told us you were dating a celebrity."

"This isn't a…" She sighed, "Just let him in."

Paul motioned Harry to come in and promptly disappeared into the kitchen forgetting to greet their guest.

Harry tentatively stepped into the narrow hallway. The man that had rallied a city appeared nervous. Eva made him out for the first time. Bathed in the soft light of the bulb above his head, he had no visible scars from the previous day's battle.

Forgetting her vow of strength, Eva grinned. "Hi. You look nice."

Look nice?

NICE?

Who the hell was this person speaking? Since when did Eva use the word 'nice' or care about what people wore? That wasn't what she was about. Sure, judge someone for what they read, their stance on social justice issues, but not the clothes on their back. Everything about Harry made her lose focus on what she believed in.

He did smell nice though.

She mentally kicked herself.

Harry rocked on his heels and nodded. "Thanks. Well, I had some help."

Overcome with a sudden sense of dread, Eva mulled that statement over. Help choosing clothes? Did he mean a girlfriend, wife? She realised she knew next to nothing about this man.

Picking up on her lost expression, Harry said, "I commandeered a younger member of staff during the day to ask sartorial questions. I chose him mainly because he had immaculate hair. I believe he first thought it some kind of test, but eventually he figured out I was a bit clueless. We went on a little shopping expedition."

With his hands, he gave a *ta-da* gesture. Wearing the rewards,

Harry was fashionable, but not over the top in his jacket, jeans and shirt combination.

With arms folded, Eva gave an appreciative nod. When did he find the time? Lead a counter-riot one day, have a makeover the next.

There was a commotion from the kitchen, voices were raised, and something smashed.

"Come in and meet everyone. That was Paul by the way."

Paul stepped out of the kitchen, tea towel over his shoulder. "What now? Someone said my name." Not waiting for an answer, he extended his hand. "Any commotion you may have heard was completely Nancy's fault and I'm willing to sign statutory declarations to that effect. Sorry about before, Evie didn't tell us much about you."

"That's because I don't know much." She hefted a challenging eyebrow in Harry's direction.

Giving a knowing smile, he said, "You'll know a lot more very soon. Believe me."

Was that a promise or was he flirting? Or both?

Harry handed over the bottle of wine he'd brought. Paul read the label and pursed his lips.

"I've never heard of it, is it decent?"

"I believe so."

"Good-oh. Come in, I'd give you the grand tour but it would take less time to complete than this sentence." They stepped from the hall. "This is what we like to call the lounge. That's the kitchen and that's my wife Nancy and upstairs is the bedroom."

Nancy stepped in from the kitchen and gazed at her husband disbelievingly. "Way to bury the lede."

"Huh?" Paul asked.

Ignoring her clueless husband, Nancy shook Harry's hand. "A pleasure."

Harry grinned. "Thank you for inviting me for dinner. Your request couldn't have come at a better time."

"Oh, *our* pleasure." The grin virtually encircled her head. She turned to Eva in the adjoining kitchenette. "I don't know what you're on about, he's not hideous. He's bloody gorgeous."

Eva rolled her eyes at her best friend as she sliced a crispy loaf. She'd expect nothing less from Nancy. She issued Harry a good natured *sorry about my friends* grimace.

This wasn't a date. She'd made that perfectly clear. When he'd found her after the riot he'd repeatedly told her he was thankful she was unharmed. They'd exchanged brief tales of cracking skulls, but then fell into an uncomfortable silence. Eva surprised herself when she'd suggested dinner. Definitely not a date though, she'd stated that firmly, it would be with her friends. She wanted to thank him for looking after her, for protecting the street.

He'd agreed, eagerly. Harry had said he understood there were to be no romantic connotations, but she didn't think he believed it. She didn't. For all her talk and self-flagellation, deep down she was captivated by the mysterious and dangerous stranger.

"I 'spose your wine's alright, Harry," Paul said after taking a sip. Eva hadn't even seen him open the bottle. "Pretty bitter though."

Nancy snorted. "Says the guy who gets his wine from one-eyed blokes in seedy pubs."

Harry motioned to Paul. "You might want to let it breathe a bit."

Eva picked up the bottle and virtually snatched the glass out of Paul's hand. She placed it delicately on the bench as one would with a ticking bomb. Poking the bottle in Harry's direction she asked, "Is this legit?"

Harry nodded.

"Christ on a bike." She cradled the bottle as if was a newborn. Eva addressed the visibly perturbed Paul, miffed at his wine being snatched away so suddenly. "This is," she sighed, "an '86 Grange."

"Couldn't afford a new one?" Paul asked.

Assessing Harry, Eva could tell he didn't know if Paul was joking or not.

Incredulously, she said, "It's probably worth a few thousand quid."

Paul's complexion turned pallid.

Harry nodded. "Something like that."

Nancy sidled up to her and admired the bottle. In a stage whisper she said to Eva, "If you don't marry him, I will."

Paul recovered enough to say, "Hey!"

Eva slid into the tiny kitchen and opened a high cupboard. "I'll put it in the decanter for a bit, shall I?"

"We have a decanter?" Nancy asked.

Eva waived it above her head "I gave it to you last Christmas. You thought it was a vase."

Nancy went to the fridge, pulled out several lagers and handed them about, including to Harry, who she hadn't asked. She motioned everyone to sit on the lounges. "So Harry, you're a bit well-known now, eh?" and promptly plopped next to him.

"I guess so. It wasn't intentional. Just kind of happened."

"Oh, so I gather from our girl here. You did a good thing, the whole city thanks you." Nancy raised her bottle in salute. "Going to have a tell-all book or reality TV show next?"

"Not really my style. I think there's enough vapidity in the world, I'm pretty sure we don't need any more, particularly with me involved."

She threaded her arm though his and leaned in. "So, family?"

"Yes, I have one of those."

"Anyone in it?"

"Parents. Two of them. A male and a female."

"Well, aren't we getting somewhere?" Nancy grimaced. "Are they Australian too?"

"Yes."

Nancy waited for more, but nothing came. She let out a frustrated sigh. "So what is it you do, Eva has no bloody idea."

"Nance!"

"Oh come on, you don't mind me asking do you, Harry?" She issued her trademark wicked wink. In spite of the unusual introductions, Harry didn't seem offended. In fact, he appeared to like her nutty friends. She loved them, but realised they could be off-putting for newcomers.

Paul was a man out of sync with time. His movements were slow, as were his reactions, but he somehow made it endearing, as if he was operating in his own timeline and was happy with that. Nancy was her Irish pocket rocket, fiercely loyal and loving. No one ever made the mistake of crossing her twice.

"Acquisitions, mostly."

Nancy nodded. "She said you were evasive too. Acquisitions could be anything from antique teapots, to white slavery, to plutonium for a flux capacitor." Nancy's face took on a hard edge. "So how's about you talk to us like we're not idiots and give us some answers."

Harry might have figured out Nancy was straight to the point, but this was extremely direct. Eva wasn't comfortable with her friend's change of tack.

"Let's just say I'm in a business that has a lot of government dealings and contracts. I'm a small cog in the big machine and being evasive comes with the territory. I'm not being vague or misleading to be insensitive or deliberately obtuse, but there's some important work going on, and unfortunately that requires some level of secrecy, at least initially, so my caginess has less to do with deception and more to do with protecting people."

Nancy nodded and frowned. She raised an appreciative eyebrow in Eva's direction. "Good enough for me. I hope you like pot roast government boy Harry, because that's what you're getting."

"It smells good."

Nancy headed towards the kitchenette. She leaned towards Eva. "He's got a gifted tongue. Always comes in handy."

For the first time Eva saw Harry blush.

"Wait, wait," Eva put down her knife and fork and wiped away a tear. "You just left him there?"

Paul frowned. "What else could we do? We didn't get him in, why the hell would we want to get him out?"

Harry put down his empty glass, a huge grin creasing his red wine-stained lips. "Yes, but he was naked–"

"Then he could find his own way out of the toilets." Paul shrugged. "We weren't stopping him."

"What time was this?"

"A bit after eight. Everyone was coming into work, reception was rather busy. He was in quite the pickle." Paul topped up his glass with the not-entirely-Bordeaux wine, seemingly having forgotten about his story.

"And?"

"Oh, right. So after a few minutes the door opens, he strolls out completely bollocking starkers, asks one of his subordinates for his coat, puts it on and strides out the front door with his head held high. If there's one thing us private school boys can pull off, it's false dignity in the face of adversity."

The three of them stared at Paul, imagining the scene, but not wholly believing it could happen in the Department of Treasury.

Eva had to ask, "So how exactly did your HR manager get to be naked in the work toilets first thing on a Thursday?"

"Uh, don't know." An expression slid across Paul's face that said, *maybe I should have asked*. It only made Eva laugh harder.

"Not exactly the end to the storly I was looking for," Harry said.

"Did you just say storly?" Nancy asked, punching him in the arm. "Lightweight."

Harry let out another riotous belly laugh. Eva liked his laugh. There was no pretence, no act. It was honest. He said, "I don't think I've laughed this hard in years, possibly ever." He touched his cheeks. "My jaw's sore."

The night had been filled with so much laughter. Eva and Harry had bonded while reminiscing about childhood TV back in Australia. They'd utterly bamboozled Nancy and Paul trying to explain the appeal of Monkey – a poorly dubbed Japanese live-action show starring a monkey born from an egg on a mountain top, which also starred a talking pig. When Eva and Harry had recited lines and re-enacted a slow motion kung-fu fight Nancy had brought out dessert in order to shut them up. That was when Paul had launched into his work story.

Managing to compose himself, Harry said, "How long have you worked at Treasury, Paul?"

"On and off for fifteen years."

"Off?"

"When he sleeps," Nancy answered for him.

Harry stretched his arms above his head. "You know, back in the day anyone who worked for MI6 used to say they worked at Treasury."

All motion at the table stopped. Nancy's and Paul's features turned grey.

"Harry..." Eva started.

Still smiling, Harry either hadn't noticed, or hadn't cared about the sudden chill he'd brought to the table. "I'm just saying that's what I heard somewhere."

"No, Harry... You don't..." Eva turned to Nancy and said, "Look, Nance, I'm sorry, he didn't..."

Nancy waved her friend's apology away. "He didn't know." She turned to Harry with a grin she reserved for shopkeepers who advised they had nothing in her size. "Our sudden silence isn't due to my husband's wine. It's just MI6 is a touchy subject in this house." She steadied herself. "Paul's father was executed as a spy in Warsaw in 1982."

All colour drained from Harry's face. "Jesus, I'm so–"

Nancy wasn't finished. "You weren't to know, but the whole spy thing is a bit of a minefield."

"Of course, of course." Harry pursed his lips in apology to Paul who tilted his glass, as if to say, *don't worry about it.*

Paul did his best to appear nonplussed and licked the remainder of a delicious crème brûlée off his spoon. "So what's it like to be the most famous man in London, Harry?"

"I hardly think that's the case. There were hundreds there, and I'm sure people wouldn't have the foggiest–"

"You're a meme," Paul said cutting in.

"–and I...I'm a what?"

"A meme. On the internet." He paused. "A meme."

"Just because you keep saying it, Sweetie," Nancy spoke quietly to her husband, "it doesn't make it any clearer."

"Oh, right." Paul reached over to the couch for his Lancing tablet computer. After a few moments of tinkering, he turned it around for all to see. It was a news site with the image seen throughout the world; Harry standing above the first of the attackers, with bold lettering: *Not. In. My. Town.*

"That's a meme?" Harry asked.

Paul grinned. "Nah, this is."

He scrolled down. The same picture, but the youth's face had been replaced with the mayor, who hadn't fared well in the aftermath of the riot. The appalling emergency response was put down to computer glitches and understaffed services after severe budget cuts. Paul scrolled through the rest, the PM, the London Eye, the King, the Wimpy Burger logo, Hitler and various members of One Direction all came in for the Harry-punching treatment. The One Direction picture made Eva laugh.

"So that's a meme, then," Harry said. "Right." He seemed genuinely shaken.

"There's hundreds of these, check it out, you've got your own hashtag too, and about a bazillion fake accounts, and…"

"He gets it, Paul," Eva said.

"Oh, right." He pointed to the TV and asked his wife. "Mind if I–?"

Nancy tutted. "Go on, news junky." She gently pushed her husband. "It's just going to be the same again. The riot's all they can talk about at the moment. At least it's a break from the usual who's Horatio Lancing crap and, oh, another story about another government he's helped out and now here's a cat that counts. Repeat."

Harry choked on his wine. Eva should have warned him about the impending hangover but decided to leave it. She suspected he didn't get many chances to let loose.

Paul kissed the top of his wife's head and went searching for the remote. "I know it's here somewhere."

"Not a fan of Lancing, Nancy?" Harry asked. He kept his pleasant air, but Eva detected an underlying current of seriousness. *Him again?*

"Like most plebs, I'm still a bit sceptical, way less than at the start, but I still don't think he's as good as they make out, you know? Loads of businesses, charity work, propping up struggling European countries, all good, right, but it doesn't affect me one dot, so why should I care who the bloke is?"

Eva filled her glass with Paul's toxic wine, knowing full well she'd pay for it the next day. "You didn't seem to mind when your charity got a slice of the funding pie."

The expression Nancy gave her was one only good friends could give each other when they'd been caught out. One of Nancy's side projects at HSBC was to run a charity for women's literature in the Middle East. They'd received a grand from the Lancing Foundation.

"Yes," she said reluctantly. "There was that. Made me think Lancing was a chick. I mean, we've never seen her, heard her speak, could be."

Paul became animated. "Could be a giant space monkey for all we know."

Harry waved his glass in Paul's direction. "How cool would that be?"

"I know, right! Now where's that sodding remote?"

Nancy shook her head. "Don't encourage him."

Harry grinned with good nature. "So, that's your take away from all this? You're happy to take his money when it suits but you don't care about the good he's trying to do? Just leave that betterment of the world to someone else?"

She recognised the change in Nancy's face, but she doubted Harry did. Her eyes became slits and Eva could see she was about to hurl a bucket of abuse. Before she could, Harry leaned over and kissed Nancy on the top of the head totally disarming her. "It's alright, politically I should put the fact that he's ensuring private corporations stay out of African water supplies at the top of my list, but if I was to be honest my favourite is taking down that minister for culture who was secretly funding the militant anti-immigration group. What can I say, I'm still a troublemaker at heart."

Nancy did her best to stifle a smirk. She failed dismally. Coyly, she said, "I can be a bit opinionated sometimes."

"Nooooooo," Harry said.

"Listen Buster, do we know each other well enough for you to be taking the piss?"

Harry tilted his head. "I'd like to think so."

"Alright then." Nancy unleashed her pinball smile, only slightly lessened by the coriander between her teeth. "I like a man who can stand his ground. I think you're overqualified."

When Harry offered his help to find the remote with Paul, Nancy gave Eva's leg a pinch. Her eyes went wide and she nodded in Harry's direction. She'd given her approval. A first.

Paul made a passing comment about how he wanted to show how the newsreader on CNN looked like a cartoon turtle and Harry laughed his manly laugh. His face lit up and Eva let out the smallest of sighs. Eva clenched her eyes closed. *No, no, no.* She wasn't developing feelings for Harry. It wasn't possible. He was far too reserved and measured for her. And *nice.* Notwithstanding his baseball bat-wielding behaviour, he seemed far more intro-verted than the usual blokes she hooked up with. *Was that such an awful thing?*

Eva's dating history was patchy at best. Or as Nancy had referred to it on more than one occasion, 'a toxic waste dump of losers and abusers'. She did love a bad boy. Harry certainly didn't fit that mould. Badass, yes, but not a bad boy. Could she suspend her bad-boy addiction, even temporarily? What would it be like to be with a nice guy?

Maybe she should give Harry a chance? Nancy had certainly dropped enough hints. He did have a lovely mouth. It could have been the cabernet sauvignon merlot pinot, but from deep within, Eva sensed the long dormant warmth of attraction clawing at some sadly neglected parts of her anatomy. She highly suspected it wasn't the wine talking.

"Isn't it time you were heading off Harry?" Eva asked.

"Uh, is it?" Harry asked, confused. "Alright." He stepped away from hunting behind the cushions and adjusted his shirt.

Paul let out a childish, "Awwww."

Nancy displayed her best poker face, which is to say, she made it perfectly clear that Eva was ruining it with Harry. She was an easy beat at card games.

Collecting his jacket, Harry went to shake Paul's hand, but Paul had other ideas. Leaping to his feet, Paul wrapped his tree trunk arms around Harry and enveloped him in a hug with so much force Harry's feet lifted off the ground.

Harry leaned down to hug Nancy. Before he could release her, Nancy held him long enough to whisper something in his ear that Eva was unable to make out. He stepped back and gave Nancy a terse nod of understanding. Eva fought the feeling to roll her eyes at her best friend. Subtle, she wasn't.

Harry thanked Nancy and Paul profusely and complimented them on their hospitality, fantastic meal and wine. Though, Eva was certain the last one was him being polite, especially after the Grange.

On the way out Harry paused at the entry to the lounge. He picked up a small black device behind the door. "Paul, I seem to have found your remote control."

"My beloved!" Paul said, launching himself at it. "How the hell did it get there?"

Harry shrugged. Eva led him quickly out of the flat and closed the door behind her. They were motionless on the small landing, staring at one another.

"Well." Eva rocked on her heels.

"Well," Harry said with a slight nod.

They both grinned.

Kiss me. Kiss me now you fucker before I change my mind.

"I really like them. They're so loving and...real. Totally utterly one hundred percent real. You have no idea how much I miss that, Eva."

She liked it when he said her name.

"You've created a couple more fans," she said not knowing what else to say.

"As long as they don't create any memes about me and by meme, I mean my meme." He grinned, showing off his red wine-tinged teeth. "Thank you, Eva, for dinner. Tonight of all nights, I really needed this."

"What's so special about tonight?"

He tilted his head and leaned down. "This."

Gently lifting her chin, he kissed her tenderly on the lips. Eva was sure she'd never been kissed so lightly, so delicately. Perhaps it was the uniqueness of his touch, or the man that made her desperate for more. Either way, it worked.

In a whisper, Eva said, "Screw it, Geronimo."

"Come again?"

Eva answered with her lips. Like some damsel in a 1950s Hollywood flick, she melted into his arms. There was no denying it. She'd fallen for Harry and there was no going back.

Gripping the back of his head, she forced the kiss into less tame, more lustful territory. He seemed to approve of the change of direction.

Hands slid around bodies, legs wove amongst legs, and kisses became more frantic, more passionate.

Unexpectedly Harry broke from the embrace and breathlessly said, "Eva, before we–"

Interrupting him, she kissed him hard and he fought to get his words out.

"–I have to tell you something–"

The more she kissed him, the more his resolve fell away.

"How about you shut up for now?" Eva brushed her lips over his. "I have other priorities."

Eva threaded her hands into his jacket and pulled him close. Harry's last semblance of willpower collapsed and thankfully he abandoned all hope of talking. Eva had bigger plans. Much less innocent plans.

Losing herself to the moment, it took a while to realise someone else was present. It must have taken four or five coughs before Eva realised Paul had opened the door and was attempting to get their attention.

Finally managing to tear herself away from Harry's firm grip, Eva turned to Paul. She almost gasped. She had known the lovable lug for eight years, but she'd never seen him like this. His face ashen, hard as stone. Every semblance of the normal jovial friend had disappeared. It had been replaced by something harder. Much harder.

"Paul, what...?"

Eyes bored into Harry, he said, "You're on the news."

"Sweetie, he's been on the news all–"

"No, there's been an announcement. An official one. You're on the news...Horatio Lancing."

CHAPTER TEN

The four of them gawked at the TV as BBC repeated the brief news conference again. Before a backdrop of the logos of the Lancing Corporation and its subsidiaries, Harry, well, Horatio, was straight-backed. Even with the air of confidence, Eva could tell he was nervous. It was in his eyes. Behind the lectern, he took a sip of water. After a bracing breath, he calmly said, "Ladies and gentlemen of the world, I am Horatio Lancing."

Cue a light storm of flashbulbs.

The reporters went nuts shouting questions. Horatio held up a hand and glanced at his notes. Steeling himself, he looked up and changed the world.

"Good afternoon. I apologise for the grandiose opening statement, but I thought it important to come to the crux of the matter quickly. I'm not a politician, I have no desire to be one, so why talk like one? Yes, I am Horatio Lancing, head of the multifaceted Lancing Corporation. My public relations team and I had planned my coming out, so to speak, in a few months, but recent public events sped up that process somewhat, and," he let lose a mischievous grin, "well, here we are."

It was the genuineness of the smile that did it for Eva. She was sure it was the same the world over. In the space of thirty seconds he'd shown himself to be likeable, charming and non-political. Quite an achievement. He either had spectacular PR training or was the real deal. Either way, Eva couldn't tear her eyes from the screen even though he was standing right next to her.

In a whisper, she asked, "Why didn't you tell me?"

In a hushed voice he replied, "Because I wanted to get to know you, and you me, without," he waved a hand at the screen, "all this."

Onscreen Harry continued his press conference. "Like many people, I was caught up in the events of yesterday, which the media have dubbed the Battle of Trafalgar, by pure accident. I was in the city on some very pleasant personal business…"

Was he flirting with Eva via the most viewed press conference of the last decade? *Damn. Way to crank up the woo.*

"…and like my fellow citizens decided to hold the line against chaos, against destruction, against those who wish to watch the world burn. And please let me add for the sake of clarity that my role yesterday has been generously exaggerated. Every citizen who stood their ground and took back their city deserves praise and admiration for their efforts and sacrifice. To label one person responsible negates the selfless efforts at the Battle of Trafalgar."

That was good spin. It reeked of PR. Denying something while repeating it only reinforced the thought in people's minds.

Horatio took a sip of water. "And I might add, the Battle of Trafalgar is somewhat of a misnomer as most of the battle took place on the Strand."

What he didn't say, Eva thought, was that the Battle of Trafalgar had a far more heroic edge to it. One that he'd already repeated twice.

"My face being associated with the riot meant there would be investigations into who I am, so, well, that brings us back here, I guess." There was that grin again. "Back in the day, when I grew up in Australia I was a geeky, pimply, socially awkward kid who clung to the shadows and went by a slightly different name–"

Eva turned to the man beside her. Her voice deliberately even. "So, what's your real name?"

"Harry. Harry Lancing. I've never lied to you Eva."

She folded her arms and returned her attention to the screen.

"If I may be so presumptuous, please let me answer some questions before you ask them. Yes, I am the Horatio Lancing who started the Lancing Corporation over fifteen years ago. There has only ever been one. Why the secrecy? I'm not one for taking the limelight and prefer my department heads, who let's face it do the hard work, to take their due credit. Guys…" He arched his back and motioned with his hand. "Guys, step forward."

Distinguished men and women of various departments stepped from behind the Lancing Corporation signage. Eva could identify the heads of Technology, Media and Entertainment.

"These are the people who rightfully deserve the praise. And to be honest, I liked the anonymity. To walk into one of my stores or ask someone on the street what they think of one of my products and to hear unfiltered opinions. I'm genuinely going to miss that."

That didn't entirely ring true with Eva. Harry told her on their first meeting that he never left his 'compound'. The man of the people routine sounded good, but she had her doubts.

"While I have your attention, I may as well advise that effective as of yesterday, I have resigned my position as head of the Lancing Corporation."

Again there was frenzy in the room, but this time it was different. The department heads were just as shocked as the press. This was news to them too. They glanced at each other to see if anyone had known. There was a round of shrugs.

The press roared and leapt out of their seats firing questions at him. Camera flashes illuminated Horatio like a floodlight. All the while he was granite-like, impervious to the frenzy before him. Horatio Lancing waited for the press' flurry of questions to die down. It didn't take long. They seemed to know who was in charge of the room.

"And while I'm here I may as well respond to some of my critics. I've been accused of bullying-tactics, using money and power to influence corporations and governments into doing what is best for their people." He paused and stared straight at the camera. "Well, they're right."

Cutting off the questions before they were fully vocalised, he continued, "So, the next question is, what will I do with all this spare time on my hands? Golf? Not my style. Lounging on a beach somewhere? Definitely not my style. We've entered a new age. The age of information. If corrupt governments who exploit their people think their lies are safe behind firewalls and security protocols they are very much mistaken. People have been demanding more of governments who have ignored them for too long, concerning themselves only with re-elections and pandering to their corporate demigods rather than caring for the very people who seek their guidance, support and leadership. They've had enough. I've had enough. That's the other reason I was planning to reveal myself before the events of Trafalgar Square. The world needed a voice, one that isn't after political gain or a fat government retirement fund. If I need to be that voice, then so be it. And to the nervous governments of the world watching this, don't be." Horatio beamed and stared down the barrel of the camera. "Unless you have something to hide."

The room was oddly silent, compared to the previous outbursts from the press. They must have been thinking the same as Eva. *Did one of the world's richest men just threaten every government on Earth?*

The BBC then cut to the studio and the news anchor introduced an important-looking panel. Eva hit mute. She turned to the other three in the room and assessed them. Horatio fidgeted like a nervous schoolboy. Nancy stared blankly, blinking at the screen. Paul in particular seemed aghast.

Shaking his head, he pointed at the screen. "Governments need secrets. It's how they operate. If every government knew every-thing about other governments the world would collapse in on itself. Things fall apart, the centre cannot hold, mere anarchy is loosed upon the world."

Eva was slightly shocked. Paul had presented a lucid argument and thrown in a poignant Yeats quotation. Sometimes he did surprise her.

"It's not like that," Horatio started.

"It ruddy well is." Paul shook his hand at the screen. It was the first time Eva had ever seen him angry.

"That's not how it's going to be. Of course governments need their secrets, of course. It's only when they're blatantly lying or self-absorbed where it hurts the people that it's meant to–"

"But who makes that choice?" Paul asked. "Who says you have the right to pick and choose which governments stand and which fall? You complain you're sick of seeing power abused but it seems you've been searching in the wrong direction. There's a mirror over there, I suggest you use it."

"Forgive me Paul, I believe you've misunderstood what I'm trying to achieve. It's about keeping individual politicians to their word. I'm not–"

"You just threatened every government on the planet by telling them that their secrets aren't safe. I think it's pretty ruddy clear, Mate." Paul's face took on a magenta hue. "How the hell have you done this? Have you been using your own systems? Because let me tell you, you'll be liable for breach of so many ruddy laws you'll die of old age by the time they've read the list of charges."

"Not at all. I know a small army of hackers dedicated to a noble cause. Nothing traceable back to me or my company. We're clean."

Paul turned to Eva and Nancy. He pointed at Harry and shrieked, "He admitted to treason and blackmail of the highest order and he thinks he's ruddy clean!"

"It's all about the greater good, Paul. Fine, okay, take for example a minister with a penchant for sodomising prostitutes. Legal, of course, it was all consensual apparently but, you know, not completely in keeping with his publicly-promoted traditional Christian beliefs. So, someone, I won't say who," he shrugged letting everyone in the room know he was speaking of himself, "just reminds him of this fact, makes a minor request for approval of a solar farm that was a pre-election promise anyway, and there you are. A better life for future generations and we're all not subjected to weeks of newspaper reports of a senior cabinet minister's proclivity for buggery while listening to S Club 7. Win bloody win."

"It's still illegal. It's still…"

"Paul, I'm just holding these guys to the standards to which they said they'd abide. I'm–"

"Right you two," Nancy said sternly. "You're not going to solve this here and now. There are more important things that need to be addressed than national security and worldwide governmental stability."

Three sets of eyes stared at her. Nancy jerked her head in Eva's direction.

"What?" Eva asked. "Me?"

Nancy nodded. "I think the two of you have some talking to do." Paul began to protest, but she held up her hand. "Without us." Nancy threaded her arm through her husband's and led him away. Over her shoulder, she hollered, "Lovely to meet you, it's been, uh, interesting."

"Likewise," Horatio shouted after them.

As Eva watched Nancy and Paul disappear up the stairs she let out a, "Huh," and scratched the back of her neck. "The remote."

Horatio shook his head. "Excuse me?"

"The remote that Paul couldn't find." She poked him in the arm. "You hid it, didn't you?"

He bowed his head. "I wanted to see you and your friends without the distraction of who I am, what was unfolding. For a little while, at least. Is that such a bad thing?"

The blatant deception was almost mitigated by the sentiment and his big puppy dog eyes. Almost.

The two of them were alone for a while. The porch seemed a million years ago.

Horatio turned to Eva. "I tried to tell you, but you kept kissing me."

Eva could still taste him on her lips. Was she seriously contemplating dating the person who could be the baddest bad boy on the planet?

Was that even a question? She knew the answer. Eva was screwed.

"I need a walk." She picked up her coat and headed for the door. "Come on."

∾

The night was crisp. Their footsteps echoed along the empty streets of Kensington. They walked separately, hugging themselves against the cold. Eva slowed as they approached a church and cut Horatio off as she entered the church's yard. They found a stone bench. He sat beside her silently. The vapour from their breath floating into the stillness of the night.

Eva glanced up at the imposing church. "Symbolic really."

"Why?"

"St Jude."

"Huh?"

"Jude the Apostle, the patron saint of lost causes and desperate cases."

"Catholic?"

"Well read."

They convened in silence for a few minutes. Horatio seemed willing for her to take the lead.

Finally Eva was ready to talk. "Well, one thing's for sure, your stock's bollocksed."

He chuckled. "Our predictions are an initial forty percent hit, then another twenty in the next week and a half. Within two months they will be back to acceptable levels."

"You seem to be in control of everything."

"Not everything." He slid towards her. "Some things are a force of nature and can never be controlled, never be contained or dominated..."

"Unless it's recreationally..." She was trying to lighten the mood. His face didn't change. He kept moving towards her.

"...and it would be foolish to think otherwise." Eva could feel his warm breath on her skin. "But to be in the presence of such beauty, such passion, even for a moment, I would give up every ounce of control I have."

Horatio slid his hand around her neck, weaving his fingers into her hair. The kiss wasn't like the tentative innocence from the porch. This was a man filled with hunger and intent. If Eva were weaker willed, her knees would have buckled. *Where had this guy been thirty minutes ago?*

Eva pushed him away. "We have to talk about this. About you. About, jeez, I don't know, the world!"

"We can." He said caressing her cheek.

"Good. Then pick me up tomorrow."

He moved back. "What?"

"If you want to talk, then that's what we'll do."

"Eva, I was hoping you and I could…"

"Nope. No rumpy and definitely no pumpy, Mister, until we get this shit sorted."

"I have a bit on at the moment…"

"Rubbish. You just quit, and it'll be ages before you're entitled to unemployment benefits."

He tried and failed to hide the smile.

Eva placed her hands on her hips. "The traders will be going nuts tomorrow and their need for artificial stimulants will go through the roof. If I'm shut for a day that's going to smash *my* business." She thought of her boarded-up windows that would make little difference to her caffeine-addicted clientele. "But I'm willing to do it for the sake of seeing if this," her finger flicked between them, "has any future. Are you?"

To her surprise, he agreed. Reassured with the sacrifice, they made plans. He walked her back to Nancy and Paul's. On the threshold he turned and gave her one last kiss. And what a kiss. Eva was no shrinking violet and considered herself experienced in the ways of men. So it was not lightly that she considered that kiss, the one in the doorway of her friend's house on a night of confusion, to be the best kiss of her life. No matter what happened, she would always treasure that instant as the moment when the entire world disappeared and she had been embraced by pure bliss.

~

Eva tilted her head as she revelled in the memory.

The impatient tapping of a pen on the metal table brought her back to reality.

"See, not what you expecting was it?" she asked smirking.

Decker brushed non-existent lint off his crisp white sleeve. "I'm intrigued. Please tell me what I expected? I'm dying to know."

"A stupid girl who met a rich a man, was swept off her feet by expensive trinkets and spent her days on the beach waiting for him to summon her with a click of his fingers. That's what you expected me to be, wasn't it? Some airhead who'd jump into bed as soon as she realised how powerful he was and didn't understand the political ramifications of the man she was with. I'm guessing that's what you were thinking. Am I wrong?"

"You're not entirely out of the ballpark."

"You know that sentence makes no sense, right?"

"A lot like your story, it would seem."

"Now it's my turn to be intrigued."

"You meet a man, he seems nice, a little heroic. How wonderful for you. Then you invite him to dinner and he reveals himself to be one of the world's most powerful men, a man who publically threatens every government on the planet. Then you organise a picnic? Really? Come on. You seem reasonably intelligent Ms Destruction, surely you were not naïve enough to think that was going to end well?"

"Excuse me, Sir," Cole piped in. "I think we're veering significantly off topic. We still don't know why she was on the island or what caused the explosions, or..."

"Yes, yes, yes, Cole. I know. As Ms Destruction keeps telling us, she's supplying context."

"Yes, but Sir," he said, glancing at his watch, "we have orders to–"

"I'm well aware of our orders, thank you Lieutenant Commander. But they also wanted as much detail as possible, I think we're getting that too."

They? Eva doubted it would be Navy Operations. They would be more concerned with moving little ships around a big map with sticks, or whatever they did. CIA? But why would the CIA trust a Navy Commander to lead an interrogation? Surely they would wait for an operative to come on board who conduct the interview themselves? It didn't add up.

Shaking her head, she dismissed the thought. She was being paranoid. Even more than usual. No, she had to keep going with her plan. Keep them occupied, ensure they stayed in the room and talking until she could find a way to escape and get back to the island. To him.

She scrunched her toes and caressed the bobby pin clasped underneath.

"You asked how I thought it was going to end?" she asked, interrupting the scowling match between Cole and Decker. "To be honest, I wasn't thinking that far ahead. As far as I was concerned at that stage, nothing had started. And no, the date wasn't a picnic. It was a little more exciting than that."

Cole and Decker stared at her, waiting for her to continue. She had their rapt attention again.

"Well for one thing, a girl might expect flowers on a first date, perhaps chocolates if he's particularly clueless. Most girls don't expect spies, kidnapping and a gunfight."

CHAPTER ELEVEN

This seriously can't be the address, Eva thought to herself.

Checking her phone again, she confirmed that yes, this was the venue of her date with Harry, *damn it*, Horatio. She still hadn't become accustomed to his other name yet. Riverside Building, Westminster Bridge Road. It didn't make a lot of sense to Eva. She assumed that Horatio would shy away from crowds, not run head first into one.

As she watched the capsules of the London Eye slowly rotate in the grey London sky, she assumed Horatio had a reason. He seemed to be someone who always had reasons.

Eva shivered against the cold. She'd only worn a woollen jumper and an icy wind had picked up. She had several perfectly serviceable coats, but they didn't enhance her curves like the jumper did. There she went again. Discarding her usual set of principles and good sense for Horatio Lancing.

The previous evening they had agreed a car would pick Eva up and they'd go on their first official date. This morning she'd received a text message from Horatio saying there had been a change of plans. Standing at the exact pillar in the message, she was beginning to regret the whole thing. She should be promising herself that she'd swear off bad boys rather than agreeing to date a man who gave the up yours to every nation on Earth. She honestly couldn't see a future for them.

Then again, by Merlin's pants, that man could kiss.

A cough distracted Eva from her pleasant thoughts. An impeccably dressed man with a severe haircut was politely attempting to get her attention. He wore a tight-fitting suit that did little to conceal a post-Hulk-out body beneath. He was huge. Like a gorilla wearing a Saville Row suit. A gorilla who worked out. A lot. He beamed a used car salesman smile and motioned her towards the crowds waiting to board The Eye.

The man mountain walked with her silently, half shoving her past the roped off hordes of tourists to a red carpeted area before an open capsule. There were minor grumblings from parts of the crowd when Eva was ushered forward. They were quickly silenced by an icy glare from her gorilla-in-a-suit friend. He pointed at the capsule, pivoted and promptly left.

Eva called after him. "Thanks. Been a pleasure. Catch you at book club."

About to step in and ask why Horatio had sent hired muscle to fetch her and not himself, Eva stopped dead. She couldn't ask Horatio. Because he wasn't the one sitting cross-legged in the capsule. It was someone else entirely.

The man greeted her casually as if they were meeting at a garden party. The man before her was clearly tall despite being seated. Neatly trimmed blond hair, muscular wide shoulders in an expensive exceptionally well-fitted suit and vest. His smile shone brighter than the dull day outside. His deep blue eyes sparkled with mischief. He was clearly pleased he'd caught her off-guard.

"Champagne?" he asked spinning a bottle in the ice bucket beside him on the bench.

"It's nine in the morning."

"Terribly sorry. Is it too early for champagne?"

British. On the posh side.

Eva folded her arms. "It's more a vodka time of day."

"Isn't it always?"

"Where's Horatio?"

"Who can say with certainty?"

"He didn't send you?"

"He did not."

"Then how did I get here?"

"I'll reveal everything if you come inside."

"My mum taught me to never fall for a line like that."

"She sounds like a wonderfully wise woman. No, I was wondering if you could join me to discuss Mr Lancing."

"And why would I do that?"

"My boyish good looks?"

"Nope. Try again."

"National Security."

"Zero for two. On three I walk."

He shifted in his seat. His demeanour told her this wasn't going as well as he'd anticipated. There was something in his manner that told Eva that didn't happen often. *Tough.*

"Alright, Ms Destruction. I shall be blunt. I work for His Majesty's Secret Intelligence Service and I've been asked to speak to you on an issue of the utmost importance."

"You're a...see, I thought one of the fundamentals of the spy game was to not to let people know you're actually, you know, a spy. When people ask you, you should say something like, 'I'm in importing and exporting', or 'I work for the embassy', or 'Hey, look over there – flash bomb!' I'm pretty sure you're not meant to come out and say you're a spy unless it's absolutely necessary."

"It's absolutely necessary."

"I see."

"Officially, I'm not here but, Ms Destruction, I wouldn't be speaking to you if this were not of the most critical importance. I'm asking for a few minutes of your time, after that you may do whatever you like, no ties. Talk, that's all. All I ask is fifteen minutes to hear me out."

"It takes half an hour for this thing to go around."

"For the last fifteen minutes you can sit beside me and we'll see what pops up."

"Jesus, I haven't heard a line like that since I was sixteen. Over-confident much?"

He outstretched his hand, his face serious. "Ms Destruction, please, I wouldn't ask if it was not of the–"

"Utmost importance, yes I got that the first time."

It was the eyes that did it. He wasn't lying. His initial cavalier attitude didn't hide the fact that he was telling the truth. Or at least, he believed what he was saying.

Eva was good at reading people. Even this Secret Service agent. He had his own secrets. The accent was Cambridge...only not. There was something distinctly working class in some of his inflection. Yorkshire probably. She scrutinised his hands. Smoother than her thighs. Probably one generation away from working class. He worked hard to conceal it, but it was there, bubbling away below the surface. The man was polished, but only to a point.

The self-confessed spy looked behind her at the crowd. "People are becoming agitated Ms Destruction. I must insist you come inside so we can continue our delightful discourse."

"Well, you insisting is a guaranteed way for me to tell you to go to hell."

"Can I politely request, then? Like I said, no obligation, just hear what I have to say and we can part with a hearty handshake and be done with it. I would ask if it weren't imperative."

Eva stared at her feet. They were firmly planted on the ground. The capsule a simple step away but in another world. She took a gulp of air and not entirely knowing why, took the step.

The door slid quietly shut behind her and she instantly regretted her decision. She was angry at herself for behaving reck-lessly again. Like a fire juggler with dynamite-filled pants, she was expecting bad things.

In contrast, his grin was incandescent. He motioned around the capsule. "Fit for a princess."

Eva's hackles weren't just up, they'd been stuffed in a rocket ship and launched into orbit. Her jaw clenched. It took all her concentration to prize them apart. "Excuse the fuck me?"

He went pale. The Secret Service agent realised he'd messed up. Far worse than before. Although, if he really knew what was going on he would have asked them to open the doors.

"Princess? *Princess?*" Eva raised her voice. "Is that what you think women want? To be put up on a pedestal and treated like an eight-year-old who's seen far too many Disney movies? Jesus, how about being treated as an equal?"

The spy's eyes darted from the door to her and back again. There was a *clunk* and the capsule slowly rose. No escape. "I didn't mean that you–"

"Sure, it was a slip of the tongue, a turn of phrase or some such bullshit, right? Well, I'm sorry that doesn't cut it. Everything we say has weight. Everything. Casual sexism is still sexism any way you slice it. I'm going to tell you I won't put up with that shit. Not now, not ever. Do you understand?"

The man who may have faced off against armed terrorists for all Eva knew, simply stared at her. His ashen face told her people didn't talk to him like that. Well, screw them. Eva wasn't other people.

Arms folded, she stood across from the spy and raised a challenging eyebrow. She wasn't sitting until she received an answer. The quality of the answer would dictate which way the conversation, or lack thereof, would go for the next half hour. She could let him off the hook with a laugh or change the subject. Only letting anyone off the hook wasn't exactly in Eva's repertoire.

"What I mean, what I meant to say was, that, look, what I mean, what I meant to say, ah…"

"I think the record's stuck."

"Nobody listens to records any more."

"Tell me exactly how that's helping you right now?"

"Point taken." He centred himself and the transformation was astonishing. "Firstly, let me apologise for my insensitive offhand remark. It was crude, offensive and thoughtless."

So far, so good, Eva thought to herself. Perhaps he was redeemable.

"I see what's going on, and it's fine." He touched her crossed forearms. "Your reaction is understandable. You obviously noticed it the moment we locked eyes, there's a chemistry here, and it's confusing. There's no need to lash out disproportionately, we're both consenting adults, we can converse respectfully despite the simmering attraction."

Eva was too shocked to respond. He grinned and touched her knee. Jesus, he was using the physical escalation technique. Maintaining the occasional non-sexual contact so when he went in for the kiss it would seem natural.

Ladies, we have a player. Eva shook her head in disbelief. *He honestly thinks he's in with a chance.* She only had herself to blame. She did have a pulse after all. Hussy! Whether he was doing the mild seduction technique to sway her to his agenda or go in for the snog, Eva was having none of it.

There was no immediate response. She tossed up between stony silence or hurling him out the window to watch him scream to his eventual and painful death. In the end she chose neither. She wanted to know why the Secret Service agent wished to speak to her about Harry. Unfortunately in this instance curiosity trumped sexual harassment revenge.

Eva flopped onto the seat opposite, as far away from him as possible. "This thing better have a fucking bar."

"Ms Destruction, it's the London Eye, not a pub with unlimited choice."

"I'm failing to see your point." Eva grabbed the bottle and took a swig. The spy did little to hide his surprise. She tossed the half-empty bottle in the ice bucket. "Horatio messaged me to change the time to an hour earlier and changed the venue, why?"

"Well, he didn't actually, that was me."

"But it was Horatio's number."

"Well, no, it was made to appear as if it were from Mr Lancing, but I can assure you it was indeed from me. We could have made it look as though it came from the King if we wanted."

"Except I don't have the King as a contact."

"Indeed. Horatio Lancing will still be waiting for you at the designated time and place later this morning. You can hang your hat on us not getting you in hot water."

"I see you know which side of the fence your mixed metaphor is buttered on." Eva glanced out at the slowly descending London skyline. "Why SIS?"

"Excuse me?"

"You said SIS, so MI6. You're on British soil, shouldn't this be an MI5 thing?"

"Let's just say it was a personal request to have me intervene. I'm here as a favour to an old friend. A close friend." He paused on the last sentence. "It's not necessarily signed off by the higher ups."

Right, thought Eva. That probably explained the almost aloofness of the spy. He was here on business, just not *official* business. So he probably thought that meant he could pull out all the misogynistic stops. *Lucky me.*

"Who made that request, this old friend of yours?" Eva planted her hands on her hips. "And don't say it's classified."

"It's a secret."

"Who else knows this secret?"

"It's classified."

"You're insufferable."

"You mispronounced adorable." The spy tapped his foot. While the veneer of calm remained the same, it was clear he was losing patience. *Bad luck.*

"What's all this about, Spy Boy?" She didn't ask his name. She assumed whatever he said would surely be a lie. As for whatever else he had to say, she'd judge that as it came.

"As you know, Mr Lancing has accumulated and continues to accumulate vast amounts of information illegally from several governments and this has quite rightly generated an excessive amount of consternation. To date, as far as we know, he has not made this information public, but he appears to have coerced, some would say blackmailed, several key members of several governments to cave to his will."

"Like ensuring water's kept out of private hands in Africa and agreeing to set up free schools for women in the developing world? What a bastard."

"Regardless of the spin his marketing team have managed to put on his current outward intent, there is a very real possibility that he may put this information to far more nefarious uses. We do not know what his intentions are, and that makes an awful lot of people tetchy. All we ask is that if you hear anything that is, shall we say, on the less altruistic side of the ledger, you contact me. I will be available to you whenever you need."

"So, basically, you want me to spy. For you."

"Spy? Of course not. Nothing of the sort. Merely advise us of a few things about Mr Lancing, his movements, any information that would concern His Majesty's government here and there."

"That sounds kind of like spying there, Dude."

Eva remembered Horatio asking Paul about spies the night before. Was it already on his mind? If he was worried, should she be too?

She let out a frustrated sigh. The spy tilted his head. "You want me to get you off, Ms Destruction?"

"Wow, you're just one big walking innuendo, aren't you?"

His grin was luminous. Eva shook her head. Under different circumstances she might find his remarks playful rather than annoying. But these weren't different circumstances. The spy possessed the charisma of Cary Grant but the subtlety of a kick to the balls.

As the capsule slowly crawled above the rooftops, the two of them fell mute. Eva had no intention of spying on Horatio or anyone else for that matter. It had been a mistake to agree to talk to this man. It was as though she was genetically programmed to make poor decisions. She had a lifetime of them and the trend didn't seem to be reversing.

Breaking the silence, he said, "Can I ask a question? I'm not trying to be discourteous, but is calling you a princess really so bad?"

"It automatically makes a woman subservient to a man." Eva paused and glared at the spy. "And that's a bad thing."

"Oh, right."

He really did seem like a cretin. She sighed. "You see, calling a woman a princess is another way to put a woman in her place. Like automatically calling a strong woman a bitch. Well, we don't need to be put anywhere, thank you very much. For a certain type of man," she nodded in his general direction, "there's nothing more intimidating than a woman who doesn't require male validation."

He nodded in understanding like a two-year-old would after someone had explained thermodynamics. In an obvious attempt to change the subject, he asked, "Eva Destruction," as if rolling it about his tongue, "I assume there's a story behind your moniker?"

"Oh yes."

"And?"

"I'm sure a man of your profession knows everyone must have some secrets."

The girl-slayer grin returned. He nodded in acquiescence.

The capsule ground to a halt. Below them passengers exited. Eventually the next set of tourists boarded. The capsule shunted and continued its meandering slouch skyward.

"You didn't give me an answer about Mr Lancing."

Each time the capsule crept forward meant it was that much closer to Eva's release from captivity.

"I noticed that, too. What's your rush?"

"Excuse me. Urgency dictates I dispense with any Victorian hypocrisy."

"You form a sentence like that but can't grasp the fundamentals of a metaphor?"

"And what do you like to take a grip of, Ms Destruction?"

"A great many things. Like when someone jumps ahead in the conversation without putting in the hard work first."

The Secret Service agent eyed her up and down slowly. To use a metaphor, he viewed her like he was a man who had wandered out of the desert and she was a glass of icy water. Also, she was thirsty.

"Believe me," he said with a slanted grin. "I'm willing to put in many hours of hard, hard work for you."

"There you go again. Settle down, Tiger. How did you know about Horatio and me so quickly? I didn't even know until last night."

"I am almost certain I mentioned the spy thing, didn't I?"

"You've been spying on me?"

"Sadly no. Mr Lancing has been on our radar for some time. Although it wasn't until a few days ago we had confirmation of exactly who and where he was."

"The man can keep a secret."

"Indeed."

"What's the big threat? I mean, he's a successful businessman, he does a ridiculous amount of charity work, his companies pay taxes in the countries they operate in. Smeg, all of London has a man-crush on him right now, he stopped a riot and made everyone fall in love with their city again. He's a hero any way you slice it. As far as this secrets business is concerned, he's only forcing shady politicians to do good things. What's the problem?"

There was a subtle shift in his eyes. The grin remained, but there was a hardening in him. "The problem, Ms Destruction, is that when one man deliberately sets out to steal governmental secrets, it's doubtful he's doing it for a lark. He's deliberately accumulating the most sensitive of governmental files, for what end, we're not sure, but let me assure you, it's incredibly unlikely to be about paying the right amount of tax or feeding the needy. The man has an agenda, it's apparent in all that he does."

Eva tried not to show the surprise. It echoed her own thoughts right before she had boarded.

"But he does all the charity work and he saved a city when the authorities didn't. Some might think you're a touch cynical."

"You've summed me up perfectly. Some would suggest in my line of work that would be an asset."

She could see his point. It didn't mean she liked it. Or him, for that matter. Cynical. Misogynistic. Aggressive. He was virtually the anti-Harry.

They reached the top of the structure and lapsed into silence again. The spy placed his hand on hers. She flinched and balled her fists. He wisely retracted his hand. He straightened his back and gave a nod.

"Ms Destruction, promise me one thing. If you decide not to trust me and select not to supply any information, I will understand. You seem like a woman of great integrity…"

It was obviously a line and they both knew it.

"…but promise me one thing – you'll be careful. Whether you choose to believe it or not, Lancing is a dangerous man. Cogs are spinning in the background, he has grand plans that span the globe. He's lighting the fuse to something gargantuan and you don't want to be anywhere near it when it goes off. This is me as a human being, not a member of His Majesty's Secret Service." He leaned in. "Eva, look out for yourself. He's not the man you think he is."

As much as she was inclined to, she couldn't dismiss the statement out of hand. It was the earnestness of the delivery that made her actually listen to the words, even though she'd ultimately ignore them. One day the world would figure out that telling Eva not to do something never resulted in anything good.

She crossed her arms firmly against her chest as an act of defiance, and so he couldn't cop another look. At least he had the good sense not to try to talk her around again. They rode the remainder of the ride quietly. When it came to an end he gave her a white card with a single phone number, no name.

Eva turned it over a few times. "Does this turn into a jet ski?"

"No."

"A hovercraft?"

"Not exactly."

"A hang glider?"

"I have a feeling you've watched far too many films. No, it is simply a phone number, you call it, I answer."

"It's a bit low tech."

"What can I say? I'm an old-fashioned kind of fellow."

"So I've discovered."

He extended his hand and out of reflex Eva shook it. He clicked his heels, gave a slight bow and departed at the exact instant the doors opened. Still in a daze, it took her a moment before she left. A large group of tourists were eagerly waiting for her to get out of the way and rushed past her.

By the time the crowd cleared, the spy was nowhere to be seen.

CHAPTER TWELVE

"You look flushed," Horatio said as he opened the limo door.

Eva waved the statement away and kissed him on the cheek. She tried to show no outward signs, but the spy had rattled her. Everything had happened so quickly, the riot, finding out about Horatio, then his coming out to the world even before she'd really gotten to know him. It had all happened so fast. Her feet not only hadn't touched the ground, she wasn't even sure where the ground was any more.

Eva didn't even hear the limo. One moment she'd had her head down reading her book, and the next a car door had opened in front of her. The Lancing Corporation were big on their environmental credentials which apparently extended to their now-former CEO turning up in a hybrid limo. At least it wasn't a stretch, but it was still on the large side.

"Good morning, Horatio." At least she got the name right.

He gave her one of his beaming grins. "I trust you slept well?"

"After I took care of things, yeah."

"Things?" He gave a slight shake of his head.

"Yeah...things," Eva replied wiggling her head from side to side and opening her eyes wide.

He still didn't get it.

"Uh, because we were getting frisky and there was no payoff and a girl's gotta sleep…"

Horatio shook his head again, but abruptly stopped. He got it. The expression on his face was less one of shock, more embarrassment. *Bless.*

Then she had a thought. *Oh god, he's not a virgin is he?* If he had spent all his time in his mysterious bunker building an empire maybe he never found time for the opposite sex. Eva didn't have the time or patience to train someone up from scratch. She tried to bury the thought, but it remained there, like a splinter in the back of her brain.

To change the subject, Eva asked, "Where are we off to?" a little too eagerly.

"Ah, now that's a secret."

Great, she thought. *More secrets.*

Noticing her downcast expression, Horatio added, "You remembered to bring your passport?" Eva nodded. "We'll pick up a couple of things at the airport. Let's just say you'll need a new bathing suit, thermal gear, hiking boots and a taste for adventure. I hope you like things fermented."

"So, Iceland then?" Eva asked.

Horatio's face fell. "How the hell…? Have you been there before?"

"No. I just read a lot." She sheepishly held up her book. "Hiking, could be anywhere, I guess, well except the Netherlands. The swimsuit and the hiking stuff don't usually go together, so that led me to thermal outdoor pools and hot tubs. Then the fermented food closed the deal. They're mad for it, apparently."

The disappointment was palpable. He'd obviously spent time planning the surprise and she had come in and popped his metaphorical balloon. Compelled to say something, she said, "At least it wasn't Paris. Whisking a girl off to la Ville Lumière is a cliché in the extreme." Rolling her eyes to emphasise the point, she patted his arm. Eva smiled and wrinkled her nose. It did the trick and his shoulders straightened. His demeanour brightened and he cordially motioned with his hand to the limo.

Did she just placate his ego? *What the hell was she turning into?* This wasn't what she was about. It wasn't in her nature to care if the man she was with felt at ease. That was his issue. She was herself, damn anyone who had a problem with that. She'd learned early on to be true to herself and moulding herself to fit a relationship was fraught with danger. Her partner, or more likely, Eva herself, wound up hating who she was trying to be. It had been many years since she'd even tried to be anyone but herself. She sure as hell wasn't going down that track again.

Attempting to dismiss the thought, she tried to focus on what the day held. It wasn't every day someone picked her up to fly her to another country in an effort to woo her. It was foreign in all sorts of ways.

The spy had rattled her, but she was determined to not let it affect her. She'd make up her own damned mind about Horatio. If she discovered things she didn't like it could all change, but so far she'd liked what she'd seen. More than liked.

Eva was still going through the motions of weighing up Horatio's pros and cons, but already knew where her heart was leading. She was developing feelings for a man unlike any she'd known before and she couldn't get enough of him.

Yes, he was ruffling feathers around the world but he seemed to be doing it for the betterment of the world, not himself. The morning newspaper had summed it up nicely. 'Lancing is like Snowden with an agenda and Assange with charisma'. She liked that. A lot.

Eva snuggled into the luxurious surroundings. If the limo wasn't new, it was certainly newly appointed. It even had that new car smell. There were plenty of computer screens and other technology fastened to the interior, but they were thankfully all turned off.

The limo set off silent and smooth, heading out of Westminster. It floated weightlessly above the road.

She cocked an eyebrow and asked, "Is this meant to impress me?"

"Would a tandem bike have been better?"

"Actually, that would have been kinda funny."

"I briefly contemplated it, but peddling to Iceland would have been a bitch. You'd have to have done most of the hard work."

"So, Mr Bigshot, travel by limo much?"

"Quite a bit, it's my mobile office when I need."

"Even though you quit?"

"One of the things I negotiated. I also kept a stapler."

She stared at the traffic. "Why did you?"

"It was a really nice one, hardly ever jammed."

Eva regarded him flatly. "No, why did you quit?"

"To be honest, the business was practically running itself and I got into the philanthropy side of things and found there were far too many roadblocks, or my funds were being pilfered by corrupt governments. I used my influence to see that didn't happen. I enjoyed it, far more than I thought, then I decided to go full time, as it were."

"Caring for the starving is a noble pursuit, but it's hardly the same as stealing state secrets and threatening governments."

"They are one and the same, Eva. They shouldn't be, but they are. When governments channel aid money to build a bigger palace or buy another yacht, then that's the same as forcing their people into a camp and watching them starve. When officials take a bribe to look the other way while a multi-national corporation pillages their resources and exploits their citizens, leaving the poor with nothing, it's the same. People should expect more from their leaders, but most of them stopped leading long ago. It's all about re-elections and taking cash from big business."

"*You're* big business."

"Was, but yes, you have a point. There were plenty of times I could have set up a factory or opened a new market if I simply supported a particular party or politician. I chose not to but, sadly, I'm the minority. Politicians are about lining their own pockets and ignoring their own people. If the people need someone else to look out for them, then fine, I'll take the job. I'm the guy with the bottomless chequebook, so if it's not me, who will?"

"Nobody uses chequebooks any more." Eva issued a smirk, quickly followed by a frown. "So, what's the end goal here? You have all these secrets that you intend to, ah, let's call a spade a bloody shovel, blackmail governments with, is that it?"

"Not really, no. It's a small component. Basically all I want governments to do is what they said they'd do. Care for the people. If that means bandying about some truths, and they are truths, so a particular government concerns itself with the poor and the environment, so be it. It's all for the greater good. My threats were only ever meant to be private, but when they hadn't garnered a reply I was forced to go public and all hell broke loose. That's when the governments of the world began baying for my blood."

"Can you blame them? You can't go around blackmailing the world, Horatio. You earned a squillion brownie points as the face of the Battle of Trafalgar, but it won't be enough. To some you're still going to be a hero, others a pariah and to others, especially governments, you'll be public enemy number one. You have to see that, surely?"

He shrugged nonchalantly. "Western governments have changed in the last few decades. Compromise is a now a four-letter word. It's seen as weakness. Everyone's too busy shouting to hear anyone else. The problem isn't that politicians aren't talking, it's that none of them are listening. They're polarised, refuse to negotiate. They're hell-bent on ideological stubbornness while people starve and die. They don't care about who elected them, after all, they're not the ones who funded their elections, that's big business. So where do you think their loyalties lie? I don't want power, Eva, I only want politicians to listen to their people again."

Regardless of Harry stepping down as the head of Lancing Corp, Eva assumed he would still hold influence over the media arms. Notwithstanding the nice stapler, he would still have connections to his former organisation. If he wanted an article or a favourable opinion piece, there was no doubt he would hold enough sway to have it at the click of his fingers. Harry was not a man to leave such things to chance.

It sounded too good to be true. The spy had been so adamant that Horatio wasn't what he seemed. Even if it was all factual, who was to say down the track Horatio's good deeds couldn't be used for more disreputable purposes? Or what if he changed his mind and decided that supporting only the good was boring him and self-interest was more fun?

Eva drummed her fingernails on her jeans. "So Mr Bottomless Chequebook, what's your limo driver's name?"

"Come again?"

"Your driver. If you travel so much, do you actually talk to the help?"

Horatio shrugged. "Let's find out."

He pressed a button on his armrest. A low whir emanated from the front of the vehicle and the partition lowered revealing the back of a man's head. Closely cropped grey hair sat neatly under a driver's cap.

"How goes it, Mark?"

"Fine, thank you, Horatio. Good day for flying by the looks of it. The plane's prepped and ready, so we're on schedule for departure."

There was no hiding the smug expression on Horatio's face. "Mark here has a very bright son." He raised his voice. "Tom, isn't it, Mark?"

"Yes Sir, Tom."

"Well Tom is exceptionally gifted, top five percent, but his family were struggling to pay his tuition. That's why Mark is my chauffeur, amongst other things. Before, he was working three separate jobs."

Horatio leaned over and whispered to Eva, "He doesn't know that I've organised for his next pay to have a little bonus that means his son doesn't have to worry about his tuition or anything about his education ever again."

She folded her arms. "Stop making it hard for me to hate you."

~

The Gulfstream touched down like a cotton ball landing on a pillow. Eva had to look out the window to confirm they were actually on the ground. The flight had been wonderful. There were no flight attendants and she hadn't seen or heard from the pilot. They were self-contained in their own bubble. Horatio had prepared her a gourmet breakfast, complimented with a bottle of Châteauneuf-du-Pape. She couldn't fault his taste. She couldn't fault much about the man at all.

He'd had her in hysterics with his awful impression of Jimmy Stewart impersonating Arnold Schwarzenegger which somehow made everyone sound Indian. He was charming, attentive and wanted her opinion on everything. He didn't always necessarily agree, but he was eager to hear what she had to say. That in itself was a welcome change from her usual dating profile.

The pilot's door opened and a man wearing aviator glasses and peaked cap emerged.

"Great flight. Thanks Mark," Horatio said.

Apparently being a limo driver qualified you as a jet pilot as well.

"My pleasure, Horatio. The limo's ready, but I suggest putting on coats. It's five below."

"Positively balmy. Cheers."

They all put on bright orange thermal coats from the plane's coat cupboard. Mark pressed a button and the cabin door slid outward. An icy snow flurry invaded the cosy warmth of the cabin. Stairs had already been wheeled up and a black limo awaited them at the bottom. It was almost identical to the one in London, although it was slightly raised with bulkier tyres.

The interior of the limo was familiar. Eva patted the plush leather and asked, "Do you get a discount for buying these things in bulk?"

Horatio ignored the jibe and removed his coat. She kept hers on to warm up. Mark slid behind the wheel and started the engine.

Horatio clicked his seatbelt in place. His eyes darted between Eva's and the untouched buckle.

She shrugged. "Dude, if we hit anything it will take me a good half hour to hit the front of this thing. Plus I'm pretty sure Iceland has slightly less traffic than Central London. I think I'll be okay."

Horatio wisely decided not to say anything. The car took off and at the first turn Eva slipped across the length of the seat and straight into Horatio. She pushed herself away. In order to avoid an *I told you so* lecture, she peeked out the window and asked, "Where are we headed?"

"Landmannalaugar."

"I dare you to say that drunk."

The road was thankfully clear of snow, but rough in places. They drove on and the scenery changed dramatically. From sparsely-located buildings the road morphed into an alien land-scape. The gravel plains were a shocking wasteland of vivid orange, speckled with snow. The approaching mountains were coated in white. All the way to the horizon no man-made structure could be seen. No building, house, power line or telephone tower. The scenery resembled a stark alien landscape. The further they drove, the more snow dominated the countryside. The deserted road only added to the unnatural feel.

It was ruggedly beautiful, unlike anything she'd ever seen. Definitely better than Paris. Eva was already falling in love with the country. And in deep like with other things…er…people…er… A particular person.

The silence was broken by Mark. "Excuse me, Horatio. You might want to give Van Buren a call."

"Trouble?"

"Not yet, but possibly. Two black Suburbans have been tailing us and they've blocked the road behind. That makes me nervous. So…"

Horatio pulled out his phone. "Calling him now." The phone was answered instantly. "Van, we've got two vehicles blocking the road behind. Is it possible to have the boys dispatched to…how far away? Well, that's hardly helpful." He smiled sweetly at Eva. "Is there any way to...? Marvellous. So we're on our own then?" Horatio ran his fingers through his hair. "No, no, there's nothing you can do about that now. Okay, I've got to go." Horatio hung up.

"Should I be worried?" Eva asked with mounting dread.

"Not at all, just adding some excitement to the day. You spoilt my surprise, so I thought I'd change things up a bit."

Eva was far from convinced. She hoped Mark was paid to be paranoid. If Horatio was at ease, maybe there was nothing to worry about. She relaxed slightly. That was until there was a crack and the chauffeur's head exploded in puff of red.

The limo lurched forward in a burst of speed and hurtled towards the side of the highway. The speed of the impact plunged the front of the limo into a ditch. With a terrifying crunch, the vehicle rolled. Eva's world spun. Everything became orange and deafening. The limo tumbled over again and again. She was thrown around like a ragdoll in a washing machine. She hit her head on something solid and everything went black.

CHAPTER THIRTEEN

The sunlight hit her like a slap to the face. As did the slap to the face.

Eva jolted awake. There was so much to take in at once. The luminescent sun shone through the limo's shattered sunroof. They had miraculously landed the right way up. Her ears rung. The smell of gasoline assaulted her nose. Horatio knelt above her, blood pouring from a cut on his temple. His face was stony and clear-eyed, like the day of the riot.

Eva rubbed her cheek. "Did you...did you fucking hit me?"

No man had ever laid a hand on her and walked away with anything less than stitches.

"Slap you, yes. There weren't any smelling salts handy. We have to run, now."

There was no apology. "We need to get Mark."

"He's dead, Eva."

Instinctively she knew that. She'd seen his head explode but she didn't want to hear it. Eva sat up and saw the wreckage that was the front of the vehicle. It was mostly a grotesquely twisted abomination. Part of the driver's side had been torn open as if a T-Rex had ripped it apart.

"Who...who shot him?"

"A question for another time. We need to go now."

Eva didn't know why, but she had to see Mark. Horatio cried out in protest and tried to hold her back. She broke free and scrambled forward. If there was some small chance that...

The thought dropped away as she crawled over the remains of the driver's partition.

Most of the engine was crumpled from the impact, there was no door on the driver's side. For an instant she couldn't see where Mark was. When she did, her stomach convulsed and she dry retched. There were shoulders attached to what had once been a human head. He was held in place by his seatbelt. Snow had already begun to land on his lifeless form.

Instead of falling apart, the horrific sight steeled her. She dropped into survival mode. Mark would be mourned later. First she had to live.

The jacket on the blood-splattered torso of Mark was open and Eva spied something metallic poking out. With Horatio protesting behind her, she realised what it was. As objectionable as it was, she retrieved it.

She squinted through where the windscreen once was. Outside, the snow was moving. White shapes slithered in a way snow shouldn't. Three figures emerged from the landscape caked in white camouflage. Crouching. Advancing. Their raised assault rifles were wrapped in white material. The only colour came from the orange lenses of their snow goggles. They'd been hiding in the snow waiting to ambush them. Their movements precise. All rifles were aimed at the limo.

Eva ducked and crawled back to Horatio. "We have to go!"

"I wish I'd said that."

There was nowhere to run in the barren wasteland, but they had to try. Staying in the limo was a guaranteed form of violent suicide.

She pushed past Horatio and opened the side door. Without waiting for him, she leapt out. The gunmen approached from the other side, spanning out in an attempt to encircle the vehicle. If the two of them didn't move, people would be mourning more than a good-natured driver and pilot by the end of the day.

Snow swirled around the featureless landscape. No tree or bush could be seen. Only the occasional low mound and snow-bank. There wasn't a single building to be seen. All of which would be fine, unless you were faced with encroaching heavily armed assassins planning to propel projectile ammunition into your person.

Eva took refuge behind the engine block as it offered the greatest protection. Horatio sidled up to her and landed with a thud. The vapour from his breath floated into the air. "If we can make it to that embankment, at least we'll have some space between us. They'll have to come at us uphill…"

He stopped talking as Eva tore off what was left of the limo's rear-view mirror. His plan wouldn't work. There was no way they could cover that amount of ground without re-enacting the final scene of Bonnie and Clyde. Eva positioned the rear-view mirror to peek above the roof so she could see how close their foes were.

Too close.

The three were positioned behind low embankments. Their exact hand gestures were directed at the remains of the limousine. While obviously highly trained, they were far too visible above the snowbanks. They probably assumed whoever had survived the crash posed no great threat. Good.

Horatio lay his head next to Eva's to share her view. "I'll distract them, you make a run for it."

She shook her head and slid off her bright orange coat. No use making it too easy for them. She didn't notice the cold.

Deep within Eva's core she knew that she had to protect this man she'd just met with everything she had. Including her life. Had she ever felt that before? Eva knew the answer was no. She also knew it was the worst possible time for such a revelation. "How about I distract them and we both make a run for it?"

"You go," he said. "The snow's not that thick on the ground. I'm a very good runner, I'll catch up. When I was ten I was a wiz at Little Athletics."

Against her better judgement, she grinned. There was something in his nature that always put her at ease. She shook her head. "You run over to that ditch and dive in. They'll need to come across the road to get to us and they'll be exposed. I'll be doing the distracting today."

He was about to protest when Eva pulled out the gun she'd taken from the corpse of the driver. It had been tucked into Mark's shoulder holster. Horatio's eyes went wide.

"I call him Captain Distracty."

Horatio stared at the pistol in her hands and said, "What would a barista know about–?"

Ignoring him, Eva cocked the Desert Eagle and spun to place the gun on the roof of the limo. "Go!"

If the gunmen were shocked that a raven-haired woman was aiming a gun in their direction, they didn't show it. They repointed their weapons. They weren't fast enough.

The first two shots went wide but her third found its target. The right-most assassin's arm splattered red across his white camouflage. He fell out of view. Eva re-aimed and fired at the second target. He'd been distracted, out of position and standing exposed.

Her shot caught him dead centre of the chest. There was no burst of blood like his compatriot. Bulletproof vest. He was thrown backwards and out of sight. The third had far longer to react than his partners. He managed to fire off a wild shot before Eva delivered bullets in his direction.

Her trigger finger spasmed and she fired off four successive shots that buried themselves into the snowbank with a puff. He dove for cover.

Not needing any further encouragement, she turned to run. Horatio was still crouched beside her. He appeared part stunned, part impressed.

She had no time to determine the appropriate ratio. Eva pulled him up by the collar. "Move!"

They ducked low using the bulk of the limo as cover and sprinted towards the ditch. Eva fired over her shoulder as they did.

They dived in and landed hard. The rocky gravel under the thin layer of snow was sharp volcanic rock that cut into their clothing. She assessed their position. The results weren't encouraging. In fact, they would probably result in their demise.

They were protected, sure, but there was nowhere to fall back to. It was safe to assume their opponents possessed more bullets than whatever remained in her handgun. All the gunmen had to do was keep her firing and they were done.

From the expression on his face, Horatio didn't seem overjoyed with their options either. With a shrug, he said, "And to think my other first date option was a knitting circle in Slough."

"Well, this is just about as exciting. You really didn't have to splash out on the terrorist package, though."

"I know, but the salesman was rather persuasive. It came with a free sun hat."

"Any idea who they are?"

"If I were to make a wild guess I'd say GRU. The Russians discovered a teensy data breach the other day. Apparently they're not overjoyed."

More shots were fired and they both ducked. Horatio shielded Eva's body. The warmth of his body was a welcome relief.

They were out of options. Eva had at best one or two bullets left. It wouldn't be enough. At least one of the gunmen, probably two, was unharmed. The one with the bulletproof vest would still be a threat. The first gunman had been winged, but she didn't know how badly. Either way, her shooting hadn't saved them. They were cornered, outnumbered and outgunned.

Eva wasn't waiting for death, but it was on its way. If she had any bullets left, she wasn't going alone. She'd make the bastards pay. Her grip on the pistol tightened.

Nothing happened.

Was Death caught in traffic? Did he do afternoon tea?

The faint sound of wheels on asphalt. Reinforcements? They had more than enough to finish them off. Were they rubbing it in?

There was more gunfire, but it was short-lived. The explosion saw to that. Frantic shouting. None of it seemed directed at them.

Repeated shouts of, "Clear!" overlapped one another. One voice could be heard over all others. He only repeated one word. "Horatio!"

Not making any movement or sound, Horatio remained motionless as he lay protectively over Eva. She rolled to see his face, and he ended up on top of her. His face mere centimetres from hers.

"I think...I think they're your people," she whispered. "You're not going to tell them you're okay?"

He gave a slight wriggle of his hips. "I'm kind of comfortable here, to be honest."

"Horatio..."

"Can you start calling me Harry again?"

"I...why?"

"It keeps me grounded...you keep me grounded. You're one of the few people who knows my real name. And, well, when we first met, and I told you my name, you weren't aware of who or what I was. It was genuine. You're the most authentic thing in my life in a very long time. To be honest, you calling me Harry makes me want to be better. Better for you."

He ran his hand gently along her cheek. Eva was sure she blushed like a lovesick teenager.

Further shouts of his name were unanswered and they became more frantic and dispersed.

"You'd better..." she said nodding to the voices.

"I know." He made no move. He stared into her eyes.

"Harry..."

He grinned. "Better." He kissed her, lingering on her lips before pushing himself up. "Van! Over here! We're unhurt."

Eva raised herself and made out six heavy-set men rounding up the white-clad assassins. Their guns pointed skyward, there was no urgency in their movements. The immediate threat neutralised.

"Mark's family...," Eva whispered hoarsely. She'd blacked out the memory of the kindly driver in order to survive, but the horrific vision returned tenfold. Eva wanted to throw up all over again.

"Will be looked after. It can never replace a husband and father, but they'll have no mortgage, no need for money ever again."

"Small compensation..."

"Insignificant. He was a good man. A good friend."

The snow swirled around them for a while. What could you say? They watched silently as each of the assassins was forced to kneel before large black van. Each had their feet and hands bound with plastic ties.

"Eva?"

"Hmm?"

"Where the hell did you learn to shoot like that?"

She shrugged. "Virtua Cop II." Harry stared blankly at her. "It's a video game. There was a pub I frequented far too often in my teens, had one in the back room. I was the diva. Smashed all usurpers. Unbeatable, I was. Also, I had a boyfriend who worked at a shooting range. But mostly the first one."

Before Harry answered a squat angry-appearing man with more grey hairs than was warranted for his age, came running towards the two of them. To Eva's mind, he had a face like a kicked-in door. Breathlessly, he said, "Horatio, you're unhurt?"

"We both are, thank you, Van." Harry patted her backside. "Thanks to Eva here."

Sneering, the man analysed her. Harry made his introductions. Van Buren was his security chief. Had been for many years apparently. As soon as his eyes fell on the pistol Van Buren's hand instinctively went to his holster.

He nodded at the gun and asked, "What did you think you were going to do with that?"

Eva gazed at the gun in her hand. It was far more comfortable and natural than she would have expected. She shrugged. "Give out free hugs."

The two of them stared at one another for the longest time. He must have concluded that she wasn't going to shoot anyone and relaxed enough to hand a silver thermal blanket to Harry. After less than subtle hints from his employer he reluctantly supplied another to Eva. Van Buren acted more like a jealous lover than a security chief.

Harry picked up the tension and broke in. "Any injuries? How are their men?"

"We rounded them up pretty quickly. Tossing a stun grenade into a party tends to do that. Police are on their way. Could take a while, none of us speak Icelandic. We've all got permits. No major injuries on either side. One of their lot was winged, must have caught in their own crossfire."

"No, that was Eva. She fought them off. She saved my life, Van."

Van Buren blinked repeatedly at her. It was if he'd been asked to solve an algebra problem while wearing boxing gloves and the test was written in Sanskrit. It didn't compute.

Eventually he nodded towards the Desert Eagle. "I'd feel a lot more comfortable if you handed that over. You're likely to do yourself an injury."

Eva growled. She ejected the magazine and cocked the weapon, expelling a bullet from the chamber. She turned the weapon over to Van Buren, handle first. "Knock yourself out."

Harry whistled, impressed. "I'd keep an eye on her, Van."

With a sneer to make Billy Idol proud, Van Buren said, "I intend to."

He stormed off and Harry went to follow, but Eva held his arm.

"I've come to a conclusion." She kissed him with all the passion she possessed, plus some added adrenaline. When she finally caught her breath, in his ear she whispered, "Definitely Geronimo."

"One day you'll tell me what that means."

"One day. Not today."

◡

Cole let out a frustrated sigh. He shook his head. "That's all fine, Miss, but–"

Decker cut him off. "You're right, she's not getting to the real point, is she, Cole?"

Cole nodded, relief obvious on his face.

Decker tilted his chair backwards and placed his hands behind his head. "It's clear that Ms Destruction here is lying through her teeth. Let's ignore the whole Iceland thing, which, even if it is true, is a mere distraction. She said at the start she fell for a man, but in reality all she was after was his fortune."

Cole's jaw dropped. Eva was pretty sure that wasn't going to be his point at all.

Decker's brow furrowed, taking on a more aggressive persona. "In reality you were just seeing Lancing because he was rich and powerful. Time to cut the bullshit. That was really the reason wasn't it? You said yourself you weren't that interested in him, but all of a sudden he's famous and rich and exciting and you're all over him like cheap celebrity perfume."

It sounded familiar. Eva had featured on all kinds of gossip websites. She'd done her best to ignore them, but the occasional word had popped out and garnered her attention. 'Gold-digger' seemed popular. It only reinforced Eva's distaste for computers. For once she was thankful for her technophobe ways.

Decker was leading up to something. He was trying to play her. Regardless, the barbs hurt. What followed Iceland had been the most intense year of Eva's life. She'd fallen for Harry. Hard. It was unlike anything she'd ever experienced, or even suspected she could. For most of it she had felt she was living someone else's life, Harry keeping her draped in a luxury she was certain she didn't deserve. Breakfast in Paris, dinner in New York, trips to Rio simply to buy shoes. Anything she wanted was hers. Not to mention the castle.

Her old life and friends fell away, as did her business. She'd hastily drawn up a contract for Anchor to be a part-owner of the café and for him to run it in her absence. Basically, Eva had suspended her life for a man. She was a sell-out to the sisterhood and she knew it.

But as much as she tried to hate herself for it, she couldn't. She was so under Harry's spell that her long-held convictions didn't apply. They belonged to someone else, like a childhood superstition, an abstract concept long since abandoned.

Not only did Eva's other life disappear, so did her sense of right. For the longest time, if Harry had asked her to do anything, *anything* at all, she would have done it without hesitation.

Her life never felt like her own, as if she were living someone else's by mistake. Nancy had been the first to notice and called her on it. Nancy knew she and Horatio had run its course even before she had. Eva never felt completely her independent rebellious self.

After the first year, slowly the dissociative fugue had cleared and Eva had begun to question her life and what she'd become. She had grown increasingly suspicious that Harry was too good to be true. That, combined with an increasing exclusion from his life had forced her hand. He'd had too many solo trips and had been away too long which had given Eva time to bring herself around without the silver-tongued Harry to talk her out of it. Fed up, one night she'd simply packed up and left Harry with a note.

She was sure there were others like Decker who believed she'd been in it all along for Harry's wealth. If that was the case, she'd be still with him. It was never about Harry's fame and money but, in quiet reflective moments, Eva had asked herself similar questions. Would she have been so drawn to him if he wasn't threatening world leaders?

She always loved a rebellious soul, a man who gave a 'screw you' to authority. Harry was the manifestation of that taken to the extreme. The world's biggest bad boy. If he'd just been Harry from Accounts, would she have been so enamoured with him? She didn't know then, and she certainly didn't know now.

Eva wasn't sure why Decker's accusations hurt so much. Maybe she wasn't in control of the room as much as she'd thought. Perhaps they were wearing her down.

Decker jeered. "Admit it, Destruction. You were after his money all along, weren't you?"

Between clenched teeth, she stared him down. "You sound just like Van Buren."

"Maybe he had your number too."

"No, that's not–"

"Bullshit, it isn't."

"What kind of interrogation is this, Decker? You haven't asked me about–"

"You've been stringing us along for an hour. Wasting our time, feeding us a cock-and-bull story. You're trying to paint yourself as some kind of innocent fawn randomly thrust into events. A cross between Mother Teresa and Lara Croft. But I'm not buying it. And as for this hokum story you're spinning. How are the London riot and a bunch of snow assassins even remotely connected? They're just random events. It's so obvious you're padding."

Sure, she was taking her time telling the tale, but she wasn't telling them anything that wasn't relevant. It had given her enough time to unpick one handcuff and work on the other. This new aggressive stance only made her double her efforts. Was she going to run out of time before she could unpick the second set of cuffs?

"They are more relevant than you know," she implored. "They all tie together, I didn't know at the time. But they're–"

"And it's all masking one point, isn't it, girly? You were after his fortune from day one, so you might as well admit it. When all is said and done, you're just a whore like every other bitch. Lie down, spread your legs and count the money."

Eva saw red. She leapt up and pounded her fist on the desk. "You have no idea what you're talking about, you ignorant fuck!"

The reverberations echoed around the metallic room. It took a moment before everyone in the room realised what had just happened.

Eva stared at her unshackled fist resting on the table, the hand-cuffs clanged on the floor. "Balls."

Decker and Cole recoiled, scrambling out of their seats. Cole thumped on the steel door and screamed for a guard. She really didn't pose that much of a threat. One wrist was still firmly secured in place.

Decker beamed.

Stupid, stupid, stupid.

He'd deliberately provoked her and she'd fallen for it.

"Guys...guys..."

Cole pointed at her hands. "How the hell did you undo that?"

"Uh, would you believe it fell off?"

"No, I wouldn't." Decker crossed his arms. Satisfaction seeped from every pore. "I thought you were too busy with your hands down there."

"Oh, I don't know. You're both reasonably attractive gents..."

Cole shook his head. "But how? I fastened them myself."

Decker showed no sign of losing the smug grin. "It seems Ms Destruction is a woman of infinite skill. Able to leap off tall buildings in a single bound, expertly wield a baseball bat in a riot, take down armed assassins and seduce the world's foremost self-appointed saviour. I believe everyone has underestimated her, probably her whole life."

Under her breath, Eva said, "Not everyone."

CHAPTER FOURTEEN

"So, Ms Destruction," Decker said reclining comfortably, sipping tea from a silver mug. "Tell us more about this spy."

"Who me?"

"You're a spy now, are you, Ms Destruction?"

"Mainly I'm a barista. I do some spy work. Occasionally."

"I see. A barista spy. What are you going to do to an enemy, make a frappé at them?"

"I'm only speaking technically here, a spy-ish. I had a crash course."

"Of course you did. Did you happen to get this qualification online by any chance? Spies R Us dot com? Did you get a certificate from the Spy University of Nigeria?"

"I can't help but think you're taking the piss…"

Eva bitterly regretted joking about the plastic ties earlier. About a dozen held her legs and arms in place on the cold metal chair. Her arms were fastened so tight she couldn't scratch her nose. Her legs were spread and secured to each chair leg. The white ties dug into her skin, making it purple in patches. She wasn't going anywhere in a hurry. Which was a shame. She really had to pee.

She had to be more careful with Decker. She'd made the mistake of underestimating him. She wouldn't do that again.

"Look…"

Decker interrupted. "Tell us about the spy. Not you, the real one."

"Why would I do that?" Eva tried to keep her voice as casual as possible. She certainly wasn't feeling it. In fact, she was fighting to keep the bile in her stomach from making an impromptu appearance.

"You seemed awfully chatty before. Don't tell me you've clammed up simply because we've taken your toys away?" He took his time leering at her restricted bikini-clad form. "You look like a woman who would enjoy using toys."

Another ploy from Decker? In her current situation she was vulnerable and they all knew it. With her legs spread wide and hands tied, if they decided to move beyond idle threats, there wasn't a damn thing she could do about it. An abhorrent violent image jumped into her mind. Believing it to be a ploy didn't make it less intimidating.

She fought the dryness in her mouth. "Oh, toys are for little children." It was a lie, Eva rather liked the adult kind. She hoped connecting them with children would create a negative connotation if he was remotely thinking of employing what he was implying. She was in a far more vulnerable position, in all kinds of ways, than minutes before.

She tried to remind herself that these were United States naval personnel. There were rules. There were ramifications for stepping over the line. It didn't alleviate Eva's fear.

Wanting to change the subject, she asked, "So we're done with Horatio, are we?"

"We'll come back to him in time. But now I want you to tell me about the Secret Service operative."

Eva's plan had been to break free, subdue the sailors, get off the ship and back to the man she'd left behind. Sure, the plan was a little sketchy in places but now it seemed like that ridiculously misguided stratagem was far less obtainable in her current situation.

A chill spread across her body. It was all her fault. The explosion. The end of a dream. It was all on her shoulders. Worst of all, she'd left him behind. The guilt was all-encompassing. The final image of him alone fighting for his life was heart wrenching. She had to get back to him. She had to do whatever it took to make it right again.

Her first plan in tatters, she now believed her best bet was to confide in the naval men. They might be on the wrong side, they might not. Regardless she had to try.

"Look, there's someone trapped on that island. You need to send people ashore. If he's still alive..."

"We are aware."

"You...you know? Well why don't you send–?"

"It may surprise you, but deploying armed troops onto an island not a part of the sovereign United States may be frowned upon by certain parts of the world. Shocking, I know, but true."

If the US Navy wasn't going to intervene she'd find another way. Eva needed something new. She needed to know more about the naval officers and where she was. She needed information. Only then could she create a new plan. A plan to go back and save him.

For all she knew he was already dead. If there was even the remotest chance he'd survived she had to take the chance. She'd made her decision to leave him behind and come back later. As with all her life decisions, she had to assume it was a bad one. But if he was still alive she would do whatever it took, no matter how vile or disturbing, to get back to him. She owed him that much. She owed him everything.

"I'll tell you about the spy if you tell me about this boat and why I'm being held. I'm not the bad guy here, fellas. You picked me up fleeing an exploding island. Hardly up there with Charles Manson or Nickelback now is it?"

"I like Nickelback," Cole said before covering his mouth.

"Ms Destruction," Decker said, ignoring his offsider. "I think it's far too late in the game to be playing Little Miss Innocent. We all know how ridiculous that is."

"You want to know about the spy? Fine I'll tell you, but you're going to have to pony up some information too."

Decker scoffed. "You're in no position to barter."

"You're obviously asking me these questions for your higher ups. Hell, you're still here after the handcuff stunt. The fact that you're not interested in the island either tells me they already know or don't care. Someone, somewhere is *very* keen on this information. If you want to be good lapdogs and keep giving them what I'm telling you, then we need to have a bit more of a balanced rapport. You don't want me to clam up, now do you?"

"What do you propose?" Decker asked leaning back and folding his arms.

"Here's what I want to know. What sort of ship this is? Why are you two interrogating me? No, actually, I'll add one more. Why are you so hell-bent on finding out about Horatio Lancing and a spy right after an island exploded and the UN went into meltdown? I would have thought that would have been right at the top of your list."

Decker interlaced his fingers and rested them under his chin. "We may be able to share some of that with you. But first, the spy. You met him at the London Eye, then at Lancing's apartment. I assume you saw him again after that?"

"Yes," Eva said firmly. "I saw a lot more of him."

CHAPTER FIFTEEN

ONE MONTH BEFORE THE ISLAND

Eva stared at a tourist boat as it floated leisurely down the Thames. If anyone could see her through the window, which she seriously doubted given where she was, they'd assume she was an office worker in her sleek pinstripe suit. It had been hanging up when she'd stepped out of the shower. The shoes were her own, she had to assume they couldn't find her size, but they matched the suit. Or was it the other way around?

They'd promptly patched her up soon after she'd arrived at SIS headquarters. She'd made the mistake of calling it MI6 headquarters but was quickly and roundly rebuffed. The title MI6 didn't actually mean anything officially. It was only ever used as a flag for the organisation, what the public know SIS as, but far from the endorsed title. Having said that, most people she'd encountered used the title MI6.

An officious and silent doctor had seen to her numerous lacerations and administered a couple of stitches from their harrowing escape from the missile attack and subsequent stranding on the side of Lancing Tower. She hadn't asked where they'd sourced her outfit. Apparently there was someone at headquarters who had a spare business suit her size. At least she hoped it was a spare.

"You look positively radiant," Bishop said as he strolled into the mahogany-lined boardroom. He appeared unaffected by their ordeal. He'd showered and shaved and was dressed in black trousers and a black polo. His gun holster clung snugly to his muscular frame. She assumed this was standard spy attire.

Bishop stopped and squinted at her. Suspiciously, he asked, "What?"

"I'm trying to figure out how you're going to turn that into a sexual innuendo."

He opened his mouth in mock offence. "Is that how low your opinion is of me? That every sentence I utter is for the purposes of luring a woman into my bed? I'll have you know I am a professional operative of His Majesty's Secret Service. I have multiple degrees, speak five languages and have highly-refined skills. Not every sentence I utter has sexual connotations. I would hope you'd think I was more erudite than that."

Maybe she really had offended him. "Sorry. Just on past form you seem to turn every conversation into a Benny Hill sketch. I apologise for calling you a walking innuendo."

"Thank you, Eva. Why do you make it so hard? I wish you'd open up for me. It would be so pleasurable for us both."

She rolled her eyes. "There you go."

He gave her a wink. He really was incorrigible. *How did he do it?* If anyone else had spouted that type of misogynistic crap out their mouth she would have slapped it. But with Bishop, he delivered it in such a way that was half serious, half come-on. As if he knew he was a parody of himself.

"How did you go with the USB doohickey thingumabob?"

Bishop held up his hands. "Hey, settle down with the technical jargon there."

"I don't do technology. Did you get what you needed from Harry's computer before it, you know, exploded?"

"Our boffins did their job marvellously. All the data was retrieved, as far as we can tell. We've identified many of the hackers, arrested a few, with others on the run. The operation was, as you Aussies say, as tight as a platypus' behind."

"Nobody says that."

The boardroom doors swung open and a middle-aged man marched in. His features unmemorable. The perfect spy face. A completely grey man. He clutched a thick folder and had the demeanour of a man who took no pleasure in his job.

Normally Eva had no trouble reading people. Even after watching anyone briefly she could tell much from how they moved, their personal ticks and gestures. This man was unreadable. A blank page.

The grey man sat on the opposite side of the huge table without acknowledging her or the spy. Eventually he glanced up and motioned them to sit.

Bishop nudged Eva. "It's about time we got debriefed."

"Stop it."

For the next hour and a half they were subjected to incessant questioning. Eva believed the grey man was merely going through the motions. Not once did he seem surprised or pause in his relentless enquiries. He either knew all the answers or was completely unreadable.

When he had pointedly asked about Harry, Eva's blood boiled. He wanted to know how she felt about him? She was pissed off! Her former lover had been spying on her, apparently tracking her every move, sending armed guards into her bedroom, oh, and there was the minor issue of leaving her for dead. Not figuratively. Literally leaving her to die with a missile up her twat. She was beyond incensed.

She didn't give a crap about the betrayal in Harry's eyes when he realised she'd let Bishop into his penthouse. That was nothing compared to the horror of him disappearing into the floor. How could a man who purported to love her be so ruthless?

The burn carried her through the questioning, through the moments where it became personal, too personal, especially in light of Eva's painful memories. As much as Harry was a threat to national security and even though she was still pissed at him, she hated the fact that deep within her soul there was a tiny flicker of affection. She crushed it as low as she could but even after the mind comes to a conclusion, the heart can sometimes lag behind.

It was Bishop who eventually called for a pause in the questions to pour her a glass of water. He took his sweet time and there was a crack in the interviewer's marble façade. He was annoyed with Bishop. She wondered if it was the momentary distraction or an ongoing frustration. She suspected the latter. Perhaps Bishop had that effect on everyone. Regardless, she was thankful for the opportunity to gather her thoughts.

After a few more questions the grey man closed the folder and advised they were done. Eva wasn't.

"So where's Harry now?"

"Who?" he asked.

"Horatio. Where is he?"

"He is no longer on English soil."

"I'm amazed. After all the hospitality you supplied, trying to give him a missile enema and all."

"I'm *amazed* you can be so flippant," the grey man advised. "We sent a SAS mobility troop to intercept him at the airport. They're all dead. Twelve men whose family and friends will never see them again. I suggest you jettison any romantic meditations you may still possess. Frankly, your ex-boyfriend is now the most wanted man on the planet. Horatio Lancing has been considered a dangerous man for quite some time. Now he's dangerous and desperate. The situation is infinitely worse."

She could see how they viewed her ex as the biggest threat to global security. But for Eva, it was far more personal than that. She wanted answers. She wanted to see his face to prove she could survive without him, even in spite of him. Eva wanted revenge. But most of all she wanted to prove to herself she and Harry were done.

"Where was he headed?"

"We are unsure at this time."

"So, you've got nothing?"

"We have some leads. Some possibilities."

"Cut the crap. You've got bugger all, haven't you?"

The grey man cast his head downward. When he raised it, for the first time she saw some humanity in his eyes. "Your summation is correct. We have no idea where he is headed. We weren't able to scramble jets to intercept the plane in time. In short, we have nothing, Ms Destruction."

She sighed. She couldn't believe what she was about to say. "That's not entirely true."

"Excuse me?"

"You don't have nothing." Eva rose. She placed her fists on the table. "You have me."

Even as the words spilled out, Eva wasn't sure she didn't want to gather them up and stuff them back in her mouth. She was pissed at Harry, yes, but to sacrifice him like that? Was that who she was?

"Eva," Bishop said. "You don't have to do this."

Eva stared at Bishop. Why would he oppose her on this? She ran it through her mind again. Harry had left her for dead. He was the one who was the betrayer. No, this surely had to be the right path. The fact that it contradicted Bishop only reinforced the idea in her head.

She inhaled deeply and addressed Bishop. "If you want to find him, I'm your only chance. I might be able to get him to tell me where he is."

The grey man seemed dubious. "I don't distrust your intent, Ms Destruction. You said yourself, he left you and Mr Bishop to die. Even if you were somehow able to contact him, and he miraculously had a change of heart, I seriously doubt Mr Lancing would divulge his location if you called him and asked. Regardless of your previous rapport."

"What if...what if..." Was she really going to suggest this? Was she mad? Was she that pissed at him? "What if he doesn't say where he is, I could ask him to come get me? What if I say I want him back? That I want to be with him? He said himself he still loves me. I could use that against him. He turns up, you nab him."

Bishop was wary. "Eva, I'm not sure you understand what you're committing to, you–"

The grey man interrupted, finally animated. "And if he doesn't come? Would you be willing to leave? To meet him? To let us track your whereabouts?"

Events were spiralling too quickly. Could Eva do it? Could she be a spy? Could she spy on him? On Harry? Could she do the things he'd done to her? Would her conscience allow it?

The last of the grey man's unemotional disguise fell away. "We would supply you with every resource possible to ensure your safety. It would be a great service to the Commonwealth."

She ignored the plea to her patriotism. Eva didn't have any. She turned to Bishop. "You need someone on the inside. You need me."

Bishop shook his head. "It's risky." He turned to the grey man. "For one thing, she's not trained."

She turned to him. "Those SAS blokes were. All those years of kung-fu classes, stupid haircuts and no sex didn't do them any good. Call me Little Miss Opposite. No martial arts, fabulous hair and plenty of rumpy-pumpy, I'd say I'm over qualified."

"This isn't a joke, Eva."

"I know. But if you want him I'm the only one who can deliver him tied up with a pretty bow."

My god, had she just agreed to deliver Harry's head on a spike? How had she turned from wondering if she still loved him to betraying him so quickly? Was she that cold hearted? Or had he hurt her that much? She had heard the old phrase about a woman scorned before and had dismissed it as misogynistic nonsense. Now she wasn't so sure.

She could see Bishop wasn't in favour, but he didn't have much choice. Regardless of the incessant flirting she had no doubt his first priority wouldn't be her. Was he trying to talk her out of it? Eva didn't believe for a moment it had to do with her lack of training. It was highly likely it was her lack of penis. There wasn't much she could do about that.

For a while the room was quiet. The grey man probably didn't want to say anything that would change her mind. Eventually Bishop said, "She's going to need a handler."

"We can draw up a list of candidates that–"

"No," Bishop interrupted. "I have just the one."

Fifteen minutes later there was a rap at the boardroom door. The grey man called for them to come in. There was a pause. When the doors parted she lost her mind.

Her brain reeled. Several thousand thoughts bombarded her brain at once. Not one of them made sense. Nothing at all made sense.

A tall man ambled into the room.

He gave a slight shake of the head as if to say *don't let on*. He needn't have bothered. Eva was so stunned she couldn't have uttered a sound. She tried to backtrack her history with the man to have his appearance as a member of MI6 make even a tenuous connection to logic.

He strode forward and extended his hand. "Hello Evie."

Holy cockwaffles.

"I look forward to working with you."

Holy cum-juggling fuck buckets.

She stared at the figure standing before her. At the man she'd known for eight years. A man she thought she'd known like a brother. Eva stared at a man she obviously didn't know at all.

"I'll be your handler. My name is Paul."

CHAPTER SIXTEEN

"Does she know?"

"Evie, please. Lower your voice."

"Does she sodding well know?"

Paul had escorted Eva to a small meeting room. As soon as the door was closed she punched his arm.

"It's not as straightforward as all that."

"I don't give a twirly fuck how complicated it is. Does Nancy know you're a spy?"

"I'm not a spy, Evie. I work at MI6 but I don't do any actual spying." Paul must have determined semantics wasn't going to win her over. "No. She doesn't know. She suspects, of course, but she's never asked directly. She's a clever clogs. Nancy knows when I disappear urgently in the middle of the night it's not a Treasury spreadsheet that needs my attention."

Eva was finding it hard to come to terms with the revelation. Paul, the husband of her best friend was a spy/not-spy. She'd placed him in the lovable oaf box and was having a hard time getting him out of it. Sure he was a news junky, sure he worked long and odd hours...but a senior member of MI6? It was hard to deal with.

A thought jumped into her mind. "Bishop…"

"What's that?"

"You sent Bishop to meet me at the Eye a year ago. That was you, wasn't it? He said an old friend sent him and that it was off the books. You sent him, didn't you? That's how he knew about Harry so soon. That's how MI6 knew my connection to him so fast, because when he came out to the world we were standing in your bloody flat!"

"You've always been smart, Evie." Paul rubbed his face. "But you need to keep that sort of talk between ourselves. Nobody here should know about our personal connection. They'd see our relationship as a weakness and hand you over to someone else. I don't want that to happen. They'd expect us having a history would mean I'd be less likely to put you in danger. I called in a lot of favours to be your handler. I haven't been one in years. I suspect there's some along the chain of command that think I fancy you. Little do they know you're not my type. Too tall, too skinny, too Australian."

The attempt at humour was welcome but Eva didn't crack a smile. She wasn't there yet. She was still far too angry at his deception.

"I can't believe you lie to your wife. Every day."

"It's my job, Evie. Without certain secrets people die. It's that simple."

"Oh, so you don't trust Nance?"

"I do with every fibre of my being, but that's not what it's about. It is about protecting her as well. Behind these walls the ability to keep secrets determines if lives are saved or lost. It's not a matter of trust. It's a matter of national security. Honestly, you have no idea what happens in the world every day. What sacrifices are made, the tragedies averted, the lives saved while you make your lattes."

"Leave coffee out of this."

Paul smirked and Eva glimpsed her old friend again. "I love my wife, but her not knowing certain things about what I do protects her, protects King and Country."

"And that's important? King and Country? Would it be so important that you'd sacrifice someone for it? Me?"

"Yes. I have and I would again. In a heartbeat."

If Paul had slapped her across the face he couldn't have shocked her more.

"This isn't a game, Evie. I love you, but if there was a choice between you and the nation I would choose the nation. You have to understand that. This isn't a lark. It's deadly. If the wrong decision is made people die. If you're not prepared for that I'll tell the higher ups you had a change of heart and I'll meet you in the pub later for a beer. But if you stay, you need to realise that it's likely lives will be lost, that you're stepping into a cloudy world where nothing is black and white. You will be forced to make decisions that will haunt you for life. If you can manage that, wonderful. If not, I more than anyone else in this building understand. The choice is yours."

Yes, the choice was hers. In a way she wished it wasn't. Being forced into it would make betraying her ex-lover so much easier. But that's exactly what she would be doing. Betraying Harry. Betraying the man she had loved more than any other in her life. As much as she could justify it logically, when the time came would she be able to deliver him to the ones baying for his blood? Irrespective of how it ended, what she'd discovered, could she hand him over and live with that on her conscience?

Paul must have sensed her wavering. "Evie, I can get you out of this if you want. But I also have a job to do. We've analysed the secrets Lancing was going to reveal. They would have resulted in our own operatives being uncovered and killed. That's not hyperbole, that's a fact. People would have died. Governments would have fallen. Innocent lives would have been lost all because of one man's hubris. We can't be certain our boffins extracted every copy of the data, or worse, he has more to threaten us with. It need not happen. It can be stopped. You can stop him."

"You really don't like Harry, do you?"

"Tell me one damn good reason why I should like the bastard?"

"You're making it personal."

"Of course it's ruddy personal. He was in my house. Ate my food."

"Drank your shitty wine."

"He also changed who you are. I had the opportunity to stop him but I didn't."

"What, you wanted to put a bullet in his head between courses? Nancy's cooking is bad, but not that bad."

"Stop making jokes."

"Stop freaking me the hell out. For eight years, eight sodding years, I knew you as a clueless lovable oaf and now you're James Bond's dad."

They stared at each other for a long while.

"Oh, and speaking of Bond, thanks for sending his sleazy brother my way. Bishop's quite the cretin."

"He's an old friend of mine. A good man, loyal, faithful."

"Does he fetch sticks too? You make him sound like a dog." Eva fidgeted in the suit. "I'd appreciate it if you could stop him humping my leg."

"There's more to him than you think."

"Yes, I'm sure he has the emotional depth of a teaspoon. But next time you send a secret agent my way could he be slightly less sexist?"

"He may have his flaws, we all do, but he's an honourable man. He's seen a lot of suffering in his time. Too much. Don't dismiss him so quickly, he may be imperfect but in a crisis you want him to have your back. Believe me."

Eva suspected there was far more to the story but knew better than to ask. The room was still again. No sound permeated the four walls.

She could imagine what cogs were turning inside Paul's head. Paul knew her well enough to know pushing her wouldn't work. He had to let her make up her own mind; would she be a government stooge or tell them to go to hell?

Eva peered down. She really needed some new shoes, not that she had the time to shop. Harry had bought her the shoes in Rio. He'd bartered hard, got a great price and ended up paying five times what they were worth anyway. The woman had hugged him and shut up shop early. She and Harry had made love under the stars that night. It had been a good day.

Quietly Eva said, "Okay."

A single word to commit to herself to a path of betrayal. It was that easy. While her justification was sound and Eva wanted revenge on Harry for leaving her for dead, there was a pang of doubt. Okay, a lot of pangs.

She was stepping into the unknown, again. She had no idea how Harry would react to her contacting him. Would he greet her with open arms or throw her off a cliff? Sure, she wanted to slap Harry's pretty-boy face, but could she hand him over to people who wanted him dead? The US and UK governments had proven that human rights and the rules of international law meant nothing in the face of national security. Would Harry simply disappear?

Eva had made a commitment. She would help Paul and his MI6 apprehend Harry. She dismissed the twinges of guilt as nothing more than aftershocks. When she had a moment of doubt, all she had to do was recall the moment when he'd saved himself and left her to fend off air-to-surface missiles with nothing but a weak cocktail and her wits.

~

Over the next few hours Eva was advised of certain protocols and asked to sign countless forms. For some reason, everything she signed had to be done in green ink. She assumed it was an MI6 thing. Paul left her alone but she saw him hovering in the hall, never too far away.

Form after form was shoved in front of her by humourless and featureless personnel. None cracked a smile. The harder Eva tried to pry some human interaction from them, the faster the forms came. It was officious to the point of clinical detachment. Don't get friendly with the bait.

It was only after the last form had been signed that she saw Bishop again. It was a relief. He was like a human lifebuoy in a sea of bureaucracy. When he sauntered into the meeting room she almost hugged him. Then she remembered she hated him.

Bishop escorted her to the elevator without a word being spoken. As the doors closed, Eva asked, "So, how are we going to do this?"

"Very simply, we're not. I'm taking you home."

"Excuse me?"

"Eva, let's be realistic. I'm not throwing you into a vipers nest full of angry bees…"

"Still haven't got those metaphors sorted out, huh?"

"…with no way of knowing if we can offer you backup."

"I signed forms and everything. I'm in. And there you go telling a woman what she should be doing again."

"If you were a man I'd be advising the same thing."

"Would you be looking at his breasts as much?"

Bishop's eyes darted to the elevator ceiling. "You can still change your mind. Go home and think about it, please. This isn't a game."

"So people keep telling me."

Eva found it odd that Bishop was the one who was trying to talk her out of it. The grey man obviously perceived her as an asset. Even one of her very best friends did. Yet, here was Bishop, a man she hardly knew, a man who disgusted her, looking out for her. What was that all about?

"Are you trying to change my mind because I'm a woman?"

"God no. No. No. I mean, no."

"The sexist brute doth protest too much, methinks."

"No, not at all. But if I were to say anything, I would say that that fieldwork for a woman is inherently more dangerous. The threats are more immediate, there are greater dangers, more psychologically damaging ones than for a man."

Eva chose not to hide the distain. "Just as well you didn't say anything then, otherwise you'd have come off as a patronising chauvinist son of a bitch. Dodged a bullet there."

Regardless of Bishop's misdirected attempt to protect her virtue, there was no way Eva could say she didn't have her doubts.

Despite her anger towards Harry she was still betraying her ex-lover and throwing herself recklessly into danger. Was that really who she was?

"All I'm saying is that I urge you to reconsider. I'll be at your house in the morning. Sleep on it."

Absentmindedly, Eva mumbled, "We are such stuff as dreams are made of, and our little life is rounded with sleep."

"What?"

"Huh? Sorry. Just a random Shakespeare quote. You said sleep."

Bishop nodded and stared at the elevator doors. "People sleep peaceably in their beds at night only because rough men stand ready to do violence on their behalf."

Eva tilted her head. "Orwell?"

Bishop nodded, still facing forward.

She didn't know if the line was general spy issue or perhaps Bishop was slightly deeper than she'd given him credit for.

She assumed the former.

CHAPTER SEVENTEEN

Bishop liked his coffee black. Like his turtleneck. And his pants. And his dive watch. And his socks. And his shoes. Eva assumed he had a bust-up with colour some time in his past. It was apparently a bad break-up. His underwear was probably black too. She assumed boxers. Or at least that's what Eva had in her mind. And then all of a sudden her imagination had him not wearing under-wear at all. *What the hell?* Bishop represented everything she hated in men. Where had that thought come from? Maybe his one-track mind had somehow infected hers.

"You okay, Eva?" he asked.

"Hmmm? What now?"

"Are you alright?"

"Yes, why?"

"You just put six spoons of sugar in your coffee."

Eva gawked at her coffee. *Dickpans.* She wanted to put her wandering thoughts down to realising how difficult the path she'd set herself on was going to be. She wanted to.

When Bishop arrived Eva had already made her decision. In fact, she'd decided somewhere around 3.00 a.m., right between the rerun of *Seinfeld* and *Only Fools and Horses*. He'd quickly discovered there was no talking her out of it.

"This is good coffee," Bishop said.

Eva shook her head at him, as if he'd said breathing was nice.

"So what happens now?" she asked.

"You try and make contact with Lancing. We get you trained up as much as we can. You're in for an intense few days. We're going to try and make you a spy in record time. I hope you don't like sleep and love pain."

"Sounds like my normal life so far."

"Don't be so facetious. You are in for the hardest few days of your life. We have the world's best trainers lined up to push you harder than you've ever been pushed in your life. You will bleed. You will beg for it to stop. You will be so rammed full of information you'll want to gouge your brain out with a pitchfork. When that's done, you'll get up and start again. You will be tested like you never thought possible."

"Can't we do a montage?"

"A...what?"

"Like in the movies. We could totally do a montage. You know, me flailing about trying to climb a rope, you shaking your head, then at the firing range, karate classes, all that shit. Over the space of a song I get better and by the end I climb that rope in record time, you click a stopwatch and give me an approving nod. It ends with us laughing and sipping cocktails at sunset."

"You know this is real life, don't you?"

Eva drank her horrific coffee. If she had been diabetic she'd have been in a coma. "It's my turn to ask if you're okay."

Bishop frowned. "Me? Why?"

"You've been here for half an hour and you haven't made one lewd remark or double entendre. I'm worried about you Bishop. Are you having some sort of stroke?"

A wry grin. "We're colleagues now. It may be hard for you to believe, but I can control myself around you."

She mulled it over. Eva wasn't convinced. She knew she wasn't completely irresistible, but Bishop with self-control was as believable as a ballet dancer's codpiece.

She squinted at him. Even though he was a spy, Eva didn't seem to have trouble reading him. "What else is going on? Have I upset you in some way?"

"No, it's...," he glanced at his coffee mug. "Today's just a bad day."

"I apologised for the hair. Some mornings it sticks up like that."

"Amusing." His eyes were bereft of humour. "No...it's...well, today's an anniversary, of sorts."

Oh god. Was he married? He didn't have a wedding band, but in retrospect she doubted any secret agent would.

Bishop must have picked up on her thoughts. "Not that kind of anniversary, no. A bad one. A mission. People died. It's...today's not a great day, okay?"

So the walking innuendo had a heart after all. Eva didn't ask. She assumed he wouldn't tell her if she did. She also didn't want to tell him she was sorry. It was a cliché and his response would be automatic.

She still loathed him, but now he was a human she loathed, instead of a cartoon of a man. Eva pretended to drink her coffee and listened to the sound of morning traffic through the window.

Eventually, she asked, "When do we get started?"

Bishop downed his coffee. "Now."

Eva was incredulous. "Wait, not even one?"

"No. Why is that so hard to believe?" Bishop pointed down the firing range. "Can you please just shoot, we need to determine how much time you'll need on the range."

But she wasn't looking at the range. "Like, not even one? How is that even possible?"

Bishop crossed his arms in frustration. "I never got around to it, my utmost sincere apologies. Now, if you could just focus on..."

"How can you never have seen a James Bond movie? You're a goddamn spy!"

"Well, yes, but those movies don't exactly represent real spy craft..."

They'd been at SIS headquarters for five hours and Eva was thankful for the distraction. "But that's the starting off point, surely. It's like someone watching Star Wars and getting inspired to become an astronaut. Or an archaeologist watching Indiana Jones. Not the same thing because you're not going to be running away from rolling boulders every day, but, I mean, come on."

Bishop must have realised he wasn't going to get Eva to fire a shot without finishing the discussion. He sighed. "I've never seen those movies, either. Now, if you could aim your gun we'll teach you how to–"

"Were you born in a lab?" She was aghast.

"Can we," Bishop ran his hand down his face, "shoot? Please?"

Eva glared at the target Bishop had set for her. It was roughly three centimetres from the barrel of her gun. It was so close a blind grandmother could have hit it. She gave him an expression of contempt and hit the button to send the target further down the range.

She rolled her neck, extended her arm and gave Bishop her sweetest fake smile. Hardly glancing at the target she fired six shots and managed four direct hits and two near misses. Not bad for being a bit rusty. And showing off.

Who needed a montage?

Bishop was dumbfounded. "How...how...?"

"Long story. Anyway, I can shoot. Surprise! So, have you seen any movies? Like, ever?"

Bishop ignored the question and made Eva shoot for another hour. Finally he was convinced that Eva wasn't fluking it and had significant skill. He, of course, didn't use those exact words. It was more of a grunt.

She was more than happy to show Bishop up. There was something satisfying about a mere *girl* finishing with a qualifying score for a field operative. Although Eva had to admit the victory dance may have been too much.

After passing her scores to a minion, Bishop said, "How about we take a break and grab a coffee?"

"That stuff in the staff room is not coffee. It is an abhorrence masquerading as a beverage. No wonder you boys can't keep up with Harry, you're fuelled by an anaemic caffeine wannabe."

Bishop shook his head and handed his weapon and glasses to the armorer. Eva did the same. They headed towards the caféteria. At least he had learned not to engage in coffee arguments.

The morning had been a series of introductions to her trainers. She was pleasantly surprised that they weren't all male. It seemed MI6 wasn't quite the boys' club she imagined.

They had no idea how long Eva had to train, or even if it would be needed. She had reached out to Harry but there was no guarantee he would respond. Even if he did get back to her, would he agree to meet?

The more time wore on, the less likely she thought it was Harry would reply to her message. Surely he had more on his plate than to get in contact with his mouthy bothersome ex-girlfriend. The expression on his face the last time she'd seen him made her dubious he'd invite her over for beer, a grilled cheese sandwich and a laugh about old times.

Regardless, the tiny kernel of hope she still carried in her gut convinced her to train for something her brain doubted would ever eventuate.

The afternoon was designated to be surveillance and counter-surveillance. She was looking forward to it, but suspected she'd fail to impress like her marksmanship had. Or was it markswomanship?

When they arrived at the caféteria, Bishop handed her a coffee without asking how she had it. They were seated in a virtually empty room. Eva wanted to grab something to eat, but everything available was exceedingly and annoyingly healthy. Fruit, vegetables and low carbs. The likelihood of finding a jam doughnut in the MI6 canteen was about the same as finding Mikhail Gorbachev behind the counter serving sandwiches in a panda suit. Sometimes Eva needed junk food. She'd kill for a chocolate sundae.

Bishop sipped loudly, his mind apparently miles away.

"Can I ask a question?" she said.

"It's never one question with you, but certainly."

"Do you have a licence to kill?"

"There's no such thing."

"Do you have a garrotte wire in your watch?"

"No."

"What's a gnafu?"

"A word you just made up."

"How many novels did Jane Austin complete?"

"No idea."

"Six. How many have you read?"

"None."

"I am surprised. What's the…?"

The phone rang in Eva's pocket. The number was blocked but the sense of dread was enough to know who it was. She answered.

"Hi Eva." The sound of the sea in the background. "It's Harry."

CHAPTER EIGHTEEN

Eva pressed 'End' on her phone. She stared at it for the longest time and Bishop let her.

She was numb. She was cold. More than anything, she felt incredibly alone. She'd give anything for an afternoon down the pub with Nancy. Her best friend would be able to sort it out over a few pints. Except that would be impossible.

When she took the call, Bishop had ushered her into the nearest office. He'd ordered the occupants immediately out with a snap of his fingers. They scurried away without protest.

Eventually she placed the phone on the table. "So...that was fun."

"Are you alright, Eva? Do you need a moment?"

A moment? She needed a lifetime.

Eva shook her head. "You got the gist of it?"

Bishop nodded.

"Do you need me to write everything down?"

"No need, we'll have a transcript."

She tilted her head. "A transcript? Wait, you have my phone bugged? Don't you need a warrant or something?"

Bishop chuckled and shook his head. He patted her arm conde-scendingly and walked off to make some calls of his own. *Prat.*

Two weeks. Eva had two weeks to become a spy. She had two weeks to wrestle with her conscience before being confronted the biggest moral dilemma she'd ever faced. Sure, she was still angry at Harry. Sure, he'd left her to die while he escaped. Sure, he'd been tracking her every move since they'd broken up. Sure, he'd deliberately sent armed guards into her bedroom while she was screwing. But still…

Harry had seemed sincerely concerned for her safety. The relief was palpable in his voice. Eva knew him well enough to know he was being genuine. He was thankful she was safe and wanted to see her. She didn't even have to ask.

She asked tentatively if he was going to unleash the secrets. He said he no longer had a copy but had other information, equally as destructive. The British government had seen the original data he was going to release. There was a slight strain in his voice when he'd said it and they both knew why. Harry said he was waiting to see if the governments of the world would do the right thing now that they were aware of what he was capable of.

The right thing.

Right.

Harry had been vague about why he needed two weeks before meeting her. 'I need to get settled', he'd said. Whatever that meant. Settled where? Eva hoped it wasn't Iceland. She'd seen enough of that place.

He'd said he'd be in contact soon to provide her with the loca-tion of their rendezvous point. When he'd rung off, she wasn't entirely sure what she should feel.

With Bishop gone, Eva took advantage of the rare moment of solitude to stare out the window. It was a horrid London day. A typical one, then. The dull grey skies had opened up and bombarded the city with icy winds and incessant drizzle. Great coffee weather.

She hoped Anchor was taking care of her coffee shop in her absence. The profit share she'd given him would hopefully be sufficient motivation. She missed him. She missed that life. Eva wondered if she'd ever return.

Bishop strode into the office. "Alright, everything's falling into place. Your next session is soon, we better get cracking."

"What is it?"

"Chemistry."

"How to make a better cocktail? That sounds like something I can get behind."

"Almost like that, but more about making explodey cocktails that go bang."

"Did you just say explodey? I am rubbing off on you? ... I said 'off on you', don't get any ideas."

"Perish the thought. We commence in five minutes."

"No rest for the wicked, then?"

"As well you know, the wicked get exceedingly little rest." He gave her a wink. And just like that the innuendo was back. "We've put you on a strict regime and I've scheduled you in for as much Krav Maga as we can."

"The Israeli fighting thingie?"

"That's exactly how they refer to it, yes. It's all about practical fighting, how to finish a fight as efficiently as possible. You're super-intelligent Eva, you read something once and you have it. That's a gift. But learning martial arts is different. You need muscle memory. You need to do it several hundred times over for your body to do it mechanically, without thought. You'll do these things so many times you'll want to crawl into a foetal position and cry. And then you'll do it again, and again. Its real-world fighting, like stripping a gun from an assailant's grasp."

"Like I'll ever need that. I'm meeting Harry, not storming Normandy."

"You never know. Our job is to prepare you for anything."

"Can you teach me to juggle? I've always wanted to do that. I should totally learn how to juggle. You never know, I might have to join a circus."

"Three thirty, Captain Bozo." He smiled and his baby blues lit up in cruel anticipation. "Come on, there's a world of hurt ahead."

"Stop sugar-coating it."

~

"Evie, a moment."

She stopped walking down the light-filled corridor. MI6 was far more modern than she'd thought. In her mind Eva had imagined an old school boys' club look, all mahogany and leather. In reality, it was merely another office building, although one with bulletproof everything, armed guards and unbelievable security at every level.

She had come from her lock picking lesson. It was meant to be two hours but was only ten minutes. The instructor had attempted to walk her through the basics, but she'd laid down a challenge. When she'd broken the lock faster than the instructor he'd advised she could skip the class.

Eva thought Paul might be after her to tell her off. She was still unclear on exactly what the handler's role was. He took her by the arm and led her to an unoccupied meeting room and shut the door.

"How's it all going? You keeping up?"

If she were talking to Bishop, she could have made something out of that, but this was Paul. He wouldn't know an innuendo if you wrapped it around a dildo and slapped him in the face with it.

"Good. So far. Bishop's keeping me busy."

"I bet he is."

Eva didn't know how to take that.

"Can I ask you a question, Evie?"

"Sure, you know that. You can ask me anything. You *have* asked me anything."

"Do you miss him?"

"Who Bishop? I saw him, like, fifteen minutes ago."

"No, Lancing. Do you miss him?"

"Miss him how? Like with a sniper rifle or like a saxophonist misses the eighties?"

"The second one. I think."

There was no use lying. Paul had seen the ugly aftermath of her relationship with Harry. Nancy had spent months putting her back together. It hadn't been pretty and it hadn't been high on dignity.

"I'll admit I occasionally miss the idea of him. Who I thought he was instead of what he actually ended up being. But do I miss the man? I don't think so, no."

"But he did buy you a castle."

"That's okay I can build my own castle out of the fucks I no longer give."

Eva held her face as neutral as she could muster. She'd been confident Old Paul couldn't read her. With New Paul, she had no idea.

Paul nodded, seemingly unconvinced. "But you've tried before, haven't you? To be free of him, and that didn't exactly work out now did it?"

So that's what the conversation was about. Paul was having second thoughts. He'd seen her as a strategic asset to capture to Horatio Lancing, but once he'd thought about it he'd remembered the frail flawed woman she really was.

"That was a long time ago."

"A year."

Eva shrugged. "Sometimes you have to fail before you succeed. Sometimes you have to release *Their Satanic Majesties Request* before unleashing four of the greatest rock albums in history."

Paul stared blankly at her as if he had no idea what she was on about. It felt like home.

She hadn't thought about the castle in a long time. It was probably still in her name. For a time she'd toyed with the idea of giving it over to an asylum seeker organisation just to piss off the current French administration. It was worth looking into when her life returned to normal. That is, *if* her life ever returned to normal.

Getting back to the topic at hand, she said, "I'll be fine Paul, really." She rubbed his arm reassuringly. Eva wanted to change the subject as soon as possible. "Any news on that front? Has anyone located him?"

He shook his head. "Not a peep. He's disappeared off the

planet. No agency has the foggiest where he is or knows of anyone that has drawn a bead on him. Only you as far as we can tell. Which, to be honest," Paul scratched the back of his neck, "makes me even more nervous. He has to make his move soon, surely. We still don't have a clue what his end goal is. So far it's been threatening politicians to bump up their green credentials and care for the poor–"

"And start the occasional revolution…"

"What?"

"Uh, he did claim to have started the latest Russian revolution."

Paul's jaw tightened. "What! When was this?"

"When I saw him at the penthouse. Before the missile suppository."

"Why haven't you mentioned this before? It's kinda important, Evie."

"I thought he was joking, or at least exaggerating."

"Has nothing he's done in his life led you to believe Horatio Lancing is capable of anything?"

Eva ground her shoe into the carpet. "There's more." She glanced up. "He made some crack about creating a new European currency and calling it ducats. He was definitely joking about that."

"Joking?"

"He always had a weird sense of humour."

"Apparently." Paul mulled the new information over. "Maybe I was right after all."

"With what?"

"We've got an office sweep about what Lancing's really after. I've put my money on world dictator. I guess I could win after all."

Eva scoffed. "Whoever heard of an Australian dictator?"

"Are you familiar with the work of Rupert Murdoch?"

"Point taken."

~

Eva jiggled like a five year old on Christmas morning. She couldn't help it. Bishop didn't share her enthusiasm. In fact, the more she became excited, the more dour he became.

"It's really not that exciting," he assured her.

"Shut up. Don't spoil it."

Finally the brown-coated technician placed a small wooden box on the counter. She'd left Eva and Bishop in the small waiting area while she went to process the requisition request.

Eva stopped jiggling. "That's it?"

The young technician pushed back her thick rimmed glasses and checked her Lancing Corp tablet. "Yes. That's all that was in the order."

She harrumphed. Still, it was something. An unknown something. She was still excited.

She beamed at the technician. "Thanks, Q."

Bishop shook his head. "Stop doing that."

The name badge proclaiming the technician's name said it was Charlie, but Eva couldn't help herself.

She flipped open the lid and failed to hide her disappointment.

"A pen?" She tilted her head at the technician, her enthusiasm waning. "What does it do?"

"You click it and it activates. The device tells us exactly where you are, anywhere in the world."

"That's it?"

"That's it."

Eva picked up the pen. It looked like an expensive writing implement, nothing more. She turned it over in her hands several times. The technician drummed her unvarnished fingers on the counter and checked her watch.

She held the device up. "Would someone be able to detect the GPS signal?"

The technician shook her head. "This doesn't use GPS. Similar, but the next step. This uses quantum positioning. Far more accurate."

Okay. Eva was slightly more impressed. She glanced behind the technician to the labyrinth of shelves and doors to the unknown. "Are you sure there's nothing else I can have?"

The technician sighed. "Like what?"

"Oh, I don't know, an underwater breathing apparatus, a magnetic watch, a lipstick rocket launcher, flamethrower bagpipes, radioactive lint, something, anything."

The technician turned to Bishop. "She watches a lot of movies, doesn't she?"

"Quite so. Especially for a self-proclaimed book nerd, a staggering amount."

Eva ignored the digs. "So, this pen, what exactly does it do?"

Like I said, "It tracks your movements."

"Anything else?"

"No, that's it."

She screwed up her face. Not entirely sure what she was hoping for. In fact, she was utterly deflated. It was as if she'd caught her parents putting out Santa's presents on Christmas Eve.

She thanked the technician who was already on her way back to her tech warren. Eva placed the pen in the case and tucked it under her arm. Bishop held the door open for her.

"Not as fun as I thought it would be," she said.

"Welcome to the Secret Service."

As they stepped into the hall the technician called out. "Excuse me, Miss!"

Eva turned. The technician behind the counter held an odd-looking object. In her hands was a bright pink frilly umbrella.

It took her a while, but she finally determined the only parts of her body that didn't hurt were her eyelids. She'd deliberated if she was still alive and the answer came back, 'possibly'.

She'd collapsed onto the bed of her MI6 sleeping quarters face first and fully clothed. She didn't have the energy to take her shoes off. The thought of removing her bra was bliss, but that would involve moving in some capacity and her muscles were on strike. Or dead.

There was a knock at the door but she didn't have the strength to answer. Perhaps it was an undertaker. The door opened with a creak. She didn't lift her head to see who it was. It could be an assassin for all she knew. The fact that she was incapable of movement rendered all the martial arts training she'd received over the last few days useless.

"Why hello, I was wondering if you'd be up for an evening jog?"

If Eva could have summoned the energy she would have given Bishop the finger. She decided to respond with the most devastating repartee she was capable of flinging in his direction. "Ugghhhhh."

That'll teach him.

She really didn't need a reminder on how much she despised Bishop.

"Indeed." She could hear the pleasure in his voice. He was enjoying seeing her suffer. "Glad to see our little training regime is having the desired effect. We have recruits who would literally kill to have the intensive instruction you're receiving. Tomorrow we'll step it up a notch. I'm sure you'll agree we've been taking it far too easy on you."

With her face mashed into the pillow, she replied with, "Bwasted."

"That's the spirit!" She could hear Bishop pacing about the room. He was probably checking out the complete mess she'd made of it in such a short amount of time. She wasn't one for domestic cleanliness. "Is there anything I can get you?"

"Vodka, a masseuse and vodka."

"It will surprise you that alcohol is not encouraged in the sleeping quarters. Shocking, I know. But I might be able to source some massage oil. I've been thinking you could use some lubrication for quite some time."

It appeared Bishop's code of not hitting on his fellow employees was a fluid thing.

Eva turned her head in order to speak. "Bishop, as flattering as that comment isn't, please don't confuse my current predicament as a come on."

"You needn't worry, fair maiden. I'm far too much of a gentleman to take advantage of a woman in such a delicate state." There was silence and she wondered if he'd left the room. That was, until he spoke. "I am, however, enjoying the view."

Eva's last session had been a high-intensity Krav Maga class. She'd worn the appropriate attire of Lycra gym gear. It was practical, but hardly the right outfit to rebuff a sexist pig. Even her straight-laced instructor had checked out her arse. The arse that was currently directed at Bishop.

She managed to summon the energy to move one hand and waved it around her behind, as if she was swatting away his glare. At least that was the intent. The physical effort made her exhausted and she buried her head in the pillow again.

"Are...are you slapping your arse at me?"

"Nwo."

"Because I have to say I approve."

"Uhhhggghhh!"

"Is there anything of mine I can slap around for you?"

"Just your face."

"I'm blessed, but not *that* blessed, Eva."

"Is there a reason you're here, Bishop? Besides the sexual harassment, of course."

"Of course. That's just a bonus. You've received a message. From Lancing. He left a voice message advising where you are to meet. Prague."

It was as if Eva's heart clenched. Everything was real again all of a sudden.

Bishop went on. "That means we'll need to ramp up your training. With the travel to the Czech Republic we'll lose a day's training, so we'll need to make that up."

"Oh goody."

"I thought you'd approve."

A thought hit her. *The cheeky bastard.* She grinned.

"What is it?" Bishop asked. "You seem happy. I'm worried."

"Prague. Harry's being a smartarse. It's an old joke of ours. I once told him I'd always wanted to go to Prague but he said it was only because of INXS."

"I don't follow. What's in excess?"

"The band. The Aussie band? INXS. They made a video in the eighties for 'Never Tear Us Apart'." Bishop stared at her blankly. "What am I thinking? Of course you missed that, you were born in a lab. Anyway, they made a music film clip, it was huge, and Harry reckoned that the only reason I wanted to go there is INXS made it look cool. He always refused to take me. It was one of those ongoing little niggly fun arguments couples have."

Bishop didn't respond. Guilt stabbed her for bringing up such a fond memory. As far as he was concerned, Harry was the enemy and there was no fond anything.

Bishop straightened his back and resumed his casual demeanour. He gave her a slight bow before opening the door. "So, about the training. I'll be here again at five a.m. Be dressed and ready to go. Or just ready to go."

"Say goodbye, Bishop."

"Goodbye Bishop."

The door closed and Eva remained motionless. She had no idea how much more they could pack into a day. She was mentally and physically exhausted. The last few days had comprised of weapons training, surveillance and counter-surveillance, computer hacking, martial arts and self-defence training. As well as specific sessions like communications equipment, sending messages that couldn't be traced. There had been more, but in her current state couldn't recall what they were.

Apparently they hadn't even scratched the surface on what Eva would learn. She certainly hoped not. She still hadn't had her juggling classes.

Finally managing to roll over, she stared at the plain white ceiling.

It was probably for the best she hadn't answered when Harry called. There was something she hadn't told Bishop about the first call. Something she'd *never* tell Bishop. Hearing Harry's voice, hearing the genuine concern in his tone, her rational boundaries had begun to crumble.

Paul was more right than he knew. Eva had tried to shake Harry off and had failed. More than once. Even before she saw him again at his penthouse, the mere sound of his name made her shake and break into a sweat. That wasn't the reaction of a woman who was over anyone.

She'd had her doubts before, but hearing him, letting their memories together wash over her, she wavered more than ever. The longer she'd spoken to Harry, the less confident she'd became. She'd hoped the more distance she had from that first call, the more rational she would feel. She was wrong.

Eva's misgivings about what she'd committed to were growing. Would she be able to give away Harry so easily? What would happen when she met him again?

Could she give up Harry for forcing the world to do the right thing? She tended to lose her self-control when in his presence, but if she was already wavering, it didn't bode well for the mission. Would she crumble before his many charms like she had countless times before? Eva assumed she'd have the answer soon enough.

She blinked her non-painful eyelids. Was all this training for nothing? Was she going to give everything up to be with the man she still loved? The ceiling blurred as tears formed. Without knowing precisely why, she sobbed and couldn't stop. Curling into a ball, for the first time in a very long time, Eva cried.

CHAPTER NINETEEN

Normally Eva avoided clichés like the plague, but it really was like a fairy tale. The architecture ranged from Romanesque, to Gothic to Baroque to Art Nouveau. She had to wonder what the rest of Europe would have been like if it had been spared like Prague during the Second World War.

Surprisingly it was more beautiful than she'd imagined. Photos could never convey the sheer breathtaking magnificence that greeted the visitor at every turn. The light snowfall only added to the surreal nature of the scenery. There was meant to be a storm overnight but the early evening skies didn't appear menacing.

She could see herself spending months there and never scratching the surface. With her face against the glass of the limo, she must look like an overeager child to Bishop and Paul, but didn't care. Driving through the city she'd fantasised about for so long she cared little for the thoughts of the others.

Eva wished she'd come under different circumstances. She wanted to stop at every street corner, get out and explore. That's what she loved to do in new cities, drop off her bags, pick a random direction and set out to discover the *real* city. It was the way she'd uncovered hidden gems in many foreign cities. And in one case, get mugged.

Perhaps she was so in love with the city at first sight, as it was in direct contrast to her last few weeks. Her training had been relentless and gruelling. She'd never been pushed so hard, or been so challenged in her life. Or frightened. The nearer she came to the inevitable conclusion of her training, the more worried she'd become.

Sleep was no longer a thing. She imagined her teeth would soon be flat from her incessant grinding. She'd need to find a way to release the building stress, one way or another.

"If you ask me, it was a dick move," Paul said breaking the silence. Arms folded, he ignored the passing scenery.

"Huh?"

"Lancing never taking you here. He dragged you all around the world, but not the one place you wanted to go. Therefore, dick."

A grin. "I wouldn't call it drag, but, it was always a joke. It wasn't malicious."

"Uhuh."

"Oh come on, you know how it goes in relationships. You have your little play digs. They don't mean anything, but it's a cute way to get a rise out of your partner. Like you do with Nance and her unnatural fear of salsa, or how she's always ribbing you about your unbridled love of *Frozen*. All couples do it, maybe not as much as you two, but I'm pretty sure everyone has their little good-humoured taunts."

She stopped, unsure if Bishop was aware of how well she knew Paul. If she was going to be a spy she had to be more careful about what she said.

Eva sensed she'd been given a test and failed. Paul must have picked up on it.

"It's okay, Bishop knows. He's even met Nance."

"You met her?"

"Yes," Bishop sighed. "But I was Clive from the office." He didn't seem pleased about it.

"You're so not a Clive."

Bishop held his hands up to Paul and frowned a *see* face. "Thank you, at least someone thinks so."

The limo slowed as they reached a five-storey hotel. It had a grand elegance that spoke of refined expense. It appeared MI6 wasn't as cash-strapped as other government departments. Bishop opened the door and got out. After checking the street he gave a brisk nod. Eva picked up her history of MI6 book and exited.

On Paul's way out of the limo, Bishop said, "Frozen? Really?"

Paul scowled. "Shut up."

"OK. I'll let it go."

"*You're* the dick."

Eva glowered at Bishop. "You've never seen a Star Wars or James Bond but you can make a *Frozen* joke? You seriously need to reassess your priorities."

On closer inspection the hotel wasn't as lavish as it first appeared. Up close it seemed dated and definitely in need of renovation. Once great, it had fallen on hard times. If Norma Desmond was a hotel, this would be it. At least it would be a good place to avoid prying eyes.

Through the revolving door emerged a tall stocky black man with a closely shaven head. His movements were precise and his course to the car was a series of straight lines. There was a slight limp in his gait. The suit cut was stylish, yet conservative. His eyes darted along the street, outwardly casually but deliberately vigilant.

Paul and he hugged like old friends. He gave Bishop a terse handshake. It was the greeting of men who'd had clashes before. It seemed Bishop had the unique ability to piss everyone off. Maybe Eva could form a club.

Finally he turned to her and smiled. It was warm but guarded. He had a friendly face, but there was concern in his manner.

"Ms Destruction, a pleasure." He shook her hand firmly. "My name is Angelis Travers. I am Station Chief in Prague."

The words 'Station Chief' brought the whole exercise back into sharp focus. She was all too aware that she had been turning into a spy. A real spy. Complete with a handler, gadgets and all the associated danger. A real life Station Chief standing before her reminded Eva that this wasn't an old spy novel, this was her life and it was in very real danger.

Angelis bowed slightly. "Welcome. Please," he said gesturing to the entrance, "we have prepared everything for your arrival."

All four headed into the foyer where it was thankfully warm. The interior of the hotel matched the exterior. Dated opulence, décor out of step with time. They sat in a deserted lobby on well-worn couches before a raging fire.

They discussed the mission the higher ups at MI6 had planned. The strategy was to lure Harry out into the open with Eva as the bait. A message had been sent for Harry to meet her at the Old Town Square. They had every operative in the city ready. If Harry didn't appear in person, she was to go with Lancing's representative while Angelis and his men tracked her. All she had to do was click on the pen and they'd take care of the rest. As soon as they could positively identify Harry they would nab him. It all sounded too loose for her liking.

Once the broad plan had been explained, the four of them dissected the smaller detail, well, three of them. At every turn Angelis excluded her from the conversation. For a solid five minutes he had his back turned to her. She wasn't sure if it was sexism or her inexperience. Either way, Eva wasn't having any of it.

"Do we have a problem?"

All three men turned to her.

"Excuse me?" Angelis asked, annoyed at the interruption.

"I'm just asking if I've done something wrong."

He scowled. "Not yet, but I find it highly likely."

"And what does that mean exactly?"

A sigh. "Please allow me to be blunt, Ms Destruction. I think this mission is a mistake. It's foolhardy and ill-considered. To have such an assignment hinge on the actions of an amateur in a skirt is nothing short of reckless. You're in my town. Anything that goes wrong in my town reflects poorly on me. And right now, your inexperience places us all in danger. I'm not prepared to put my men in harm's way without feeling one hundred percent comfortable, and to be honest I'm far from it. Far from it. You know nothing of spy craft. How to read a scenario, a person, or how to act naturally when the situation is anything but. There are thousands of things that can go wrong, and to be frank, that's all I'm seeing right now."

The sentiment was nothing Eva hadn't thought herself, but she'd be damned if she'd let someone else insult her. Screw him.

"How was it?"

Angelis eyed her suspiciously. "How was what?"

"The Gulf War, the first one, how was it?"

Visibly taken aback, he asked, "How did you...?" His hand ran over his leg. "Are you trying to make a point?"

"I don't know, am I?"

Angelis appeared partly shocked, part angry. Paul gave the slightest shake of his head, as if asking her to drop it. Bishop seemed to be having a marvellous time.

Eva gave a tilt of her head. "I'm just a silly girl, what would I know?" She shrugged. "But I'm guessing that's how you got your leg injury, wasn't it? In the Gulf War. It seems you've come a long way since growing up in Liverpool."

"How the hell did you know any of that?" He eyed Paul and Bishop.

Paul held up his hands. "We've told her nothing."

Bingo. "Liverpool, well, it's obvious. You try to sound more southern, be more crisp with your pronunciation, but really, it's like trying to hide an elephant with a blanket. As for coming from a military background instead of hired directly out of university, which is the norm, it's in the way you move, for one. The way your hand went straight to your leg when I mentioned the war. The way you move in straight lines, your efficiency of movement. Minimal and deliberate. You move like you were born in khaki."

His face had softened, but only slightly. "I could have been in the military and not have fought in a war."

"A military man who hadn't seen combat wouldn't be as reluctant as you to get in a firefight. You've seen action. Given your age, that's either the Gulf War or Bosnia." Eva paused and gave a weak grin. "The Gulf War *was* actually a guess."

"A good one."

"You also eyed the street taking in all the dark corners."

"That's what spies do, we look for dangers."

"Yes, true, but a spy would stick to the shadows themselves. You march in a straight line out in the open. I use that word deliberately. March. Like you spent half your life on a parade ground, you even turn precisely. I bet your bed has corners you could cut yourself on. So," she folded her arms, "if you don't mind, please stop underestimating the skirt."

The smirk hiding in the corner of his mouth spread like wildfire across Angelis' face. "Oh, I like her."

Eva raised an eyebrow. "I like me too."

"You pass."

"Smashing, do I get a lollipop and a pat on the head?"

"Oh, I really like her."

Paul beamed. Unlike her earlier test, she seemed to have passed this one with flying colours.

For the next twenty minutes, the conversation returned to the mission, although in a more collaborative manner. Eventually the points of discussion whittled down and she yawned. Angelis handed out room keys and recommended everyone rest up for the operation in the morning.

Eva shook everyone's hand and headed towards the lift. Bishop shadowed her. As the rickety doors to the ancient lift closed, Bishop nodded towards the room key. "We should see if the bridal suite is still available." His eyebrows virtually danced off his forehead.

There were times when she could let Bishop's comments slide, sometimes even find them amusing. It wasn't one of those times. She was already tense from the mission, and had just had a confrontation with someone who had no faith in her abilities. She wasn't entirely sure why Angelis had decided to dislike her, but she had a strong suspicion it was her gender. In short, she didn't have the patience to put up with Bishop's sexist crap.

Eva grunted. "Sounds like someone got out of the regular side of the bed this morning."

"What's that meant to mean?"

She groaned. "It means I look forward to the day you don't hit on me, make a chauvinist remark or twist every statement into a Carry On double entendre."

"I feel you have me categorised as something I am not."

"I feel I've categorised you pretty bloody well."

"Can I say anything at this stage that wouldn't frame me as a boorish misogynistic sycophant?"

"I don't know? Have you ever tried?"

The elevator pinged and the doors slid open.

"You've taken it all the wrong way…"

Eva exited and turned on Bishop. "But that's the problem, isn't it? You and all those in your exclusive boys' club probably say to yourself you're just joking, having a bit of fun. But when you can't have a civil conversation without throwing in a sexual innuendo you've gone beyond a joke and have become a sad parody of yourself." Eva wasn't entirely sure why she was so fired-up, but there was no stopping her. "What I'm saying, Bishop, is you're not having a joke, you *are* the joke."

Bishop grimaced but his hand shot open to stop the door from sliding shut. His face stripped of all humour it seemed her barb had cut, though it seemed he wasn't going down without a fight. "Righto. You're the paragon of the women's liberation movement but you can't see we're here because you've disregarded your own principles?"

"Excuse me?"

"You're always telling me off for my sexist ways, but do you think maybe some of that anger is misdirected? Perhaps you're hard on me because of the guilt you feel for accepting all those dresses, the jewellery and trips from Lancing, in return for giving up large chunks of yourself, what you believed in? I mean, it doesn't sound terribly suffragette, now does it?"

Fucken ouch.

"No. But nice try on misdirection by saying I'm using misdirection. You're more like Harry than you know."

Bishop stopped walking and stayed in the elevator.

Eva pointed at his key. Annoyed, she said, "This is your floor, too."

The doors began to shut. "I just remembered I have a meeting. In the lobby. With a bottle of scotch."

The doors slid noisily closed.

Eva couldn't sleep. She'd lain awake contemplating the ceiling for hours. Her final conclusion was that, yes, it definitely was a ceiling. Time well spent.

Lightning flashed and she counted the seconds before the thunder. Four kilometres. Rain pounded the window while the wind buffeted her new favourite city. There were already reports of flooding further south.

When she'd retired earlier she'd claimed it was to rest up for the mission the next day. It was also to avoid Bishop. She'd probably been too harsh on him. He represented everything she despised; the unashamed sexism, the incapacity to speak to a woman as an equal, or at the very least not as a sex object. Unfortunately, no matter how much she loathed everything he represented, there was something Eva found most horrid. She was oddly attracted to him. That was what offended her the most.

There was a confusing melange of thoughts bouncing around her brainpan. The mission itself was at the forefront, dangerous and unknown. She was already conflicted about working for MI6 to apprehend her ex-lover. Then there was Bishop. How could she be drawn to a man that represented the antithesis of everything she wanted? Maybe it was due to the stress she was under and she was looking for a form of relief. Perhaps Bishop represented the best way to release that tension. Maybe not. Either way, she'd spent a good hour chastising the bad-boy chip in her head.

In an effort to clear her head and hopefully assist with sleep, she decided to take a shower. Unfortunately her room didn't have one. The building dated back to before the time when having a private bathroom was the norm. The hotel had been luxurious, if not convenient. Luckily the bathroom down the hall had a shower with the water pressure of Niagara Falls. Eva was sure she'd used the hotel's supply of hot water, but it was worth it. She felt better.

As it was 2.00 a.m. local time, she didn't see the need to get dressed to go back to her room. She wrapped a towel loosely around her body and stepped into the hall. The door to the bathroom was an original fitting and heavy. It closed far quicker than Eva had anticipated. So quick, in fact, that she had to leap out of its way. Unfortunately she wasn't quick enough. The white towel became wedged between the door and the door frame.

"McSlutnuggets."

She tugged and tugged but the towel was firmly stuck. She tried the handle but it didn't move. It was then she remembered the bathroom required a room key. Like the one sitting neatly on top of her clothes. In the bathroom. That was locked.

Eva glanced at the empty hall. Her wet hair dripped on the ostentatious oriental carpet. Her only worldly possession was a single white towel that was impossible to dislodge from its current position.

In the following ten seconds Eva uttered every swearword she knew and invented a number of new ones. A thunderclap added to the atmosphere.

She contemplated her options, or rather, lack thereof. There was no hotel phone on the floor. She had the choice of leaving her towel behind or getting in the elevator and having a quiet nude chat with the receptionist. Not exactly up there on her list of desirable scenarios. Eva wasn't ashamed of her body, far from it, but taking her naked, tattooed form across a public hotel lobby wasn't exactly in keeping with a low profile.

There was only one choice.

Cum-absorbent waffle stompers.

She took one last look at the towel wrapped around her body

and stepped away. It fell to the floor with a soggy plop. She stood without a stitch of clothing, every inch of her feeling the cold. If anyone saw her standing in the hall they'd be able to make those two determinations for themselves.

Eva strode down the hall about ten metres and paused in front of Room 25. She placed her forehead on the cool wood. She didn't want to do it, but just as equally, didn't have a choice.

She knocked quietly on the door and waited. No response.

Eva tried again, a little louder. Again, no response.

Her third knock was less subdued, and more a pounding. Eventually she heard movement behind the door. A groggy voice murmured, "Who is it?"

"It's me. Can I come in?"

There was a pause. "Go away."

"Bishop, please…"

"I must apologise, I'm busy being terribly sexist right now, I simply don't have the capacity to entertain."

"Bishop, you don't understand–"

"I'm in no mood for your feminist abuse, Ms Destruction. We have a mission tomorrow, er, today. Please go away."

"Bishop…"

"Go."

She realised she was gritting her teeth.

"Bishop…I'm naked."

The door flew open with a *whoosh* of a jet engine. Eva did her best to cover herself. One hand over her genitalia and her other arm attempting to cover her breasts. Bishop wasn't attempting to cover anything. He was, like her, completely naked. Unlike her, however, he had no compunction about standing in front of her in his birthday finest.

"Christ, did you strip off to open the door?"

A flash of lightning silhouetted him against the window, a flashbulb moment highlighting his muscular physique. Eva blinked to return her eyes back to normal light levels. She promised herself she wouldn't look down. Well, she'd already seen it, so she promised not to look again. But she did.

Oh my.

It seemed Bishop could back up his swagger and have plenty left over.

"My eyes are up here Ms Destruction."

"Mmmm?" She shook her head. "Yeah, uh, I took a shower and got locked out. No key, no towel. Can I have yours? Please. A towel. Not a key. A towel. Thanks."

Bishop placed his hands on his hips. "Quite the predicament." His self-satisfied grin was unbearable. He was loving every second of it.

Eva repeated in her mind, Don't look down. Don't look down.

She looked down.

This wouldn't have happened if she'd known Paul's room number. If she'd been able to knock on his door he'd have thrown a towel at her and never peeped in fear that Nancy would somehow find out. Bishop wasn't Paul.

"Towel," Eva growled.

"My, you are demanding when you're naked, aren't you? I like it."

It seemed they were having some sort of naked Mexican stand-off. She was about to unleash a tirade when Bishop opened his cupboard and held out a towel. He made no movement towards her. Taking the towel would mean moving closer and exposing herself. The grin on his face told her he was perfectly well aware of that fact. *Git.*

Screw it.

Eva dropped both hands, exposing herself fully. Bishop's grin morphed into something less arrogant. He took his time exploring her body. He appeared to like what he saw.

She stepped forward and grabbed the towel. Bishop held onto it. They both clasped an end, a minor tug-of-war. Eva took another step forward until their faces were nearly touching. She could smell his masculine scent and the scotch on his breath.

She stared into his eyes. Huskily she said, "You're enjoying this aren't you?"

"How could I not? Eva, by any measure, you're a stunning

woman, an amazing woman. You're in my room in the middle of the night. Naked."

There was no mention of her brain in the compliment, but she was okay with it. She wasn't exactly thinking with hers.

He tucked a lock of stray wet hair behind her ear. "I think that is a pretty accurate summation of enjoyment. I apologise if I've come off as a chauvinist bore. I thought we were playing. I'll be much more attentive to your desires from now on, if you'll let me."

Every atom of her body screamed at her to grab him and kiss him. Ignoring the man he was, Eva had desires, she needed release. She had no idea what the next few days would hold, or even if she'd be alive at the end of the week. Their respiration became deeper, panting.

She leaned further in, tilting her head slightly. She murmured, "Fucking bad boys."

Throatily, he asked, "Why am I a bad boy?"

"A gentleman would have handed me the towel straight away."

He leaned in. "Then the gentleman," his nose brushed her ear, "would have been an idiot."

Bishop's hand slowly ran up her thigh. *Wait.* That wasn't his hand.

My god she wanted him. Old Eva would have already thrown Bishop on the bed. But that was the thing, she wasn't Old Eva. Chasing bad boys only led to heartbreak, torment or sometimes, both. No, she was better than that. She was better than him.

Eva stepped away. Bishop's mouth opened in surprise.

She nodded to the towel. "Please."

He stared at it, as if was surprised he still held it. "Indeed."

She wrapped the towel around her and opened the door. "See you tomorrow."

"As always, I look forward to it, Ms Destruction. Sleep well."

The door clicked closed behind her and she exhaled. Had she just grown? Had she royally messed up? She didn't know.

The one thing she did realise was that she still didn't have a room key. That would mean she'd need to head to reception. At least she was less exposed. Eva strode towards the elevator trying to position both the towel and her face to convey the greatest amount of dignity possible.

～

The next morning, the hotel restaurant was practically empty. She wasn't sure if it was due to a special arrangement, everyone out assessing the storm damage or if the hotel wasn't that popular. The only other diner was situated at the far corner devouring the huge meal before him.

Eva helped herself to a bowl of Rice Bubbles and sat opposite the man. She dropped her backpack on the chair beside and Angelis stopped shovelling in bacon long enough to wish her a good morning.

"Been Station Chief here long?"

He chewed quickly to reply. "Six years. The first two unofficially after the previous Chief disappeared with the wife of a Czech cabinet minister and never officially resigned. He eventually sent word from the Maldives, apparently he and the missus needed access to his government pension because they needed cash for cocktails while working on their tans."

"That's suspiciously un-spy-like talk."

"Oh, my dear, this whole city knows that particular sordid tale. Prague is almost Parisian in its lust for juicy gossip and I have to admit, that one is delectably sleazy."

It appeared Angelis held no grudge by being called out by Eva the previous evening. In fact, she suspected standing up to him had won him over. There was a mischievous twinkle in his eyes that Eva found enchanting. Like a favourite uncle who told the best rude jokes at family gatherings.

As he sliced into a tomato, he asked, "I'm dying to know, the name. Is it real or do you partake in a spot of roller derby?"

She smiled. It was more polite than most of the questions she usually received.

"Real. Well, real enough. My mum changed her last name as

some sort of feminist statement back in the day. When she finally had me she thought adding Eva was some kind of political declaration."

There was no mention of the fact that she hadn't spoken to her mother in the years leading up to her death. Eva shrugged. "I didn't choose the name, I just lived with it."

He frowned. "I was looking for something a little less pedestrian."

"Aren't we all?"

He raised his fork in agreement. Angelis' face suddenly fell. He leapt away from the table, stumbling backwards. She twisted to see what he was staggering from. Storming through the restaurant door surged three black-clad figures wearing balaclavas.

Eva reeled around to ask if this was some kind of a test. When Angelis drew his gun she had her answer. Before she could do anything, Angelis' chest exploded in a spurt of red. His body flew backwards and hit the wall.

She dove under the nearest table and covered her head with her hands. Angelis was dead and she'd soon join him.

Who the hell were these men? They didn't act like Harry's security force, she doubted they'd kill a man in front of her. Then who?

Eva had never been so petrified in her life. She could see Angelis' gun lying on the floor about three metres away, but froze in fear. Even if she wasn't petrified, there was no way she could take down three heavily armed attackers. All that training wasted.

Heavy boots clomped their way towards her. Eva shook her head. She wasn't one to pray, but wished with all her might to be somewhere, anywhere else. Her fists balled. *No.* If she was going to die she'd go out swinging.

The table she cowered under was kicked away. She glanced up to see an Uzi aimed at her. The figure held a finger to his ear, and in thickly-accented English, said, "Target acquired."

His fingers flexed on the trigger. The hot barrel burned into her temple.

CHAPTER TWENTY

Eva heard a small pop. A tiny one. Then another. A fraction of a second later the assassin's head burst apart. One second he had a face, the next it was gone. His lifeless husk collapsed to the floor like a marionette with cut strings.

She raised her head and witnessed another gunman fall. At the door a lone dark figure rushed towards her, gun raised.

"Are you injured?"

"No, I'm...I'm okay."

"How many are there?" Bishop shouted, his gun sweeping the room.

"Three."

Bishop crouched. "Bollocks."

A shadow crept into the doorway where Bishop had been and Eva gasped. She needn't have bothered. It was Paul. A gun in her friend's hand seemed so unnatural, so otherworldly that she had a hard time believing it. It was like seeing your grandmother in a sex dungeon – it didn't connect. The way he held himself, it wasn't natural for Paul either.

Without a word or even a gesture exchanged, the two took a side of the dining hall each, their guns scanning the room. Eva slid across the floor until she reached Angelis' gun. As soon as her fingers wrapped around the grip, she was more secure, less fearful. And, most importantly, enabled to exact vengeance.

Scurrying footsteps echoed from the end of the room Paul and Bishop had come through. The assassin leapt through the door as it was peppered with gunfire from the two. They were too slow, he made it through without being hit. Bishop ran after him.

Paul knelt beside her. "You're unhurt?"

"Angelis, he's…"

"I saw. Evie, are you alright?"

"But your friend…"

"Will be mourned later. The last thing he'd want is for us to sit around lamenting his passing and being shot in the goolies. He'd say, 'get your lazy arses moving'. He was an awfully practical bastard. Now come on."

Paul wrenched her from the floor and virtually flung her towards the exit. She shook him off and retrieved her backpack. She slipped it on as Paul propelled her onward. They paused at the door. She felt sick.

Bishop bounded in breathlessly. "Not that way."

Eva snuck a glimpse around the door. The foyer was filled with balaclava-clad assassins. There must have been at least eight of them, all of their guns trained on the three of them. Paul and Bishop fired indiscriminately, causing the attackers to dive for cover. It would slow them, but there was no way it would be enough to stop so many.

Paul checked his magazine and nodded at Eva. "Take her out through the kitchen, I'll cover you."

Bishop shook his head. "You go with her, she's your friend."

"And because she's my friend, she's going with you." Paul sneered grimly. "I'm not a field man, never have been. If she's going to survive this, she goes with you." He fired four times. The shots were wild and poorly aimed. His grip was all wrong and he winced every time he pulled the trigger. Paul was right, he was no field man. "That's final. Call it an order if it makes you feel better."

"Do I get a say in this?" she asked indignantly.

198

Paul grinned, more genuinely this time. "No, you really don't." His big bear arm wrapped around her in a lopsided hug. "I love you Evie. Now fuck off."

She was prepared to protest the point, but Bishop had other ideas. "You heard the man."

He pulled Eva to her feet. As Bishop dragged her away, she struggled and broke free of his grip. His hand clasped her arm again, harder this time. "The longer we wait, the more likely everyone will die. Do you want to distract Paul in the middle of a firefight? Operatives are on the way, they'll come in from behind, opening a new front. He'll be okay, Eva. But if you stay, you'll place Paul between them and you, and by the looks of it you're what they really want. They had no issue with murdering a Station Chief to get to you, so the sooner we get you out, the sooner Paul will be safe. So you need to move. Now."

Her body sagged as she realised she wouldn't be winning the argument. Bishop tossed Paul a magazine and led the way.

With a grimace, Bishop said, "Just like old times."

Paul snorted. "I hated the old times. Go."

They ran towards the kitchen and she took one last glance at Paul. He fired single shots, deliberate, focussed. She doubted she'd ever see him again. The thought almost paralysed her, but Bishop pushed her on. Eva wanted to be sick. How could she leave her friend behind like that? As if reading her mind, her companion positively carried her away. She swallowed hard, fighting the wave of tears forming. Eva wondered what she'd say to her best friend. How could you apologise for causing the death of someone's husband?

Bishop and Eva slammed their backs to the wall on either side of the kitchen door.

He nodded towards the gun in her hand. "Safety off?"

"Never went on."

"Good girl." He winked. "Stay close to my gorgeous arse and you'll be fine."

From the far end of the room there was a series of shouts and an escalation in gunfire. Bishop shoved her through the door.

Smoke filled the kitchen. Pans billowed vile black vapour, food burning unattended. At the first sound of gunfire the staff probably scrambled out leaving everything to burn on stovetops.

They crouched their way to the only door at the far end of the galley. Their guns were held at torso height, ready.

Sunlight shone under the door frame. Without preamble, Bishop kicked the door open and leapt into the void. No gunfire. He aimed his weapon at every window, corner and rooftop. He seemed pleased enough to jerk his head for her to follow.

The thin cobblestone alleyway was quiet enough, but Eva knew they were far from safe. Bishop raised his gun and yelled, "Down!" He fired three shots at the rooftop. It was a distinct pattern. He'd taught her the technique. One head, followed by two heart. Brutal. Effective.

A body fell in the alleyway with a stomach-churning thud. Bishop scanned the rooftop for more. "We need to get out of here." His gun raked the skyline. "We're sitting ducks wearing t-shirts sponsored by Target."

She tugged his sleeve and pointed to the only thing in the laneway. "Over there, the little Skoda 130."

Bishop shook his head. "No keys."

Eva rolled her eyes. She sprinted to the rusting once-yellow car. She rested her back on the driver's side window and in one swift movement used her elbow to smash the glass. She opened the door and shook off her backpack. From the front pocket she pulled out a flick knife and threw the backpack into the back seat. She deftly pried open the steering column cover and pushed aside two of the three bundles of wires. With the remaining bundle she cut the red battery wire then the brown. She sheared two centimetres of plastic off both and twisted them together. The radio came on and she turned it off. She then cut and stripped the blue wire. She sparked it against the exposed battery wire and the engine roared to life.

She unlocked the passenger door for Bishop. "Come on Gorgeous Arse, get in."

He slid into the passenger side. "We didn't teach you that."

"You're right, but I'm sure you didn't get all your unlawful skills from MI6."

Eva put the car in gear and released the handbrake.

Downcast, Bishop said, "Well, I did actually."

A shake of her head. "You guys seriously need to expand your hiring practices."

Bishop's eyes darted between her and the steering wheel. "Maybe I should drive."

Eva sneered. "Why, because I'm a girl?"

"No, it's, ah, I did a course."

"A half-day defensive driver's course has nothing on me, baby."

She put her foot down. The pre-end of the Cold War Skoda sped along the alleyway and Bishop's hand fumbled for the grab handle. When they reached the road, Eva wrenched the wheel and narrowly missed two black Humvees bowling down the street. She didn't exactly know where she was headed, but she was getting there in a hurry.

During her preparation for the mission she'd managed to commit a map of Prague to memory, but with adrenaline pumping she found it hard to translate actual streets to map references. To clear her mind and put herself slightly more at ease, she asked, "What car colour would you call this? Diarrhoea yellow?"

Bishop ignored her and used his mobile. It went unanswered and he punched the dash. Eva glanced in her rear-view mirror and spat, "Jizzlobsters."

"What?"

"You remember ages ago when we passed those Hummers?"

"Like, two seconds ago?"

"Yeah, then. They, ah, seem to be chasing us."

Bishop's head whipped around and saw the black monoliths careening towards them. "Shit."

"Mine was better."

Bishop opened the glove box and pulled out an old folding map. She didn't need the help. Able to get her bearings she had a firmer idea of what street they were on.

She planted her foot to the floor and the engine gave her everything it had. The car screeched in protest wanting to be placed into fifth but she needed the torque. She took the next corner at speed, taking a solid racing line. The car held firm. At least the tyres had adequate grip. Especially in the post-storm wet.

She made a small amount of ground on their pursuers. Either the drivers of the Hummers were too tentative or inexperienced. Either way, Eva needed to choose a route with the most corners if they were going to have any chance outrunning them. Given the state of the elderly car, it seemed a stretch.

They still had no idea who had killed Angelis and why they were after her. All she knew was they weren't altogether too friendly. But who? Then an odd thought struck her. There was one way she could exclude Harry from being part of this.

Bishop gazed up from the map and pointed forward. "Keep heading west, we can meet up with the secondary team at–"

Yanking the wheel the car did a sharp turn onto a smaller street. She narrowly missed a fallen branch from the night's storm.

"What the hell are you doing? Go west!"

Eva concentrated on her driving so could only imagine the expression she was receiving. She gulped as she narrowly scraped through the gap between a parked car and another coming the other way. "We'll head west, but I have to make a minor detour first."

"There's no time for sightseeing."

She glanced at the rear-view mirror. Both Hummers slowed to get past the parked car, but soon made up for lost ground. The vehicles were impractical for Prague's ancient winding streets. She had to assume they were American. Brute strength versus practicality.

Eva was giving it everything she had, but they would close the gap soon enough. Distant cracks could be heard over the howling engine. The car shook as it was pockmarked with gunfire. Bishop wound down his window and returned fire.

With his head halfway out the window, he yelled, "I hope you know what you're doing."

"As much as I always do."

The two exchanged glances. Bishop regarded her in horror. Eva tried to appear as adorable as possible.

She tore the wheel and careened towards her objective. With a *crash* the rear window was shot out. Bishop fired again then collapsed into the passenger seat.

"Gave up?"

"Out of bullets."

"No buwets?" Eva said in her best Bugs Bunny voice.

Bishop stared at her blankly.

"You seriously need to...," she barely missed a tram that had stopped to pick up passengers, "...work on your pop culture references." Once the car had straightened, she held up Angelis' gun. "Want mine?"

"No point. Armoured. We'll need it when they catch up to us. Let's see what we've got."

Bishop leaned into the back seat and rummaged around. Eva approached a roundabout knowing she'd lose precious ground.

Her eyes flicked to Bishop. "What have we got?"

"The best defensive weapons we have is a tennis racquet, several strings missing. A small ball-pein hammer for thumb-sized terrorists and this." He held up an ancient fire extinguisher. "Not sure why you'd need it in a car. It looks more suited to putting out a fire on a ye olde paddle steamer."

She'd hit the roundabout too fast. They barely missed hitting a tourist bus and bumped the lip of the roundabout, the left side of the car lifted into the air. It landed with a sickening thump, but lost little momentum. Eva hit the accelerator.

She peered behind as the Hummers careened into the intersection. The first connected savagely with the rear of a painter's van which sent ladders and paint flying. The second Hummer overtook it but smashed a Citroën out of the way. It still managed to gain on them. The first Hummer re-entered the fray close behind. Heedless of the carnage the two Hummers were closing in.

Eva wiped her nose with her sleeve. "I'll tell you why they need a fire extinguisher." She heaved the wheel and entered

Smetanovo nábreží, the roadway that ran alongside the Vltava River. "Because this Skoda has all the safety features of a piñata."

The Vltava of today was completely different to the serene river from the day before. The storm surge had seen to that. The river was fast flowing, chaotic and dangerous. She could sympathise.

Before them, the road opened up. There were no longer any turns. The Hummers were gaining. Fast. They couldn't outrun them. They would be on top of them before they reached the nearest turn off.

Eva pressed the accelerator so hard she was surprised her foot didn't go through the ancient car's floor.

"If they want to ride my arse so hard..." they darted around a slow moving BMW, "...the least they could do is pull my hair."

In acknowledgement of their current dire predicament, Bishop didn't respond. Her mind raced for options, but could only come up with one. And it wasn't great.

There was a slight bend in the road ahead. Over the sound of the increasingly strained engine, she yelled at Bishop, "Toss the extinguisher into the middle of the street."

"What? Why?"

"Just do it."

"But why?"

"Throw it out the fucking window, Bishop!"

Bishop did as he was told.

There was a loud clang as the fire extinguisher hit the asphalt. Eva took her foot off the accelerator, turned the wheel sharply and yanked the handbrake. Before the tail of the car slid out she stepped on the accelerator. The car spun in a circle on the wet road. She grabbed Angelis' pistol.

The extinguisher tumbled end over end. The Humvees zoomed towards them. In an instant the world slowed. Eva held the wheel firm and as the car spun she aimed at the extinguisher and fired two shots. She missed. The car revolved. The extinguisher rolled. The Hummers closed. On the next pass she fired two more shots. One hit. The extinguisher erupted in an explosion of white powder.

She tapped the brake, whirled the steering wheel in the opposite direction and hit the accelerator. Bishop bounced off the passenger door with an, "oof!"

Behind her, she watched as one of the Hummers emerged, roaring through the thick white fog. Too late to notice the bend in the road. The driver hit the brakes in an attempt to correct his trajectory but the second paint-splattered Humvee hurtled through the fog and rear-ended it.

The first vehicle, propelled by the second, crashed through the low railing and leapt over it. The Hummer flew in the air momentarily until it splashed into the ferociously flowing Vltava River.

The second Humvee smashed into a light pole and bounced violently backwards. She doubted it could continue the chase but wasn't hanging around to find out.

Eva drove on.

Dazed, Bishop said, "That's seriously some of the best driving I've ever seen." He paused. A wry grin crossed his lips. "From a girl."

She squinted. "If this thing had an ejector seat..."

Bishop flashed his baby blues. He touched his scalp and winced at the blood from a small wound. "Where exactly are we headed?"

"Here."

The Skoda turned a corner into the old part of Prague. She slowed as they approached the Old Town Square.

Bishop's face was confused. "Why are we...?" Then he got it. "Oh, Eva, you don't need to..."

"I need to know, Bishop. I need to."

Near the centre of the square was the huge Jan Hus statue. Due to the weather, it was more or less deserted. But not quite. In front of the memorial was a lone figure. He was dressed, as agreed, in a white trench coat. He seemed to be scanning every passing car, assessing the occupants.

She couldn't help it, an enormous wave of relief swept over her. Harry was there. Waiting. If he was waiting then he didn't send the armed men after her. They weren't his. Who they were could be answered another day, but all Eva cared about was that Harry wasn't responsible.

She couldn't be sure, but Bishop may have actually growled. "Keep moving, we can't stop here."

"I know." Eva was guilty for feeling so relieved about Harry. She felt even worse that Bishop had seen it and knew her dirty little secret.

If she wanted, she could still meet Harry. She had her backpack, after all. But none of the MI6 agents would be in place. They were incapable of nabbing him. *Would that really be so bad?* Her traitorous mind whispered.

She shoved the old car into a reluctant third gear. Another engine could be heard above theirs. A guttural, angry vehicle sound screamed from behind. Eva looked in the mirror and glimpsed a blur of colour splattered across black. The Skoda shunted violently forward from the impact of the Humvee. They mounted the sidewalk and she grappled with the wheel to keep the car on the road.

She dropped a gear and hit the accelerator. The little car jerked to attention and darted to the left to avoid another collision. The Skoda sped off with the Hummer looming large in the rear-view mirror.

At the far end of the square lights flashed. Police cars sped in their direction. Apparently their little parade of carnage had been noticed. The Humvee backed off and turned onto a side street. Eva sped on, heading back towards the Vltava.

She had tried to outrun cops before and it hadn't ended well. The previous pursuit had been brief and ended in the front window of a discount vitamin store. It was the beginning of the end for her car-thieving ways. Within months she'd distanced herself from her worst influences and had enrolled in university again.

After a couple of blocks the police car either didn't have a handle on where they were or wasn't interested in them.

"Can we head west now?" Bishop asked.

"Sure."

Eva made a series of quick turns to confuse the police just in case. They'd have to ditch the car at the earliest opportunity.

They entered a wide street parallel to the Vltava. The river was choppy and carried with it the debris from further up the river. She felt a wave of nausea wondering how the occupants of the Humvee had fared.

She turned onto Palacky Bridge and was about to bring it up with Bishop when he cried, "Look out!"

The paint-splattered Humvee crashed into the side of the tiny Skoda causing it to spin. She lost control. Nothing she did changed their direction. They careened towards an oncoming tram and they braced for impact.

The collision was vicious. The tram screeched against its track and the front of the Skoda disappeared, disintegrating on impact. The tram was knocked from its tracks and the two vehicles became one. Eva was thrown violently against her seatbelt. Bishop, who wasn't wearing one, bounced against the dash horribly. The windscreen exploded and they sprang backwards into their seats.

The world blurred and her ears rang. She was grateful to see that Bishop was still conscious. Bloody, but conscious.

The valiant car was dead. It had done its part bravely. Steam poured from under the Humvee's hood. Its motor spluttered and died. The driver attempted to restart it.

Eva frantically removed her seatbelt and slapped Bishop's arm. "We need to get out of here, now!"

He gave a vacant stare. She tried the door but the impact of the crash had fused it shut. She threw the backpack out onto the road. She crawled through the shattered windscreen and grasped Bishop under his arms. He tried to help her but appeared half-concussed. He was conscious enough to have grabbed Angelis' gun from the footwell. Finally free, they rolled onto the road.

She threw Bishop's arm around her shoulder and they limped around the derailed tram. The Humvee's engine roared to life. It had survived far better than the Skoda. There was a screech of tyres and a thunderous boom as the Humvee collided with the tram. It flipped on its side and careened towards them. The roof of the tram lurched towards them, threatening to pin them between the tram and the bridge railing. There was no way for them to outrun it. They'd be crushed.

The roof of the tram hit her square in the chest and the overhead wires from the tram struck her like a whip. She launched into the air and over the railing. The world toppled end on end. She saw water, sky, bridge. Water, sky, bridge.

Abruptly, painfully, she came to a halt, halfway between the bridge and the river. She was tangled in the tram wires, suspended precariously above the raging Vltava. Eva unleashed a primal scream. Her foot was painfully wedged in the mangled tram cables. Bishop was below her, his wrist caught amongst the tangled mass of wires. His hand had to be broken. He hung by one arm, his foot weighed down by the tram's large metal contact strip. He gazed up at her with panic-stricken eyes.

Every time he tried to unhook his wrist she screamed. The wire Bishop was bound to was wrapped around her foot. Every move he made wrenched it tighter and shot excruciating pain to her foot.

Above them, the whole structure shrieked and shuddered. They both slid another metre closer to the raging waters. The descent stopped abruptly and she screamed in agony. Eva's vision blurred around the edges and she was close to blacking out.

She looked at the ferocious river and had no doubt they'd fall and be enveloped in seconds. She could swim, but even an Olympic swimmer couldn't beat that current or avoid the mass of debris hurtling along its vicious flow.

Bishop cried out in his own pain. She was amazed he was still conscious. He was bloodied and damaged, his hand jammed amongst the wires. He swung one-handed, suspended above the river.

She did her best to sound hopeful. "Hang on, Bishop. We'll make it."

"No." Bishop looked at her dejectedly. "We won't."

He raised Angelis' gun and aimed it at Eva. She gulped.

Bishop's lips parted in a bloody, humourless grin. "Take care, Princess."

Bishop lowered the gun to just below her, above his head. She realised what he was about to do.

"No!"

He fired one shot, severing the wire that held them together, that held him above the chaos below. Bishop fell into the fiercely surging river, weighed down by the mass of wires and tangled metal.

He hit the water and disappeared from view instantly. Eva tried to keep up with where he would be in the fast flow, but he never emerged from the river.

Bishop was gone, forever.

The man she had saved and had been saved by, despised and desired was lost somewhere in the chaos of the Vltava River. There was no hope. He was too injured, the river too violent and all encompassing. She'd never again hear one of his lame double entendres.

Weak and with little left, an image flashed before her about sharing Bishop's fate. She hoped death would be quick. Apparently drowning was like going to sleep. She doubted it would be that peaceful.

Never one to give up, it took all of Eva's might to try to lift herself up. She was upright, but she didn't know for how long. Without Bishop pulling her down, she managed to unhook her ankle but had no energy to climb the metres of slippery cable. Her grip slipped and she clung desperately to the wire that cut into her hands. There was commotion above, odd shouting and noises she couldn't identify. Suddenly there was a tug on the wire and she ascended.

As she reached the edge of the bridge, a figure leaned over and reached for her.

"Looks like you could use a hand."

His strong arms pulled her to safety. Thankfully she planted her one good foot on the bridge. Her vision blurred and Eva collapsed into Harry's arms.

CHAPTER TWENTY-ONE

The pina colada made it better. And Eva didn't even like pina coladas. All she could ever think of was that horrific song.

The tropical sun caressed her bruised body. As she lay on the sunlounge overlooking the calm cobalt sea the gentle lapping of the waves lulled her into a dreamlike state.

The drugs also helped.

"You know, you shouldn't be drinking on that medication."

Harry hadn't left her side since Prague. She waved a floppy dismissive hand in his direction. He ran a reassuring hand over her leg. He always had a gentle touch.

She took another sip and closed her eyes. In reality, she wanted to forget.

The image of Bishop falling into the surging river had meant she'd been unable to sleep on the flight out of Prague. She didn't know if Paul was still alive and couldn't ask Harry to check.

Oh god, Paul. Her friend. Her best friend's husband. Was she the cause of his death? Had he died saving her like Bishop had? Why had she lived? Did she even want to any more?

Harry had anxiously brought her to see his personal physician when they'd arrived on the island. He'd prescribed Valium to help her sleep. After forty-eight hours of consciousness she'd fallen into more of a coma than sleep.

When she'd awoken Harry had suggested they relax on the beach. It was Eva who'd requested the cocktails. Her skin was so used to the English climate it was probably already burnt. She didn't care. She'd been numb since Prague.

It was like all her feelings had been turned off. She was a zombie. She was an emotionless husk. The whole spy thing had all been a bit of fun for a while, then people died. People she cared for. She wondered if she'd ever feel again. Everything since Prague had just kind of happened, she'd paid little interest.

Harry had told her how he'd found her dangling from the bridge. When he'd been waiting for her at the Old Town Square he'd seen the Humvee smash into the Skoda. He said he'd instinctively known it was Eva. Carnage tended to follow her. Even in her traumatised state she could see the sense of his conclusion. He'd called his people and they'd tried to track her. When they'd heard over the police radio about the accident on Palacky Bridge they'd sped there. When Harry found the wreckage of the Skoda he'd feared the worst. He was the one who'd found her hanging from the tram wires.

Everything else she'd managed to piece together from fragments of her sluggish memory. Harry had hoisted her into the back of his limo, the same type he always used. They'd driven to a private airfield and had taken off in his personal jet. There were a couple of minor stops along the way. The airfields were makeshift, or near enough. The refuelling was done via commercial trucks instead of official-looking airport vehicles. She assumed the airfields were abandoned and only used because Harry had arranged it. Off the books.

MI6 must think she was dead. Perhaps they'd recovered Bishop's body to emphasise the point. Maybe MI6 blamed the assassins, maybe they thought it was a terrible road accident, Eva didn't know. She wasn't sure she even cared.

The only thing she was sure of was that she was on her own. There was no help on the way.

MI6 had blown its one chance of capturing Harry and all because she'd failed. There was no possibility of tracking him either. There would be no cavalry. There would be no knight in shining armour. It was just as well. Chainmail in this heat would be a bitch.

Eva sipped her cocktail and thought about her options. Or rather, lack thereof.

She could try and find a computer and send a clandestine message, but what would she tell them? She was stuck on an island somewhere, she didn't know exactly where, but it was picturesque and they had lovely pina coladas.

Eva felt broken. The thought of moving from her sunlounge seemed impossible. She wondered if they should have left her to die in Prague. Would that have been better? Did she have any strength to go on living? She honestly didn't know. If it hadn't been for Harry scooping her up and tending to her wounds, would Eva have let herself fade away?

All this doubt and confusion because of Harry. *Bloody Harry.* She was meant to hate him. She'd sworn revenge. But there he was saving her life. Eva was out at sea and the only buoy was Harry Lancing.

Everyone had an ex in their past, someone whom logic seemed to bounce off, that you couldn't say no to. You knew you should, but there was something magnetic, something inescapable about them. They were like a piece of popcorn stuck in your teeth you can never dislodge. Harry Lancing was that kind of ex blown up to gigantic proportions.

In many ways, Harry was Eva's nemesis. The harder she fought him, the stronger her feelings became. It was illogical. But since when did the heart ever listen to the head?

Since he'd found her in Prague Harry had been so attentive, so loving. It was just like it had been. It was hard to forget the love she'd experienced with this man. It was too much like before. For a man supposedly hell-bent on destroying the world, he was spending a lot of time by the side of an ex-girlfriend. Eva was sure she hadn't earned that kind of care.

If MI6 really thought she was dead maybe she could simply disappear. Her mother was dead. Anchor could have the coffee shop. She'd miss Nancy terribly. But if she'd been the cause of her husband's death Eva was certain she'd never be able to look her best friend in the eye again.

Ever since Harry had left her for dead in his penthouse she'd been furious with him. Livid. In the weeks at MI6 she'd focused on that hate. Then why had it all fallen by the wayside in Prague when he'd held out his hand for her? He was still the same man who'd spied on her. Who'd sent armed goons into her bedroom. Why did that not seem to matter? What was wrong with her?

Was she really contemplating giving up? Everything? There was no way this was Eva. She was a warrior queen. She was a fighter. She never gave up. And yet…

It had to be a passing moment of weakness. She'd get back to hating Harry momentarily, surely. Maybe it was the drugs. Then again, what if it wasn't?

She closed her eyes and let sleep envelop her.

∽

"Better?" Harry asked, knowing perfectly well what the answer would be.

"Oh baby."

Eva licked her lips and let the ecstasy overwhelm her. It had been too long. Far too long.

Her hands clasped either side of his face. "How…?" She hesitated, "How much more have you got?"

Harry smiled down at her. "I can give you as much as you want."

Eva wasn't sure, but she may have let out a breathless *squee*.

Her breathing became shallow. She was determined to enjoy the blissful sensation while it lasted.

Harry slid his hand along her sweaty cheek. "More nuts?"

"More everything!"

He scooped another pile of crushed peanuts over her chocolate sundae followed by more whipped cream. The small private kitchen overlooking the beach had suddenly become her favourite place on Earth. After weeks of calorie-controlled uber-healthy MI6 foods, a simple dessert had permitted a brief moment where the rest of the world had fallen away.

Sitting there in her pyjamas, Eva knew she should feel guilty for it but couldn't muster the energy. Next she'd ask for pizza. Her mouth watered at the thought of it.

For the first time since Prague, she sensed tiny tendrils of normality creeping back. Her head was still clouded. Everything was out of sync, but she was beginning to feel human again.

Harry's guest house was amazing, jaw-dropping even. All sides opened to allow the sea breeze to flow through. The décor was dark wood, bohemian-like furnishings and all the finest fixtures. The gourmet kitchen had a fully-stocked walk-in pantry. There was a sunken lounge to hide in, as well as a bath into which you could invite six of your closest friends. The overall effect was luxurious, manly and everything you could ever want. Harry all over.

She was thankful Harry hadn't assumed she'd be staying with him immediately. He seemed to be taking it slow, never assuming. She'd agreed to come with him to the island, but he knew her well enough not to expect she'd be sharing his bed on the first night.

Eva wondered how long she could put it off. A full night's sleep had revived her body and cleared her muddled head. It had taken time, but she'd overcome the shattered thoughts she'd had on the beach. Giving up was not an option. Eva had a mission.

It was ridiculous to think she could live on the island, to be happy. It was naïve and she knew the initial feelings she'd had when she'd arrived were ludicrous. The logical part of her brain had come in screaming and ruined the party.

She determined her softened feelings for Harry were temporary. Regardless of her thoughts for the man, he was still hell-bent on destroying the world and rebuilding it as he saw fit. Paul had been right, it didn't matter about his aims, Harry shouldn't be allowed to succeed. If the governments of the world capitulated this time, what next? Where would it end? Would Harry become a tyrant dictating which governments fell, which ones survived because they defied or obeyed him? Despite her misgivings about democracy, it was the best system they had. One man's will should not be allowed to override the will of the people, despite his intent.

Eva was reminded of the Lord Acton quote: 'Power corrupts; absolute power corrupts absolutely'.

Although he had made her sundaes. Beautiful beautiful sundaes.

Eva was in a defiant mood. In other words, more like herself. Giving up and lying on the beach wasn't her. Would never be her. She was stronger than that. The momentary doubt when she'd first arrived had been just that, momentary. A mere blip. She had a mission. Even without Bishop or Paul she had to succeed.

The thought of Paul made her nauseous. She stomped it down. She had to.

To complete her assignment she had to become the actress. She'd never been a great one, even in the bedroom. Her brief time as a stripper taught her she could act when needed but she had no desire to be on stage and much preferred to be in the shadows. The limelight never suited her and she shunned it like an albino vampire.

She could do this. The alternative was failure and that was an option she'd never accept. Perhaps pretending to be Harry's girl-friend was the role she'd been born to play. Eva hoped she wouldn't become typecast.

She glanced up. Harry was watching her with a weird expression. She hoped he hadn't learned to read minds. "What? Do I have something on my face?"

Harry grinned. Oh how she'd missed that face of his. "No. Well, actually you do, but that's not it. I'm glad you're happy. I haven't seen you this way since... I haven't seen it in a long time. It's nice to see."

"Thanks," she said wiping every inch of her face.

How did he do it? Make her so at ease so quickly? She'd woken in his ridiculously huge guest bed and there he was at the door, offering to make her breakfast. Anything she wanted. He had probably been expecting to cook a batch of his famous pancakes, but she had reminded him he'd offered her anything. So chocolate sundaes it was.

As she finished the bowl, he asked, "Can I make you a coffee?" and they both laughed.

Harry knew better than to ever attempt to make Eva a coffee.

"I flew in your favourite Ethiopian beans last week. There's a Lamazoco in the main house."

"Thanks." Eva licked the spoon. "How many buildings are there on this island?"

"There's the main house, five guest houses like this one. Staff quarters, the power plant and a couple of other buildings on the far side of the island."

Somewhat evasive, but she didn't want to push too early. She remembered seeing the expanse of the island when they landed. It was larger than she'd imagined when he first told her he was taking her to a tropical hideaway. She still had no idea what ocean they were in. She thought it best not to appear too inquisitive.

Eva thought she was doing well. She acted as natural as possible. Sure, it wasn't an Oscar-worthy performance, but it would do. Perhaps a Daytime Emmy. The most important thing was that Harry thought she was genuine.

The island was beautiful. And isolated. There seemed to be nothing to the horizon in any direction. Except for one thing.

"What about the other island?"

"Sorry?"

"I saw another island when we were coming in. Is there anything there?"

"No. I haven't been over there, to be honest. We've had a hell of a time setting this lot up."

"Why did you exactly? I mean, set this up. I'm guessing you didn't run an extension cord from your house."

"We tried the extension cord, it kept on getting snagged on chair legs and scared the cat when we tried to loop the cord over.

No, we run off thermal power. Less of a carbon footprint, almost limitless supply. More than adequate for our needs."

"But the logistics to set this up would have been a bitch. Why go to all this trouble?"

"Because everywhere else has been so hospitable? I think you recall the lovely reception I had last time I was in London."

They both looked away at that. Painful memories for them both.

He continued. "I wanted somewhere I wouldn't be swayed by the hosting government, or more likely dissuaded. We are a tiny nation unto ourselves here. It's the last place anyone will look."

Eva's heart sank at that. "Does it have a name, this island?"

"It did once. I changed it. It is now known as Nice Bum."

"No it isn't."

"You're right, it's not." He put on his serious face. "I've always referred to it as Eva's Island."

～

The path between the guest house and the main house was curved so there was no direct line of sight. Palms overhung the paved footpath providing shade, but they also made guests feel like they were walking through a tropical paradise. Which is exactly what it was.

Harry had left her to get dressed and encouraged her to roam the island. She veered off the main path and followed an unmarked one. After a short distance she'd discovered a hidden oasis built next to a small stream. There was a fire pit and several hammocks strung between palm trees. It was far too inviting.

Eva lay on a hammock. The wind meandering through the trees swung her gently. She listened to the brook and the distant sound of waves crashing on the beach. The chaos of her previous life seemed like a fever dream, someone else's life. She could even forget her current deception towards Harry. Right then it was as if she'd always been there.

For a brief moment she was content. Her mind clear.

Eva was determined to complete her mission. She needed a plan. She needed to contact MI6. The only practical way she could determine was to find a computer and send a clandestine message. Her least favourite subjects at MI6 had been computer-related. Computers and Eva had never seen eye to eye. She never saw the point. Like leaf-blowers and white chocolate.

She decided to turn her mind to the best way to gain access to a computer, tablet or phone. Thoughts of computers weren't exactly stimulating and it was so lovely and warm. She drifted off to sleep.

She awoke when a shadow fell across her.

A deep guttural voice said, "You owe me an apology."

Eva shot up. Holding up her hand to shield her eyes from the sun, she asked, "For?"

"For this damn scar, whore."

Van Buren loomed over her, which was an effort for the short troll. His disfigured face showing the recent prize for interrupting a screwing Eva. She still thought he'd gotten off lightly.

"Yeah, no. That's not going to happen for all sorts of reasons."

Her blissful moment of peace disappeared faster than anticipated.

The Security Chief stood before her in barely restrained rage. If it wasn't for Harry's presence on the island she was sure Van Buren wouldn't have hesitated to place a bullet between her eyes. With or without the use of a gun.

But Harry was present. And if she was playing a role, she may as well play it to the hilt.

"Listen VB, I suggest you stop blocking my sun and stow your homoerotic frustrations, okay? I'm on the island at Harry's request. He wants me here, so get used to it. If you have an issue with it, how about we go up to the main house and let him choose. You or me. Do you have that much faith that Harry's going to choose you? Wanna gamble on that one, buddy?"

His knuckles turned white. "You're nothing to him, bitch. You're a pet. A distraction. Don't dare to assume you mean *anything* to him. He knows you're only good for one thing and that's the shit between your legs."

Why did men continue to distil a woman's worth down to only one thing? Had history not shown the countless wealth every woman brought to the world? That *one thing* was the most creative power humans had. Men could only destroy, it took a woman to create. Why did society continue to let it be so easily dismissed? Why did it not smash the trite worthless argument every time it reared its ugly head? Probably because weak spineless men like Van Buren continued to steal oxygen.

Eva tilted her head and smiled a viper's smile. "Good for one thing, eh? I have to congratulate you, VB. I underestimated you, I really did. I never thought you could count that high. Well done you."

She wondered if a pat on the head would be too much. Probably. She did it anyway.

Van Buren reeled backwards swatting away Eva's hand. His face flared fiery red.

"Such the little Aussie wise ass, aren't you? You think you know him. Think he trusts you, yeah?" He snorted. "I bet you believe he stumbled into your café by chance the day you met. Just wandered by for no reason. You really have no fucking clue, do you? Like hell he trusts you, you know nothing." He sneered. "You think you're untouchable, don't you? Good, keep thinking that. I can bide my time. And when he's bored with his skinny little bitch of a play thing, and he will, believe me, I'll enjoy feeding you to the sharks. Feet first and slowly."

"You're sweet, but I'm already spoken for. I'll tell you what. You keep those sharks hungry. I'm sure they won't discriminate between a bitch whore and an overcompensating Security Chief when the time's right."

It was a good performance, the aggrieved girlfriend. Worthy of a Golden Globe, Eva thought.

Van Buren pursed his lips and shook with anger. He must have determined that if he spoke to her for a moment longer he'd end up strangling her. He stormed off, a dark cloud hovering above his head.

In direct contrast to her outward calm, her hands shook. Van

Buren had terrified her. Never in her life had she been face to face with so much hatred, so much anger directed at her. He was scarcely under control. Given the slightest provocation, Eva had no doubt he'd kill her in an instant. Vomit rose in the back of her throat.

The island paradise wasn't as idyllic as it first appeared. A flock of tropical birds flew overhead. She needed to calm herself.

Mumbling, she sang, "If you like pina coladas and getting caught in the rain…"

～

Cole rubbed his bloodshot eyes. "At least we're on the island. I was beginning to think this story would go on forever. Like Lord of the Rings or something."

Decker and Eva stared at him.

"Because it was a long story." Cole's face took on a reddish tinge. "That never seemed to end…" He shifted in his seat and coughed into his hand. "Right. Can we get back to the explosions? I want to know why–"

"Who attacked you in Prague, Ms Destruction?" Decker interrupted. "You never mentioned who it was. You said it wasn't Lancing, then who?"

Eva flexed her hands. The white cable ties were restricting her circulation.

"I later learned it was the same group who attacked us in Iceland."

The two naval officers leaned forward.

She needed a flick blade. Even a small one would do. If she could remove the ties she could grab the gun in front of Decker. She'd then have leverage to bargain with. She was in a far worse position than when she first woke up with Cole in the room. And worst of all, she was running out of story.

She sniffed. "Before I answer, we're trading information, remember? I told you about the spy like you asked. Now you tell me about this sham of an interrogation. Cole seems to be asking the right questions. What caused the explosions and such. Why don't you care Decker? Why do you give a shit about how well I knew a spy or my feelings for Harry? Who are you reporting all this to? I'm certain it's not Navy brass. Then who?"

Decker's index fingers rested on his chin in an attempt to appear contemplative. Eva didn't buy it. She perceived the flash of panic in his eyes. What was he hiding?

He blew out slowly. "If I tell you, will you tell us about the teams in Iceland and Prague?"

"Yes."

Cole tilted his head. It seemed he wanted to know why the interview had gone off the rails as much as she did.

She attempted to still every atom in her body.

Decker took on a bombastic tone. "The person who has been feeding me these questions is the President of the United States of America."

"I'm...excuse...what now? And by what now, I mean what now?"

Decker folded his arms. "That's what I have been told. The line of questioning I'm following comes, indirectly, from the Big Man himself. If you have a problem with it, I suggest you take it up with him."

Eva repeated it in her head over and over. The President, the most powerful human being on the planet, was asking her questions. Indirectly, but even so...

She wasn't that important, surely? It was far too much to comprehend. Little Eva Destruction was being interrogated by proxy by the President of the United States. It had to be a ploy. Had to be.

"So," Decker said interrupting her disbelief, "if you don't mind, how about we get on with it, eh? Where were the assassins from?"

"Huh? Oh..." She tried to steady herself. "They, ah, they were Russian. Or at least a faction thereof."

"I'm afraid you're going to have to expand on that. Why were the Russians trying to assassinate you?"

"No, not me, Harry. Iceland was a straight-up assassination

attempt on him. Same with the Bulgarian in the alleyway, although that was pretty amateur. Prague was trying to get to him through me. At least, that's how Harry explained it. Back when Iceland happened, the Russian government believed Harry was a threat. They must have known what he had on them and wanted him gone. The Prague thing was after the government had fallen, so Harry assumed it was an old faction left over that wanted him dead. That's why they wanted me as bait. They were going to murder Harry. Their corrupt regime had already collapsed so all they had left was revenge."

For Eva, the wounds of her time in Prague would never heal. For a brief moment it had been her favourite city in the world. Now thoughts of it brought nothing but pain.

"So you arrived on the island," Decker resumed his business tone, "then what?"

"Then," Eva said with a sigh, "everything went to hell."

CHAPTER TWENTY-TWO

"You're invited to dinner at the main house, Milady," Harry said with a bow and a large dollop of irony.

Eva stretched on the guest house couch and scratched under her arm. Just like a lady.

She felt better in herself, despite the run-in with Van Buren. The chocolate sundaes had worked miracles. Energised, she was ready to get cracking on her mission.

She was more like her old self, and that self was in the mood to be cheeky.

"That's what you call it? The main house? Not anything else?"

"What would you have me call it?" he asked.

"Oh, I don't know. Something cool like the Forbidden Citadel or Skull Fortress. Something befitting an evil lair."

Harry asked mockingly, "You think I'm a supervillain?"

Eva counted off her fingers, "Mysterious identity, check. Hideously rich, check. Brings down governments, check. Threatens world leaders, check. Has secret island hideaway and personal security force, check and check. Has slightly unstable and aggressive 2IC, check."

She hadn't mentioned her run-in with Van Buren to Harry yet.

She intended to hold that one close to her chest until needed. Also, not running to Harry might be the first of many steps to get Van Buren on side. Possibly not. She doubted they'd ever be poker buddies. If she never caught sight of the little weasel again she'd be happy, but at some stage she would need to deal with him, one way or the other.

Eva took a sip of her ice tea and waved a finger at Harry. "Face it, dude, you have an evil lair. You're Lex sodding Luther."

Harry did his best to appear offended, but it was mitigated when he failed to hide a smirk. For a fleeting moment, it was like old times. Good times. It didn't last. There could be no future. Even if she was inclined to really be with Harry and not just act like it, the world would end it long before she managed to sabotage their relationship.

If Eva were with a guy called Harry from Accounts they might have a shot. But with the world's most wanted status, assassins, not to mention her own position as a temporary MI6 agent, she anticipated a few more hurdles than the usual relationship. Not that she was searching for one, of course. She had an assignment to complete. Van Buren had been the dose of ugly reality she needed.

In spite of all this, Eva still enjoyed Harry's company. He was magnetic, charming and made her feel like the most important person in the world. Hell, he'd named an island after her. And a castle.

Besides the occasional reassuring caress Harry had kept his hands to himself. He was waiting for her to let him know when she was ready. Harry may have taken the lead on most things when they dated, their travel destinations, accommodation, where to eat, but Eva took care of the important things. In the bedroom she was the one to steer that particular ship. But she had to admit, Harry had brought some game to the table. And bed. And closet, bathroom, terrace, plane, cloakroom and opera balcony.

Even with his years of isolation, she highly suspected he hadn't lived like the monk he claimed. He was too skilful for that. Harry slowed everything down, taught her to take her time. She didn't have to run headlong to reach her goal, and could slow up, enjoy the journey as much as the destination. The feel, the smell, the taste, the sensation; taken as a whole or in the minutest detail.

He was, by far, the most considerate lover she'd ever known. Generous without being timid, he knew when to take control, when the moment called for it. Harry had also discovered a part of her neck, just below her ear, which when licked, sucked or nibbled at the right moment would send her crazy. No one had ever found it before. Even thinking about it made her toes curl.

Realising her mind was wandering, Eva reminded herself that she was playing a part. Admittedly, she was playing it well. She may as well choose a dress and start writing her acceptance speech thanking The Academy because that baby was hers.

That reminded her of something. "Is the dinner formal?"

"Very," he said in mock seriousness.

"I don't have anything to wear."

"I don't recall having an issue with that previously." Harry did his best George Clooney. He strolled off to the right where he'd parked his golf cart, the island's only mode of transport. He brought back a dress on a hanger. Actually, it wasn't a dress. It was a work of art. Jade, silk, long and elegant. It was the most beautiful dress Eva had ever seen.

"It's from Elie Saab's latest spring collection. Haute couture, daahling!" Harry carefully laid it beside her. "I thought you might also need a killer pair of heels to go with it." He picked up a large box with *Christian Louboutin, Paris* on the lid.

Eva may have squeaked. She wasn't sure. Maybe Harry was reading her mind because this would be the perfect Oscars outfit. It was breathtaking.

"I'll see you for dinner in an hour. Enjoy your pretties."

Harry made to leave. She wondered if there was a law against making out with apparel.

As he reached the golf cart Harry snapped his fingers, remembering something. "Oh, I almost forgot. I have something else for you."

"Listen, Harry, if it's another dress, they're really quite beautiful, but…"

"Oh, no not that. Wait."

From the passenger side he lifted the black bag. It was filthy and torn. But intact. *How?*

"Sorry, I should have had them leave it in your room when you first arrived, but it slipped my mind. I had a couple of things going on. I don't know if there's anything of use in there, but it's all yours."

Harry held it out for her. Like Frankenstein's monster she lumbered forward. She took it from him with a weak smile and held it at arm's length. Finally she placed it on the couch, not believing it real.

"My guys found it on the bridge in Prague. I assumed you'd want it. We don't exactly have a vast library here."

Harry said his goodbye and drove off. Eva stared at the backpack.

Everything was still in there. A change of clothes, her favourite lock picking kit, books and a bright pink frilly umbrella. She'd thankfully had the good sense not to pack the history of MI6 book she'd been reading. She rummaged around the bottom and found a small wooden box. It was damaged, probably during the crash. She extracted the pen. It was bent. It appeared worse for wear and she doubted it even worked. Without thinking, she clicked it.

Nothing happened.

No ninjas burst through the ceiling. The Eighty-Second Airborne didn't kick down the front door. Eva would have to rely on her computer skills after all.

She really was screwed.

∾

The chef cleared her plate and she followed it out of the dining room with her eyes longingly. "That was...bloody amazing."

"And to think I found him cooking for tourists on a junk in Halong Bay. Chen can make even the most basic ingredients into a sumptuous banquet." Harry patted his napkin on his lips. "Since he's been cooking for me he's had ridiculous offers to open his own restaurants in New York but turned them all down."

"That's loyalty."

"Not really. I pay him a preposterous amount of money. That's not loyalty, its capitalism."

Eva rolled her tongue around her mouth determined to savour every last skerrick of flavour. They were seated at a booth in a dining room that would put most of those New York restaurants to shame. The warm wood panelling, velvet drapes, old-style wooden chairs. It certainly wasn't in keeping with the tropical theme. It reminded her of John's Grill in San Francisco. She and Harry had dined there one night and Eva had fallen in love with its old world charm and history. He'd even offered to buy her the original Maltese Falcon on display. It occurred to her that the décor may not be coincidental. She chose not to mention it.

It had been obvious to her as soon as she entered the main house that Harry had been building this outpost for some time. It was a cathedral to modernity and luxury. It certainly wasn't a few huts slapped together. It had been executed with an unbelievable eye for detail. The house was opulent and magnificent.

She had to wonder why she never heard about the island when they dated. This wasn't something Harry had thrown together since London. How long had he been planning all this?

The chef interrupted her thoughts by announcing their next course would be in five minutes. Eva salivated. Pavlov would have been proud.

Thankfully there was no sign of Van Buren. In fact, there had been little sign of anyone. Apart from Harry and Chen, Eva had only seen one other human, a butler who had escorted her to the dining room. She had to expect there were more than Harry, Van Buren, Chen, the butler and Harry's physician on the island. She assumed Harry wouldn't be fixing his own toilet. Although the idea did amuse her.

Harry, as usual, was excellent, attentive company. The night had all been extremely pleasant. There was something on Eva's mind that would make it significantly less so. She couldn't let it wait any longer.

Eva picked up the glass of Spanish Dominio de Pingus wine and took a polite sip. She then gulped down the rest of the glass and refilled. It was an attempt to brace herself for what was to come. There was one burning question she'd failed to ask since Harry had rescued her in Prague. Something that had scorched her insides since it happened. The image forever forged in her brain.

If she was to play the part of the returned ex-girlfriend, there was a question in that particular script. Strictly to appear as the upset ex, nothing more, of course.

"So, Harry…"

"Hmm?"

"Here's a fun question." Eva traced lines in the tablecloth with her knife. "How could you leave me to die at the penthouse?"

Harry's expression was frozen in a grim half-smirk. It was as if he'd pressed pause on his face while he went off to make a tea and cultivate an appropriate response. Finally he spluttered and guzzled a glass of water. "Well, that came out of nowhere."

"Sorry for blurting. You know me, when something's on my mind. One of those questions that occasionally pops up. Like what happened to Richie Cunningham's brother or why the Germans are so obsessed with reserving poolside seating. So, uh, why did you want me to die?"

Harry inhaled deeply and smoothed his already straight trousers.

"Eva, I didn't…I never…look." He blew a lungful of air towards the ornate ceiling. "I was rattled. When I saw you with that man I panicked. I hit the button and a split second later regretted it. The single biggest regret of my life, and I've been to a Hootie and the Blowfish concert." The attempt at levity fell flat. It probably wasn't the time to make light of leaving the person sitting opposite you to die. He forged on. "I tried everything to reverse it, Eva, I did. Screamed at it, punched it, everything, but it was a one-trip deal, straight to the basement. Van Buren was already there and bundled me out. I kicked and screamed the whole way, but he was following standing orders, my orders actu- ally. I think I gave him a fat lip."

"The poor baby."

"I'm so sorry Eva. I've relived that moment every day since. It is honestly the biggest regret of my life. That's why I was so relieved when you contacted me. I needed to start making amends. I know I have far to go, I do. That's why I didn't assume you'd want to stay at the main house. Small steps. I intend on making it up to you every day. It will take years, the rest of our lives. If you'll let me."

It was a good answer. Not a great answer, but good enough. She hadn't made her mind up if she believed it or not. Academi- cally, Eva could understand poor split-second decisions. She understood regret. She understood hurt. While it was all logical in a theoretical sense, her heart was not along for the ride. *Not that it had to be*, she reminded herself. She only had to *appear* like she cared.

Chen materialised and filled the void in conversation with the next course. Eva picked up her fork but she'd lost her appetite. She put down her cutlery. "I wasn't with that man. I didn't know him."

Harry shrugged nonchalantly. "You looked pretty cosy to me."

"I'd met him once, the spy. He tried to warn me off you when we first started dating. It didn't take. That was the only time I'd seen him before, honest."

Historically, Harry had been pretty good at reading her. She hoped sprinkling in truth would make her act more believable.

"Yet you let him into my home, Eva. Colluded with him." Harry lowered his gaze. "Betrayed me."

Eva shook her head. "Nope. Too soon to play the guilt card. I'm talking about being wronged here, okay? I go first. You'll get your turn."

And he did. For the next hour they opened old scars. It was brutal. Food went uneaten. The looks Eva and Harry exchanged were enough for Chen to simply remove the still-full plates and leave them to it. There were raised voices, accusatory fingers and more than a few truth bombs lobbed. It was a knock-down, drag-out affair. No one was coming out unscathed.

If she was to be convincing, Harry shouldn't be let off the hook lightly. Her role dictated she act as habitually as possible, and that meant she would make Harry pay for leaving her behind. The spying. Everything.

Eva found the role so natural she wondered if she was acting at all.

~

Chen hadn't called it anything, but she viewed it as a kind of mutant Eton Mess. Every spoonful was like a tiny little mouth orgasm. She told Harry this and he laughed so hard cream came out his nose.

After two bottles of exquisite wine and four ports, the earlier unpleasantness was more or less forgotten. But not entirely. What-ever version of Eva she was playing, there would be no letting Harry off the hook any time soon. In fact, she refused to acknowl-edge the existence of a hook.

He had always been a bit of a lightweight when it came to drinking, so she thought it may be the time to prise some informa-tion. If she was feeling tipsy she could only imagine how Harry was feeling. Though, as she stared at him glassy-eyed across the table he seemed as sober as a Mormon judge.

Eva licked her spoon. "Why are you still doing all this, Harry? The blackmail, the threats. Surely you've made your point by now?"

"And what point is that?"

"That governments shouldn't be dicks and should listen to their people. You bringing it to the fore has resulted in change, but the harder you push the more governments will push back. I think destroying your penthouse shows they think you're pretty much public enemy number one."

He shrugged. It was a ploy. Harry was never unsure about

anything. "I'm merely making everyone to do the right thing, is that so bad?"

"Making them. That's just the point. You're bending people to your will. You can't make everyone on the planet do what you think is right, Harry."

"Why not?"

Was he playing with her? "Because people have free will."

Harry tilted his head. "Do they? Really?" He put down his spoon. "Okay. Free will verses being happy. What would you choose?"

"Can't I have both?"

"No."

He did love his moral conundrums. She rolled her shoulders in readiness for the debate to come. Early in their relationship it had become an almost nightly ritual. It had been as if Eva was his moral sounding board. "Alright. I know you're expecting me to say free will, aren't you? That's what us lefty types always say, right? Give me liberty or give me death and all that? But you're going to counter by saying what good is free will if I'm starving in a cave somewhere eating squirrel and my only friend is Roger the corn chip?"

"It's uncanny how you read my mind sometimes."

"Well, I'm going to shock you. I'd choose being happy. Most people would."

"Would they?" The condescending tone riled her.

"Of course they would. Take Facebook or any other major social media outlet, most of yours, too. Everyone knows they on-sell everything about you to corporations but at the end of the day you need somewhere to post a picture of a cat wearing a sombrero, so what are you gonna do? Same with freedom. When it comes to the crunch, people really would sacrifice some free will, some liberty. Why? Because being happy is preferable to being miserable and living in a cave sucks monkey balls. Plus, I think Roger is seeing other people."

"Sometimes you surprise me, Ms Destruction."

"Sometimes." Eva held up her index finger and waggled her eyebrows.

Harry blushed and shuffled his backside from side to side. "Well, yes, that was surprising. Tokyo, wasn't it?" Regaining his composure, he said, "You're equating freedom to the internet, but I'm talking larger than that. Most of the world has some sort of democracy, some way to elect their leaders and unfortunately the vast majority of those leaders don't give a tinker's cuss about their people. Do you think voters would sacrifice a tiny bit of democracy for a government that looked out for them? That had their best interests at heart and made the right decisions without being stonewalled by self-interested parties propped up by multinationals and vested interest groups only after profit?"

"So, a dictatorship then?"

"I wouldn't use that word. I'd call it compassionate leadership guided by principles with slightly less democracy than some are used to."

Harry was deliberately twisting things. Like he always did.

Her eyes narrowed. "Margret Thatcher said a benevolent dictatorship was the most efficient way to govern."

"Old Maggie may have been onto something. Democracy is hard work. People don't like hard work. When it comes down to it, they'd prefer to be at the pub, reading a book or hanging from the chandelier naked."

They both grinned at that. Memories are a wonderful thing.

Where was he going with this? It seemed to be more than just one of their theoretical debates.

He was being deliberately obtuse but was up to something. That was part of the problem that had ended them. When they first started dating, Harry had shared everything with her. It was as if she had been invited into his secret world and he couldn't wait for her to be a part of it. Slowly, imperceptibly, that had changed. His meeting explanations had become more vague and clandestine. She had never known if it was something she'd done or if he was trying to protect her.

She pushed the bowl away. "Is this related to your crack about a European currency? Are you angling for more than just environmental policy and supporting developing nations?"

"We're simply talking about theoretical musings, Sweetie."

And trying to piss her off. *Sweetie.* He would have seen her eye twitch. Eva was no Sweetie. "No, I know you too well, you're planning something. Something big."

Another shrug. The fact that he had no words told her more than an outright denial would have.

"So when does this thing drop?"

"Soon. Very soon. The next phase is already in play. An escalation of what I had planned when in London. They've just called a special meeting of the UN, so that's a good start."

"What are you really up to?"

"I'm only encouraging a more representative government, so it's not all white guys in blue ties who have already made their fortune."

"Encourage how?"

"A well-timed article in one of my papers, a signal boost on my social media platforms, some opportune campaign funds. Whatever is needed to have greater diversity and representation. If they recall my assistance later down the track, all the better."

"There's more to it, there has to be. The island wasn't created on a whim, Harry. You've been planning this for an exceptionally long time. What are you aiming for, and don't tell me for people to be good."

Harry clasped his hands in front of him. He took a dramatic pause like when he gave a press conference. He was calling on his media training and she didn't care for it. "The world is sick, Eva. Physically and emotionally. The environment's shot because politicians have made global warming a political football and ignored the science. Governments are self-interested, ineffective and directionless. I'm trying to save the world from itself, Eva."

"By doing what *you* think is right."

"Correct."

She didn't like this side of him. The megalomania side. From a distance she could understand what he was trying to achieve. She really could. But she wasn't at a distance. She was across the table from a man who wanted to control the world.

Harry leaned forward and took her hand. "Green energy, better distribution of wealth, universal healthcare, clean cheap water, food distribution that's efficient and feeds all, not for most, but *all*. These are not ignoble pursuits. Nearly everyone agrees these are good and desirable things but they assume someone else will make it happen. If I have to be that someone else, then so be it."

"By threatening those who legitimately came to power? By making them petrified you'll release every lurid detail about them?"

"I'm simply reminding them why they're there. Governments are in power because they govern on behalf of us, not over us. That's democracy, something they've forgotten. I'm simply reminding them of that. If they go along with it because they don't want the world to know about their internet search history for pictures of young boys, or the affair with an intern or what they really think of the prime minister, fine. No politician is going to fear threats of a pillow fight."

"There's that word again."

"Pillow?"

"Fear."

"See, that's the thing. You think that given the chance people will intrinsically do the *right* thing, but I'm here to tell you, Sister, that's nonsense. If every person on this planet did what was right we wouldn't need laws, or lawyers, or police, or armies, or CCT, or contracts, or religion, or…"

"Or dictators?"

"Exactly! Now you're getting it."

"So, what?" she said waiving her arms about. "You're going to blackmail politicians into voting you in as European dictator?"

The comment was flippant. The reaction wasn't.

"Again, I wouldn't use that word, no."

Eva was aghast. "Jesus titty-fucking-Christ, you're serious?"

"I think the history books say Jesus didn't titty-fuck anyone."

"You don't know, he totally could have. So you're going to

appoint yourself Emperor. Tsar. Monarch, whatever. That's your end goal? To rule Europe?"

"For starters."

"You're insane."

"Do you doubt me?"

She must have been drunk. She'd always said Harry was capable of anything, but he was surely taking the piss. Eva was still in shock at the audacity of his plans. For once she was speechless. She should have been outraged but was too anaesthetised for that. Her mind would need time to catch up. This wasn't about 'doing good' any more. This was manipulation on a global scale. She'd always loved his passion and drive. In all honestly, she probably still loved the man too. But this was too much.

"You can't blackmail every European politician into voting you in, that's nuts."

"The end result is what's important. It's for the greater good. I don't need to, as you say, blackmail them all, just enough. Everyone, and I mean, everyone has something in their past they want to keep away from the public or loved ones. Everyone has a trigger. The fact that I'm getting them to do good deeds only smooths the way." He sipped his port and his eyes wandered off contemplatively. "But that's a long long way away. People need to see the results of my influence, get over the distaste of having someone influencing their leaders. They need to get on with their lives. Once things settle down, in a few years, a few select respectable politicians can suggest bringing me into the fold. Oh, that guy from the Battle of Trafalgar? Sure, why not? It will appear to be the most organic of ideas. Then," he smiled, "we'll see what happens." He pulled his shirt cuff, a move he always made when he wanted to appear nonchalant but actually had a point to make. "You could always be my first lady."

Eva's eyes narrowed. "I'm not the marrying kind."

"First partner then."

"I'm not a decoration either"

"But it would be more than a mere token position. How would you like to be the chief advisor for women's issues? You could guide key policies for education, domestic violence, anything you liked. You could affect real change."

It took a moment for it to sink in. Did he just offer Eva Destruction, a lowly barista from Melbourne, the role of guiding governmental policy? For all of Europe?

By the balls of Bill Murray…

"You're serious?"

"Deadly." Harry slid around the booth until his thigh rested on hers. He ran his hand along her cheek, his fingers through her hair. She asked for another port. She'd need it.

Her query went unanswered. His warm breath caressed her ear. She turned to see his gorgeous face. She recognised the look in his eyes. The hungry look.

The performance she was putting on dictated she should react, respond lovingly to his advances. Yes, the performance. So many confusing thoughts coalesced in her brain at once.

"I missed you." He kissed her neck. "My whole body has missed you." He kissed her nape, then around to just below the ear. Her toes curled in ecstasy. *God damn it.* He knew all her buttons. All her triggers. She forgot about the port.

Eva had lost her place in the script.

The sand squelched pleasantly between her toes. Eva held her shoes in one hand and held the hem of her dress in the other. She took in the crystal clear stars. With the moon the only source of light every star in the sky could be seen. It was awe-inspiring. The waves crashed against the shore, soothing her mood.

Finally alone she realised how utterly confused she was. She hoped it was the booze. Was Harry a good man using bad methods to achieve good results? Was he an insane Machiavellian tyrant? Was he simply a good kisser?

She gazed along the uninhabited stretch of beach on the island. Eva's Island. She shook her head. What had she done to deserve a whole island? Or castle. Or, for that matter, Europe?

She remembered the night he'd given her the castle. They had been high on the hills of the Rhone Valley on the balcony of a beautiful old villa. She hadn't been able to fault the Châteauneuf-du-Pape, it had a kick like Touché Turtle. The night was clear and crisp, but not cold. The torchlight was more for effect. The two of them had sat alone overlooking vineyards below. Harry had made a big show of the reveal. He'd clicked his fingers and the lights of the castle were illuminated.

At first she thought it was a joke. A million-dollar joke. It was actually more like twenty-million Euro non-joke. A castle of her very own. It had all the modern appointments, old world charm, spa, sauna, and helipad. You know, the basics. It was dazzling, amazing, but ultimately hollow.

She'd realised it for what it really was. The desperate act of a man who knew the truth but refused to admit it. Their relationship had stalled, stagnated. They didn't have a future. He knew it, she knew it. The castle didn't fix it.

He'd excluded her too much. Kept her at arm's length too long. She'd been wavering. The frustrating thing was, she'd cherished every moment she'd spent with him, but they had become too infrequent. She wanted more time from a man that had none to give.

Eva realised she'd become someone she didn't recognise. She dressed differently. Long gone were the jeans and t-shirts. She wore refined clothes during the day as they often had private tours of museums or lunches with powerful figures. Dinner attire was generally graceful silky dresses to please him.

As she walked along the beach she glanced at her dress. She'd fallen for it. Again.

The night's drink was starting to wear off and the brisk tropical night brought everything into sharp focus. Harry's plans were too extreme, too destructive. Her former lover *was* a megalomaniac. Harry *was* a supervillain.

She also shouldn't have slept with him.

There had been opportunities during the night where she could have resisted. She really could have. There were so many excuses she could have given. 'It's too soon'. 'I'm not ready'. 'We need to reconnect properly'. Something. Anything.

Mad at herself for her stupidity, she tried to convince herself that sex with Harry was part of the role, a facet of her mission. Deep within her core she knew it wasn't true. She'd joined him willingly.

Sure, five screaming orgasms had cleared her mind, but with that clarity came a realisation Eva wasn't altogether comfortable with.

To escape, she'd told Harry she couldn't sleep because of the time zones. By the time she'd reached the door of his bedroom he was asleep. As she strode along the beach the regret weighed down on her shoulders burying each step further into the sand.

Regret and sex hadn't mingled together in Eva's mind since the age of sixteen, and yet, there she was. She was in unfamiliar territory in every sense.

She glanced back at the main house and gave it the finger. Though it wasn't really a main house at all. It was the evil lair of a supervillain.

Why had he invited her there? *Really*. Was it to make him feel better? To be an ornament, a trinket? Was she there to be at his beck and call? She didn't have any particular skill, well, not one that would be useful to his plans.

The thought was so sudden she actually gasped. It seemed like the entire island had fallen silent, so complete was the revelation.

Fucking hell, I'm a Bond girl.

CHAPTER TWENTY-THREE

Eva was sure the entire island could hear her breathing. She tried to stop, but it was a habit she found hard to break. Like biting her nails or falling for bad boys.

The sweat dripped off her, unfortunately not all of it. A bead managed to find its way down her back and between her butt cheeks. The startled shriek wasn't in keeping with her stealthy endeavour. She wiped her brow and hoped no one had heard her. *It has to be here.*

It had taken her the better part of the morning to wander about the main house and figure it out. Harry advised he'd be in phone interviews all day, decrying his innocence while pushing his political barrow. Not knowing the location of Van Buren had caused most of the sweat.

It had taken far longer to find than she'd anticipated simply because of the sheer size of the mansion. Or evil lair. Eva had compared all room sizes and doorways, searching for inconsistencies. She was searching for hidden rooms.

For someone who had founded their fortune on technology there seemed to be a distinct lack of it on the island. Harry had a few tablets – all password protected, she'd tried. She'd gone in search of more. In her mind there would be a temperature-controlled room of maybe four or five servers.

Harry had claimed there was no other technology room on the island. She didn't believe him for a second. Even a computer-averse entity like her knew there was no way a tech genius would not have a dedicated server room of some description. If there was a server room, there would be a computer. If there was a computer, there would be a chance she could get a message to MI6. Without it she'd be stuck on the island forever.

The revelation she'd had on the beach as to what Harry perceived her role on the island to be had jolted her into action. She was no Bond girl. She was a feminist firebrand. She was a self-sufficient independent woman who defended her beliefs and was confident in her views. She'd travelled the world alone, forged her own path, built her own business, and taken no shit along the way. Eva wasn't someone's ornament.

Unfortunately, she also wasn't a technological wizard. She didn't know anything about computers. She had to admit, a self-confessed technophobe hacking into what was most likely to be the most protected computer on the planet was going to be prob-lematic.

Harry claimed to only have hackers on his team to accumulate the data on politicians but she suspected he'd at least need some local storage. She'd read enough tabloids to know information and nudie photos were always being leaked from 'the cloud' so she was sure Harry wouldn't risk storing it exclusively there. And according to a book she'd read about Julian Assange, the physical servers, whichever country they were located in, would be liable under the laws of the hosting government. And there weren't many governments sympathetic to Harry's cause. So there had to be a server room here somewhere.

All she had to do was find it.

After two hours of searching, she'd done just that. Following the mental map she'd made in her mind, she'd determined there was something between the library, kitchen and master bathroom.

In the bathroom she'd spent a good half hour pressing every tile and pulling every tap, soap holder and switch – nothing. Next she'd tried the library. As Harry had warned, it was sparse. Much to her disappointment, Eva had tilted every book but the bookshelf steadfastly refused to spin around to reveal a hidden room. Did he have no respect for clichés?

Eva paced out the rough length in the kitchen, well the secondary kitchen. There was the main kitchen for the staff, where all the meals were prepared. Chen had shown her around the night before. The staff could prepare a fifteen-course banquet in there. She was looking in the kitchen you went to when you couldn't be bothered walking the distance to the *other* kitchen. Billionaires.

She'd determined the secret room had to be in the pantry. If the entrance was there, it would make the most sense. Wandering into the kitchen for a snack was a perfect cover. Also, she was peckish.

For ten minutes she lifted cans of beans and packets of maca-roni and cheese. Nothing. In retrospect, it would be dangerous to be so obvious. You wouldn't want a guest stumbling onto a hidden room because they felt like baked beans on toast.

Just when she was about to put the whole thing down to a quirk of architecture she spotted a metal support piece. It stood out as all the others were wooden. She ran her hand along its length until her finger came to the bottom end, nearest the wall. The metal slightly gave way when pressure was applied. Eva pushed it in. There was a faint *click* followed by a *whir*. The entire wall swung open.

The victory dance was brief, but expressive.

Instead of a bank of computers flashing at her, she was confronted with a downward sloping corridor. This was no server room. It was a secret passage. Fluorescent lights flickered on. The first twenty or so metres of the wide corridor were drywall but as it descended it cut into the bedrock of the island.

Having come this far, she had no choice but to see where it lead. The passageway descended into darkness. There was no way of telling what was at the other end. It was silent except for a distant whooshing sound. To Eva, every footfall sounded like a bass drum. If anyone was coming the other way she'd be discovered in an instant. There was nowhere to hide.

In contrast to the chilly atmosphere, she was sweating bullets. There was no way to explain away her presence. There would be no, 'I took a wrong turn' excuses. If she was discovered it would be all over. Van Buren would come in his pants at the prospect.

The further she descended, the louder the whooshing noise. It wasn't the sea. *So what was it?*

Again she was struck by the thought that the island wasn't a fly-by-night operation. Not only would the mansion have taken significant planning and effort to execute, so would whatever this passage led to. Harry had planned this for years, possibly decades. *What was he up to?*

Did she even know Harry? She thought she had once, but was that the delusion of a love-struck fool?

Thoughts of foolishness brought her thoughts back to the night before and sleeping with her ex-lover. It had been far too easy. So natural. So effortless.

Eva could fool herself that she was playing a role and had done what she needed to do for her mission. But no matter how she examined it, she'd gone to Harry's bed willingly. Wantonly.

What did that make her?

It had been naïve for her to think she could keep Harry at arm's length on the island. There was no way she could stay in his orbit and not come crashing down to Earth. His pull too great, her strength around him far too weak. There it was, *weakness*. How did Harry get to her so easily? How did he negate everything she held dear? What did you do when the man you thought you loved cancelled everything that made you unique?

Eventually the passage flattened out, came to a bend and narrowed. Muscles tensed, her senses heightened. Another loud *whoosh* stopped her dead in her tracks. Silence fell again and curiosity propelled her forward.

Stepping through a slender doorway at the end of the passage, Eva's mouth hung open. This was no server room.

The completely circular tunnel was dimly lit, but there was no mistaking what it was. The single rail line gave that away. She was standing on some kind of monorail platform.

A small blue sign stated; *ETT Station – Main House Entrance B.* Looking at the monorail, she guessed that ETT signified Evacuated Tube Transport. She assumed it was some kind of superconducting maglev train. A form of transport she'd read about in some speculative article. It may well have denoted Elephant Training Terminal for all she knew.

Why the hell would Harry need a train? On a damn island? He'd claimed the island was a simple affair, a smattering of residences and not much else. The main house was large, but certainly not big enough to justify a technologically advanced railway. So what was it for?

On the wall next to her, a small computer screen flickered on. A small blinking message appeared onscreen. *One minute.*

One minute to what? A train? Armed guards to capture her? The launch of intercontinental ballistic missiles? Eva's mind reeled. Everything made as much sense as Japanese Ikea instructions.

The *whooshing* sound increased in volume. Should she run? Would she make it back to the kitchen before being discovered? Should she stay and find out what the hell the island really was?

She stayed.

Light shone around the corner. A quiet train carriage hurtled towards her. It was egg-shaped, glass and apparently unmanned. It slid noiselessly in front of her. With a small *hiss* automatic doors glided open. The carriage was empty. Having come this far, Eva stepped in.

There was an electronic panel with four buttons.

Main House Entrance A.

Main House Entrance B.

Warehouse Entrance A.

Warehouse Entrance B.

How big was this operation? The main house had two stations? It was big enough, maybe. It made theoretical sense. If there was another entrance Eva had missed, but it would be logical to have another. If one entrance was blocked, by an innocent guest or hostile force, you'd want another option. But what the hell was the warehouse and how big was it to justify two train stations?

For no reason, she pressed the *Warehouse Entrance A* button. The doors hissed closed. The jerk of acceleration made her stumble. She only retained balance by holding onto a strap hanging from the ceiling. This thing was fast.

Expecting a short trip, she was surprised when the train showed no signs of stopping. In fact, the tilt of the carriage seemed as if it was going deeper. The longer it went on, the more confused Eva became. It didn't make sense. The carriage was travelling at speed and should have come to a stop relatively quickly. The island wasn't that big.

After what seemed like minutes the automatic train slowed and ascended. For all she knew it would end in a room full of Van Buren's security guards and she would be done for. She clenched her fists and crouched.

The train came to a station, slowed to a halt and the doors slid open. There was no reception committee waiting for her. There was not much of anything. It looked exactly like the station she'd just left. Plain walls, a small computer display, a doorway and nothing else.

She'd come this far. Eva stepped off and headed towards the exit. The air was freezing. Goosebumps broke out on her skin. Choosing not to wait before doubt enveloped her, she stepped through the threshold.

What was on the other side made her reel backwards.

It was, in every sense, awe-inspiring.

Before her was a cavernous space, easily the size of a football field housing hundreds of banks of computers. It appeared forged from a natural cave. Overhead were a series of pipes that criss-crossed the entire roof, most likely sprinklers. If she had to guess, there would be tens of thousands of servers. Each blinking and doing computer things.

No wonder she was freezing, the amount of computer power would need a ridiculous amount of air-conditioning. That's why Harry needed unlimited thermal power.

Again, it didn't add up. Harry had always claimed the information used to manipulate politicians came from hackers. If that was the case, why would he need all this? Harry wouldn't require that much computing power to blackmail a few politicians, surely?

Eva had walked the island several times, she couldn't place where this warehouse was located. Then it twigged. It wasn't the island at all. At least, not the one she'd been on. This was the other island. That was why the train trip had taken so long.

She remembered the exact words Harry had used when she'd asked about it, 'I haven't been over there, to be honest'.

Another lie. What was he up to?

Eva stared at the banks of servers. Each rack had many blinking servers, but no monitors. There were no labels to signify, even remotely, what they did. She stared like a primate before a great black monolith.

She slunk towards the only desk she could see. One computer monitor sat alone on the table. There was no keyboard or mouse. She placed her hand on the table in frustration and the glow of a fluorescent keyboard appeared magically on its surface. Eva pressed a few random keys followed by enter and the monitor flashed *Access Denied* on the screen.

Well, it was never going to be that easy. She tried a few random words. Eva. Nice Bum. No success. She stared dejectedly at the screen.

The sound of voices pierced her malaise. There was nowhere for her to run. The entrance to the station was too far, the voices too close.

She dove under the table.

The voices grew louder and she could make out three distinct men. Only one she recognised and it wasn't a welcome recognition.

The three were joking about the size of some woman's breasts.

Eva hoped it wasn't hers. Not that it should matter. They sounded like twats. All three loitered by the desk, far too close. One sneeze and she'd be discovered and likely killed.

Cowering as much as she could into the corner of the cavity all she could see was the lower half of the men. A real, 'Hey, check out our crotches' moment. Not an enticing prospect for several reasons.

She could imagine the expression of glee on Van Buren's face as he gutted her like a pig. That was the best-case scenario. There were no rules on the island, they could do anything to her before slashing her throat. The thoughts circling in her mind were terrifying.

Eventually their conversation wound down and Eva did her best to remain motionless. If any one of them decided to sit at the desk she'd be done for.

Thankfully none did. They all wandered off with promises to catch up for coffee later. She stayed under the table for what seemed like decades. Eventually she was confident there were no human beings nearby. Tentatively she poked her head out from under the desk. No guns were pointed at her. A good start.

Crouching, she made her way as fast as possible to the station. On her way, she noticed a wall-mounted computer display she hadn't seen before. The display showed only one thing, *Current Server Numbers 27,457*.

What the hell was going on?

~

The sun soothed her skin, but nothing soothed her mind. Lying on a towel on the beach Eva had all the outward appearance of calm. Inward, the story was different.

This spy stuff wasn't like it was in the movies. She wished there was a plan to follow, but in reality she was winging it.

If she had been able to contact MI6 she might have been able to ask for guidance, but even that wasn't inside the realm of possibility. She'd found a warehouse full of computers, great, now what was she meant to do?

If this was a movie she'd slap her hands together and type away. If Jeff Goldblum could hack into an alien spacecraft with a nineties laptop, surely she could get a message to the outside world. But life wasn't that simple. She'd found computers, but her mission had become extraordinarily more complicated, not simpler.

What was the island really? It was obviously more than a getaway to escape the pressures of being a wanted man. The island had purpose. And she had no idea what it was.

Why was Harry being cagey about it? It was plain to see the island was a long-term project, so why had he mentioned nothing about it? He'd promised there would be no more secrets, the main reason they'd broken up. Yet, there it was, possibly the biggest secret in the world and he'd not even hinted at it.

Eva dug her hand into the sand and let it run through her fingers. She had the beach to herself, well, except for the ibis who seemed under the impression she was in possession of chips.

The tide was coming in and waves crashed nearby. She'd have to move eventually, but not yet. First she had to figure out how to find out what all the computers were for, how to get a message to MI6, find out what Harry was really up to, stay alive and keep away from Van Buren while she did it. Simple. *I'm going to drown.*

The ibis fluttered away, startled. Eva rose from her towel and shielded her eyes from the sun. Something emerged from the water. The sun was too bright for her to focus on exactly what it was.

The figure was human and waded through the surf towards her. Slowly she was able to make out details. Male. He wore nothing but blue swimming trunks. His frame was more muscular than Harry's.

Distant shouts turned her head and she saw heavily-armed guards sprinting up the beach. They were trying to run on the sand, aim weapons, gesture and shout at the same time.

The figure emerged from the waves and towered above her.

Not until she fell in his shadow did she know who it was. She was too gobsmacked to speak.

"I was wondering if you could return a favour and lend me a towel?"

Eva gaped at the man open-mouthed as Bishop dripped on the sand.

CHAPTER TWENTY-FOUR

Eva did her best impersonation of a sideshow laughing clown. Her head swivelled from side to side, mouth open wide. Not believing him to be real she proceeded to blink blankly at Bishop. Eventually she moved onto squeaking incomprehensively.

The secret agent appeared remarkably unharmed from Prague. Either he'd been seen to by some exceptional doctors or his injuries were less severe than she'd imagined. Bishop raised a roguish eyebrow and seemed to revel in her disbelief. He looked suspiciously as though he'd walked off the set of a Diet Coke ad. Hair tussled just so, two-day growth, chiselled body, wry grin. He looked perfect. Right up to the moment an armed guard brutally rugby tackled him to the sand.

They landed with a collective *oof*. Bishop spat out sand as the guard grappled to pin his arms behind his back. Bishop didn't resist. He seemed to be expecting the reception.

A ball of wheezing sweat staggered towards Eva. Van Buren was so out of breath he could only rasp orders about hauling Bishop to the main house for interrogation.

Regaining his composure as best he could, he turned to her and said, "Stay out of it."

Eva rose up. Placing her hand on her hip, she said, "I find that highly unlikely."

As the guards shoved Bishop along the beach, she shouted to Bishop, "I have to know. Is Paul...?"

"He's fine."

The warm tropical sea water lapping her feet was nothing compared to the wave of relief that enveloped her. Paul was 'fine'. As in, 'not dead'. Eva allowed herself a brief moment to choke back the emotion of finding one of her best friends hadn't died saving her life.

One less thing to worry about. But that wasn't entirely true. With Bishop on the island things had become a shit-tonne more complicated.

~

"Why do you want to see him?"

Harry had asked an excellent question. It really was. Insightful and to the point. Eva didn't care for it.

Standing on the veranda of the main house, she studied her shoes. She really should have thought this one through.

Asking to see Bishop was bound to raise further questions. Yet she asked anyway. Eva had always assumed Harry believed her interaction with Bishop had been limited. The warning on the London Eye and fraternising with her in his apartment bathroom. Which for a brief period of time had been the case. It's everything past that moment she hoped he was unaware of.

In retrospect she should have wondered if Harry had known Bishop was with her in Prague. They had both gone over the bridge, but only one had climbed back. Did Harry know she hadn't been alone? He hadn't mentioned it. She didn't want to ask.

Harry leaned against the doorjamb of the huge double doors. Dressed casually in white t-shirt, jeans and no shoes. He wasn't confrontational in his question, but his crossed arms indicated he wouldn't let her speak to Bishop without a good reason.

Unfortunately, she didn't have a one. Before him, cogs turned in her head, but no ideas fell out. Something must have been jammed up there because the cogwheels weren't spinning like they should.

Without speaking to Bishop, Eva had to assume he'd found her via the quantum positioning pen. It had worked after all. Having supplied her with the backpack she doubted Harry would like to know he was indirectly responsible for Bishop's arrival.

"How does he know Paul?"

The question was practically nonchalant, but she detected an undercurrent. Was he beginning to distrust her?

"I'm sorry?"

"Van Buren said the spy mentioned something about Paul being fine to you. I assume that's your mate Paul."

If she could have, Eva would have smacked the side of her head to get those cogs spinning. *Focus.*

"Yes, my Paul. That was one of the ways he tried to make a connection at the London Eye. Said he went to school with Paul. Pretty sure it's untrue. In fact, I never asked Paul about it because it sounded like utter bullshit. I was being sarcastic when I asked him. I guess Van Buren doesn't get subtlety. Surprising. When Bishop confronted me on the beach we hardly spoke, but it was enough to remind me he's still a twat."

A lie with a pinch of truth and a smidgeon of desperation. Harry gave a slight tilt of his head. He seemed to buy it. She decided to push her luck.

"So that's part of the reason I wanted to talk to him. Find out where he gets off accosting me when I was having a lovely day on the beach. He pissed me off. I wanted to see him because I wanted to vent, I guess. And remind him not to use my friends as some sort of letter of introduction. I'm certain Paul wouldn't have the foggiest who he is."

The last part had been true as far as she'd known until a few weeks before.

Harry nodded. "I was wondering what the link was. I thought perhaps Paul was connected in a more professional manner."

Eva laughed and hoped it was convincing. "You've met Paul,

does he look like a master spy? He buys wine from dodgy blokes in pubs, he doesn't fly around with jetpacks, saving the world and snogging the damsel in distress. Nancy would kill him for one thing. He couldn't get dressed in the morning without his wife laying his clothes out for him."

"I guess you're right." Harry seemed to accept it, but there was something in his manner Eva couldn't place. Was it nervousness about Bishop being on the island or something more? "Come back in a couple of hours, dressed for dinner. I've invited him to dine with us. We'll get the bottom of this. I've sent an entire wardrobe over to your villa. Wear something nice, a dress. A slinky one would be good."

He leaned over and kissed her lips. The door closed and Eva was alone on the vast terrace.

She pushed down the distaste of Harry telling her what to wear, again. What would Bishop say? Did Harry know more than he was letting on? Was he playing her? Was she being paranoid? If she was safe, what did Harry intend on doing with Bishop? She doubted Harry would hand him a packed lunch and send him on his way. Dinner with the two men was fraught with countless potential chasms to fall into.

Muttering, she said, "The spy who came to dinner."

Heading back to the guest house the image of Bette Davis flashed before her. *Fasten your seat belts, it's going to be a bumpy night.*

~

"No, I won't be doing that."

"Oh come on. It'll be fun." Harry's mischievous eyes twinkled.

Eva wasn't buying it. "This has to be some hitherto unknown definition of fun with which I am unfamiliar."

He sat cross-armed on the edge of his huge mahogany desk. As with all things Harry, the room was opulent, yet tasteful. It was decked out with Edwardian scientific instruments; barometers, microscopes and the like. A large stylised wood carving of a monkey dominated the room.

Harry was resplendent in his white tuxedo, if a little over-dressed. Not that Eva could talk. Her elegant black lace and satin Givenchy gown was low-cut and figure-hugging. The bare arms showed off her tattoos, her hair pulled back in a ponytail. Her feminist sensibilities riled at being told what to wear by a man, but damn if she didn't feel confident and masterful. And sexy as hell.

Where she did draw the line, however, was being told where to stand. "I'm not going to pose like a damn Barbie Doll. I'm not a prop, Harry."

"It's not that at all. I want to see his face when you're standing behind me like a goddess and I do the swivel around on the chair thing. It'll be fun. Just messing with him a little. You of all people should know about messing with people's heads."

"What the hell is that meant to mean?"

A knock at the door interrupted them. The butler advised he was about to bring Bishop in. Harry leapt into the chair and spun it so the back of the chair would face the spy as he entered.

Eva rolled her eyes. "Do you need a cat to stroke?"

"Shhh, you'll ruin it."

"You're kind of being a dick right now."

"Eva," Harry scowled with a hint of humour, "not in front of the monkey."

The door opened and Bishop strutted in as if it were a cocktail party and he was the guest of honour. He knew how to own a room, that's for sure. Eva wondered how much was put on bravado and how much was natural Bishop swagger. His black tuxedo was so well-fitted she had to squint to check it wasn't painted on. Did Harry have a tailor on the island? Bishop strode towards the desk as if he didn't have a care in the world.

Harry's chair swivelled around. "Mr Bishop, welcome to my island."

My island? Eva had thought it was hers. At least in name.

There was no reaction to the chair turn, which must have

annoyed Harry. Bishop gave a slight bow and said, "Harry Bala-
fonte I presume?"

She snorted and Bishop turned his attention to her. While his
face remained impassive, his pupils dilated at the sight of her. Eva
would have blushed if she was into that sort of thing. Which she
totally wasn't.

"I do believe we've met, but we haven't been properly introduced. Miss...?"

"Oh come now Mr Bishop, please drop the pretence. I am fully
aware of your history with Eva here."

"Fully?" Bishop smirked.

Behind Harry, she gave a slight shake of her head. *Don't.*

"Yes, she's told me about your aborted attempt to talk her out
of our fledgling romance and, well, we all recall the minor alterca-
tion in my apartment. Incidentally, I'll be sending your government a bill for the tidy-up on that one."

"And I'm sure they will enjoy ripping it up." Bishop slid his
hands in his pockets. "So, if I may be ill-mannered, why am I here?"

"A question I very much want answered as well. But first,"
Harry stood and motioned to the far doors, "dinner."

Unimpressed, Eva said, "Oh goody, dinner and a show."

Chen cleared the plates silently. Eva began to feel sorry for the
chef. He possessed amazing skills yet was also tasked with serving
and clearing the table. Given the amount of human resources
required to build Harry's buildings, underground high-tech rail
system and huge data centre, surely he could have forked out for
at least one lousy waiter. The secret infrastructure was something
she was eager to speak to Bishop about, but Harry seemed determined to give them no time alone together.

So far they had talked generalities. Weather: tropical, not much
to expand on there. Sport: the upcoming World Cup held
England's greatest chance of winning the title in quite some time,

as in, little possibility at all. Food: Chen was remarkable and Michelin stars were overrated.

Eva was on edge. The conversation was far too polite and the false civility only made the situation worse. It was as if someone had thrown a hand grenade into the middle of the table and she didn't know how long the fuse was. All she could do was sit there and wait for the inevitable explosion.

"I must say," Bishop said, "I have to commend your wine collection. This DRC La Tàche is sublime. Seventy-four?"

Harry nodded, with an impressed expression.

Bishop took another sip, savouring it. "Although the seventy-eight is when they reached the zenith. This is good too."

A smirk crossed Harry's lips. "Unfortunately the seventy-eight is hard to come by. Even for me."

"Oh, I know a gentleman who has some in his collection. I'd be happy to supply his details."

"That would be marvellous, thank you."

Eva was ready to scream. "Would you lot stop being so bloody civilised? It's doing my head in."

"I believe Werner Herzog said civilisation is like a thin layer of ice upon a deep ocean of chaos and darkness."

The quote was a good one. The fact that it came from Bishop made the situation more confounding.

"What would you have us do, Eva? Pistols at ten paces?" She hated it when Harry took on a haughty tone.

"What I want is for everyone to drop the pretence and deal with the situation." She pointed at Bishop. "He swam to shore and interrupted my sunbaking. Aren't you the slightest bit interested in how he got here?"

Harry sighed. "Alright, Eva. If it makes you happy." He took a sip of water biding his time. "So, Mr Bishop how did you come to be on our little island?"

"Would you believe I swam?"

"I would not, no. The nearest land is three thousand kilometres away." Harry glanced up. His thinking face. "At best that would take you over forty days without breaks. If you could maintain Olympic speeds."

"You calculated that in your head?"

"I looked it up recently." Harry paused. "Not a lot to do on this island."

Bishop turned to Eva. "Nothing to do on the island?" His demeanour flirtatious. "Such a shame for a man to have such little imagination." His voice dripped innuendo. This was more like the Bishop she knew.

She shook her head. "Stop it."

"One day." He grinned. "Not today."

Harry tapped his knife on the table to get Bishop's attention. "How exactly did you find my island?"

"It's rather amazing actually," Bishop said threading his hands behind his head. "I was in the office and every Tom, Dick and Harriet was asking where's Horatio Lancing? Where's Horatio Lancing? So there I was in front of a globe of the world with a dart in my hand. So I gave it a spin, threw the dart and here I am. I mean, what are the odds?" He waited a moment and added, "That was rhetorical. I don't actually need to know the actual probability."

Harry's lips appeared to have been run over by a truck. "Is this the kind of childish answering I can expect?"

"I guess it all depends on the questions." He turned to Eva. "And who asks them."

Chen interrupted with a tray of soup. He ladled it in silence. Everyone at the table eyed the others. When Chen wordlessly escaped to the kitchen, Harry recommenced his line of questioning.

"Am I to understand you're here in an official capacity, Mr Bishop?"

"Let's just say I am not on vacation."

"And am I to assume you have a submarine or commandos at your beck and call and other such threats?"

"Not at all, not at all. I'm here on my lonesome. No backup. No threats, veiled or otherwise. Just little old me. Let's call it a good-will mission."

"Of course, a goodwill mission. But let me tell you, if only for the sake of openness, that if, theoretically, there was an assault on this island we would have the ability to defend ourselves."

"Oh, no doubt. And theoretically, the British Navy could flatten this island with a press of a button if it so chose. Again, theoretically."

She expelled a frustrated breath. "Jesus guys, why don't you flop them out on the table and be done with it?"

Eva didn't want to mention she already knew the answer to that particular conundrum.

Bishop tutted. "In the middle of a soup course? I think not. Dessert, by all means, that possesses all kinds of delectable possi-bilities. But not soup, that's fraught with danger."

A napkin to Eva's lips attempted to hide the smirk. She hoped Harry hadn't seen it.

"I think that's enough of that talk, thank you." Harry said in his best schoolmaster voice. "I think we should come back to the subject at hand."

Bishop let out a childish, "Aww," and tilted his head. "Just when we were getting close to the fun bit, like the colourful tattoo of a lily on Ms Destruction's inner thigh."

It took a moment for her to realise what had just been said. She still didn't believe it. Harry raised an eyebrow. Eva raised two. Bishop raised a glass.

Smarmy git.

Jesus, he was deliberately being provocative. To what end? Little did he know Harry wasn't so easily baited.

The napkin was torn from Harry's lap. He screwed it up and flung it into his half-eaten soup. "We're done here." He pushed out his chair. "Back to the lock-up with you. My limited hospitality is officially over."

Maybe she had been wrong.

Without a further word being spoken, armed guards entered the dining room and hauled Bishop unceremoniously away. His last action before disappearing behind the large wooden doors was to give Eva a wink.

She turned to Harry. His fists were clenched and he fumed. It was the first time she'd ever seen him jealous.

He grasped her arm. "Come on, let's go to bed."

Eva shook him off. "Like hell. What was all that about, really? Were you trying to show off for me and it didn't work out? Tough. And I won't be the target of your hate fuck either. I'm not here for you to take out your frustrations on, Harry. If you want that, I'll give you some hand cream and can recommend some excellent pornos, but I won't be your on-call relief, okay? That's not how it works. Are we clear?"

Chen rolled in a serving trolley and stared at them for a moment, perplexed. He wisely pushed it back into the kitchen noiselessly.

Harry's jaw was clenched like a bear trap. He inhaled deeply for a while, gathering himself. "Sorry. It's...he got to me. He shouldn't have, but...he seems to have a way of pissing people off."

"Really? I hadn't noticed."

Harry ran his hand along her cheek tenderly. "I apologise for being so churlish. That's not me. You know that. I regret treating you like some lady of the night. It was uncouth and thoughtless."

It was incredible that Harry had taken umbrage to Bishop's, admittedly provocative, chauvinist remarks when it had been he who'd told her what to wear, where to stand. Pot, kettle, black. Eva was about to mention it when he interrupted.

Harry ran his hand along her arm. "Oh, and I wouldn't worry about the spy."

She found that difficult to believe.

Harry kissed the top of her head and continued. "This was to be his last meal. He'll be executed in the morning."

CHAPTER TWENTY-FIVE

Decker put down his coffee mug. "Oh, don't stop there."

Eva sighed. "Kind of have to. I really need to pee."

Tilting his head, Decker said, "So pee."

Even with her restricted limbs, she sensed she was gaining some ground back in her conversation with the Navy men. She had their attention again and Decker was less threatening. She decided it was time to push her limited advantage. Plus she really did have to pee.

"Look, I know some guys get off on that and I'm sure there are websites dedicated to watching chicks pissing their pants, but I really have no time for your fetishes."

"It's not like that, Ms Destruction. We want to make sure you don't free yourself from your restraints again."

"You mean the handcuffs you put on a lone woman, in a locked room, on a ship full of armed Navy personnel in the middle of the ocean. They're the restraints you're referring to? Also, let's not even go into the fact that I'm not the bad guy here. All I've done is cooperate with you and you tie me to a chair and make me wet myself. Have you informed the President of that little titbit? How about you release me and I'll forget all about it when I write my memoir. What do you say?"

Regardless of his gruff exterior, Eva could see Decker waver. The mention of the President caused his eye to twitch slightly.

"Come on guys. I'm sure this tub has a toilet or two. Surely you can let me…?"

"Not a chance in hell." Decker shook his head.

"How about a bucket then? Something. Anything. Hell, give me that cup."

"It was a present from my mother."

Eva paused. "Do you like her?"

"Yes."

"Alright, a bucket then."

Cole interjected. "If we ever want to get to the bottom of this, how about I go to the infirmary and grab a bedpan. Otherwise we'll be here for hours."

It was the first time Eva had seen Cole assertive. The timing for him to man up couldn't have been better. Decker gave a slight nod and Cole left.

Shifting in his chair, Decker said, "Please, continue. If your bladder can hold on for a few minutes."

Eva wasn't sure it could, but they would find out soon enough. "Where was I? Oh, yeah. I was about to find out the truth. A terrible unbelievable truth. I was about to choose my side and decide the fate of the world."

~

Eva stormed down the hall after Harry.

"What the hell do you mean he'll be executed? Since when do you execute anyone? You're not an execution kind of guy. You're all justice for all, I donate to Amnesty, Kumbaya, I'll have the free range eggs, guy. As far as I know you aren't the, hey let's put a bullet in this bloke's head because he annoyed my girlfriend, guy."

"You're my girlfriend?"

"Yeah, because that's what we should be talking about right now."

Harry stopped walking. "Eva, he represents a threat to everything I have established here. Everything I–"

"You're killing him because of what he *represents*? Can you even hear yourself?" Eva ran her fingers through her hair. She couldn't believe she was having this conversation with Harry. "Why kill him? Why kill anyone? I thought you were about taking the moral high ground and setting the example. Slap him on the wrist and stick him on a plane with a note from the principal. Anything is better than executing him. He hasn't threatened you or your operation."

Harry continued his walk along the corridor. Eva had no choice but to follow.

"Despite what he said, the man isn't here for a lark. Somehow he's stumbled on our location and he's unwilling to divulge how he did it."

Eva did her best to show no change in her demeanour. She needed to destroy the pen.

Throwing his hands in the air, Harry continued. "But the fact remains he is currently the only person on this planet who can bring down everything I've meticulously planned. I refuse to let decades of ceaseless work be destroyed by an arrogant sexist buffoon."

Harry turned and she realised where they were. The bedroom. The place where only the night before she'd fallen into old habits and spent an amazing night with a man she thought she could love again. But everything since then had shattered those rose-coloured glasses.

The more time she spent with Harry 2.0, the more she believed he really was a supervillain, or at least was charging towards being an evil dictator. Perhaps without the total evil, but still. Sentencing Bishop to death would only tilt him further in the wrong direction.

Harry Lancing possessed unnatural gifts in all areas and Eva honestly believed he wanted to improve the world for the better. Free healthcare, no war, free trade, just labour laws for all, not only the rich countries. Although for him to achieve all that he'd need to become, for want of a better term, a benevolent dictator. Did the end justify the means? Did the death of one man justify the benefits for millions?

Eva came back to the murky question of who wore the white hat and who wore the black. Deeper than that, there were the differences between the two men themselves. Harry was like honey; sweet to taste, sensual, something to roll around on her tongue and savour. Bishop on the other hand was like a shot of bourbon; sharp, strong, making her whole body tingle. And ultimately something she'd regret in the morning.

Once again, Eva came back to what Harry believed her role was in it all.

"Why am I here, Harry? I want a real answer this time."

"Because I love you and you make me a better human being."

Suddenly his words seemed hollow to Eva. Devoid of significance. She was beginning to regret not only agreeing to find Harry for MI6, but possibly her entire relationship. Was the man underneath worth all the pain and compromise?

Whenever she was around him Eva became someone else. Something less than the sum of its parts. Was Harry worth her becoming less than herself, less than whole?

"Tell that to Bishop." Dread gurgled in her gut. "Executing a bloke is a major step, Harry. It's making me question you, us." That caused a reaction. His face flashed with a fracture of fear. *Good*. She decided to push it. "Why are we even together? Why me, Harry?"

"Because you are exceptional. One of a kind." He slid his hand along her cheek. "I came back to the café the day we met because you were unlike anyone I'd ever met in my life. You're devastatingly intelligent, you are my moral compass, you challenge me when needed and, let's face it, you're a bit of alright."

She pushed away his hand. Something in what he said triggered the memory of a niggling thought that had been rolling around her brain since the conversation with Van Buren when she first arrived. At the time she'd tried to dismiss it as the ramblings of a jealous Security Chief. Now it began to ring true far more than she was comfortable with.

She inhaled deeply. "Harry," she said almost inaudibly, "why... why were you near my café that day?"

"What?"

"The day we met. You said you were in the area. Your exact words were that you were trying to 'familiarise yourself' with the area. You've got no parts of your corporation anywhere near there. So," she gulped fearing the answer, "why were you near my café? And Harry, don't you dare bullshit me, I'll know."

His face was sombre. "You want the real truth?"

"I wouldn't have asked if I didn't."

"You won't like it."

Eva crossed her arms. "Why were you there, Harry? On that day."

"I was just poking around. Checking things out."

Things. Eva's spine turned to ice. "Did you...did you know what was going to happen? The terrorist attacks? Did you know, Harry?"

Harry said nothing but gave a small smile. That bloody smile. The smile he thought was cheeky, but right at that moment it was only sinister.

Eva felt ill. She had to leave or she'd throw up on Harry's expensive rug.

The foundation of everything – their entire relationship – was based on a lie. The Battle of Trafalgar wasn't some random event. It had been planned by a madman. The day she'd fallen in love with Harry was also the day he'd manipulated the world. Lied to it. To her. He was never the hero of the Battle of Trafalgar, he was the cause.

It had never made sense to her why the youths had been so ready to attack the streets so soon. They had been far too organised. There was good reason for that – because Harry had organised them.

"You set it up? The whole Battle of Trafalgar was..." Eva fought the dizziness that swirled around her, "...you caused everything? It never had anything to do with those Freedom First nutbags did it? The explosions, the riot, just for some, some, fucking PR?"

Harry shrugged. "Threatening world leaders was never going to win me friends, Eva. I needed a way to have the public on my side. To show them I was their champion, not some rich man with an agenda. I needed a way to generate goodwill and leverage it as long as I could."

"Leverage! People died in those explosions, Harry. Innocent people."

"A few, yes and that was unfortunate. That shouldn't have happened. The warnings weren't heeded, the stations weren't evacuated. But in the end it was a small sacrifice in the whole scheme of things. For decades, hundreds, probably thousands, of years civilisation has been waiting for the world to right itself, to rid itself of evil, to do the right thing. It hasn't. For every green energy bulb, hundreds die of starvation. For every treaty signed, thousands of refugees die in limbo. For every charity dollar given, billions languish in poverty."

"So you killed innocent people so you can appoint yourself as the world's saviour?"

Eva's response was automatic. She sensed herself floating away from the conversation. She needed to run until her legs gave out. Only, on an island, she could never escape what she knew.

She could have fought on, argued with Harry. If she really was his moral compass, maybe she could talk him around. But she didn't have the strength. She wanted to collapse in a ball and let the world spin on without her.

Harry took her hand and gave it a slight squeeze. "You need time. It's a lot to take in, I understand. Go and sleep on it. Tomorrow it will make a lot more sense, believe me. It's all for the greater good, it is. You'll see. We can change the world, Eva. You and me. Together we can be the best thing to happen to Europe since the Renaissance. We have to forge through a little pain, and it will all be for the better."

Eva stared at him with impassive eyes. She didn't know what

to think any more. Stumbling towards the door she tried to convey an outward appearance of calm. She failed.

She mumbled some vague excuse about not feeling well and needing a lie down. Harry nodded and kissed her cheek. As she entered the hall, Harry grasped her arm. "Oh, and I know you wouldn't, but don't bother trying to speak to Bishop either. For your safety I have two layers of armed guards, as well as an exceedingly pissed off Van Buren in charge. He really doesn't like you, does he?"

They both knew it was rhetorical. Harry lowered his gaze. His expression stern.

"And tonight is your last night in the guest house. It will be far better for us both when you move your things into the main house tomorrow. I'll give you tonight to come around." His expression was emotionless. "Otherwise we might need two blindfolds tomorrow morning." The laugh was meant to convey a joke. Eva detected no humour.

He shut the door and she staggered along the hall. It was too much to take in. The lies, the betrayal, everything she held dear for so long was all twisted and wrong. She found the nearest pot plant and threw up.

She wiped her mouth and straightened her back. She headed towards the guest house.

Harry had made a mistake.

He said Bishop was the only one on Earth capable of bringing him down.

He was wrong.

~

Eva counted her advantages. Surprise, sure. Plus she also knew the main house intimately as she'd cased it extensively searching for hidden rooms.

The disadvantages seemed disproportionately stacked against her. She was mostly unarmed. The guards were not. She didn't know exactly where Bishop was being held, nor how many guards were between them. She also didn't know when or where they planned on killing him. Then there was the minor point that Van Buren would have a hard-on for a week if she gave him an excuse to shoot her between the eyes.

There was another advantage. She looked like a Hollywood cat burglar in her black turtleneck, black leggings and her black hair tied back in a ponytail. Screw Harry and his expensive dresses. In fact, just screw Harry.

It was astonishing how quickly Harry had unravelled their entire life together. The final fall had been swift but the crash landing stung like a bitch. Irrespective of what Harry had become, one day she would mourn their relationship's passing. That day wasn't today.

At the moment she was focussing on anything but Harry, but, of course, everything was still about Harry. It took all of her already significant powers of denial to filter him out. Thankfully she had a mission to accomplish and if that involved taking out the bastard who had lied to her since the first day they met, so be it.

As she hid in the tropical underbrush across from the main house, Eva tried to focus. She had spent an hour circling the house, watching every movement. The quarter moon made it easier for her to be veiled by shadows. The only lights on in the main house were in the western wing. Guards only seemed to be patrolling that side as well. Reason dictated Bishop would be languishing in a cell on that side of the house.

That was the easy part. All Eva had to do was get past the armed security force, rescue Bishop and get off the island. *Piece of piss.*

Eva went back to the mental map she'd made of the house. Logically any outward-facing rooms should be excluded. Too easy for Bishop to escape, or someone else to get in. There were a few open lounge areas in that part of the house, so they would be out as well. She narrowed it down to two or three possible rooms.

A thought struck. The secret railway. She recalled the main house had two entrances. Therefore there must be another entrance somewhere. The one she had used was on the eastern side. It was plausible the other entrance would be far removed from that one. She frowned. It was worth a shot.

Taking a wide arc around the house, Eva entered undetected through the eastern entrance. She made her way quickly to the secondary kitchen. She didn't slink, in fact, she marched down the halls like she owned the place. Over her shoulder was her backpack. If she was discovered, her explanation would be she was heading back to Harry's bedroom to start their happy life together as soon as possible. If she could say it without gagging.

As soon as she pressed the button to open secret door to the underground railway her excuse became moot. The *whir* was the same. Eva stiffened. Nobody was on the other side, the corridor was as empty as it had been the first time.

Eva exhaled slowly. She stepped into the underground passageway. Not being shot was a good first step.

As stealthily as possible, she made her way to the train station. She pressed the button labelled *Main House Entrance A* and hoped it didn't trigger some sort of alarm. A message appeared on the computer display, *30 seconds*. It may as well have said thirty years. Eva was alone and exposed. She ground her teeth.

Eventually the noiseless train carriage arrived. Empty. She stepped in placing her backpack on the floor. All she had in her arsenal was a lock picking kit, a lighter and of course Greta. The name she'd decided to bestow upon her MI6-issued frilly pink umbrella.

As the carriage moved off, Eva was dramatically undergunned. She'd seen how many weapons the members of Van Buren's security force had carried when they'd captured Bishop on the beach. By her estimate roughly a couple of hundred. Each possessed a short-barrelled machine gun, a pistol on each hip and a shotgun strapped to their back, plus who knew what else.

Eva had a lighter and an umbrella. Hardly Delta Force.

What the hell am I doing here?

The trip was brief and the train slowed to a halt. The doors opened automatically to a vacant platform. So far, so not-dead.

She slunk through the only exit. Like the other side of the

house, the passageway was cut from the foundation of the island. It climbed upwards and eventually met a more finished drywall hallway.

Tentatively Eva approached the abrupt end of the passage. Just like its counterpart at the other side of the house, there was a metallic button to open the secret door. Unlike the other side of the house, she didn't know what was on the other side.

There was a strong stench of chemicals. Whatever was on the other side, it didn't smell pleasant. For at least five minutes Eva held her ear to the door listening for the slightest of noises. She heard nothing, not even a mouse fart.

Reluctantly her finger hovered over the door release. She exhaled silently, chastising her weakness. Her free hand gripped the handle of Greta. Blood surged through her veins. She envisaged as many permutations of attack that she could possibly face on the other side of the door. Pumped up, she was ready.

Eva's palm smacked the open button and there was a tiny *whir*.

Taking a Krav Maga fighting stance, she wielded Grata like a baseball bat.

She needn't have bothered.

There was no army waiting for her. There were no guards. In fact, there was nobody at all. Eva had entered a cleaning storeroom.

That explained the stench. It smelt like a public swimming pool. Luckily she didn't smoke any more, the whole place could go up. Dozens of containers of industrial cleaners were stacked on the shelves. Not having seen any cleaning staff, she hoped Harry hadn't tasked Chen with that too.

She crept across the storeroom and carefully opened the door a crack. A quick two-second glance showed nobody in the hall. Feeling emboldened, Eva stuck her head out the door. There was less good news.

Two sets of guards. One group of five men were about ten metres way. They lounged in a common area on sofas and casually chatted. They were facing away from her. They appeared to be the first line of defence, which Eva had bypassed by taking a secret route.

The second set of guards were more problematic. Two guards bookmarked either side of a door about five metres down the other end of the hall. Motionless, their hands were draped over machine guns strapped to their chests. Their bodies were so bulked up they looked like black condoms filled with walnuts.

Thankfully there was no Van Buren. He was probably in his room carving Eva's name onto bullets.

There was no way she could take down these highly-trained militia. She was a barista not some ninja assassin.

Eva's skin flashed with heat at the realisation of how utterly insane her position was. She couldn't rescue Bishop. She'd be found soon and executed alongside him. Harry would continue his crazy world domination plans undaunted. There was nothing she could do. The odds were too insurmountable.

Then Eva remembered who she was, but more importantly, *where* she was. She was standing in a cleaning storeroom.

A cleaning storeroom full of chemicals.

Explodey chemicals that go bang.

CHAPTER TWENTY-SIX

Eva removed the rubber gloves and leaned back to admire her handiwork. It had taken forty-five careful, nerve wracking minutes, but she'd done it. She'd created a bomb out of household objects. Well, two kinds of bomb, four in total.

Thankfully the chemistry instructor at MI6 insisted on homework, which she'd reluctantly read through that night. It had stuck in her near-photographic memory. The storeroom was well stocked and had all the ingredients for freeing Bishop in the most explosive manner possible.

If they didn't go off in her face first.

The first type of bomb had been the easiest to make. The box marked 'Party Stuff' had been a godsend. The packet of fifty sparklers was exactly what she'd needed. She finely crushed them all, except two, and poured the powder onto aluminium foil. She then placed an aerosol can of air freshener on top and wrapped it up. An uncrushed sparkler its fuse. She had two of these bombs. They would make a very large bang.

The second type were smoke bombs and were the most painstaking to put together. Mostly because of the high likelihood of blowing up in her face. She balled up pieces of aluminium foil and positioned them in the cap of a screw top container, held in place by rubber bands. Drain cleaner was poured in the container itself. Eva had chosen the latter as it had the highest percentage of sodium hydroxide she could find. The delicate step had been screwing on the lid without letting the foil drop into liquid. If the two ingredients mixed too early it would cause a toxic chemical reaction that Eva didn't want to be around in a confined space. In fact, any space.

It had gone past two a.m. and the boisterous banter had all but disappeared from the guards in the common area. *Good.* They'd be at ease, if not asleep. Eva had the cure for that.

As quietly as she could, Eva opened the door. Only one of the five guards in the common area was standing, the others lounged about in various stages of ennui. Even the two burly men posted outside Bishop's cell had more of a slouch.

She had to act. There was no time to ready herself. That would only slow her down. Protective goggles slid into place and the disposable face mask pulled up. Eva picked up the two smoke bombs and shook. She stepped into the hall, planting her feet. It was vital to know where she was when everything went to hell.

One was lobbed towards the centre of the common area and exploded in a ball of grey smoke. The second she threw as the two guards by the door realised something bad was happening. They were too slow. The smoke bomb exploded before they'd drawn their weapons.

Coughing, choking and confused shouts rang out in the chemical-filled air. Everything was grey. Visibility was less than a metre. Half-orders were issued before the officer gagged on the toxic fumes.

With her lighter she lit the sparklers on the explosive bombs. Sparks flew, but it was anything but a children's party. She had dubbed them Mr Explodey I and Mr Explodey II. She rolled the first aerosol bomb along the ground towards the largest group of guards.

The explosion was magnificent. In a blinding flash the sparkler powder ignited, followed directly by the aerosol can. It had come to a halt under a couch which was lifted into the air by the explosion.

Flames engulfed the couch. Someone fired a machine gun indiscriminately. Panicked cries and incoherent shouts filled the room.

There was one thing she hadn't taken into account. The smoke bombs of sodium hydroxide and aluminium created hydrogen. Hydrogen is extremely flammable. The fireball was immense and all encompassing. Eva was swayed by the blast, but held her position firm. If she lost her footing she'd become disorientated in the blinding fog and everything would be lost.

Spot fires burned in the common area.

Eva turned her attention to her prize. The longer fuse on Mr Explodey II was getting low. She hurled it like a cricket ball at the door with the guards. The second explosion was more spectacular.

Unhindered by a couch, Mr Explodey II detonated in an incandescent fireball at the base of the door. The explosion so intense the door was blown off its hinges.

If Eva waited even a second she would lose the advantage. She wasn't prepared for that to happen. She pulled out the only remaining weapon strapped to her back.

Greta was wielded like a baseball bat.

With a banshee cry she hurtled towards the two burly guards. Her only advantage was her goggles and face mask. She intended to utilise them.

The two guards staggered around blindly, charred and smoking from the fireball Eva had inflicted on them. She leapt into the air and struck the nearest with every ounce of strength she had left.

Greta struck him on the side of the head and he flew backwards. Greta was no ordinary umbrella. Reinforced with high-tech components she was virtually unbreakable. Eva was wielding the equivalent of a lead pipe. Greta's bite was something you would never expect from a pretty little thing.

Just like Eva.

She hooked the handle around the neck of the stunned guard.

Using her body weight as leverage she wrenched his head and propelled it into the door frame. The crack was sickening. He fell to the ground, a dead weight.

The second guard, alerted to her presence, issued threats and brandished his gun. His puffy glazed eyes told Eva he could barely see her, if at all. But pistol beat umbrella. She may have overplayed her hand.

It was no time for timidity. A slow exhale of breath steadied her. So what if he was the size of steroid-munching gorilla? He could hardly see, was dazed, probably deaf from the blast and didn't even have a fancy pink umbrella.

From within the confines of the room came a guttural growl. Eva aimed the tip of the umbrella at the guard and pressed the release button. The shaft extended like a welterweight's punch and propelled the off-kilter guard into the threshold of the door. The growling ceased. A dark shadow leapt out of the smog, connecting viciously with the guard and they crashed into the hall.

Despite the formal tuxedo, Bishop looked like a caged animal unleashed, which is exactly what he was. Gone was his British restraint. Bishop was a brutal weapon. His fists a blur. His enraged roars primal and savage.

If Eva hadn't hauled him off the unconscious guard she was sure he would have killed him. He was still swinging wildly when she used hushed soothing tones in his ear, telling him he was safe, that she was by his side and they were getting out of there.

She shoved Bishop through the door of the storeroom before he succumbed to the hydrogen gas. From a bucket near the door, she threw a pre-soaked towel over his head. He was singed, but unhurt. Thankfully the noxious fumes had hardly penetrated the storeroom and visibility was good.

With her ear pressed to the door, Eva heard angry shouts and urgent orders contradicting themselves. Footfalls echoed, none came towards them.

Bishop convulsed, hands on knees. He sucked in non-poisonous breaths. Eva tilted his head up and poured distilled water in his eyes. With a dry towel she patted his face. For the first time Eva saw a vulnerable soul. At that moment, he was like a defenceless child, and she his guardian, his protector.

She was sure it wouldn't last.

His gasps rushed, he asked, "SAS?"

"No, me."

"And?"

"Me."

"And?"

She threw the towel at him. He could dry his own stupid face. In her best southern drawl, she said, "Just little old me and my book learnin'."

Blinking in return, Bishop said nothing.

Evenly, Eva added, "And you're welcome."

"Where are we?"

Apparently they didn't teach gratitude at Cambridge.

"Safe." When that didn't garner a change in his furrowed features, she added, "In a storeroom. And we're about to leave."

"I don't much care for the party we just left. Too many cocks on the dance floor."

"Not to worry, I have a private party organised."

"Now you're talking."

She ignored the innuendo and pushed Bishop roughly towards the back of the room. In keeping with the man he was, Bishop proceeded to unbutton his shirt. Eva gave him a disbelieving expression.

Staring at the wall she'd entered, she realised a major fault in her plan. She didn't know what triggered the door to open from their side.

"Balls."

"Steady on, I've still got my jacket on. We haven't even snogged yet."

"What? No, you letch. I don't know how to get out of here."

"The way you came in?"

"Funny."

"Traditionally speaking, one exits via a door."

"Traditionally speaking, one offers thanks for saving another's life. And secondly, there's a secret passage behind this wall," Eva searched for a lever, "we only have to find it."

Continuing her hunt, she turned and stopped dead. Bishop's face was a mere centimetre from hers. The grin was equal parts playful and lustful. Before she could voice an objection his lips were on hers. His warm mouth enveloping hers, his kiss commanding but yielding. Knowing it was wrong but unable to stop herself, her lips parted and she invited his exploring tongue. He was nowhere near as tentative Harry had been the first time. Bishop was man with experience.

His strong arms held her firm, his caress tender. Eva saw stars. Bishop wasn't all braggadocio. *My god, the man knows how to kiss a woman.*

Bishop leaned backwards and in a whisper, said, "Thank you."

The slap surprised them both. Well, mostly Bishop.

He reeled backwards, rubbing his face.

Eva lowered her gaze. "You haven't earned that kiss."

His red cheek morphed into a smirk. "But you have."

Bishop's arrogance knew no bounds. Ignoring the cretin, she pushed herself away and continued her search. Every bottle, jar, container and packet near the wall was pulled and poked.

With her back to him, Eva tasted her lips. The memory and ecstasy of the kiss still fresh, burned into her memory. If she had been elsewhere and if Bishop had been anyone else, at least one of them would be naked by now. But they weren't. And he wasn't.

She searched harder for the elusive trigger.

"What happened out there? It was like Guy Fawkes Night. You really did all that?"

"I did." There was no concealing Eva's satisfaction with the rescue she'd pulled off. "I made a few smoke bombs and home-made grenades out of this." She motioned to the shelves of chemicals. "I'm like the mother-fucking A-Team." She paused. "The A-Team was a TV show in the eighties…"

"I've seen the A-Team."

"Oh, *that* you've seen."

Running her hand over cleaning products at the back of the

shelf there was a spray bottle that didn't budge. She yanked, but it remained locked in place. When the trigger was pulled there was a slight *click* followed by a *whir*.

Eva spun around expecting to see Bishop's jaw agape in wonder, instead he viewed the opening secret door impassively as if it was an everyday event. Perhaps it was for him. He may very well have a secret room at home. In all likelihood a sex dungeon.

Clearly not getting a deserved round of applause, Eva picked up her backpack and pushed Bishop into the secret passageway. The door closed behind them.

The bare walls of the tunnel seemed colder than before. She hoped the guards didn't figure out she had used the underground railway because there wasn't anywhere for them to hide. The best they could do was get away from the main house as fast as possible, find a place to hide and start planning their escape off the island.

They were only five metres down the passageway when Bishop tugged on her arm.

"Eva."

"Hmmm?"

"I know I can be flippant at times."

"No!"

"But, sincerely, thank you. I owe you my life. It's a responsibility I take tremendously seriously. I owe you a debt. A debt I intend to repay."

"Let's not count our chickens before the well runs dry."

"That's an awful analogy."

"It's a metaphor and I learned from the best."

The two walked on cautiously. Bishop glanced in Eva's direction, either taking in her outfit, or checking out her arse. Probably both.

"If I may ask, why did you save me? You seemed cosy enough with Lancing. I thought you may have turned and lost your nerve."

"Nope. Harry's lost it."

She gave a brief rundown of Harry's plans, or rather, her limited knowledge of them. All the while she attempted to hold back the emotional damage of Harry's duplicity. No matter how much logic she applied, or how much she reminded herself that reuniting with Harry had only been for MI6, it stung. The love of her life had met her while planning a terrorist attack and had pursued her to appear good on camera. It was sickening and painful. She needed Nancy and a case of gin to thrash it out. But first they had to get off the island.

The more Eva explained Harry's plan, the paler he grew. She went on to explain the data centre on the other island and the underground railway. "What I want to know is, how could he have built it? I mean, the thing's massive. How could he have created it without word getting out?"

"That, I can answer. Chinese labourers. Mr Lancing hired hundreds of labourers from an isolated province and paid them extremely generously. He also funded the town's schools, library and sporting field. They love him. That's what did him in."

"I don't follow."

"We wouldn't have known anything about it, but the CIA became interested when satellites detected a statue erected in the town square of a little Chinese town. Not Chairman Mao, but Lancing. They sent in a local agent to do some digging and found the locals were being flown in and out of some isolated island in the Pacific, but no one knew where."

"Until I clicked on that pen."

"Exactly."

"His own statue? He'd love that," Eva said bitterly. "So is the British Navy awaiting your orders?"

"We haven't had much of a presence in the Pacific since World War Two. No, I was dropped in a few miles off shore. We've no support."

"You didn't think to bring a gun maybe?"

"You saw the reception. Any equipment would have been confiscated immediately. I parachuted into the ocean, took a leisurely scuba scooter, then a nice little swim. A one way endeav-

our, I'm afraid. So from here on in we'll have to rely on my ingenuity and dashing good looks."

"*Our* ingenuity."

"That's what I said."

They reached the end of the passage and the entrance to the
underground train station. After tentatively checking for anyone
planning to use them as target practice Eva approached the
console. It lit up giving the four destination options.

"Where to?"

"May as well find out about this data centre I've heard so
much about."

Eva pressed the button labelled *Warehouse Entrance B* and
waited.

She gripped Greta tighter and hoped the guards above hadn't
called for reinforcements who could be arriving on the same train.

To fill the void in conversation, she asked, "Why did you
deliberately provoke Harry at dinner? I've never seen him
so angry."

Bishop shrugged. "We weren't getting anywhere. Plus I didn't
come here to see him, I came here for you."

"To save the damsel in distress? So far the only rescuing has
come from me, Buddy."

He sighed. "Are you going to turn this into a feminism thing
again?"

"Feminism thing? I'm sorry, do my opinions bore you?"

"Not at all." Bishop rocked on his heels. "All I'm saying is
sometimes with all the feminist talk, it just...I feel it gets a might...
I don't know, tedious? Everything doesn't have to be about feminism, does it? If I say I don't like liquorice it doesn't mean I hate
women and need a fifteen-minute diatribe on a female's eternal
struggle. Sometimes I feel like I'm trapped in a first year women's
collective meeting where you're holding the talking stick way
too long."

The train carriage arrived empty. Eva was proud of herself for
not pushing Bishop in front of it. She must be growing. If it was
another time she may even have found the statement amusing.

Her hackles were up but she was far too nervous and exhausted to debate him. She flicked him the bird instead.

The train journey was conducted in silence. The further the carriage descended, the deeper her trepidation. In retrospect selecting the second warehouse station may have been a mistake. For one thing, they had to go via the first entrance, subjecting them to potential discovery as the transparent egg passed through the station. Secondly, for all they knew the second warehouse entrance was the guard's station. Dread gurgled in her gut.

As the train climbed towards the second island, Eva crouched and gripped Greta like a weapon.

"What are you doing?" Bishop asked, slouched against the carriage wall.

"Getting ready. I suggest you do the same."

Bishop gave a nonchalant shrug and pushed himself upright. He hunkered into an old school boxing stance and rotated his wrists mockingly.

"You can really be a massive dick sometimes, you know?"

They stared at one another as the last sentence sunk in.

Eva raised a finger. "Don't!"

"Perish the thought."

Bishop was being more obnoxious than usual. Perhaps it was that she had rescued him and not the other way around. Maybe this was his default setting when in danger. She suspected the former.

The train carriage flew through the first station. There was not another human being to be seen. It slowed as it approached the second. In contrast to his flippancy, Bishop's body became rigid. The carriage slid quietly to the second warehouse platform. It was empty. The doors hissed open and they exited. Eva found it hard to move as every muscle was tense.

Bishop jerked his head and sprinted towards a dark corner. She followed. They stopped in front of a large blank barrier. Above them a series of walkways were built into the concrete wall. Eva could faintly hear the sound of crashing waves, as if they were hitting the other side. It seemed the area had once been a cave mouth. It must have been closed up to accommodate Harry's server farm.

They squatted, listening for any human activity. There was only the constant purr of air-conditioning and the occasional bleep of a server doing something computery.

After a few minutes, Eva thought it safe to whisper. "How did you survive Prague? I was sure you were dead in that river."

"I almost nearly was. Fortunately I am blessed with high cheek-bones and exceptional good luck." His expression turned more serious. "I was underwater for a long time, but eventually managed to free my leg. When I was finally able to pitch my head above water, the storm surge had swept me well down the river. I managed to latch onto some flotsam and float for a time. When I finally reached shore I was rescued by an amenable farmer's daughter. When I advised she would be rewarded handsomely for her kindness she took me in and I showed her my unrestrained gratitude."

Eva groaned. "Did all that really happen?"

"You may substitute farmer's daughter for an elderly farmer's wife."

"And the showing of unrestrained gratitude?"

He waggled his eyebrows.

"You're incurable. You have the restraint of a dog in heat..."

Bishop raised his head in alertness, held up his finger and in a hushed tone said, "Shhhhhh!"

Eva stopped and became watchful, shrinking into the wall. As quietly as she could, she asked, "Did you hear something?"

"No. I just wanted you to stop talking."

Fists clenched, she ground her teeth. "You're pissed off that I saved you, again, aren't you?"

"Of course not, why would you say that?"

"Because you've been a surly git since I blew you out of there. You didn't like that, did you? Being saved by a girl? What's the matter, bruised male ego? Diddums."

"I'll have you know I was working on my own fiendishly

clever escape plan when you came barging in. I was waiting for my moment."

"Right. Admit it, you're narky because you weren't the one to save the day."

Bishop's shoulders dropped a fraction. "I will concede it's not usually my role to be saved, no."

"As in, the male role, as in the prince sweeping in and saving the defenceless fawn of a princess? Well, bad luck but the rules have changed, it's a whole new millennium. Gender roles are all fucked up, get used to it."

About to launch into an all-out tirade, Eva stopped when she spotted distant movement. Only a flash, but it was enough. In the distance a shadow darted between two banks of servers. It was a stooped run, not a casual stroll.

A guard. Harry's men knew they were there.

A finger went to her lips and she pointed where the figure was. Bishop nodded curtly, alert. The figure was fifty metres away, but they literally had their backs to wall. Not a lot of options. They could make a run for the train, but the carriage had gone and it would mean at least one of them would need to wait unarmed in the open until the next one arrived.

A *click* echoed through cavernous hall. Actually, in was less of a *click*, more of a cocking sound. A loud, close-by cocking sound.

They turned and glanced up to see a group of five heavily-armed guards above them on the walkway. Front and centre was a furious-looking Van Buren. Lips hard, he said, "Oh, hey guys. Cosy?"

It had happened all too fast for Eva to process. She went to rise, but Van Buren aimed a gun at her chest and tutted.

"Sorry to interrupt." His tone implied the opposite. "You seemed to be having an awfully interesting debate about equality." His trademark sneer returned. "This is the side you've chosen? Incredible."

Eva chose not to respond. He really did act like a jealous ex-lover.

Van Buren sucked in air. "Well this is all very awkward, isn't it?

You've left a whole mess of my guys bruised and blinded. You really are a destructive little bitch, aren't you? Destroy everything you touch. Destruction by name…"

"Harry was going to execute him. I think that's a pretty decent reason."

A bitter laugh echoed around the cave. "You're such a stupid whore, aren't you? Horatio was never going to execute him. He just wanted to see what you'd do."

A strange kind of relief washed over her. Had she read all this wrong? Was Harry as innocent as she'd always assumed? After the brief blip of thought, reality sunk in. It sounded too good to be true, because it was. Eva recalled the London bombings and the death and destruction that came with it. She hated herself for forgetting who Harry was for even a second. She remembered she was a fighter and her fight was with Harry Fucking Lancing.

Bishop gripped her wrist and squeezed.

Van Buren went on. "As it turns out, what you'd do is betray him. Again." Van Buren positively glowed. "I guess I will really have to execute you now. Both of you."

The guards raised their guns.

CHAPTER TWENTY-SEVEN

Eva's mouth fell open, but no sound tumbled out.

If Harry had been there she could have talked him out of it. Appeal to his moral compass. But with Van Buren, there was no appeal. Nothing appealing at all. They really were dead.

She lost her balance but Bishop wouldn't let her fall. He held her firm, his gaze bore into Van Buren like a laser.

Bishop's demeanour was casual, but Eva could feel his body become taut through the tuxedo. "So, Van Buren, do you have a first name?" Stony silence was his reply. "Fine, I'll go with...Reginald. I have only one question for you, Reginald. This lot," he threw a thumb towards the cavern of servers behind him, "isn't about blackmailing a few politicians, is it? You've got more grunt here than the NSA. Lancing's no longer about blackmailing a few select officials, is he? He's collecting information on everyone, right? You don't need this kind of power to play a few games of *Tetris*." Bishop slapped his forehead. "Of course! I'm going to take a wild stab and say you've tapped into the submarine communications cable." He waggled his finger at Van Buren. "That's why you're on this island, isn't it? You've hooked into the intercontinental communications line?"

DAVE SINCLAIR

Van Buren's face could have been carved into Mount Rushmore. The lack of response was confirmation enough. Eva should have known Harry wouldn't have chosen the island location on a whim. Like everything the man did, there was a purpose.

Bishop continued. "I assume all of this is so you can comb everyone's data, correct? Lancing's moved beyond the odd bit of blackmail to spying on everyone he can. You might want to be careful associating with your boss. Do you know how many thousands of laws he's broken? He's violating the privacy of every internet-connected citizen on the planet. My question is, why?"

Van Buren tilted his head, like a lion assessing its prey. An amused smirk crossed his strained lips. "What you see here is the work of a great man. A brilliant genius whose vision you will never comprehend. What he's doing is not as malicious as your tiny mind obviously thinks it is. The metadata retention on private citizens will only be used to persuade individuals who try to oppose his vision. A brainless blogger who wants to criticize, a turd-munching journalist who's getting too nosy. Every moron out there has something to hide, everyone. Do they really want the world to know they've cheated on their husband or have been siphoning company funds? Is a blog post worth a family's happiness or one story more important than their home? Is it really?"

"So everyone can have freedom unless they oppose the great and powerful Horatio Lancing?" Bishop's tone was mocking.

"You know nothing. It's not like that."

"Isn't it?" Eva was amazed she'd regained the ability to speak. "Because it bloody well sounds like that. Harry's become what he always claimed to be fighting. He's become his own enemy. 'Four legs good, two legs better'. He's twisting the world to only his way of thought. Freedom means people have the chance to choose the option that isn't him. Otherwise it's not freedom, it's a dictatorship."

"What Horatio is doing is for the greater good." Van Buren was repeating the same phrase Harry had used countless times. *The greater good.* He'd drunk the Horatio Lancing Kool-Aid long ago. The Security Chief shook his head, as if he was addressing a partic-

284

ularly stupid child. "Any woman on the planet would have given her left nut to stand by his side. Any woman but you."

"Or man, as it turns out," Eva said.

"What?"

"Nothing."

Van Buren spat on the walkway. "You stupid slut. You squandered your chance to be part of his vision."

Eva's finger stabbed at the banks of computers. "This isn't what I thought Harry's vision was, not even close. I always believed in the core of what Harry wanted to achieve, but what he's trying to do now is sick, it's twisted. Surely even you can see that? It flies in the face of everything he said he stood for. I doubt he'd want all this to get out. Will his loyal acolytes love him when they find out he's snooping on their email, their private messages? Harry's become what he despised, he's become a man with secrets he wants to hide."

Van Buren glared at her with a face carved from rock. "Nice speech. Tell me exactly how that's gonna stop me from killing you?"

"If you kill me now Harry will never trust you again." That got through. There was the slightest turn of Van Buren's head. "If you shoot me, even if you claim it was self-defence, Harry will always wonder. He knows you hate me and would be boning for an excuse to murder me. 'Did it go down like VB claimed, or...?'" Eva shrugged. "The seed would be planted. He'd never fully believe a word you said again. And once that happens, well, you know as well as I do how it ends. Is it worth it? Contact Harry, let him make the call."

Van Buren scoffed. "It's obvious you're filibustering. What's the alternative? Lock you up? Yeah, that's been a smashing success so far."

She ignored him. "You want to take the chance? If you want to always be on Team Harry, I suggest you call him."

He assessed her, part loathing, part reluctant resignation. Van Buren grunted. He took out a walkie talky, turned his back and had a hushed conversation.

Eva tried not to think about what she'd discovered about Harry. She had to focus on survival first. One day, hopefully soon, she could take her time to think about the scumbag douchepoodle lying sack of baboon shit that was Harry Fucking Lancing. But later. Presently she was all about avoiding death.

It was inconceivable that Van Buren wouldn't win the case for getting rid of them. The logical portion of her brain could see that she and Bishop posed too much of a risk. The only way for them not to be a threat to Harry's operation was for them to die.

If she could only see Harry, she'd have a chance. Talking him out of it wasn't impossible. She could do it. She could convince her former lover not to harm them. She could. Probably. Possibly. Maybe. She had to try. It was their only chance.

"Hey." Bishop's quiet voice tickled her ear. "Give me your bra."

Her head snapped around. "What? Uh, hell to the no."

Did he want it for his trophy wall? He probably had a trophy wall.

He unleashed his girl-slayer grin. "Do you trust me?"

"Not even slightly."

"It's important."

She was too numb to be pissed at him. His problems must be genetic or something. Like expecting a rat to stay out of the garbage or a randy dog not to hump your leg. Maybe he wanted to build a slingshot. What did she have to lose?

Keeping her eyes on Van Buren in an intense but quiet argument, Eva unhooked her black lacy bra. She wriggled her arms out of the straps under the turtleneck. She extracted the bra from her sleeve like some sleazy magician.

Bishop gave her a slight nod of thanks. "It still fascinates me."

"Boobs?"

"No. Well, yes, but I was referring to the ability of women to take a bra off while clothed. It's beguiling for us mere males."

Eva turned her attention back to the conference on the walkway. Van Buren's hand on his hip, a faint smile across his scarred face. *Diarrhoea monkey farts.* He'd won. They'd be hauled up to the beach and shot by firing squad. It was over.

A flicking sound came from behind. She turned to see Bishop attempting to start a lighter. *Her* lighter.

"How did you get that? It was in my pocket."

He splayed his fingers, jazz hands-style, and said, "Spy craft."

In one hand he held the lit lighter, in the other her bra. He was trying to light it on fire. Was he making a feminist statement?

Finally the flame caught the bra on fire. Holding the smouldering underwear Bishop stepped out into the open and held it aloft. Every man on the walkway turned to him.

Thrusting the burning garment in the air, Bishop yelled, "We will never advance as a society until we rid ourselves of the shackles of male oppression!"

As if stirred by his words, the bra erupted into flames sending a plume of black smoke skyward.

As if realising what Bishop was doing, Van Buren stretched out his hand and yelled, "No!"

It was too late.

An ear-splitting siren shattered the stillness of the yawning cavern. Red flashing lights blazed in every corner. A thunderous hissing sound seemed to come from everywhere. From the rooftop pipes a pallid fog descended rapidly.

Bishop had triggered the fire suppression system. *Clever bastard.*

Everything turned white. Visibility disappeared. Eva held up her palm and couldn't see it. Harry's men shouted but were soon muffled by coughing fits.

Bishop's strong hand gripped her wrist and wrenched her away. They ran into the labyrinth of servers. Eva was completely blind, following Bishop wherever he was headed. He pulled her hand low, forcing her into a stooped run. She hoped he knew where he was going. She was completely disorientated.

They had to be careful. There was at least one guard lurking around the floor. Possibly more.

She tried to ask a question, but choked on the fumes before she got a syllable out. Bishop stopped his run, turned to her and grasped either side of her face. A few centimetres inch away from her nose, he shook his head. *No talking*. Before she could respond, he was off again, dragging her with him.

Each turn was deliberate. His course ceaseless. Did he know where he was going? How was that possible?

The flashing lights and siren suddenly ceased. The fog remained. Things were infinitely more difficult. There was a huge droning sound like an airplane turbine starting up. They'd started the gas extraction. Any advantage would soon be lost.

He increased his pace.

Navigating around a server rack Bishop bounced off a huge black shadow. A guard. A big one. The guard's first punch was high and Bishop ducked easily. That was all he needed. His entire body leaned into a punch to the guard's sternum. The guard doubled over and Bishop didn't spare a moment. His second blow connected with the side of the guard's head, the succession of blows was so fast it became impossible to distinguish one from another. Bishop was unrelenting. Despite his size, the giant guard collapsed to the ground like a felled grizzly bear. Out cold.

Her hand yanked, they were off again. They neared an outer wall, opposite to where they'd come from. Headed for a door labelled, 'Explosives – Keep Out!'

Bishop tried the door. Locked. He stepped back as if ready to kick it down, but Eva shook her head. She pointed to her ears. *Too loud*. In a flash she had her lock picking kit out and went to work. Taking longer than she wanted, she eventually heard the satisfying *click* as the tension wrench turned in the unlocked deadbolt.

Without hesitating, Bishop hustled them in and shut the door.

The room was larger than she thought. Wooden crates were stacked to the roof behind a series of chain-link gates.

In hushed tones Eva asked, "What is all this?"

"This data centre isn't in a natural cavern."

"So?"

"So, it means it was probably blasted out."

"And if it was blasted out…"

"…they would need things that go bang somewhere."

"Okay. But why keep them down here, isn't it dangerous to be close to the servers?"

"Temperature-controlled, away from the natural elements, heavily-guarded, fire suppression systems. I'd say it's the ideal position."

"How did you know it was here?"

"My superior spy training, intuitive ability and countless hours of honing my skill." He paused. "Plus there was a map on the wall near where we were standing. But mostly the spy thing."

Bishop held out his hand. "Hand me the umbrella, please."

"Greta."

"Hand me the umbrella please, Greta."

"No, the umbrella's called...whatever." She handed him Greta.

Bishop wedged Greta into the chain binding the fence to the gate. He gave it a sharp twist. The ridiculously strong umbrella broke the chain and it fell to the floor.

The next few minutes entailed Bishop investigating the contents of boxes marked with warnings, exclamation points, and skull and crossbones.

When he had piled a succession of explosives and gadgets on a desk, Eva asked, "So what are we going to do?"

A droll grin crossed his lips. "Make things go explodey."

Twenty minutes later Bishop had assembled an impressive arsenal of weapons. He knew his explosives. Sticks of dynamite were attached by wire to small electronic devices. Eva was disappointed there was no big red digital readout like they had in movies. She'd been informed that never happens. It was a bomb. It went off when it went off, no need to advertise the fact.

Every movement Bishop made was precise and deliberate. There never seemed to be any danger of explosion, so complete was Bishop's mastery of bomb-making. He had split the bombs into two groups; those on timers and those detonated by remote control. Both triggers were plentiful. They all served a specific purpose. She had to admit it was more professional than some sparklers and an aerosol can.

Eventually he stood back with folded arms, admiring his work. He gave a curt nod and said, "Let's not dilly-dally, time to cause a ruckus." He turned to Eva, his face soft. "Oh, and Eva. I do apologise for being a chauvinistic windbag before. I am thankful for you saving my worthless hide. I know this experience must have been incredibly hard for you, working against a man you once loved only for him to…have turned on you. I keep forgetting you haven't been trained for this…uh…that is not a dig, I mean, I… In short, you are exceptional."

"And…?"

"Very exceptional?"

"No. I mean I'm waiting for the sexist punchline."

"No punchline. No inappropriate kissing. No towel stealing. Just me being genuine for once."

Eva rocked on her heels. "It's a bit weird, you not saying something inappropriate."

"I know. It is, isn't it? Would it help if I fondled your bottom?"

"In a weird way, it might." Eva grinned. "But seriously, don't. You look better with two arms attached."

He nodded.

"And Bishop…"

"Mmmm?"

"Thank you for saving me back there. That was some nice work. And I hate to tell you, but with that whole bra burning thing, you're positively Germaine Greer."

"Scary isn't it?"

"Incredibly."

He picked up a bomb and asked, "Are you ready to do something ridiculously dangerous and stupid?"

"Have you met me?"

∾

Eva checked the watch. Did the second hand go backwards? It

seemed like it. Time had slowed. The stupid thing said Bishop had left an hour and a half before, but it obviously lied. It seemed like at least a day to her.

The lack of gunfire was a good thing. She put that in the pro column. No unscheduled explosions, also pro. The fact that Bishop said he'd contact her via walkie talky in an hour 'at absolute most' was definitely in the con column. Underlined. With an exclamation point for emphasis.

Eva checked the battery on the walkie talky. Still good. She tried calling Bishop, for the tenth time, no answer. Every second that ticked by brought her closer to the detonation of the timed devices. She stared at Bishop's expensive oversized black dive watch. He'd given it to her so she'd know when the explosions would occur. When he handed it over it was as if she was receiving his first born child, such was his reluctance to relinquish his grip. She could only stare at it knowing he was long overdue.

It had been risky enough to place bombs in the facility they were in, it was far riskier for him to go back to the main island and place bombs there. The longer Eva waited, the more dangerous it seemed.

Beside her was the detonator for the remote-controlled bombs. They would be the first to go. As soon as Bishop told her he was on the surface of the island, Eva would be clear to find her way out of the data centre to meet him on the surface. Then they'd blow it to pieces. Bishop should have already placed the bombs at the base of the wall where they had been confronted by Van Buren and his goons.

Bishop had told her repeatedly that she wasn't to detonate them early or she'd die. Once the first bomb went off every living thing in the manufactured cave would be dead. No escape. She had to be nowhere near it. That's why the first bombs needed to be remotely controlled, they couldn't risk mistiming their escape and being caught in the aftermath.

After the first set of bombs, Harry's evil scheme would be all but destroyed. The timed devices would see to the rest of his operation. The power plant, the main house and anything else Bishop could find on the main island would go up to be sure. Harry's carefully constructed empire would be destroyed.

The rational part of Eva's mind had been steadily working on her loathing of Harry. The emotional side lagged behind, but was running to catch up. It's not every day the man who purported to love you gives the order to have you killed, real or imagined. Normally they'd just unfriend you from Facebook. Add to that the whole invasion of privacy on a global scale and the trifling little issue of killing innocent people in a mock-terrorist attack. The man was a megalomaniac, plain and simple.

Eva tried not to backtrack their relationship and find more times when he'd obviously lied to or manipulated her but she failed. The time in Rome when they'd been spotted by a pack of paparazzi and photographed having a romantic dinner happened to coincide with a few negative news stories. In retrospect the 'He can't be all bad, he's in love' stories made her sick. Of course they were in Lancing newspapers. The times Harry had been 'stuck' in Hawaii were probably him taking side trips to the island.

Their relationship wasn't just built on a bedrock of deceit, it was constructed with it too. Take away the bricks of lies, did she have anything worth salvaging left? She'd loved the man once, not as long ago as she should have. Eva was going to need some intensive therapy. And booze. And Nancy.

Adjusting her bikini, she checked the stupid watch again. It ticked mockingly slowly. She'd changed into the bikini from the backpack just in case. There was a high likelihood they'd need to do some swimming in the near future so swimwear was more practical than a turtleneck and leggings.

The main drawback was she would be forced to ditch the backpack. She'd have to move fast and would need her hands free to carry the detonator and the two guns Bishop had found in the armoury. Sig Sauers. Nice find. Exceptionally-balanced and superbly-crafted pieces of machinery. They cried out to be fired.

Faint footsteps approached and the handle of the door jiggled. She was relieved at Bishop's return. It was short-lived. It wasn't Bishop.

In the doorway stood Harry. Behind him were two heavily-armed guards. Eva went to lunge for the guns.

"Don't. Please."

The pistols were too far away. Harry's plea appeared genuine. If she dove for the guns she'd be cut down before she was halfway.

Eva straightened her back. "How did you find me?"

"It was Van Buren who came up with the idea. Simply turn off the lights in the main hall and see if any rooms still have lights turned on. I knew there was a reason I kept him around."

"Not his winning personality and faultless personal hygiene?"

"Always with the jokes."

"Always with the condescension."

"Eva, you know that's not true. I loved you from the moment we met."

"Lied from then on, too." Running her fingers through her hair, Eva frowned. "All this," she pointed behind him, "is wrong, Harry. It's evil and against everything you said you believed in. You always said you needed me. I never knew until now that was actually true. You said you needed a moral compass, so here I am telling you that what you're doing is immoral. What you're trying to do goes against everything I thought you stood for. You're no longer the truth's guardian, you're its oppressor."

Harry's face was unmoved. Her impassioned plea was too late. A decade too late. He was too far down the rabbit hole to come back. The opinion of an ex-girlfriend who had betrayed him counted for nothing.

Eva readied herself to dive for the guns, damn the consequences. She must have telegraphed her move because the guards tightened the grip on their weapons. Harry didn't stop them. Van Buren must have won. She would be executed.

Harry Lancing, the man she'd loved more than any other, the man she'd suspended her values for, her Geronimo Man, was lost to her. In a way, he may as well have put a bullet in her. Eva's insides were ripped apart.

The situation was grim. No sign of Bishop. Harry and his guards stood in her way. She couldn't take them all down, even if she had the guns. The larger guard's head was bandaged, the other sported a charred uniform. They'd been in the house when she'd set off her homemade bombs. She doubted they'd be signing up for her fan club newsletter.

Harry bowed his head. When he raised it, his face was gentler, like the man she once fell in love with. "I'm truly sorry, Eva. This has all gotten out of hand. You were never a prop. Honestly, I've always loved you and only ever wanted to be with you. I know I'm the one who screwed it up with all this." He waved his hand behind him. "Every day I wish I'd done things differently with you, been more open, told you about this place. I was stupid. I see that now."

She didn't know where he was going with his apology. As she listened with her hands behind her back, Eva's fingers caressed the detonator for the remote-controlled bombs. Her finger hovered over the trigger.

In a strange kind of way she held the fate of the world, literally, in her hands. She had the ability to save Harry's vision or destroy it. The future of Europe, the world, could be irrevocably changed depending on Eva's actions. It was a lot for an everyday barista to take in.

Even with his soothing words, she could no longer trust a single word from the man standing before her. He was making apologies with armed men at his back. There was no way she could have a life with him.

She had to escape, not just from the room, but from the planet-sized pull of Harry Lancing. Even after all she'd been through and all she knew he made Eva doubt herself. She was stronger than that. No man had made her concede her values like he had. She should have been tougher than that, but wasn't. Her mother hadn't raised someone so easily bent to the will of any man. Eva was an amazon, a fighter. No one should ever gauge their worth by the opinion of another.

No more.

She had no idea where Bishop was. She was cornered.

Harry was still talking. "We were close, though, weren't we?"

His face tender. "We were almost happy. We almost had the life we both wanted."

She held out the detonator. The panicked guards aimed guns at her.

"Harry…"

"Yes, Eva."

She looked him dead in the eye. "Almost only counts in horse-shoes and hand grenades."

Eva pressed the trigger. The bombs exploded.

CHAPTER TWENTY-EIGHT

The sound of the explosion was horrific. The blast inside the expansive chamber reverberated with ear-shattering intensity. The guards were knocked off their feet. Harry only managed to remain standing by clinging to the door frame.

There was no chance Eva would let the slightest of cracks of opportunity go wanting. Grabbing Greta, she lowered her shoulder and charged. Still disorientated, Harry never saw her coming. The man she had shared countless embraces with received one last less intimate one.

Her shoulder connected with his ribs. The wind knocked from his lungs, Harry flew backwards. Greta swung like a sword and connected to the side of the head of the already bandaged guard. At least it was the other side. Pivoting, Eva continued the swing and connected with the other guard's head as he raised it.

Both down, Eva went back to pick up the pistols and tuck Greta into the straps of her bikini like a samurai sword. She planned to race to the train station but something held her leg.

"Let me go, Harry."

"If only I could."

He didn't know what was coming next.

Eva did.

She glanced at the watch. "About high tide, right?

"Yes," Harry said, confused. His face contorted. "Oh, Eva, no."

The roar of water was deafening, its devastation total. The tsunami engulfed row upon row of servers knocking them over like children's sandcastles.

The only sound that could be heard above the tumultuous waters was the cry of grief from Harry. Eva turned her back on him and ran.

The train station was thankfully elevated and hadn't been hit by the first surge of encroaching sea water. It didn't mean it was safe. The underground monorail wasn't a great option in a flooding facility but she didn't have time to find another exit. There was a chance that the slight incline before the railway descended into the tunnel would be enough to hold back the waters. If she was lucky she'd make it from one island to the other before the tunnel flooded. Or lose power first. She had to concede it wasn't a great plan.

As she dashed she searched for any sign of Bishop. It would be impossible for him to have lived if he was on the floor of the data centre. Barely a server stack survived the initial wave. Debris littered the chaotic waters. Eva prayed he was topside when she'd detonated the bombs. She couldn't bear to lose him to raging waters twice.

Sprinting, Eva was relieved there was a train carriage at the first warehouse platform. On the control panel, she pressed *Main House Entrance B* and leapt in.

Behind her another rush of water engulfing what was once the data centre. The ruin she had brought was total. Nothing had survived.

Regardless of how right she thought her actions were, Eva had caused this. She had brought this destruction on Harry and his dreams. *What have I done?* Eva wanted to throw up.

Her plan was to get to the main island, commandeer a boat back to the second island and begin her search for Bishop. If he was even alive. He was meant to be somewhere on the surface. She

glanced at the watch. The power would be cut via the timed deto-
nations in forty-five minutes. If Bishop had managed to place the
explosives in time. It would be pushing it to get back before then.
She had to try. Eva owed him that much.

Tapping her foot she willed the glacial doors to go faster.

"Eva."

Her head snapped around. Before her was a broken human
being. He stumbled towards her, a shell of a man. He hardly
resembled the hero of the Battle of Trafalgar, the crusading extor-
tionist of governments or the man who had once been her entire
world. With five metres to go, Eva lifted her gun. Evenly she said,
"This carriage is taken, Harry. Find another one."

Harry was horrified. "You can't leave me here."

"It seems I can." The door continued to close.

Appalled, Harry's eyes pleaded. "What can you possibly get
from leaving me here?"

Eva lowered her gun. "Closure."

His jaw dropped. Eva could have pressed the door release
button. She could have. But didn't.

An expression of horror flashed across Harry's face. She'd
gotten her wish. She was over Harry Lancing. The doors finally
hissed shut.

A roar of inundating water surged forward and engulfed the
statue-like Harry. The water was only waist-high, but it was
enough to lose his footing. He stumbled and was swept away by
the surge. The last Eva saw of him he was struck on the back by a
server rack and went under the water. He didn't surface again.

Despite his evil transformation, Eva couldn't bring herself to
wish harm to come to Harry. She wasn't heartless. She searched
the desolation before her and couldn't find him. She asked herself,
who the hell are you? Is this who you are now?

With a clench of her eyes, Eva tried to focus on what came next
but the bile in the back of her throat told her it wasn't that easy.
Had she killed the man who had once meant everything to her?

As the train gained momentum, Eva's attention was drawn to a
flash of light on one of the upper walkways. A bloodied figure ran

as two uniformed guards fired machine guns at him. He returned fire. The son of a bitch was still alive. Wounded and limping, but alive. And in a firefight. Of course he was. He always managed to find someone to piss off.

Annoyingly, Bishop was still immaculate in the tux. The stupid bastard was meant to be on the surface. He'd just made Eva's job a hell of a lot harder.

She pounded her fists on the train carriage's glass. With every ounce of strength left, she screamed, "I'm coming for you!"

He didn't hear her. The train darkened as it entered the tunnel and descended. Eva collapsed on the floor. It was all too much. Everything happened too fast. There was nothing left in her bloodstream but adrenaline.

Deep breaths were sucked in as she stared at the ceiling. The overhead lights flickered past as the transparent egg glided along the monorail. She was exhausted in every way possible, in fact she may have even created some new ones to add to the list. All Eva wanted was to close her eyes, for a moment, and wake up in her own bed. If only she could sleep for a week, wake up and call Nancy and Paul for brunch. Take a walk. Read a book. Be human.

Eva sensed herself drifting off to sleep. Her eyes flashed open. She'd said if she was lucky she would be through the tunnel before it flooded.

She wasn't lucky.

The awful sound reached her before she saw it. When the water finally came, it was terrifying. Behind her was nothing but a churning, violent, all-encompassing wall of fury. The flooding waters came at her at an incredible rate. As fast as the train was, there was no way she'd outrun it. It was too fast. Too powerful.

There was nothing Eva could do but brace for impact. The sea water was going to smash into her and it was going to be ugly. Grasping two handrails, she planted her feet like a surfer. This was going to hurt.

The wave hit and the train carriage lurched forward viciously. With a petrifying metallic *rip* the rear of the train shot upwards. The carriage shook as if it were a tennis ball in the mouth of a dog.

After a final shredding noise the train was no longer attached to the monorail.

Unshackled by rail, the surging water propelled the egg-shaped carriage like a bullet from a gun. Eva lost all sense of balance. She had no idea which way was up. For a moment she blacked out. When she opened her eyes she wished she was still unconscious. At the peak of the wave, she saw ahead. Approaching fast was a solid, definitely conclusive wall, signifying the end of the tunnel.

The torrent of the water started to slow as the tunnel rose to the main house, but it wouldn't be enough. The train carriage was going to crash into the end of the tunnel. As best she could, Eva braced for impact.

The collision was terrible. Screeching metal, sparks and teeth-chattering shudders vanished instantly when the whole structure crushed into the rock wall. Grinding metal soon gave way to razor-sharp glass flying in every direction. The sudden stop nearly pulled her arms out of their sockets but could have been worse. The receding water made the impact less catastrophic. The final few metres were slowed by the lack of water, only momentum propelled the carriage forward. The crash was still painful but in the aftermath everything was still attached.

Unhooking herself from the straps, Eva spat blood. Her vision blurred. At first she thought it was sweat, but then realised it was more blood. A cut on her head had trickled into her eye. Various lacerations scarred her body. But she was alive. That was enough.

Allowing herself the luxury of a moment to gather her wits, she surveyed the situation. She watched the water retreat down the tunnel, but it would be back soon enough. The train carriage was the right way up but cracked and destroyed.

She had to evacuate the tunnel before the surging water returned. Eva collected her weapons and kicked out the door. It shattered on the monorail track. The closest station was fifty metres away. Eva staggered out and limped towards it.

The rumble of the rushing water was deafening. It was coming back. *Too soon. Too bloody soon.* Ignoring the pain, she broke into a run. She had no idea if she'd make the station in time. She'd come this far, she'd be damned if she'd give up now.

The rumble soon morphed into an ear-splitting wall of noise. So sluggish was Eva's progress it was like she was running underwater. She urged herself on because if she didn't make it, that's exactly what she would be doing.

Slowly, far too slowly she neared the train station. The cacophony grew in intensity, but she couldn't see the gushing sea water. Yet. She ran on.

Finally managing to reach her goal, Eva leaped onto the station as the wall of water came into view. It was close but she'd beaten it. There was no time to celebrate. Legs on fire, she darted through the exit and up the incline.

As her lungs screamed in protest, Eva sped on. A fleeting glimpse behind showed the water reach the end of the passageway but encroach no further.

Completely spent, her legs buckled and she fell. For an eternity her crumpled form did nothing but breathe. Lovely, plentiful air filled her lungs. The smooth cold surface of the passageway soothed her aching body. She could have stayed there for years. If only she had that luxury.

Her tortured arms reluctantly pushed her broken body up. Every muscle screamed for respite but was ignored.

Eva whispered, "Fuck weakness." A call back to the Battle of Trafalgar. A different time. A different life.

For all she knew, Bishop may have been dead but there was no way in hell she'd leave him behind if there was a chance. They'd saved each other's lives numerous times, Eva wasn't about to break the chain. If he was alive in the ruined facility she would find a way to get him out. She had to. That was what drove her forward. That was why she couldn't fail.

Hobbling forward, Eva fought every ache her body tormented her with. She had no time for pain. Wheezing, she slapped the release of the secret door to the cleaning storeroom. It seemed so long ago she'd been there, but in reality it was mere hours. She made her way across the room and opened the door a crack. No human activity.

Ambling into the hallway, Eva realised there was daylight. Bishop's watch said she had a little less than half an hour to find a boat and get off the island before it blew. Then all she had to figure out was a way to save Bishop. *Simple.*

"Hey!"

Eva heard the voice, but didn't turn. She ran. The only person she wanted to hear from was Bishop and he was trapped in a flooded underground cavern.

Plus he probably wouldn't be shooting at her.

The door frame splintered with bullets as she leapt through to the outside world. She ducked and sprinted towards the jungle. The gunman must have been far down the hall for her not to have seen him. She'd be well out of sight of the house by the time he reached the door. Eva sped on just in case.

The island sounded deceptively peaceful. She knew better. Between her and the pier were armed men who wanted to do her harm.

She had a mission, two Sig Sauers and a kickass umbrella. Eva vaulted into the underbrush and disappeared into the jungle.

∼

"Which brings us, gentlemen, to where we came in."

Cole and Decker stared at her.

Eva stared back.

Her story was done. It seemed nobody knew what to do next.

"So," Eva plastered on her best shit-eating grin. "How about that pee break?"

During the last part of her story, Cole had returned with a bedpan that was tantalisingly close in the corner.

Decker folded his arms. "So, the spy is still there? On the second island?"

"That's what I've said all along. I still don't understand why you won't send someone ashore or why you two are so arse-licking informal. He could be drowning for all you know. He set the bombs that saved the world from Horatio Lancing, he deserves some level of appreciation and, oh, I don't know, rescuing."

Neither of the two Navy men moved. Not for the first time Eva wondered what was really going on. The two of them were far too casual. The lines of questioning seemed to go down paths that the US Navy would never be interested in. She had seen no other Navy personnel since coming on board. Plus she had never once detected the ship manoeuvre which she took as extremely odd, even for a large aircraft carrier.

Decker straightened his pen to be in line with his note paper on the table. "I'm afraid that's not your call, Ms Destruction. I know it's hard to believe but it is actually the President of the United States of America and not your good self who decides if we are to engage in hostile action on foreign soil. So far we only have your word and," he casually flicked through Eva's large Interpol file, "that is, shall we say, of debatable credibility."

She'd grown to despise Decker. He struck her as the type of arsehole who claimed to prefer instant coffee over the real stuff. She could never trust anyone like that.

Proud of herself for not growling, she said, "So, after everything I've told you you're not going to save him?"

"I'm not entirely sure there is anyone to save."

By the end of the day Eva was sure her teeth would be ground down to nubs. How could he not believe her? All he had to do was send out a party to search the island. All the evidence would be right there. In pieces, but there nonetheless.

Eva took a deep breath. New strategy. "Can I at least go to the toilet?" She nodded to the bedpan for emphasis.

Decker's eyes narrowed. "No funny business?"

"I'll be like a high school comedy review. Absolutely no funny business."

Decker's terse nod to Cole signalled his first mistake in some time. Cole proceeded to cut the white cable ties that had locked her body in place for far too long. The release was bliss. She was a butterfly freed from a stifling cocoon.

Muscles tensed and released. The bruises and cuts still smarted. Eva rolled her neck, feeling blood finally circulating. Unsteadily she rose. For a moment the room spun, but it was fleeting. Gathering herself, she managed to walk towards the corner of the room and pick up the bedpan.

She turned to see Decker standing before her. Cole was seated behind the desk, but no less observant.

"Ah, guys, some privacy?"

Decker fingered the pistol in his holster. "I think not."

"Perve." She approached Decker. "You're afraid of a girl? You have a ship of armed guys but you can't let a woman urinate by herself? Do you have some sort of fetish disorder? What do you really think I'm going to do?"

After a shake of his head, Decker ran his hand over her Interpol file. "I think your file indicates that you–"

The base of Eva's palm drove Decker's hand onto the table. Her free hand grasped the back of his head and slammed it into the table. The loud metallic *clang* echoed around the room. The Navy Commander slumped to the floor out cold.

Cole bolted out of his chair and ran at her. Eva picked up the bedpan and connected with the side of his head. Cole staggered backwards. He was stunned but not unconscious like his commanding officer. Still a threat.

An angry Cole readied himself for another attack, but she had other ideas. She leaned down and pulled out Decker's pistol. The naval officer raised his hands.

Eva brandished the gun. "Back the hell up or I'll kick you in your fucking soul."

Cole did as he was told.

"The handcuffs," Eva nodded to the devices that had held her in place during the first portion of her incarceration. "Put them on Decker, then you." They were welded to the table and would do the job. The gun ensured there would be no argument.

Did she really expect to be able to take on a whole naval vessel? Eva knew what she was doing was insane. She did it anyway. If nobody else would save Bishop, she'd do it her bloody self.

Confident the officers were secure, her attention was drawn to the next, not insignificant, part of her 'plan'. She'd spent too much time in the room, she could spend no more regardless of what she was about to face. A brief moment to steel herself was all she allowed.

She spun the escape wheel handle and wrenched the large bulkhead door open. Pistol in hand she bounded through.

Tropical birds fluttered away and Eva had to shield her eyes from the bright sunshine. The familiar smell of the sea mixed with the pungent perfume of fresh earth and exotic flowers assaulted her.

Eva froze in place, her feet planted on the hot sand.

There were no naval personnel to fight.

It never was a US Navy boat.

She'd been on the island all along.

"Hi."

She spun around.

Harry Lancing stood before her.

CHAPTER TWENTY-NINE

"What the actual fuck?"

Her ex-lover sported a large bruise on the side of his face but otherwise seemed unscathed from his run-in with a server rack in the underground cavern. Not that Harry's wellbeing was exactly on Eva's list of priorities.

A pistol hung loosely in his hand. Decker's gun was held tightly in hers. He seemed in no hurry to raise his weapon, but it was there, waiting. A low level stand-off. If it came down to a shootout, Eva had no doubt she'd come out victorious, but she needed answers first.

"You did this?" she pointed at what until seconds before had been a US Navy cabin. "Those two idiots work for you, don't they? What did you do, get Leroy and Jed from maintenance to put on a uniform and play along to your script?"

Harry's impassive face didn't move.

"You were listening to every word in there, weren't you? Fed them the line of questioning and listened in like a voyeuristic sleazebag." She waved her arms in the air. "Oh, bloody hell, of course you called yourself the President. An Admiral would never have been enough, would it?"

The man that had been Harry, Horatio and then Harry again was motionless before Eva's fury. Hands placed behind his back, he was impassive. Quite a feat since she had destroyed his entire island operation, his dream of European dictatorship in tatters, decades in the making.

Dressed in a white linen suit and loafers, apart from the bruise, Harry appeared as if he'd walked from the summer catalogue of *Multi-Billionaire Leisurewear Monthly*. Face neutral, he said, "You left me for dead."

Eva tilted her head. "It's only fair. You did it to me."

Mind playing catch-up, Eva backtracked everything that had happened since she'd been shot and collapsed into the sea. The US Navy had never picked her up, it had been Harry's goons. They'd patched her up and thrown her in a room that had a passing resemblance to a ship's cabin.

The restraints made a lot more sense. The handcuffs, the cable ties. They knew what she was capable of and didn't want to take any chances. Where they'd sourced the uniforms from was the least of her questions. The most important was blatantly obvious.

"Why?"

"Why do I still love you after you've destroyed a lifetime's work? Betrayed me, again. Lied to me. Worked against me with MI6. And, oh, blew up a facility that could have brought order and civility back to the world. You ask why?"

"I ask why, specifically, you kept me in a room for hours, subjecting me to endless questions about you, of course it's all about you, and strapped me down to spill my life story. I want to know why, Harry. Why?"

His expression melted from its hardened state. "I had to know...I had to know if there was any chance for us. I had to know why you came here, without filters. I guess I know now. To spy on me. It was never about love."

"It was once...then you went balls-out crazy."

"I did? You're the one who sold her soul to MI6 and screwed their lead pillar of debauchery."

"I thought you were listening to every word. Didn't you hear? I never slept with Bishop."

"No, merely frolicked naked in front of him. That's why I had to find out. There had to be a reason he knew about that private tattoo of yours."

Eva was aghast. "*That's* what this is all about? Jealousy? The whole fake sailors thing was to find that out? You really have lost it. The man who threatened the world is in turn threatened by one flirty misogynist. You really are just a frightened little boy in the end, aren't you?"

Ever since arriving on the island there had been moments when Eva had wondered why she'd been invited in the first place. Was Harry aware of her MI6 connections and wanted to know what they knew? In the end, it was far simpler than that. He really did love her that much. His offer to make her European Minister for Women and rule by his side wasn't an idle proposal, it was spawned by love. For her.

If it was another time Eva might have even been humbled that she could have such an effect on a man. The affection she had nurtured had made Harry so love-struck that he'd created an elaborate play where she was the unknowing star performer.

On the other side – the harsh reality, let's-look-at-the-facts side – the story was less rose petals and champagne. The man who purported to love her had incarcerated her under false pretences, threatened her, stage-managed her and forced her to divulge intimate details all for his personal gratification.

Then there was the minor issue of trying to take over the world by threats and manipulation. Oh, and killing innocents along the way.

When it came down to it, Harry was deluded, be it in his plans for world domination or a future for them both. It was a sad end for a man that had once been her everything.

Harry stood before her with a hangdog expression. Eva sighed. She would have a lifetime to debate it all in her head, but at that moment she had other priorities.

"I really don't have time for this. I'm glad you got out...actually, how did you get out? Last I saw you were taking an impromptu swim in the data centre."

Harry winced. It wasn't anything physical, it was purely recollection-related. "I managed to find an exit, the last one, I think. I scampered for the surface. What can I say, you don't do things by halves, Eva."

That meant Bishop was trapped. If he was alive. No more time could be spent yammering on. Eva had wasted too much time on Harry's deception. She had to move.

She stepped forward but stopped when he raised the gun.

"You're pulling a gun on me?"

"It's only fair. You did it to me."

"Touché."

It was the first time Harry had ever shown any aggression towards her. His timing wasn't great.

"What exactly do you think is going to happen now, Harry? I drop the gun, fall into your arms and we scoot off to plan your next adventure setting up a utopian socialist commune on the moon where there's nothing but free love, mutual respect and space goats for all?"

Harry ignored her impudence. "You still love me, that much is apparent. The way you spoke about us, how we were, there's no way you still don't share those feelings."

"Wow. Just, wow. You still think I'll come back to you? Jesus, Harry. It's over. I loved you completely. But what you've done, what you've become, it's too much. There's no way I can come back from that. Not now, not ever."

Harry's face became a mask. She knew that mask. It was the one he wore when he gave interviews or spoke to high-level politicians. It was his, 'Hey, let me convince you' face. Eva had seen it countless times. It was how she'd abandoned her principles so readily.

Whenever Harry spoke, he made the most rational arguments on Earth. Everything made sense when it came from his lips. Of course I'll abandon my friends and follow you around the world. Of course I'll let you buy me expensive gifts and truss me up like an exceptionally high-priced hooker. Of course I'll abandon my feminist sensibilities and become subservient to a man simply because he has a way with words.

He'd browbeaten diplomats, outsmarted kings. She'd seen an unarmed Harry talk an assassin out of murder in an alleyway and rally a city to fight in the streets. Despite how adamant Eva was, she couldn't afford to let Harry's silver tongue into her ear. She stepped forward. He stepped forward, expectant.

Eva was over Harry's manipulation. She was over him holding sway over her thoughts and actions. There was no way she could let him in again, not even a crack.

Harry opened his mouth and Eva punched it.

She didn't have the time.

She had to rescue Bishop.

But also to pee.

~

The boat's hull rumbled as it bounced over a wave. The tropical waters were becoming choppier. A storm was on its way. Eva leaned into the wind and held the throttle firm.

As the second island loomed large on the horizon, she hoped she wasn't too late. Harry had said he'd been last out of the data centre and the last time she'd seen Bishop he was being shot at by a couple of guards. He'd probably said something derogatory about their mothers.

She'd carefully skulked about the island after subduing Harry. There were still guards unaccounted for and worst of all, Van Buren was on the loose somewhere. Without Harry to reel him in Eva didn't want to entertain thoughts of what he'd do to her if he found her. Thankfully she'd made it to the boat without mishap.

She'd found the powerboat tied up on the pier she'd almost escaped from the first time. As she loaded it with supplies she'd urgently scavenged, she'd seen a beautiful sight. At the bottom of the hull sat a bright pink frilly umbrella. Greta hadn't been lost at all. It was like she'd been reunited with a long-lost friend. A friend who could crack skulls when needed. The best kind.

With only a rough idea where the sea side of the data centre was, it didn't take Eva long to find it. The debris in the water helped. Parts of servers and other unidentifiable wreckage flowed in a steady stream from one point on the coastline. The tide was going out and with it, Harry's twisted dream.

Finding a foothold on the rocky cliff nearby, Eva tied up the boat. The hole they had blown was underwater as there were no physical signs above the waterline. Just as well one of the items she'd pinched was scuba gear. She strapped it on, checked the air, placed on the face mask and dove into the rough sea.

The debris swirled in the churning waters. The waterproof torch allowed some visibility, but it was limited. Eva kicked downward and headed towards a dark fissure in the rock.

The bomb had been more devastating than she'd first thought. Grey rock gave way to lighter concrete where Harry's Chinese construction workers had closed up the cave. Most of their work had been blown away in the explosion. The gaping hole that had let in the destructive tsunami of water was the only means of egress.

Eva had no idea when she'd last slept, it was possibly days. She kicked with every scrap of energy she had left. Which wasn't much. She swam on and entered the cave.

Dodging a couple of floating server racks, Eva saw a faint glow of light above the surface of the black water. But the power had been cut, so surely...?

She clicked the torch off so as not to betray her position and swam towards the surface. As slowly as she could manage, she emerged in the gloomy cavern. Still as a tomb would have been an appropriate cliché. The cave was almost completely pitch black, the occasional shadow only emphasised the desolation that had been inflicted on the facility.

It was the 'almost' of the pitch black that concerned Eva. In a far corner of the giant cavern the occasional orange flicker could be seen. A fire.

As quietly as possible, Eva swam to the nearest walkway and removed the scuba gear. She extracted Decker's gun from a waterproof bag. Stealthily she made her way towards the fire, fearful of what she'd find.

Both hands tight around the grip of the gun, she came to the corner near the fire. There was no chatter, in fact, there were no human sounds at all, just the gentle crackle of flames.

Eva blew out a silent breath and rounded the corner, gun pointed and ready.

"Good morning." The words echoed noisily about the yawning cavern.

Sitting in a dishevelled tuxedo, Bishop reclined casually in front of the fire. His wry grin conveyed he'd been expecting her all along.

"I like the bikini. Very warrior cavewoman." He looked about what had once been a data centre. "Rather apt when you think about it."

Eva relaxed. "So you're not dead then? Should have known I wouldn't be that lucky."

Bishop shrugged and nodded towards the fire. "Glad you gave me your lighter."

"You stole it."

"Semantics. So the next question is, where's Horatio Lancing?"

"In a room."

"I was hoping for something slightly more specific."

"He's in a room handcuffed to a table where a couple of other blokes dressed in fake US Navy uniforms are also handcuffed."

"I see. Is it possible to have a level of information that's somewhere between the two?"

Eva filled Bishop in. The escape from the data centre. The flooding tunnel. The dash through the jungle. The almost-escape on the boat. The bogus naval vessel along with Cole and Decker's fake interrogation. Harry Lancing's sad fixation with her.

Bishop's face relayed his astonishment at the extent Harry would go to to find out her true feelings for him. He wisely chose not to request further detail.

"So what do you reckon, Bishop? Time to get out of here?"

"A marvellous suggestion. I'll need to bid farewell to my new friends though."

"New friends?"

Bishop jerked his head towards a nearby room. Inside were three bloodied and ragged-looking figures. Each was strapped to a server rack, gagged, but alive, including one very bruised and livid-looking Van Buren.

"I caught your mate here trying to sneak up on me. All the stealth of an elephant in tap dancing shoes. I tied him up and spent the last couple of hours flicking rubber bands at his balls."

Van Buren screamed through the muzzle, his eyes crazy with rage.

Eva tilted her head at Van Buren and addressed Bishop. "Did you learn that trick at MI6?"

"Boarding school."

"Figures." She sighed. "Want to get out of here?"

"I thought you'd never ask."

They left to the panicked shrieks of Van Buren.

If Van Buren had made his way into the data centre, it was good news for them. It meant there was another way in, therefore out. All they had to do was find it.

As they strode along the concrete walkway Eva was overcome with an enormous sense of relief. Was that it, was it all done now?

She yawned. "All I want to do is get off this island, find a quiet spot to curl up and sleep for a week. Maybe take another week to catch up on my reading."

Bishop nodded. "Perhaps you could take a holiday? Uh, I'd suggest a non-tropical destination."

"I do have a little shack in France I haven't tried out."

"I'd love to."

"Nice try, but I think I'll be doing this one solo."

It was then Eva realised something. All those years of dating bad boys, she suddenly realised – it wasn't them she was attracted to, it was the danger. The Battle of Trafalgar, Iceland, Prague, everything on the island. Regardless of the fear, she had thrived on the peril of it all. Perhaps she didn't need bad boys anymore.

"When you come back from this holiday of yours, you'll need a job. You could always join MI6. There's at least a couple of well-respected gents who would put in a good word for you."

Eva's natural reaction was to scoff at the idea, but if she wanted to embrace her love of danger it wouldn't hurt to entertain the idea. If she worked for MI6 she wouldn't need a man for danger. She could create her own.

The decision came faster than she'd thought. "I'm in."

THE END

~

Want special offers, heads up on new Eva Destruction stories and free stuff (who doesn't like free stuff?), you can sign up for my VIP Book Club -
https://davesinclair.com.au/newsletter/

THE AMNESIAC'S GUIDE TO ESPIONAGE

EVA DESTRUCTION IS BACK!

Eva is an MI6 agent who wakes to find armed men in her apartment hell-bent on revenge.

The only problem is, she has no idea what they're talking about. Someone has stolen the last sixth months' worth of her memories and the fate of the world rides on getting them back.

On the eve of the G8 summit, Eva is thrown headlong into globe-trotting assassinations and gun battles on the trail of the mysterious plan known only as Halcyon. Together with a besotted CIA agent and a misogynistic MI6 operative, Eva races across the world to retrace her steps in the hopes of finding answers.

With the clock ticking, Eva must track down those behind her memory loss, as well as battle a foe she can't remember.

The globetrotting takes her from London, to exotic Macau casinos, to Hong Kong hydrofoils, to French castles, to English mansions, to a car chase between an ice-cream van containing a nuclear weapon and black SUVs through the streets of London.

With betrayal at every turn, Eva discovers she can't trust anyone, including her own organisation. Eva must face down nuclear annihilation alone and she hasn't even had her coffee yet.

<u>Pick up your copy today!</u>

ABOUT DAVE SINCLAIR

Dave Sinclair is a novelist, a screenwriter and a really excellent parallel parker.

He lives in Melbourne, Australia with his two crazy daughters. He's also an award-winning filmmaker, a title that sounds far more impressive than it really is. He won a best comedy screenplay and cinematography award for a short film he wrote and directed, though at the time he didn't really know what cinematography was. A completed screenplay is currently doing the rounds.

Dave's overflowing bookshelves include many works by Douglas Adams, P.G. Wodehouse, Dashiell Hammett, Raymond Chandler, Janet Evanovich, Ian Fleming, Zadie Smith and John le Carré.

The Eva Destruction books are stories Dave wanted to read, full of action, laughs and fascinating characters. Eva has many more adventures up her tattooed sleeves.

To find out more, you can stalk Dave at his semi-reputable website: https://davesinclair.com.au

ACKNOWLEDGMENTS

I used to have a romantic view of how a book was written. The author sat alone at a grand desk, smoked a pipe, crafted the words on a typewriter and, when finished, yelled to their assistant:

"Take this to the printers immediately! Another masterpiece! Now get me my cognac and slippers, minion!'

Now I realise that this never happens – unless you're James Patterson – because no author ever writes a book alone. The Barista's Guide to Espionage: An Eva Destruction Novel is no exception. This novel exists because a great many people believed in the story and in me.

To my daughters – Quinn and Essie – thank you for giving me time with the strange people in my head. Added to that lot is my amazing sister, Alli, who is a fantastic writer in her own right and great at keeping me on the path.

The other writers I've met and now call friends have also been a huge support. The brilliant Boa Collective (Kerrie, Peta, Cher & Clare) were my cheer squad through numerous false starts. The crazy G-Mob (Luke, Steve, Justin, Nathan, Craig, Amanda 1 & Amanda 2) thank you for your support, guidance and laughs.

To the original publisher of this book, Fahrenheit Press, who took a chance on a crazy story with spies, explosions and a mouthy Australian broad, thank you.

And finally, to you the reader, thank you for picking up this book up and reading. Every new author appreciates every single reader (and review if you're so inclined). There will be more books coming and hopefully some cognac as well.

Made in the USA
Coppell, TX
18 July 2021